STAR TREK™

PICARD

FIREWALL

Don't miss these other essential tales based on

STAR TREK™
PICARD

The Last Best Hope
Una McCormack

The Dark Veil
James Swallow

Rogue Elements
John Jackson Miller

No Man's Land (audiobook)
Kirsten Beyer and Mike Johnson

Second Self
Una McCormack

STAR TREK™
PICARD

FIREWALL

David Mack

Based upon
Star Trek: Voyager
created by
Rick Berman & Michael Piller & Jeri Taylor
and
Star Trek: Picard
created by
Akiva Goldsman & Michael Chabon
&
Kirsten Beyer & Alex Kurtzman
and
Star Trek: Prodigy
created by
Dan Hageman & Kevin Hageman

GALLERY BOOKS

New York   London   Toronto   Sydney   New Delhi   Fenris

G

Gallery Books
An Imprint of Simon & Schuster, LLC
1230 Avenue of the Americas
New York, NY 10020

This book is published by Gallery Books, a division of Simon & Schuster, LLC,
under exclusive license from CBS Studios Inc.

First Gallery Books hardcover edition February 2024

GALLERY BOOKS and colophon are registered trademarks
of Simon & Schuster, LLC

Simon & Schuster: Celebrating 100 Years of Publishing in 2024

For information about special discounts for bulk purchases,
please contact Simon & Schuster Special Sales at 1-866-506-1949
or business@simonandschuster.com.

The Simon & Schuster Speakers Bureau can bring authors
to your live event. For more information or to book an event,
contact the Simon & Schuster Speakers Bureau at 1-866-248-3049
or visit our website at www.simonspeakers.com.

Interior design by Kathryn A. Kenney-Peterson

Printed and bound by CPI (UK) Ltd, Croydon CR0 4YY

10 9 8 7 6 5 4 3 2 1

Library of Congress Cataloging-in-Publication Data is available.

ISBN 978-1-6680-4635-7
ISBN 978-1-6680-4637-1 (ebook)

FSC
www.fsc.org

MIX
Paper | Supporting
responsible forestry
FSC® C171272

For all who were ever made to feel like outcasts
and became better and stronger because of it

Historian's Note

The main events of this story take place in 2381, approximately two-and-a-half years after the *Starship Voyager*'s return from the Delta Quadrant (*Star Trek: Voyager*, "Endgame"). The framing sequences take place in 2386, less than one year after the Federation abandoned its efforts to evacuate Romulus ahead of its star's supernova (*Star Trek: Picard*, "Stardust City Rag").

The impediment to action advances action.
What stands in the way becomes the way.

—Marcus Aurelius,
Meditations

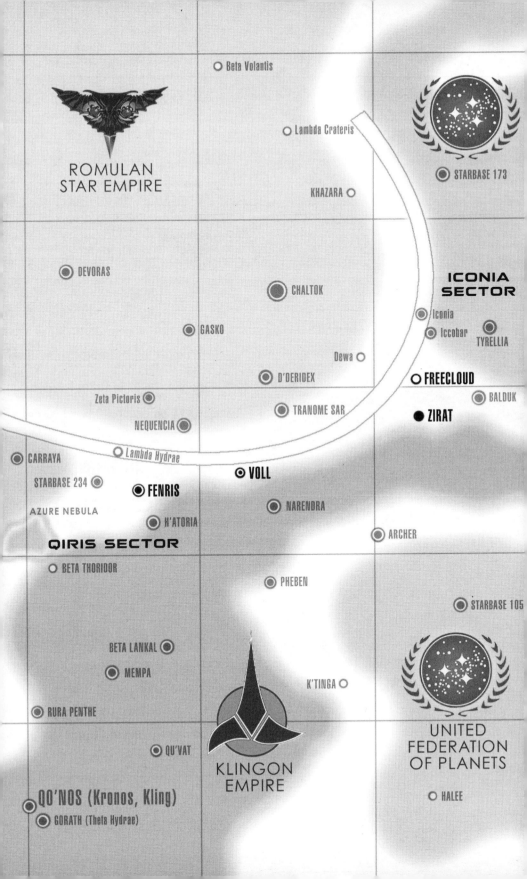

1

2386

Fenris

The Romulan sun was dying, and what a billion souls called tragedy, a legion of parasites called opportunity.

Epic disasters tended to spawn their own unique ecosystems, complete with figurative watering holes where predators and prey mingled freely, their struggles and pursuits paused in the name of thirst. The Kettle was just such a watering hole, and one of the busiest in Fenris's capital city. It was full of dark corners and deep, shadowy booths with high-backed wraparound banquettes, its transactions and interactions all veiled by a persistent smoky haze. Furtive whispers hid beneath synthetic music like strangers hiding behind aliases. Its owners claimed the establishment served food, but no one could remember the last time they saw anyone eat within its walls. The Kettle wasn't known for its bill of fare. Its overstocked bar, however, verged on legendary.

It was there, surrounded by disaster capitalists and sudden pilgrims, that Seven sat alone, craving the fleeting peace from haunting memories that could be achieved only through a sufficiency of booze. She had long since grown tired of the company of others, the pointless effort of small talk, and the ceaseless tedium of sussing out which smiles were lies.

Once, The Kettle had been a quiet place to unwind after a long patrol—until, less than a year earlier, the Federation's fragile house of cards had come tumbling down. First had been the synth attack on the Utopia Planitia Fleet Yards on Mars, in the Sol system. Thousands of lives lost. Countless ships earmarked for the Romulan evacuation destroyed. Soon afterward, Admiral Jean-Luc Picard's great mercy mission became the next casualty of the Federation's growing isolationism, canceled in a flash of fear and suspicion. That morally questionable choice had left hundreds of millions of souls stranded on Romulus or in one of its nearby systems, all of which would soon be annihilated by the imminent supernova of Romulus's star.

Within days of Starfleet and the Federation beginning the withdrawal of their fleet and its convoys of material aid, the first wave of Good Samaritans had landed on Fenris. Since then, they had just kept on coming, more than Seven could count. A handful in each wave came looking to join the infamous Fenris Rangers. Most of the others came looking for ways to help, but there were always a few driven into the Qiris sector by a need to escape their checkered pasts. Those always seemed to be the ones who found Seven here at the bar.

Seven avoided eye contact with the other patrons, and most of the time her focus on her beverage was enough to ward off those who hoped to engage her in conversation. Nonetheless, she remained aware of everyone around her. Every lowlife pickpocket working the crowd at the end of the bar, every lush flirting for a free round in exchange for a favor they'd never deliver, every piece of hired muscle trying to pretend they weren't hiding at least four weapons on their person. Gait, stance, posture—everything about a person's carriage was a tell, if only one knew what to look for, and Seven had spent five long years learning how to read the clues that were right in front of her.

Which made the enigma who sat beside her doubly intriguing.

A dark-haired woman, slender as a reed and just as willowy, settled onto the barstool to Seven's left. She had large, dark, expressive eyes accentuated by intricate patterns and layers of makeup. Her complexion was as pale as it was perfect, and when she caught Seven's eye she momentarily flashed a smile of impossibly white teeth. Her clothes were clean but not in a prissy way; her boots had seen some wear and tear. She was neat without being fussy.

The woman was unreadable. A cipher.

She gestured at Seven's empty glass. "Can I get you another?"

"No." Seven pretended to ignore the newcomer while studying the woman's reflection in the mirror behind the bar's shelves of liquor. "I buy my own drinks."

"Please?" Like a magician revealing a palmed card, the woman set a credit chip on the counter. "You *are* the Fenris Ranger known as Seven, aren't you?"

Hearing her own name gave Seven pause. She realized the woman had picked up her tactic of watching her reflection and now was looking back at her via the mirrors. "I am." She shifted her right hand toward the phaser pistol holstered on her thigh, her movements glacially slow. "How do you know my name?"

Her question made the other woman laugh nervously. "Are you serious? Who *doesn't* know about Ranger Seven? I've heard Tellarite merchant marines spin stories about you in bars from Pollux to Qo'noS. I knew that if even a tenth of them were half-true, I had to meet you."

The stranger's enthusiasm was flattering, but Seven was in no mood for it. "I'm not giving autographs."

"I'm not asking for one."

There was something sly and mysterious about the woman's confidence, tempered by a quality of awestruck admiration. It was enough to make Seven curious about her ulterior motive. Regardless, she feigned nonchalance. "So what *do* you want?"

"To talk."

"About what?"

"How to become a Fenris Ranger."

Seven stifled a cynical laugh. "Why would you want to do that?"

"Because I want to help. Every night I see vids on the news: People suffering. People with no homes. No food. No water, no medicine. Decent folks left in the lurch when the Federation lost its nerve. Law-abiding colonists left to the mercy of a growing caste of warlords. And if I'm to be perfectly honest with you . . . it makes me sick. Sick with rage. I told myself there wasn't anything a single person like me could do about it. But then, it all just got to be too much. The news, night after night—I couldn't take it anymore. I know I can't save the galaxy. But maybe, as a Fenris Ranger, I could save a few souls that otherwise might not make it."

It all had come pouring out of the woman, a confession like a river in flood, and it overwhelmed Seven. She remembered once hearing herself say something markedly similar years earlier, and now, being on the other side of that declaration, she was amazed at how persuasive such passion and naïveté could be when delivered in concert.

Even so . . . she couldn't let someone leap blindly into such a precarious life. She looked the other woman in the eye. "I get where you're coming from. Really, I do. But being a Fenris Ranger isn't a game. It can be dangerous, but it can also be boring. We protect good people when we can, but sometimes we need to make deals with the devil just to keep the peace. To paraphrase a good Ranger I once knew, it's not just an adventure—it's a job."

Not a word of what she said seemed to dim the other woman's fervor.

"I'm ready for it. Hard choices, bad food, the long silences of deep-space patrols, all of it. Somewhere out there is a person who needs a Ranger to stand up for them. I want to be that Ranger. Can you help me?"

Seven shook her head. "I don't know. You seem sincere. But part of me is afraid you don't know what you're getting into. Or that you're doing it for the wrong reasons."

"What were *your* reasons for joining the Rangers?"

"Long story."

"S'okay. I've got all night." The dark-haired woman waved over the Tiburonian bartender and motioned toward Seven's empty glass. "Another for the Ranger, and a Belgarian Sunset for me." She nudged her credit chip across the bar top. "And open a tab, please."

The large-eared barkeep scooped up the credit chip, nodded at the stranger, and then set to work preparing her and Seven's new drinks.

Unable to suppress a grudging amusement at the woman's tenacity, Seven gave her a sardonic side-eye. "You don't like taking 'no' for an answer, do you?"

A coy glance full of mischief. "No, I don't."

Seven chuckled softly. "That makes two of us." She paused as the barman delivered the stranger's multihued Belgarian Sunset cocktail, alongside Seven's neat measure of bourbon. The fruity effervescence of the former seemed out of place beside the smoky vanilla notes of the latter. Seven cracked a half smile and pretended not to notice. "Fine. As long as you're buying, I guess there's no harm in telling you how I got here."

The other woman leaned closer, her eyes wide and her smile wider. "I'm all ears."

2

2380

Earth – Cape Town, South Africa

Seven packed the last of her clothes into a synthetic-fiber duffel and set it on a chair. Cool morning air tainted with the sulfuric odor of rotting seaweed gusted through her bedroom's open window. From outside the beach house, she heard waves shredding themselves across the rocky sprawl of Macassar Beach, followed by long, ominous rumbles of thunder, low and distant, somewhere out beyond the waters of False Bay, where a leaden sky dotted with black-bellied clouds threatened rain. If her luck held, she'd be gone before it arrived.

She was about to begin gathering her effects from the living room when she heard the semimusical wash of a transporter beam outside, on her front porch. Moments later came the knocks on her front door that she had been dreading now for weeks, but from which there had never really been any serious prospect of escape. She faced the door. "It's open."

Kathryn Janeway, now attired in the uniform of a Starfleet vice admiral, opened the front door and took two steps inside the house. "Seven? Is this a bad time?"

Seven tried to sound untroubled. "Not at all, Admiral." With a gesture she directed Janeway toward the futon sofa. "Make yourself comfortable."

Janeway eyed the minimalist piece of furniture with suspicion. "I think I'll stand, if that's all right."

"As you wish."

Self-consciousness overwhelmed Seven with doubts and criticisms. *She is appalled by the condition of my home. By its lack of comforts. By my failure to live like other humans.*

Desperate not to betray her anxiety to the admiral, Seven masked her dismay with a practiced facsimile of a smile. "Would you like a coffee? Or a *raktajino*?"

Janeway declined with a small wave of one hand. "Maybe later."

Pivoting slowly, Janeway surveyed the living room. She nodded approvingly at the various holoframes, which displayed candid images of their former shipmates from *Voyager*. In one, Tom Paris was laughing while B'Elanna Torres scowled at him. Another had captured Commander Chakotay from a discreet distance, at a moment when he was deep in thought. One frame cycled through images of Harry Kim posing in front of a waterfall during an away mission, the Doctor applying a spritz of liquid-skin bandage to a scrape on the knee of young Naomi Wildman, and Neelix cooking in his kitchen. The last of Seven's holoframes was devoted to a single image: a portrait of Janeway.

The admiral looked back at Seven with a playful gleam in her eye. "Love what you've done with the place."

"Sarcasm, I presume?"

"Actually, no. I'm serious. Your home reflects who you are—or at least, the way that you see yourself. I look around and see efficiency, a cleanliness born of discipline—and perhaps just the smallest trace of sentimentality when it comes to absent friends." After a pause she asked, "Speaking of which, have you and Chakotay stayed in touch?"

"Not since he left for his new command."

"Why not?"

It was an upsetting subject for Seven. "We grew apart. What else is there to say?"

"I suspect that's not the whole truth."

Struck by nostalgia, Seven picked up Chakotay's holoframe. She was still processing her guilt about the end of her relationship with *Voyager*'s former first officer. Her attraction to him had been genuine, and she had never doubted the sincerity of his feelings for her, but events in recent years had left Seven harboring an anger and envy so toxic that it had driven him away.

She suspected those same events had brought Janeway to her home again this morning.

She set the holoframe down. "I presume you didn't come to South Africa to critique my love life."

Janeway kept her smile in place, but it was becoming forced. "You've grown your hair out. It looks good."

Reflexively, Seven touched her golden hair, which now brushed the tops of her shoulders. "Kind of you to say."

"And you've certainly been keeping fit."

"It helps to have a private beach for jogging and swimming. But we both know you're stalling, Admiral. Why are you *really* here?"

Janeway grudgingly abandoned her façade of cheer. "I wish I could say I'd come with good news."

Seven nodded in understanding. This was a continuation of a series of disappointing conversations in which the two of them had been engaged for several months. "Our appeal to the Federation Council for my citizenship . . . ?"

"Rejected. Again. And I'm sorry to say, Starfleet refuses to reconsider its denial of your application to Starfleet Academy."

"As we expected."

"As *you* expected. I thought the C-in-C would see reason when I said I'd resign unless they found you a place in the next class. Turns out . . . I was wrong."

Seven moved around the room and slowly gathered up the holoframes. "Did they say *why* they rejected my application?"

"They tried very hard not to say it, but, in the end, your fear proved to be correct."

"Because I'm still part Borg."

Janeway heaved a sigh of frustration. "It's just so damned shortsighted! I tried to tell them you're free of the Collective, that you deserve to be treated like any other person, but they see your implants and your nanoprobes, and they convince themselves you're an infiltrator bent on assimilating Starfleet from within."

For her friend's sake, Seven maintained her stoic front despite the tempest of shame and rage that roiled inside her. "Their decision is disappointing, but not surprising."

"Let's call it what it is, Seven: a racist, reactionary decision born of fear." Janeway shook her head and frowned. "I can't let this stand. I'll take it to the courts if I have to, but—"

"Please, don't. Not for me."

Seven's plea left Janeway looking perplexed. "Why not?"

"You have done all you can, more than I could ever have asked or expected. But this isn't a fight we can win. The longer you tilt at this, the more enemies you will make, in the government as well as in Starfleet."

"So what?"

"You're an admiral now. Which means you have more to lose. Please don't risk your career fighting a lost battle for me."

"Seven, you know me well enough to know I don't care about rank, or power. I care about my family, my friends, my crew—and about standing up for what's *right*. I can't just watch Starfleet and the Federation deny you a fair chance at fulfilling your potential because they've given in to fear and prejudice. I *know* they're better than this—and I mean to remind them of it."

"*Are* they better than this? Are you quite certain?"

Janeway's mien turned wary. "Why would you ask that?"

Seven tucked the deactivated holoframes inside a second travel bag and then beckoned Janeway to follow her. "Let me show you something."

She led the admiral through the kitchen and then out the back door. The two women plodded through soft, shifting sand dotted with patches of dune grass until they reached the side of Seven's beach house—which someone had defaced with crudely painted graffiti that read DIE, BORG BITCH. Janeway immediately recoiled from it in horror and disgust. "Who did this?"

Seven shrugged. "The local police tell me it was probably teenagers, but so far they haven't seemed especially motivated to find the culprits."

Janeway crossed her arms as if to defend herself from the evil sentiment on the wall. "What do you intend to do about it?"

"Nothing." Seven headed for the house's back door.

Janeway's anger boiled over as she followed Seven back inside. "What do you mean 'nothing'? Someone has to answer for this."

"It no longer matters, because I'm leaving."

"Town?"

"Earth."

Her declaration left Janeway looking stunned. Seven retrieved her duffel from the bedroom and returned to find Janeway pacing in the living room. The admiral apparently had recovered her wits and her voice. "Leaving Earth? Don't you think that's an overreaction?"

Seven set her bags by the front door. "No." She paused, unsure how much she ought to share about her recent misgivings, but then she decided Janeway deserved to know the truth—not just some of it, but all of it. "To be honest, I've felt out of place on Earth since the day we arrived. Everywhere I go, people see my implants and assume the worst. They think I can't hear their whispers or see how they look at me, but I do."

Janeway struck an apologetic tone. "It can't be that bad, can it? Certainly not everyone treats you that way?"

"You remember my Aunt Irene?"

"Of course."

"Even after a dozen visits, she still flinches when she hugs me, and she refuses to address me as 'Seven.' She insists on calling me 'Annika' no matter how many times I tell her that name no longer has any meaning for me. When I protest, she points out that's the name the Federation put on my identification documents. My real name frightens these people—even my own kin."

"And you think leaving Earth will change that?"

"Perhaps, if I go far enough."

"And what do you think you'll find out there, Seven?"

"I don't know. A fresh start, maybe." Her enhanced auditory nerve detected the thrumming of an approaching civilian transport shuttle's engines. "I just need some time, some space. Some room to breathe while I make sense of all these *feelings* that have been welling up inside me ever since I came to Earth. Every day my own thoughts get more confusing, and all I want is a chance to be on my own. A chance to figure out who I *am*. Who I'm *meant* to be."

Janeway looked up, evidently having heard the shuttle's engines as it passed over the house to land on the beach. "I can understand wanting some time alone. We all feel like that sometimes. But you don't need to leave Earth to find solitude. There are places in Mongolia, or upper Norway, or—"

"My shuttle is here."

Desperation crept into Janeway's voice. "Please, Seven, just give me a little more time to sort this out. I can work new angles, leverage other friendships, call in other favors—"

"I've made up my mind, Admiral. Thank you for all that you've done, but please let this go. Don't become a pariah for me. As Tuvok always liked to tell me, the needs of the many—"

"Outweigh the needs of the few," Janeway interjected.

"Or the one." Seven clasped Janeway's hands. "Time for me to go."

Tears shimmered in Janeway's eyes as she hugged Seven. "Be careful out there."

"I will."

They let go of each other. Seven opened the front door to reveal the idling shuttle parked on the dusty ground outside, and then she picked up her bags to leave.

Janeway looked out at the sleek vessel. "Where are you going?"

Seven paused in the open doorway and gave Janeway a sly smile.

"I'll know when I get there."

3

2381

Skånevik Prime

The white noise of a steady tropical downpour muffled the Fenris Rangers' splashing footsteps. Walking point, Keon Harper silently cursed his luck. He and his deputy trainee, Leniker Zehga, were surrounded by a vast jungle that had vanished into absolute darkness when night fell. If not for the ultraviolet-amplifying filters on the two Rangers' holographic starshades, they both would have been as good as blind.

It didn't help that the smugglers' camp they sought was pitch-dark. Harper had expected to catch a break by now. He hated looking stupid in front of a rookie, even one as restrained and respectful as Zehga. The young Zakdorn man remained a few paces behind Harper, who raised his hand and closed it into a fist, signaling Zehga to halt. With a downward gesture, Harper directed his deputy to kneel as he did likewise.

Harper surveyed the jungle ahead of them as Zehga whispered with evident disgust, "Dozens of planets in the Qiris sector, and we get the one made of mud."

"Could've been worse, kid. At least we didn't wind up on TaQ'hor."

"What makes there worse than here?"

"TaQ'hor is where the Klingons train *targ*s to hunt."

"You always take me to the nicest places, Harper."

"It's nothing personal, Len. We go where the bad guys are."

"Why don't the bad guys ever go to Risa?"

"They do, just not for business. Mooks dig *jamaharon* as much as the next guy." Harper looked over his shoulder at Zehga and pointed toward their right flank. "Tell me if you see anything over there."

Zehga frowned. "Shadows and more shadows."

Harper had no reason to think that a Zakdorn's eyesight or hearing were innately superior to those of humans, but he had hoped the deputy would have better luck seeing through the dark. "These Nausicaans are pissing me off, Len. Where'd they learn such good light discipline?"

"Such good what?"

"Light discipline." It took a second for Harper to realize Zehga had never heard the term before. "Hiding any light used after dark so as not to betray one's location. On ancient Earth, it was used to avoid being targeted by bombers or snipers."

In a tone of voice that sounded perplexed, but which Harper had learned to recognize as mocking and sarcastic, Zehga asked, "So, on Earth, learning to sit quietly in the dark is considered an advanced tactical skill?"

"Don't make me slap those ridges off your face."

Zehga suppressed a small chuckle, but then his mirth vanished, replaced by a singular intensity of focus. "Contact, bearing two seven point five. Range, fifty-nine point two meters. Steady artificial light."

Both Rangers squatted lower. Harper tweaked the settings on his holoframe spectacles and squinted as he looked where Zehga pointed. "I see it. Could be a status light on a power pack."

"So much for 'light discipline.'"

"Maybe not. It might've been covered 'til a breeze blew something loose." Harper undid the clasp that secured his pulse phaser inside its thigh holster. "Let's get a closer look."

Slow, careful steps. Harper and Zehga skulked through the jungle floor's dense growth of leafy plants, whose upper fronds entwined with the ends of vines dangling from the canopy dozens of meters overhead.

As they approached the smugglers' camp, Harper discerned long drapes of camouflage netting stretched like giant cobwebs between native flora. Beyond the mesh curtain lay a camp of ramshackle buildings, dilapidated huts, and poorly maintained surface vehicles. There were no signs of guards or patrols. He figured they could thank the rain for that.

Harper signaled Zehga to stop when they were twenty meters from the camp. "I'll bet one of these big perimeter buildings is their depot for that cache of small arms they bought from the Klingons, and another is where they likely store any heavy ordnance they're trying to move."

The Zakdorn's mental gears were clearly turning. "If you're right, we could take out their whole camp by arming a grenade with a delayed timer inside their ordnance shed."

Harper wondered if his trainee had heard a word he'd said during their mission briefing. "Kid, we're cops, not commandos. Stop thinking like a soldier and start thinking like an investigator. Remember what I told you: quick and quiet. Get in, document the presence of contraband as evidence—and then what?"

Zehga simmered, clearly resenting Harper's criticism. "Then we fall back and summon a corsair. When reinforcements arrive, we surround the camp."

"And . . . ?"

"We arrest the smugglers and take them back to Fenris for booking and trial."

"Correct. That wasn't so hard, was it?"

"Blowing them up would be faster."

"It would also be murder, and then I'd have to arrest *you*." Harper drew his pulse phaser from its holster. Zehga, in turn, unholstered his stun pistol—the only weapon deputy Rangers were allowed to carry during their probationary training periods. Harper pointed to either side of the encampment. "I'll head left. You go right. Cut through the netting, and once you're inside, get eyes on something we can use to get a warrant." The rookie nodded and turned to start his infiltration but paused as Harper said, "And, kid? Watch your step, yeah?"

"Copy that, boss."

"I'm not your boss, I'm your partner."

"Copy that, partner."

"Now you're messin' with me. Get movin'. See you inside."

They split up, each of them keeping to a low crouch as they circled the camp's gauzy screen of disguise, in search of concealed points at which to cut through.

Less than a minute later, Harper was at the netting, knife in hand, ready to slice and dice. Then came a blinding flash of white-orange light and a concussive boom whose shock wave knocked him on his ass. Stunned and disoriented,

Harper fought to get his bearings—and then he saw a rising plume of fire and smoke from the other side of the camp, and he knew the op had turned to shit.

Harsh white lights snapped on throughout the camp, and an alarm siren wailed from loudspeakers mounted atop tall wooden posts. The camp resounded with the clatter and clamor of Nausicaan mercenaries scrambling to respond to the emergency.

Harper struggled to get up. His head was spinning, and a swarm of electric-purple spots clouded his vision. As he forced himself into motion, he stumbled and caromed off one tree and then another. He heard angry shouts from inside the camp, voices growing louder because they were heading in his direction. Weaving and staggering like a drunkard after a bender, he lurched through the tangled undergrowth, hurling himself in clumsy strides toward the fire and smoke, until he found Zehga.

The young Zakdorn had been savaged by the blast. His hairless face had been scorched black on one side, and his thin crown of slicked-back dark hair had been burned off. His field fatigues smoldered, adding a chemical stink to the charnel odor of his burnt flesh. The blast had torn open his torso to reveal several of his internal organs, many of which were half-cooked. His entire body trembled as Harper took his hand.

"Good God, kid—what happened?"

Zehga forced out a reply through a mouthful of bloody sputum. "Trip . . . wire."

Panic and rage and grief collided in Harper's head, paralyzing him with indecision. He kneeled beside Zehga with tears in his eyes. "I'm sorry, Len, this is my fault. We should've stayed together. I should've—"

"Not . . . your fault."

A disruptor pulse screamed past Harper, just behind his head. Instinct took over—he pivoted and fired a shot that landed a phaser pulse dead-center in a Nausicaan's face. The ugly bastard fell and hit the ground like a sack of stem bolts.

He holstered his weapon and tried to lift Zehga's mangled, bloody body from the mud. "Hang on, kid, it's just a couple klicks to the prowler, we—"

"Go."

"We don't leave Rangers behind."

"You . . . won't make it . . . with me. *Go.*"

Harper was ready to argue, but there was no more time. A dozen Nausicaans rounded a building's corner and saw him next to Zehga. Disruptor pulses filled the air with searing light and a high-pitched cacophony as Zehga let go of his last breath and went limp.

Harper returned fire as he retreated alone into the jungle. If he had been thirty years younger, he might have tried to carry Zehga's body, just to deny the Nausicaans the perverse pleasure of desecrating it. But those days were behind him now. Harper was in his midsixties, but even more damning than his age was the wear and tear he had inflicted upon himself over the years—a state of degradation that once had been referred to colloquially as "mileage." He couldn't have hauled Zehga's deadweight back to the prowler and still been able to outrun the squad of angry Nausicaans who chased him all the way there.

The Nausicaans' disruptor pulses ricocheted off the hull of his Starfire 500 prowler—a fast, maneuverable, two-seat patrol ship with formidable weaponry—as he pushed it into a nearly vertical run to orbit, a ballistic climb so fierce that even with inertial dampers he still felt fifteen g's of acceleration slam his back against his seat, crushing the air from his chest and forcing his blood into his already throbbing skull.

He didn't ease off the thrusters until he saw the haze of atmosphere melt away to reveal the star-flecked sprawl of the cosmos.

Cruising away from Skånevik Prime, Harper switched off his comms so no one else would hear him shout, swear, and howl out his grief for a good, brave young soul who had become a Fenris Ranger simply because he had wanted to help people—and who had died because Harper had pushed him too far, too fast, and had left him alone too soon.

Never again, Harper vowed, staring with rage and sorrow at his reflection in the prowler's canopy. *Never again.*

Starheim, Utsira III

The factory was a cathedral of automation. A vast sprawl of titanic machines and endlessly recursive conveyer belts, it hummed with purpose and pulsed with heat. Its fabricators ran around the clock, every day, as millions of parts moved in constant harmony, a tireless dance of creation. Working alone inside this symphony of the synthetic, Seven felt safely anonymous.

She was aware of the irony of her circumstances. Of all the worlds she could have fled to within Federation space, of all the jobs she might have taken to make her feel as if she were actually a contributing member of society, she had found a menial-labor role in an industrial setting that bore a chilling resemblance to the inside of a Borg cube, only not as humid.

Her occupation consisted of waiting at the end of an assembly line's conveyer belt until something arrived, and then she crated whatever gadgets or gizmos the factory had churned out. When the crates were full, she used an antigrav lifter to stack them on shipping pallets. When the pallets were sufficiently full, she marked them ready for departure and watched them dematerialize.

Seven had no idea where the pallets of goods went. No clue who had bought them or what anyone had paid for them. And she had learned the hard way on two worlds before this one not to ask questions of people who were willing to pay for labor with anonymized credit chips.

Her work was tedious. It required no judgment or creativity. It was a job the factory manager had said would be "a waste of a synth," and when he hired Seven to do it, he seemed almost apologetic, as if he had condemned her to some infernal punishment detail. She kept to herself the truth that she found being surrounded by machinery oddly comforting.

A long, low-frequency buzzer sent a shiver through the entire factory.

It was the signal for morning break, when the factory's handful of organic workers converged on the east-side auxiliary landing pad. That was where Maxx, a portly Bolian food vendor, landed his "chow scow," a short-range, suborbital shuttle he had converted into a mobile restaurant. Once Maxx had secured his craft on the landing pad, he would open panels on the starboard and aft bulkheads to reveal an array of hot sandwiches, sweet or savory snacks, smokable and chewable stimulants, and an assortment of hot and cold beverages.

The other workers used the morning break to socialize, stuff their faces with greasy handheld food, and smoke during the brief outdoor recess. Seven's routine consisted of a double-strong *raktajino*, which she sipped while staring out at the bleak vista that surrounded them.

Utsira III was a remote, sparsely populated world on the far edge of Federation space. It was technically a Federation protectorate, but not a member world, which meant it had no representation on the Federation Council—but also no tax responsibilities. That detail made it attractive to Seven as a place to live incognito—but she had discovered upon arrival that pretty much nothing else about Utsira III was the least bit appealing.

Most of the planet consisted of a single climate, whose defining traits were cold, damp, gray, and bleak. A leaden blanket of cloud cover shrouded nearly the entire planet, but only occasionally dispensed any rain. Though the weather was likely at least partly to blame for Utsira III's failure to secure large-scale colonization efforts, a more obvious culprit was the planet's principal industry: resource extraction. Which Seven had learned was a euphemism for *mining*.

The town of Starheim, which had been just one population boom shy of becoming a city for roughly thirty years, was about average for settlements on Utsira III. Most of the jobs here were in mining, demolition, construction, and sorting scrap metal for matter reclamation. Heavy-duty, dangerous work, such as deep mining, was performed by robotic machines, which in turn were supervised by teams of nonsentient androids, better known by the slur "synths." A fraction of the local populace was employed in the service sector, by necessity. And for those adults unfortunate enough to have found themselves living on this filthy rock, there were bars.

Lots and lots of bars.

Seven was halfway through her *raktajino* when she noticed her coworkers crowding around the chow scow's holovid projector, which Maxx had tuned to the Federation News Network. Fear and pragmatism told her she should keep her distance. She had done a fairly decent job of obscuring her Borg implants by wearing gloves on the job and letting her hair grow long and wild so she could wear it hanging down to conceal the implant around her left eye. But whatever was going on had captured everyone else's attention, and her curiosity compelled her to investigate.

Next to the hologram of a well-coiffed, serious-sounding female Bajoran news anchor was a graphic of a star map riven by a sword and a lightning bolt, captioned CHAOS IN QIRIS. *"Unrest continues to swell in the Qiris sector,"* the anchor said. *"Several worlds that had been dependent upon Federation aid delivered by neutral, non-governmental agencies have been left to fend for themselves as Star-fleet and the Federation turn their attention toward the rapidly worsening crisis on Romulus. Many unscrupulous parties have begun to capitalize on Starfleet and the Federation's sudden absence from the sector, leading to fear of civil wars."*

The anchor continued, but Seven could no longer hear the holovid over her coworkers' increasingly loud, overlapping commentaries on the news.

"Fear of civil wars? Little late for that."

"I hear there's a warlord getting ready to seize power out there."

"If a bunch o' nobodies want to blow each other up, what do I care?"

"The real problem's the smuggling. And the sentient trafficking."

"The Fenris Rangers are shutting that stuff down."

"The Fenris Rangers? Bunch of damned vigilantes."

"Says who? The Federation government? What else would they say?"

"If the Rangers want to impress me, they ought to find a way to stop the price gouging. Have youse guys heard how much refined deuterium goes for out there? We'd make a fortune if we could get a tanker ship."

"And sell it to who? Nobody out there's got any money."

" 'Cause no one out there's got a job. All they do is protest. Bitch and moan. Cry me a river. I bust my ass on this mudball of a planet; you don't see *me* protesting."

"Yeah? *Spell* 'protesting,' ya goon."

The discussion seemed on the verge of escalating into a brawl, so Seven took that as her cue to leave. She wasn't going to risk losing her job by getting swept up in a donnybrook on a landing platform, just as she wasn't going to draw attention to herself by opining about interstellar politics, the Romulan crisis, the Fenris Rangers, or anything else.

She had taught herself not to care about any of those things.

All Seven wanted now was to do her job.

And be left alone.

Icy water surged from the faucet into Seven's cupped hands. She had never been fond of the cold until she worked a full shift as a human being in a factory like a hotbox. After ten hours on the line with only a few short breaks, she would come home coated in sweat and grime. It was all she could do to shock herself out of her stupor by splashing frigid handfuls of water in her face.

Seven refilled her cupped hands and did it again. Each time felt just as good as the one before. It was invigorating.

She couldn't say the same for her flat's tepid shower. It was cursed with weak water pressure in a grimy, badly lit stall that reeked of mildew. Compounding her disgust was the stink that belched up from the shower's drain whenever the water was running. The town had no public services administration to speak of, so even after months of making inquiries, Seven had not yet received any explanation for the odor. Her best guess was that something had died in the town's sewage tunnels. Not that anyone else seemed to care.

The rest of her flat was just a few small rooms with a view of an alleyway and a leak in one corner of the ceiling because of a hole in the roof. Her vid unit could serve up thousands of channels of distraction via the planet's FTL satellite network, and for her first few months in exile Seven had devoured all kinds of popular media, from assorted genres of music to fictional narratives of drama, comedy, mystery, and anything else one could imagine—and a few she would rather forget. The entertainment choices available here were far greater and more varied than those she had been able to access during her time on *Voyager*, but without the benefit of her friends' cultural insights, she felt like much of it went over her head.

She brushed her long blonde hair while looking in her bedroom's cracked wall mirror. *Is anywhere ever going to feel like home? I never feel like I know what's going on.*

Loneliness and frustration followed her everywhere. Shadowed her every word, her every action. The longer they weighed upon her, the closer they came to degrading into even darker emotions. Envy. Anger. Resentment.

She closed her eyes and purged her feelings. *Stop fixating. Be here. Just breathe.*

It was the start of a weekend, and Seven was intent on socializing. Because that often seemed to involve imbibing unsafe amounts of alcoholic beverages, she had learned the importance of having something to eat before going out. Unfortunately, her flat's temperamental old replicator had chosen that evening to pitch a fit.

"Computer: vegetable lasagna, recipe version Seven-alpha, one hundred fifty grams, serving temperature warm."

With a spinning whorl of shimmering particles and a pleasant wash of sound, the replicator delivered a piping-hot bowl of hyperpungent kimchi packed with enough red chili pepper to leave Seven vomiting for the rest of the weekend.

"Computer: a bowl of sweet corn chowder, non-dairy recipe, sixty-five Celsius, with a slice of warm corn bread, one hundred grams."

Another musical mini vortex yielded another bowl of killer kimchi.

"Computer: produce any vegetarian entrée *other* than kimchi."

The unit chirped, hummed, and buzzed for a few seconds. Then it spun up another funnel cloud of energized matter with a mellifluous sound . . .

And delivered another bowl of kimchi.

Seven took all three bowls of kimchi with her as she left her flat. Outside her door, she dumped out the bowls on a patch of weeds that she was confident would be dead by morning.

Out on the streets at night, she felt vulnerable. It didn't matter that she was stronger, more agile, and more durable than most of the humanoids she might encounter. What she feared was any encounter with several of them at once. Outnumbered, surrounded, alone, she would be just as vulnerable as anyone else. And she had learned through bitter experience that many people in the Federation and its neighboring galactic powers would see her as a valid target.

All because of these damned implants.

A desire to hide her alterations as much as possible had been part of her reason for growing out her hair. But that wasn't enough, not when a stiff breeze on a rainy night might whip her hair away from her face and leave her ocular implant exposed. Seven had accustomed herself to wearing jackets with deep hoods, preferably of heavy fabric or synthetic leather. She kept the hoods draped low as she navigated her way through the mean and dirty streets of Starheim.

Seven hated feeling self-conscious about her implants. They made her feel unwelcome in so many settings now, as if she were a pariah, or a criminal. It was a condition she hadn't needed to confront in any significant way before arriving in the Federation. Her shipmates on *Voyager* had worked hard not to make her feel ashamed of who she was, or embarrassed by her lingering body modifications and nanoprobes. Part of the credit for that, she knew, belonged to then-Captain Janeway, who had welcomed Seven with unexpected openness and trust. While Janeway's faith in Seven had been tested by a few crises during their early years together, her staunch support of Seven had set the tone for *Voyager*'s crew—and for Seven's new life.

I wish I could be with them now. I never knew how much I would miss them until we all went our separate ways. I didn't know how much I'd taken for granted the support they gave me, just by being there.

An "emotional safety net"—that was how the Doctor, *Voyager*'s emergency medical hologram, had once described the crew's support of Seven during the early years of her transition from an abandoned Borg drone back into a human being—a metamorphosis that she felt was still very much in progress. Reflecting on that analogy, Seven found it cruelly ironic that she had cast away that safety net just before she was about to need it most. Living alone had awakened new, unfamiliar feelings in Seven, who now struggled to make sense of her many conflicting desires.

Luck and caution brought Seven safely to the door of a seedy nightclub called Monsoon. She had sampled many of the other watering holes in Starheim, which had a "sub club" to suit every taste and clientele. Monsoon was a dive bar that catered to the city's queer and trans residents who liked their music fast, loud, and furious. Of all the joints Seven had haunted, this was the one where she now felt most like herself.

She paid her cover at the door, and the club's weekend bouncer, a massive female Balduk named Gurkha, welcomed Seven with a nod as she opened the door for her.

As soon as the door was open, amplified music hit Seven like a wave. She shouldered her way inside and wedged herself into an open space at the bar. Using hand signals she had learned through trial and error, she ordered a round of neat whiskey, and then she turned her attention to the band on the stage. It was a neopunk quartet called Amyl's Night Rate: a huge, shaggy alien drummer pounding out 240 beats per minute; one heavily inked, bearded human man playing a massively overcranked electric guitar; a Tiburonian girl thumping out a bass line so loud and low it could bruise ribs; and a short, manic, wild-eyed, platinum-haired pixie of an Orion woman whose banshee screech could make your ears bleed.

The bartender delivered Seven's drink. She paid with a credit chip, downed the sweet heat of the bourbon with one tilt of the glass, and then left the bar to wade into the slam-dance scrum in front of the stage.

This was what she lived for, looked forward to all week long: a night of release, a night to purge her anger, her sorrow, her loneliness, by surrendering herself to the chaos of the mosh pit. Bodies colliding and caroming, driven by the music to lose themselves in moments of wild movement, a maelstrom of flesh and bone.

It had intimidated Seven when she first encountered it, but in time she saw the truth that was hidden in the pantomime of violence. No one was in the mosh pit to hurt people. They were all hungry for contact, for connection, for a sense of belonging to something greater. And the moshers protected each other in ways that others outside the pit usually couldn't see. If someone fell, the other moshers pulled them back up. Couples or groups often laid claim to spaces by clutching one another and spinning around. The pit wasn't competitive. It wasn't territorial. It was communal. It looked like chaos and danger to the uninitiated, but to those inside it was safety in numbers, a huge embrace of like-minded souls.

Letting herself flail and crash and spin, Seven felt as safe as she once had . . . inside the Collective. Maybe her ex-therapist on Earth would call this behavior backsliding, or self-harm. Seven called it the closest she came to being happy anymore.

But even in the wild mix of the mosh, Seven felt alone. Cut off. Lonely. She saw so many others find sexual or romantic partners in Monsoon—at the bar, or in the mosh pit, or in the back booths—but the art of flirting continued to elude her. It was as if everyone around her were speaking a language she had never been taught.

She was rarely close enough to hear what others said to initiate romantic assignations, and she had no idea how to introduce herself in this setting or any other. The few times she thought someone might have been flirting with her she had become awkward or suspicious. And neither her brief romance with the semiliberated Borg drone Axum inside the virtual realm of Unimatrix

Zero, nor her short-lived and ultimately self-sabotaged relationship with Chakotay, had prepared her in any way for how to date as a queer adult woman.

She was about to remove herself from the mosh pit when she felt the gentle, tentative contact of a soft hand on the back of her neck. It arrived like a feather touching down on snow, gentle enough to capture her attention without triggering her alarm.

Seven moved with the music, careful not to pull away from the unexpected touch. She turned to face a tall, young Andorian woman. The bone-white hair on the right side of the woman's head had been shaved down to stubble, revealing her azure-blue skin, and on the other side it had been styled into a wild wave of ombréed teal, white, emerald, and orange. Her clothes were scant and stylishly torn in all the right places, and like Seven she wore ankle-high boots that were as practical as they were flattering.

Seven let her right hand cup the back of the Andorian's neck, mirroring the younger woman's hold on her. And then they spun, whipping each other in ever-tighter circles, every move adding to the magical gravity growing between them, feeding Seven's belief in the inevitability of their merging, of their union, of two becoming one.

The song crashed to a halt as they slammed together into an intimate clutch, sweaty and exhilarated. The Andorian's fragile antennae twitched as she smiled at Seven.

Without thinking, Seven kissed her. She didn't know what to expect. Would she be pushed away? Had she misread the moment?

The Andorian's mouth opened to meet Seven's, and their tongues entwined.

Another song spun up, and the pit churned back into motion. Seven and the lovely young Andorian stood looking into each other's eyes and let the storm swirl around them.

The Andorian woman took Seven's hand.

She led Seven out of the pit. Out of the bar.

They stepped into the street, which seemed eerily quiet compared to the club.

The Andorian nuzzled Seven's neck. "I live near Jofur Park. You?"

Realizing the woman was asking which neighborhood of Starheim she lived in, Seven replied, "Fafnir Heights."

"You're closer." Another flash of that blinding white smile. "Take me home with you."

Seven stirred from a restless and broken slumber. Uneven shafts of predawn light snuck in around the bent and missing slats in her window's drawn blinds. Even when dull and gray, daylight was still enough to hurt Seven's weary eyes and deepen the booze-fueled pounding inside her skull.

She listened for the Andorian's breathing in the bed beside her but found only silence. Slowly, Seven rolled over until she saw enough of her flat to know she was alone. The other woman's clothes were gone. Except for a few dyed-teal hairs on the pillows, there was nothing to show the Andorian woman had ever been there at all.

Maybe it was for the best. As had so often been the case over the past year of Seven's life, her emotions overwhelmed her with conflicting reactions. She felt betrayed by the other woman's clandestine exit but also relieved to be spared the need to make pillow talk with a stranger. It was a comfort to wake up in her own space, but a curse to once more do so alone.

The embarrassing details of their intimate encounter haunted her. Her fumbling gropes, the shifting of bodies in the dark, the Andorian's attempts to guide Seven verbally through the rudimentary elements of erotic foreplay. So many times Seven had fantasized about how elegant such a liaison would be, how sublime it would feel. Instead, all she could think about now, hours afterward, was how awkward she had felt. Naked in another woman's arms, Seven had felt clumsy and self-conscious, too focused on what she thought she was expected to do or say to actually let herself go and live in the moment. Several more rounds of potent alcoholic drinks had failed to compensate for the couple's lack of romantic chemistry.

Seven winced in shame and self-loathing.

I doubt either of us really enjoyed last night as much as we should have. She was so beautiful. I couldn't believe she wanted me. And then I made a mess of it. Even after she told me to just lie back and enjoy it, I couldn't keep still. What's wrong *with me?*

She tried to imagine what their evening had looked like from the other woman's perspective. Some Andorians were said to have telepathic skills, or maybe empathic abilities.

Not that she would have needed either to sense my fear of intimacy from a light-year away. I never even asked her name. Or tried to tell her mine. I can only imagine the lecture I'd be getting from the Doctor, or from Janeway, if they could see me now.

It had been over seven years since Seven had been forcibly separated from the Borg Collective while acting as its representative on the *Starship Voyager* in the Delta Quadrant. Since that fateful day, what she had longed for more than anything else was a sense of belonging on a par with what she had felt as a drone in the Collective. Despite her prolonged yearning for a genuine experience of connection with someone or something beyond herself, she remained baffled by many of the subtleties and contradictions of interpersonal relationships conducted by individuals. Where she sought intimacy, all she ever found was isolation. Her latest interlude had left her feeling more cut off than ever, alone with an aching emptiness she couldn't assuage.

I thought it would be transcendent. But it just feels . . . tawdry.

Seven made herself get out of bed. Her headache protested, but she willed herself to push on, through its petty torment, and stagger to her shower. Most nights her bloodstream's residual battalions of Borg nanoprobes were able to counteract the worst effects of what she had come to learn was called a hangover.

The previous night, alas, had not been one of those lucky evenings. Whatever spirits she and the Andorian had quaffed as social lubricants had proved more potent—which was to say, toxic—than run-of-the-mill libations. The commotion inside Seven's skull consisted of not just pressure but also heat, as if her brain were being boiled by a plasma drill.

She stuck her head inside the shower stall and turned on the water. A near-freezing, pressurized spray doused her head and the back of her neck. Imagining the torrent of icy water leaching the excess heat from her brain slowed the pace of her head's throbbing. It wasn't much as hangover remedies went, but it was a start.

Without bothering to towel dry, Seven gathered her clothes from the previous night, intending to wear them again. A brief search of the room turned up all but one small piece of her hastily removed ensemble. Everything else had landed with fairly random distribution on the floor and furniture, but her panties were nowhere to be found.

After a moment's thought, Seven concluded there was only one logical answer: the Andorian woman must have taken them. Since the Andorian hadn't left her own behind, it likely wasn't a case of mistaken appropriation. The woman had taken Seven's underwear intentionally. As a trophy of conquest. The notion led Seven to lift an eyebrow and smile.

Maybe I wasn't as bad a date as I thought.

She grabbed a fresh pair from her underwear drawer and dressed quickly, hoping to get ahead of the next phase of her hangover. It was building, like a wave gathering strength as it approached shore, and she planned to preempt it if she could.

Standing in front of her wall-mounted replicator nook, Seven gathered a few crucial ingredients from the cabinets and dumped the requisite quantities on the shallow countertop. With the pommel of her knife, she crushed several tablets of two distinct varieties into a fine powdered blend of analgesics and antacids. Then, with her hand, she scooped the medicinal dust into a tepid cup of *raktajino* that she had left sitting out since the previous morning, stirred it in until the powder was fully dissolved, and dumped the bitter concoction down her throat.

She sleeved caffeinated foam from her lips. *What was it Tom Paris used to call this drink? Ah, yes—"the breakfast of champions."*

The trick, she remembered Tom confiding to her, was to follow up the drink with a plateful of carbs, "to give your stomach something to hang on to."

She powered up her replicator. "Pancakes, short stack, hot, with buttered syrup."

Inside the replicator nook, a whorl of brilliant particles shimmered into being with an atonal electronic whimper. Within seconds the miniature storm coalesced . . . into a bowl of kimchi so pungent it made Seven's eyes water.

Something flashed with fire and went *poof* behind the replicator's front panel, which fractured and half-melted. Smoke poured from its fried control pad, acrid with the stench of burnt isolinear chips and scorched EPS conduit wiring, and yet somehow still smelling more appealing than the bowl of kimchi inside the nook.

Seven breathed a weary sigh of resignation, grabbed her ID card, and left her flat in search of breakfast. And a new replicator.

It had sounded like a lie at the time, and Seven was fairly certain she still didn't believe it all these years later, but once, long ago, aboard the *Starship Voyager*, a Talaxian named Neelix had told her that it was a truism of the galaxy that some of the best-cooked meals one would ever eat would be found in establishments that looked utterly unfit for food service.

Most run-down starport greasy spoons Seven had ever seen had failed to live up to that promise, but she had been drawn in by the white-and-chrome art deco style of the prosaically named Starheim Diner, and then she had found herself pleasantly surprised by the simple perfection in its execution of its limited menu of comfort foods, which included an all-day and all-night full breakfast menu. She didn't remember much of her childhood as Annika Hansen, but she dimly recollected that one of her favorite things had been having breakfast foods for dinner.

So strange, the things that make us happy. Even if we don't know why.

She sat alone at the counter and skewered her last bite of French toast—an impulsive choice, one she had been unable to resist after seeing another customer's order of the dish leave the kitchen—and used it to mop up the last small puddle of maple syrup from her blue oval platter. Its sweet mélange of flavors delighted her: vanilla, cinnamon, and nutmeg all were present, none overwhelmed by the syrup. It was so good, she almost didn't mind being up at the break of dawn on her day off.

The server behind the counter, a gray-maned male Tellarite with round-lens glasses, paused on his way to the kitchen to ask Seven, "Can I get you anything else, miss?"

She shook her head. "No. Thank you."

He smiled, nodded, and continued on his way.

Seven dug in her pocket for a credit chip with which to pay her bill. She was still searching when a trim, handsome human man in a dark suit entered the diner. He was in his forties, black-haired, with a tawny complexion, and his face was freshly shaved. To her surprise, in defiance of the social norm of respecting strangers' personal space, the newcomer settled onto the stool beside hers at the counter. He greeted her as if he knew her. "Good morning."

She leaned away from him ever so slightly and fixed him with a suspicious stare. "If you say so." She found a credit chip with a balance sufficient to cover the cost of her meal and set it on the counter. She was about to stand when the stranger spoke again.

"My name is Arastoo Mardani."

"Didn't ask. Don't care."

"You should, Miss Hansen. I'm here to help you get everything you ever wanted."

She narrowed her eyes, sharpening her glare. How did he know her old name?

Likely anticipating her reaction, Mardani continued, "Your Starfleet dossier is riveting, even the redacted version they let us read at the FSA. Though I should say, I think they made a grave mistake in refusing your application for service."

Seven was still wary but also curious. "FSA? Federation Security Agency?"

Mardani reached inside his suit coat and pulled out an FSA badge in a faux-leather flip-fold. "As advertised." He tucked away his badge and looked at the menu posted high on the wall behind the counter. "What's good here?"

"Minding your own business."

She knew it might be a risk to antagonize Mardani. The FSA was the Federation's civilian counterintelligence and interstellar-jurisdiction domestic law-enforcement agency. Its reach was long, and its agents had a reputation for tenacity and thoroughness. All the same, Seven was in no mood to be pushed around or intimidated, not by Mardani or by anyone else.

He put on a genial smile that looked well practiced. "Let me try this again. Excuse me, miss? I apologize for bothering you at breakfast, but as it happens, I'm here to make you a generous offer. One that I think you'll want to hear."

She swiveled her stool so that she faced him directly. "I'm listening."

"It was a mistake for Starfleet to turn you away. They couldn't see past a few residual bits of Borg augmentation to see how remarkable you are as a human being."

"I'm not joining the FSA."

"No one's asking." His demeanor turned businesslike. "I'm not looking for a new agent. What I need is a new covert asset."

"A spy."

"A nonofficial field operative."

"No, thanks." Seven once again shifted to get up.

Mardani motioned for her to stay. "Please. Hear me out. No one wants you to do anything illegal. Just observe and report. Gather information and pass it to me. And not for long. A few weeks, maybe. A month or two at most."

"What's in it for me?"

"Help us get the intel we need, and we'll get your citizenship restored, as well as pull strings with the Starfleet brass to get you the commission you deserve. With any luck, you'll be a serving line officer on a capital ship by the end of the year."

It was a more tempting offer than Seven had expected. Clearly, Mardani and his superiors had done their homework. They knew where her emotional weak spots were, and how to entice her. Regardless, something about Mardani's proposition felt wrong to Seven, and she suspected she was about to learn what it was. "What kind of intel?"

Mardani took a small breath and held it, as if he were gathering his courage. There was a note of trepidation in his voice as he said, "Infiltrate the Fenris Rangers and get us detailed intel on their operational strength and tactical capabilities."

Seven stood, picked up what was left of her *raktajino*, and dumped it in Mardani's lap. Setting the mug back on the counter, she looked Mardani in the eye. "No."

She made her exit without looking back to see if he had recovered his composure, because she no longer gave a damn about him or his proposal. As she pulled open the diner's front door to leave, Mardani called after her, "I'll be at the Starport Inn 'til tomorrow morning if you change your mind."

Positive she wouldn't change her mind, Seven kept on walking.

4

Earth – San Francisco

It often seemed to Vice Admiral Kathryn Janeway that, for a culture that prided itself on having evolved beyond the pursuit of wealth as a motivation for individual achievement, the United Federation of Planets had a knack for lavishing perquisites upon those whom it perceived as having earned *status*. In her case, those perks took the form of a sprawling, three-level San Francisco town house complete with a backyard garden, an indoor basement natatorium, and a rooftop terrace with a commanding view of the city's majestic skyline and the Golden Gate Bridge, which stretched across the sparkling waters of San Francisco Bay toward the halls of Starfleet Command and Starfleet Academy.

A cool breeze wafted over the city as dusk painted the sky in hues of violet and vermillion. Reclined in a lounge chair, Janeway poked and swiped at her padd, reviewing the previous week's reports and her superiors' orders for the weeks to come. She had been home long enough to have changed into comfortable civilian clothes and to have conjured a Tom Collins from her replicator. The gin-based cocktail had helped to soften the edges of her tedium-laden day at Starfleet Command, and the rest of her agitation was being exorcised by a recording of Yo-Yo Ma's virtuosic performances of Bach's unaccompanied cello suites. Many of her peers had evangelized the merits of listening to twentieth- and twenty-first-century American jazz, but despite her sincerest efforts, Janeway had never developed an appreciation for the genre.

Call me old-fashioned, she mused with a half-smile.

She was closing her latest work file when her padd chirped to inform her of an incoming comm signal, directly from one of Earth's orbital high-speed subspace relays. She didn't recognize the comm's tracing data, but she had a feeling she knew who was calling. She straightened her posture in the chair and accepted the incoming signal.

As she had hoped, Seven of Nine's face filled her screen. Her countenance brightened at the sight of Janeway. *"Admiral. I hope I'm not disturbing you."*

"Not at all, Seven. It's good to hear your voice. How have you been?"

"I continue to seek a meaningful outlet for my energies, but with limited success." Seven seemed to Janeway as if she were trying to hide something. Predictably, her next conversational tactic was to deflect and volley. *"Do you still enjoy your new role at Starfleet Command?"*

"It's been over a year now. Not exactly new anymore."

Seven cocked her head, conveying curiosity. *"Do I detect a note of dissatisfaction?"*

"Let's just say the bloom is off the rose." Janeway noticed Seven's attempt to mask her confusion at an unfamiliar idiom, so she added, "In other words, the novelty has worn off."

"I see." After a brief, seemingly uncomfortable pause, Seven asked, *"Have you kept in touch with any of* Voyager's *senior officers?"*

"As best I can. Chakotay has the *Protostar* out for a shakedown cruise. Starfleet Command recruited Tuvok for a role in its tactical division. Harry finally got a long-overdue promotion and a new starship posting. And Tom and B'Elanna . . . now that you mention it, I haven't heard from them in over a year."

"And the Doctor?"

"Still on his whirlwind speaking tour, telling anyone who'll listen that sentient holograms are people, and that they are just as deserving of rights under the law as sentient androids."

"I must confess a grudging admiration for his tenacity."

"Likewise." Janeway thought she saw a flicker of sadness behind Seven's eyes. "He, Tuvok, and Chakotay have all asked how you're doing, and where you are. What should I tell them the next time they ask?"

"Tell them I miss them. And that I don't regret leaving to find my own way, even if I get lonely sometimes. As for where I'll be? I honestly don't know."

Janeway sensed that Seven's melancholy was deepening because of something unsaid. "You didn't send a real-time interstellar comm just to make small talk—did you?"

"No." Seven withdrew slightly, as if she felt vulnerable because Janeway had so easily pierced the veil of her ruse. *"Something's happened, and I need your advice."*

"Of course. I'll always be here for you, Seven. So . . . what's going on?"

Seven's mood shifted to one of grave concern. *"I was approached today by a man who said his name was Arastoo Mardani. He claimed to be an agent of the FSA. He knew my name and about the Council rejecting my application to Starfleet."*

"That is troubling. Did he show you any credentials?"

"He did. An FSA badge and ID."

"Did they look authentic?"

Seven shrugged. *"Authentic enough. I'd never seen a real FSA badge or ID before, so I had no basis for comparison. I looked them up later; his seem to be legitimate."*

"Perhaps, but a forgery would be hard to spot with just a glance, even for you. Did he state a reason for approaching you?"

The younger woman nodded. *"He wants me to serve as a covert civilian asset."*

That detail stoked Janeway's feelings of alarm. "To what end?"

"He wants me to insinuate myself somehow into a role close to or within the Fenris Rangers so that I might gather operational and tactical intel about them for the FSA."

"He wants you to be his spy."

"Essentially, yes."

"That could be extremely dangerous, Seven. What made this Agent Mardani think you'd even consider such an assignment?"

"His proposed reward was quite . . . tempting."

Dreading the answer, Janeway asked, "What did he offer you?"

"He said the FSA would intercede on my behalf with the Federation Council and Starfleet Command to secure my citizenship and the commission I requested."

Janeway shook her head in anger and disappointment. "If it sounds too good to be true—"

"I had the same thought. So I dumped my raktajino *in his lap."*

"Well done."

"But now that I've had time to consider his proffer—"

"Don't tell me you're thinking of doing this."

Seven turned defensive. *"His terms were not unreasonable. Basic intelligence gathering, in exchange for the career track I deserve, but for which I was unfairly denied."*

"Maybe. Or it might be a one-way ticket to a death sentence. The Fenris Rangers are *dangerous*, Seven. Ruthless vigilantes who think they have the right to enforce their own brand of frontier justice. I can't imagine they'd take kindly to a spy in their ranks."

"Your objection is duly noted."

Perhaps it was the tone of Seven's voice, but something in the younger woman's mien sent a chill down Janeway's spine. "Please don't do anything rash. Give me a chance to check out this Mardani person, to see if he's even remotely trustworthy."

"He's waiting on my answer. I need to make a choice in the next ninety minutes."

"Seven, please—that's not enough time."

"It's all the time I have."

"Well, whatever you do, please promise you'll be careful."

Seven's stern expression softened by just the slightest degree. *"I will."* She reached toward something out of view, and her signal ceased.

The screen of Janeway's padd went dark. Setting the device aside, all Janeway could do now was swallow her fears.

Good luck, Seven. I hope you know what you're doing.

Utsira III – Starheim

Dawn was less than an hour away, but the sky overhead remained impenetrably dark, thanks to the dome of clouds that had spent the last hour dousing Starheim with precipitation. Seven stood alone in the open doorway of her flat and stared into the night. A steady, numbingly cold drizzle of acid rain soaked every centimeter of the town, but not with sufficient force to strip away its wretched patina. It was just enough to turn streets to mud and put a slippery sheen on the filth.

Distant flood lamps spilled harsh white light down misty alleyways. Curtains of steam and foul-smelling vapor, belched up from the sewers, drifted like phantoms in the street. Nearly everything within sight of Seven's residential complex was closed, and there wasn't a soul to be seen on the desolate boulevards of Fafnir Heights.

Regrets plagued Seven's thoughts, keeping sleep at bay.

What am I doing here? What did I expect to find?

She looked over her shoulder. Surveyed her meager dwelling, with its cold shower, useless replicator, and indelibly stained floors. Took note of her few, drab possessions. She had brought little with her from Earth, and she had resisted acquiring much during her travels.

This was the third world on which she'd lived in the past year, and it was about to become the third from which she would fly by night, in pursuit of a desire she couldn't define, and in retreat from a pain she didn't want to face.

All she saw, wherever she looked, was emptiness. Her barren flat, the deserted streets, the naked sky, her unshared bed . . . they all served to remind her how alone she felt in the universe. Self-pity and regret were triggers for her eremophobia, her fear of being alone, a psychological malady that had afflicted Seven since her separation from the Borg Collective. Her most severe episode of the phobia had occurred during *Voyager*'s long, silent crossing of a starless void between two adjacent arms of the Milky Way, but Seven felt the old terror lurking close beneath her conscious thoughts, like a predator of the benthic deep waiting to surface and strike.

Her forlorn gaze landed on her unmade bed.

Even the lowliest of Borg drones lead lives of greater connection than this. Have more of a sense of purpose. There's never any doubt as a drone. No fear. No regret. No sorrow.

A defiant voice of resistance welled up from deep inside to remind her what else Borg drones never knew: *Joy. Friendship. Pride. Love.*

Seven shut her eyes to hold back tears.

No! I won't give in to weakness. I have to own this.

Everything about her life depressed her. *It's my fault that I live like this. I let my shame and embarrassment lead me into this colorless exile. I told myself I wanted to spare Janeway any further embarrassment, but it was my own shame I wanted to escape. I felt humiliated when I was rejected. When I failed in front of my friends. In front of her.*

Outside, a brisk wind parted the curtains of drizzle and shredded the mist before circling around and stinging Seven's face with a chilly spray.

Seven plodded around her flat, gathering only the most essential of her personal effects into a faux-leather satchel. Her few changes of clothing. A handful of credit chips. A small holoframe programmed with images of her *Voyager* shipmates. Her Federation ID, which insultingly used her old name and categorized her as a non-citizen "alien permanent resident."

When she was satisfied she had all the things she truly couldn't live without, she closed the bag and took a final look around the room.

This isn't a life. This is existing just to exist. It's meaningless.

She turned out the lights. Walked to the door. Left it open behind her as she trudged out and down a single flight of stairs into the cold, wet, pitch-dark morning. Her footfalls splashed and squished through the mud.

The complex's landlady, an elderly Tiburonian busybody who seemed never to sleep, pulled open her ground-floor flat's door and hollered at Seven in a voice like gravel, "Packed a bag, eh? Where ya goin'?"

Seven stopped and looked back at the old woman. "Away."

"Comin' back?"

"I hope not."

"But you're paid through the end of the month."

"I know." Satisfied her point was made, Seven resumed walking.

Confused, the old woman called out to her, "What about your stuff?"

Seven shouted back, "Burn it."

The FSA contract governing Seven's agreement with the agency was needlessly long, absurdly verbose, and obviously designed to make one's eyes glaze over with weariness and boredom as a precursor to abject surrender. It was obvious to Seven that whoever had written it had not counted on an ex–Borg drone with a capacity for prolonged hyperintense focus being on the other end of their attempt at intellectual strong-arm tactics.

While Seven sat at the desk in Mardani's hotel room—which was far more functional, comfortable, and aesthetically pleasing than her own now-abandoned abode—the FSA agent leaned against a wall near the door. On the edge of her vision, Seven noticed that Mardani was checking his chrono roughly every ninety seconds.

He must be in some manner of a hurry. Unfortunately for him, I am not.

He stole another look at his chrono, and then asked in a tone meant to conceal his mounting irritation, "How are you doing with the contract?"

"I continue to make progress." She dragged a fingertip across the padd's screen and scrolled to the next page of the deal. "On line 718, please change 'may' to 'shall.'"

"Agreed. Anything else?"

"I shall let you know."

Mardani pinched the bridge of his nose and then he rubbed his bloodshot brown eyes. "If I'd known you meant to be this thorough, I'd have ordered breakfast."

Seven tapped at the padd to red-line some verbiage she found dangerously ambiguous. "I am striking line 762 in its entirety."

"Sure. Whatever." Mardani sighed, and then he stifled a yawn. "I have to confess, I admire your legal acumen. And your attention to detail."

Seven answered without looking up from the padd. "One must take care when executing legally binding agreements. A friend taught me that."

"Sounds like a good friend."

At last, Seven reached the end of the document. She initialed the summary of amendments and then handed the padd to Mardani for his countersignature. "I am satisfied that our agreement is now equitable and free of legal ambiguities or conflicts of interest."

He accepted the padd and lazily added his signature with his fingertip. "It didn't have to be this hard, you know."

"Your agency drafted this agreement. If you or your superiors had wished it to be simple and succinct, you could have written it with an eye for clarity and brevity. I take no responsibility for the delay created by your legal department's penchant for verbosity."

"I trust you see no irony in the complexity of your retort?"

"Should I?"

"Forget it." He put the padd into a slim briefcase, which closed without a sound. As the two halves of its smart-metal shell met, the seam between them vanished. "From here we'll go directly to the starport. My ship, the *Bolvangar*, is berthed there. Once we're aboard, I'll read you in on the mission brief, and issue you some field gear."

"Your terms are acceptable." She gestured toward the door.

Agent Mardani opened the hotel room door and held it open for Seven, who stepped past him into the corridor. He followed her out, and they walked together toward the lifts. Seven was already thinking ahead, imagining scenarios that might enable her to infiltrate the Fenris Rangers without arousing suspicion, when Mardani spoke and interrupted her train of thought.

"Before we go, do you have any unfinished business?"

"Such as?"

"Anybody you want to tell good-bye?"

Seven rolled her eyes. "No one here knows my real name."

"Except me."

"You cheated."

"It's called doing my job."

They stopped in front of the lifts. Out of habit, Seven reached for her personal comm device to check if she had received any messages while she had been offline reading the FSA contract. There had been no incoming calls or other messages.

She hid her dismay. She had hoped to hear from Janeway before crossing a point of no return, but when she perceived that her window of opportunity for a second chance at a Starfleet career was swiftly closing, she felt compelled to seize it before it slipped away again, this time possibly forever. Once she left Utsira III, however, she would be unreachable via her comm until the next time she used it on a world with links to the Federation subspace relay network—and that might not happen for a long time if she needed to go undercover.

Mardani glanced at Seven while she was staring at her comm. "Something wrong?"

"No." Seven put away her comm and set her gaze upon the lift doors. "Just making sure I didn't miss anything."

The handsome agent smiled. "I doubt you miss much."

Seven kept her expression a cipher. "You might be surprised."

FSA Tactical Cruiser *Bolvangar*

From the moment Seven had stepped aboard Mardani's vessel, an FSA tactical cruiser named *Bolvangar*, she had been able to tell it was a ship of secrets. Its entire aesthetic was geared toward withholding information. Aboard a Starfleet vessel, if one looked closely enough, one would see that nearly everything was marked and identified. Every bulkhead, intersection, doorway, and overhead pipe or conduit bore a unique identifier, and if one ever got lost on a Starfleet vessel, all one had to do was access a ship's directory from a companel. It was as if the designers of Starfleet's vast interstellar navy had built its ships to be read like open books.

By contrast, nothing aboard *Bolvangar* seemed to have been labeled. As Seven followed Mardani through its narrow, dimly lit corridors, she inspected her surroundings. There were no exposed conduits, pipes, or Jefferies tube access points. Not one door was marked with anything more than a string of numbers and letters indicating its respective deck, section, and compartment number. No names. No department designations. No functional descriptions. And though Seven didn't have the time to test every door she encountered, she was almost certain that each one she saw was locked. As for the companels? She could use any of the glassy black interfaces that she wanted . . . as a mirror.

Regardless, Seven still had a good idea where she was within the tactical cruiser. Most Federation vessels, whether Starfleet or civilian, followed certain design principles. Command decks were usually set toward the top of the ship, while main engineering was often located just aft of amidships. Fuel storage tended to be adjacent to main engineering, with antimatter pods in the belly of the ship to facilitate their emergency ejection in the event of a magnetic containment failure. Shuttlebays typically resided in the aft portion of either section of a ship's hull. Sickbays were situated as closely as possible to the ship's center, alongside the reinforced bulkheads that shielded the ship's primary computer core—in theory, the safest, best-protected section of a ship's

interior—and crew quarters tended to radiate out and away from sickbay, leading toward escape pods and emergency accessways.

Once in a while, some starship designer would try something different, like
putting officers' bunks in a pass-through corridor for no good reason, or berthing enlisted crew in a starship's secondary hull near the antimatter, without any
clear path to the escape pods, but such "innovations" tended to be short-lived,
as did the unfortunate souls forced to endure them.

Assuming the designer of *Bolvangar* had been of the sane variety and not
one of the "experimental" types, Seven reasoned she and Mardani were in
an outer section of deck four, where one would expect to find maintenance
bays—and very likely the ship's armory.

Mardani stopped at a door, pressed his hand against a biometric scanner
beside it, and then ushered Seven through the door as it slid open with a soft
whoosh. She stepped past him into what looked like a security division ready
room: a row of lockers along one bulkhead, with a long bench in front of
them. Along the opposite wall stood a long shelf lined with small arms and
various bits of tactical equipment. Through a viewport on the outer bulkhead,
Seven saw warp-streaked stars slip past, their heightened distortion a testament
to the ship's tremendous speed.

She looked at Mardani and tilted her head toward the viewport. "We appear
to be at high warp. Would you mind telling me our destination?"

"Otroya II." He closed and secured the door once he was inside.

"What, may I ask, is on Otroya II?"

"A city named Arendel. The FSA has signal intercepts that suggest the Fenris Rangers are tracking some smugglers who've made a deal with Nausicaan
middlemen to meet there."

Seven nodded. "I see. And what is to be my role in this transaction?"

Mardani's reply was stern. "*None.* You're to observe and report."

His order confused her. "Is that all?"

"That's all. See how the Rangers handle themselves in action. Maybe record it."

"How does that further my mission of insinuating myself into their ranks?"

"It's important to learn all you can about your target before you engage
with them. And the best way to stay safe while conducting reconnaissance is to
be inconspicuous." Mardani opened one of the lockers to reveal some civilian

garb of a more utilitarian style than what Seven had accustomed herself to wearing in Starheim. "This ought to help you fit in."

Seven examined the garments inside the locker. A few pairs of dark cargo pants. Rugged boots made to be durable but also light enough for running. A few lightweight pullover tunics. A jacket with paramilitary styling and a profusion of hidden pockets. Plenty of places to hide weapons and equipment without looking like some kind of pack animal.

She nodded. "Yes, this will do."

"Glad you approve. Now let me show you the fun stuff."

They left the lockers and stood in front of the long shelf. Mardani gestured at the assorted pieces of gear. "None of this is FSA issue. Most of it isn't even Federation made."

"Why not?"

"Plausible deniability. If something goes wrong out there and you end up making a mess or starting an interstellar incident, we need to be able to say we've never met you."

"Reasonable."

"Also, the Rangers'll see you coming a parsec away if you go in loaded up with FSA standard-issue anything. Your best bet of getting close to the Rangers without getting yourself killed is for you to look believable as a soldier of fortune."

"A what?"

"A mercenary. A soldier for hire."

"Understood."

"So, let's see what Santa brought you." He picked up one of a matching pair of energy pistols. "Talarian Stingers: pulsed plasma. Punches through light armor plate, ignites fuel and other flammable objects, destroys personnel."

Mardani set aside the pistol and picked up a bandolier of small, silvery cylindrical grenades, most no larger than a human's thumb. "Gorn shock grenades. Punch the red trigger, they'll jolt most living things into a coma for a week. They'll also knock out force fields, powered systems, and energy weapons in a twenty-meter radius. Give the center ring a twist to magnetize the mine. Push the black trigger for a high-yield detonation. Great for breaching walls and hulls." He handed Seven the bandolier. She slung it over one shoulder as

Mardani continued. "Holographic binoculars. Emergency medkit. A personal sensor blind, to hide you from everything from starships' life-sign sweeps to smart weapons' targeting sensors. And"—he dug a fistful of latinum strips from inside his jacket and gave them to Seven—"enough cash for you to pick up whatever else you think you might need once you hit Arendel."

Seven pocketed the Ferengi-issued currency. "Do you really think it would be wise for me to risk purchasing unusual or illicit equipment on Arendel?"

"It'll help establish you as a member of the local underworld economy, which is a first step to setting up your new legend."

"My what?"

"Your legend." He looked mildly embarrassed at his faux pas. "Sorry, that's spy jargon for 'cover identity.' It's not easy explaining away your residual Borg implants, but we've got a few personas that should fit you."

"No, thank you."

"Excuse me?"

"I have no use for a false identity." Seven surveyed the array of equipment on the shelf. "This all appears to be adequate, but I won't need your *legend*."

"Without a cover ID in the system, the Fenris Rangers will identify you the moment they scan your face."

"That's the idea."

Her rebuff left Mardani looking uncomfortable. "Are you sure? There are dangerous people out here, Seven. Some even make the Fenris Rangers look like Buddhist monks."

Seven gathered up her new cache of weapons and gear. "I am well aware of the sorts of persons who make the Qiris sector their playground." Strapping on the double holster rig for her pulse-pistols, she felt strangely at ease. "I won't be their prey, Mister Mardani. They'll be *mine*."

5

Otroya II – Arendel

Like a dream willing itself into existence, the city of Arendel took shape and solidified around Seven as she materialized from a transporter beam in a deserted alley deep inside the sprawling megalopolis. Majestic towers, some several kilometers tall, stood packed together tightly enough to shut out the rays of the setting sun, plunging the streets into premature night.

Seven made a check of her person, her gear, and the large satchel she carried over her left shoulder. All was well. A look at her chrono confirmed it had adjusted to local time upon her arrival. Keenly aware of the need for discretion, she pulled up her jacket's cavernous leathery hood and let it droop low in front of her face. Sufficiently disguised, she left the alley and merged into the dense throng of pedestrians that choked the streets, the skywalks, and pretty much every cubic centimeter of open public space.

The people of Arendel walked more quickly than Seven had expected. She had grown accustomed to the more relaxed atmosphere of cities on the Federation's core planets. Out here, there was a faster tempo to the communal consciousness, and a harsher quality of light unique to this city's streets. People moved in angular masses that defied delay or penetration.

And the city itself—Seven had never seen anything like it. Not up close, anyway. Every bit of it was an assault on her senses, and an insult to sentient dignity.

Entire façades of great skyscrapers were covered in blinding animations of neon. A shimmering holographic Colossus, naked and enviably endowed in every respect, dwelled in the spaces that yawned between the buildings, which themselves looked as if they had been hewn by titans from mountains of crystal and duranium. It was a metropolitan profile drawn in weeping curves, entwined helixes, partially hollow pyramids, and hundreds of dartlike spires.

Threading her way through the city's labyrinthine warren of streets, Seven couldn't help but feel small. Isolated. Alone. The mission briefing had indicated there were more than forty-five million people of various species residing and working in Arendel. Forty-five million souls. All of them living stacked like cargo in silos. Workers and consumers trapped in an endless routine, each repeating the same functions, the same rituals, the same laments every day . . .

Like drones in a Borg cube, Seven realized with sudden, grim clarity.

I tell myself we had unity inside the Collective. But did we? None of us knew one another individually. We were all One, but none of us was anyone. A trillion souls lived united—in loneliness. In desperation. In an illusion.

The buzzing roar of a speeding hoverbike derailed Seven's maudlin train of thought. She shook off her dour mood. *I must stay focused.*

A single strip of latinum bought her a monthly pass for Arendel's metropolitan transit system, with maybe enough change left over for a *raktajino.* Riding the maglev train, Seven stared down at the neighborhoods blurring past beneath her and caught glimpses of the seedy underbelly of the city. Fleeting moments of street-level violence. Red-light districts where licensed socialators had to work next door to their illegally trafficked peers. The starport sector, whose bars overflowed with mercenaries, smugglers, thieves, con men, assassins, drug peddlers, and a thriving open-air black market that stretched for several city blocks in every direction.

Wailing sirens and strobing blue-and-red lights blazed past above the train. Seven looked up at the convoy of airborne police cruisers, firefighting hovercraft, and ambulances, all racing through the night to some calamity out among the arcologies that ringed the city's farthest edges.

The maglev slowed to a halt in the midst of this decrepit zone of urban decay. When the doors opened, Seven stepped out onto the platform. The cool, damp night air was thick with the reek of uncollected garbage rotting in the streets. At least, she *hoped* she was smelling trash.

It was a quick walk from the train station to the hotel Mardani had instructed her to use. Despite the short distance, it was more than far enough to show Seven a parade of sentient cruelty, suffering, and injustice. Children abandoned to live in the shadowy spaces beneath deserted buildings. Scores of the unhoused starving and withering from exposure. Sickly stragglers, dressed in tatters, wandered the streets with rolling carts, collecting bits of detritus in the hope they might be worth a paltry sum because of their metal content. A burly young Orion man with a bruised and swollen-shut left eye, his white tuxedo shirt torn and spattered with blood, staggered beside a skinny Cardassian woman wearing a stained white cocktail dress, who limped down the street because she was missing one high-heeled shoe.

Not knowing how to help, Seven saw it all and kept on walking until she arrived at the drab but serviceable Far-Away Hotel. She entered and approached the front desk, where a Selayan clerk sat, engrossed in some kind of noisy audiovisual entertainment on his padd. Without looking up, the reptilian said in a sibilant voice, "No vacanciesssssss."

Seven pushed a few strips of latinum into his scaly hand.

The clerk greeted her with a fanged smile. "Let me ssssee what we have open." He put down his padd and checked the hotel's computer. "You're in luck. We have a balcony room open on the twenty-ninth floor. One hundred ssseventy credits per night, and I'll need to ssssee ID."

Staring into the vertical irises of the Selayan's eyes, Seven clandestinely pushed several more strips of latinum across the desk and into his hand.

"Ah, yessss. Cash rate. And anonymoussss. Very good." He handed her an isolinear chip card. "Room 29-05."

Seven took the chip card and headed for the lift.

Her room was nothing special. Boring layout. Soulless corporate artwork. Ugly but functional furniture. Spare but clean. In other words, perfect for her needs.

Seven set her satchel on the bed. Checked her chrono.

If Mardani's intel was right, the smugglers' meeting was in just a few hours, and the Fenris Rangers would be sending someone to disrupt the deal. Seven planned to be there well in advance, with a front-row seat to the best show in town.

She opened her satchel to choose her gear. The first thing in her hand was a pulse-pistol. Mardani had told her to keep her distance and not go looking for a fight, but Seven had never needed to seek out conflicts—they had always found her, all on their own.

So, just in case, tonight she would come prepared.

And if trouble got the best of her again anyway?

She steeled herself for violence. *Then I will simply have to improvise.*

Never swim alone. It was good advice, both literally and figuratively. Keon Harper's father had drilled it into him, day after day, every summer until Keon finished college. Even after Harper had left home and ventured out on his own, that sage advice had stayed with him.

As a law-enforcement officer, Harper had internalized the philosophy of the buddy system—which made him only more anxious than ever to be working solo. The death of his partner Len couldn't have come at a worse time. The Fenris Rangers were running short on money, and as the Qiris sector grew more dangerous, many of the Rangers' most experienced veterans were turning in their badges and hanging up their sidearms. Recruitment was getting more difficult with each public defeat the Rangers suffered, and being tarred by Federation-based news services as "vigilantes" and "renegade regulators" had only made matters worse. It had never been easy to find good people willing to bear the risk and responsibility of putting on the badge, but over the past year it had started to seem nearly impossible.

Harper eased his prowler down through drifting veils of misting rain, into a graceful landing inside an open-air berth at Arendel Starport. The hum of his engines hadn't yet fully faded to silence before the starport's maintenance robots scurried into action, assessing whether his ship needed fuel or repairs. He opened his cockpit canopy, squinted into the cool spray of breezy drizzle, and climbed down into the 'bots' midst. "Top off the fuel tanks but leave the rest alone. Got it?" A robot that looked like a stick figure drawing of a person rendered into duranium snapped Harper a crisp salute.

As the squad of machines set to work, Harper opened his ship's starboard storage compartment. From inside he retrieved a spare stun pistol, which he tucked under his belt at the small of his back, and his dark brown duster. The long coat would offer some protection from the storm system forecasted to soak the city for the next few days, and it also would help Harper keep his sidearms and other field gear hidden. His years on the job and then out on the frontier had taught him the value of discretion and concealment.

In minutes he was out of the starport and onto the teeming streets of Arendel. Half the population seemed to spend their lives staring at gadgets in their hands, even while walking, so Harper felt reasonably sure no one would notice his occasional glances at a tracking scanner, and that they wouldn't care even if they did. He had set the tracker to follow a rare isotope found in some of the more exotic weapons the smugglers were hoping to unload here. The signal was clear, but it was also moving quickly, which suggested it was aboard some kind of vehicle.

I could spend all night chasing this stupid thing.

He stepped out of the flow of pedestrian traffic and took shelter from the rain beneath the awning of a streetside food cart. It took him a moment to catch the food vendor's eye and then point at what he wanted. "Two *kesha* kebab. And a can of Skyhaven."

The vendor handed Harper two wooden skewers, each loaded with charcoal-grilled meat. Harper gave the Denobulan woman a strip of latinum, and then she dug his can of cold Tellarite-made ale from an insulated cooler attached to her cart. She pressed the can into his hand. The metallic cylinder was numbingly cold and dripping wet.

Harper nodded his thanks and took shelter beneath a nearby overhang. Pressing his back to a stone wall, he ate his lunch of spicy meat and washed it down with frigid malt liquor. When he was finished, he crushed the can in his fist and tossed it into a nearby recycling bin. He cleaned the grease from his hands by holding them under a torrent of runoff from the building above until they were clean, and then he palmed the remnants of lunch from his white beard.

Calmer now that he'd eaten, Harper took a fresh look at his tracking device and replayed its last few minutes of data. The signal was traveling in random directions, doubling back on its route, and circling various blocks of the city.

I knew it. They're trying to shake any tails they might've picked up.

He pulled out his comm and stole a quick look at the tip he'd received. The smugglers' meeting with the Nausicaans was set for a specific location and time. Whatever they were up to at the moment was just a Kabuki dance designed to make them feel safe.

No point shadowing these idiots all over town. I might as well head for the meet-up site and find myself a place to hide until I'm ready.

He walked a few blocks to a metro rail station and hopped on a maglev headed for the right part of town—which was to say, the part of town no one in their right mind would visit.

This would be so much easier with a partner. We could split up. Triangulate. Cover alternate routes of escape. Not to mention having another pair of hands.

Working alone was going to mean making a difficult choice. In a perfect world, Harper would have been able to count on destroying the smugglers' shipment of weapons while also being able to recover their contraband medicines and untraceable latinum. But that was a lot of steps to carry out alone under fire.

Thirty years ago I might have been fast enough and dumb enough to try a stunt like that. But I'm not the man I used to be. No way I can blast the arms shipment and get away with both the meds and the money. I've got three possible victories, but at best I can only get one. So . . . which one? I don't even want to guess how many people might die if I let the small arms and munitions get away. If I take the latinum, that might help the Rangers, but a lot of colonists really need meds. So—guns, money, or meds? I can only get one. What saves more lives? What does the most good for the most people?

On the tracker, the signal was on course for the meet-up site.

On the maglev, Harper was only a few minutes from his destination.

He had to make a choice, and he was running out of time to do it.

I'll just have to wait until I see the facts on the ground.

He imagined his superiors snapping back, "And what then, Ranger?"

Then . . . I'll just have to improvise.

Mardani's intel had started out solid. Seven followed the instructions he had sent and reached the Arendel Starport in time to see the Starfire 500 prowler land in one of the open-air bays. Minutes later, however, she spotted only a single Fenris Ranger as he exited the starport.

That's odd. The briefing said the Rangers always work in pairs.

Tailing the Ranger proved more difficult than Seven had expected. She had never received any formal training in espionage tradecraft. Consequently, while she had become quite adept at blending in and evading detection and pursuit herself, she was unsure how to transfer those skills into following another person without betraying her own surveillance.

Unable to solicit help from Mardani while in the field, Seven relied on her common sense. She did her best to remain a safe distance from her subject, avoid drawing attention to herself, and watch out for signs that her observation had been detected.

He nearly led Seven into a blunder when he stopped unexpectedly to procure food from a street vendor. All she could do was shelter in an alleyway and let herself slowly get soaked to the bone by the steady, cold drizzle blanketing the city that evening. Watching him eat had another unexpected consequence for Seven: by the time he finished, she herself had grown rather peckish, and she felt annoyed that she had no time to grab a bite of her own when he moved on, his broad shoulders blading with ease through the crowd.

Once he boarded the maglev, Seven knew where he was headed.

He's on his way to the meet-up site. I'd better get ahead of him.

Like many modern cities, Arendel had a network of automated rental stations from which citizens and visitors could rent hoverbikes and aircars. With the wave of a credit chip over a payment sensor, Seven detached a hoverbike from a charging stand. She swung a leg over its seat, settled into a forward-leaning pose behind its windscreen, and powered up its engines, which purred to life. A quick check of its status display confirmed it was in good order and fully charged. Seven gripped its steering handles and with the push of one foot on the accelerator launched herself and the sleek machine like a missile into the night.

Flying the hoverbike through urban traffic put Seven's reflexes to the test. Aircars, other hoverbikes, and a maze of skyscrapers separated by the narrowest of canyons all threatened to turn her into a stain on the cityscape. Wind roared in her ears and whipped her long blonde hair behind her like fluttering serpents, while the city screamed past her in a blur on all sides.

It took only a few minutes for Seven to get ahead of the maglev. Despite a few near-collisions along the way, she reached her destination in the city's industrial quarter and slowed while descending to street level two blocks from the meeting site, well in advance of the actual participants in the gathering. As soon as she stopped the bike, she experienced a wave of vertigo. The rush of acceleration and high-g turns had set her pulse racing.

This seems similar to what Tom Paris spoke of when he described the exhilaration of piloting ultrafast experimental small spacecraft.

Seven dismounted the hoverbike. Because she was paying by the hour for the vehicle, she considered releasing its rental lock. Emancipated from her control, the slender vehicle would pilot itself to the nearest open charging station. Looking around at the drifting walls of mist and the generally deserted nature of the industrial sector at night, Seven decided it was worth the additional expense to make certain she had some way out of this blighted neighborhood. As insurance against thieves, she guided the hoverbike to the end of a nearby alleyway and camouflaged it with a dirty tarp and a few pieces of loose debris that had been left on the street.

Keenly aware that the Ranger, the smugglers, and the Nausicaan black marketeers would all soon converge upon this area, Seven hurried to the tallest building adjacent to the sheltered intersection of alleyways where the meeting was planned to occur. The building was entirely dark, suggesting to Seven that it was unoccupied, so when she discovered its front doors were locked, she unceremoniously kicked them in.

I can apologize after *this assignment is over.*

The whole building seemed to be without power. When Seven looked for active energy service ports, she saw that many of them had been torn out. The few that remained had no safety lights. Both were signs of trouble. In a moment of letting her hope overcome her reason, she pressed the call button for the lift. From beyond the lift doors there was no sound except the eerie groans of wind circulating inside the lift shafts.

No lifts. Which means I have less than ten minutes to climb more than thirty flights to the roof access door. She looked around, found the door to the closest stairwell, opened it, and began her brutal, full-speed sprint up the stairs.

No ordinary human would have been able to accomplish it. Very few genetically enhanced humans would have succeeded, either. But Seven ascended the stairs with unflagging speed thanks to the regenerative and energizing properties of the Borg nanoprobes that still suffused her bloodstream. Versatile and acutely responsive to her needs, they knew when to turn their energy to repairing damaged flesh and nerves, or to enhancing her blood's oxygen-carrying capacity to superhuman levels while simultaneously helping break down and purge waste gases.

She reached the roof access door in four minutes and fifty-one seconds.

At the roof door she checked her scanner. There was no one else on this building's rooftop. Activating her life-sign blocker to hide herself from scanners, she eased the door open.

The wind was stronger on the rooftop than it had been at street level. Harsh sprays of rain stung Seven's face as she crouched low and scouted the vantages from the roof's low perimeter wall. All around her the truly gigantic towers of the cities climbed into the clouds, which flashed with pulses of color from animated displays on roving airships.

But one hundred meters below was where the action would be.

The other buildings surrounding the intersecting alleys were all shorter than the one on which Seven had planted herself, but they also offered more cover for snipers, were closer to the ground (which meant easier targeting), and were generally more accessible. Consequently, armed men had already taken up positions on the lower rooftops overlooking the warren of alleys, which converged and overlapped at peculiar angles to one another. Adding to the tactical complexity at street level were several industrial-size garbage receptacles, of the kind often used for collecting debris from buildings undergoing demolition.

The more Seven observed, the more anxious she became.

Factor in the steam from sewer vents, as well as the fog and rain, and visibility down there will be almost nothing. If any of the smugglers or Nausicaans are using life-sign blockers, the Ranger might not see them coming until it's too late.

She considered using active motion tracking to identify targets concealed by the vapor choking the alleyways, but then she remembered this wasn't her fight.

Observe and report, Mardani had said. *Don't get involved.*

Seven frowned. *Easy for him to say. He's not the one in the line of fire.*

There was movement in the alleyways' joint intersection. Seven pulled out her holo-binoculars, looked down, and adjusted their focus.

A surface vehicle rolled into view, emerging from a bank of fog like a creeping gray beast. Armed figures walked alongside the vehicle, and also behind it. They slowed as they neared the center of the intersection.

Gliding into the crossroads from the opposite side was another large vehicle, but this one looked like an aircar of some kind. Like its counterpart, it was surrounded by a large squad of armed defenders.

Seven panned to one side and then the other. She was sure the Fenris Ranger had to be down there somewhere. But where?

Then she saw him. Lurking behind one of the industrial waste-collection canisters. He was well concealed. Seven's holo-binoculars failed to pick up his heat signature or any life signs, which suggested he had his own sensor-blocking tech. Only Seven's enhanced eyesight had enabled her to discern his outline from the surrounding shadows.

Okay, I see where you are. What are you planning to do?

In the intersection, the smugglers—a large band of suspiciously well-armed Anticans—faced off with their Nausicaan prospective buyers. The two sides appeared to be haggling. A short distance away, the single Fenris Ranger was preparing what Seven speculated might be small, low-yield munitions, or perhaps smoke bombs to mask his actions.

What can he possibly be thinking? Does he mean to hijack the entire shipment of contraband? They'll gun him down before he gets anywhere near that armored truck. So what's his plan? He can't be here just to steal the money, can he?

The longer she observed the Ranger, the more certain she became that he was in way over his head—and that he likely had come to destroy the contraband.

She also saw something that she knew the Ranger couldn't, because of the limitations of his concealed, street-level position: in one of the alleyways on his left flank, a backup squad of Nausicaans was standing ready to attack, probably as insurance against the canine-looking pack of Anticans trying to double-cross them.

If he runs in there, guns blazing, he might get lucky enough to reach the truck. But once that second squad of Nausicaans moves in, they'll pin him down and cut off his only route of escape. That man will never know what hit him.

There was no way she could warn him from her position on the rooftop, not without giving away her position and putting her own survival at risk.

I want to warn him, but those are not my orders. The mission brief specifies that I am only to observe. But if I do not intervene, he will die. She pushed back against her upswell of emotions. *I do not know this man. He is a surveillance subject. Nothing more.*

Every word of what she told herself was true—but the part of her that was awakening to her humanity couldn't help but feel that her rationalizations were a kind of lie.

What would Janeway want me to do? What would she say if I watched that man die and did nothing? Then she realized what she was really asking herself: *If I stand silent and let this man die, what will I become?*

Once she stopped telling herself lies, she knew the answer.

As soon as Harper saw latinum changing hands, he opened fire. He peppered Nausicaans and Anticans alike with a rapid barrage of heavy-stun pulses, and the smugglers and their customers collapsed on the cracked pavement like marionettes with severed strings. Their comrades on the other side of the vehicles from Harper scrambled to cover and shot back wild flurries of disruptor energy, but by then Harper had broken from cover and moved up to the vehicles, turning them into his new de facto barricades. He squeezed off a few blasts of suppressing fire, then ducked.

I just need a few seconds to work. Let's see if these goons can dance.

He pulled two sliver-thin metallic disks from his belt, activated each with a press of his thumb, and then he flung them over his vehicular cover, one to each flank on the enemy's side. As soon as they settled on the ground they filled the air with thick, eye-stinging red smoke. Then the arrays of miniaturized stun-beam emitters along their edges unleashed furious prismatic sprays of stun pulses at varying angles in seemingly every direction. All who had been sent into the blinding haze to find him collapsed in twitching heaps.

Sorry, kids, Harper gloated. *Gotta be quick to trip this light fantastic.*

He slapped transporter-enhancing beacons onto the containers of medical supplies that laid exposed in the open cargo compartment of the smugglers' vehicle. The enhancers activated on contact, sending out signals that would help focus the transport sequence.

All I need to do is hold the line until—

A disruptor pulse hit the vehicle just above Harper's head. Hot sparks stung his face, and he swatted them away. *Where the hell did that come from?*

More shots screamed in from his rear left flank. Harper dived for the ground and tried to roll beneath the smugglers' vehicle for protection, but its chassis was too low—he couldn't fit under it. In a panic he scuttled backward, firing random shots into the drifting red smoke.

I guess it's too late to hold up my badge and say they're under arrest.

He squinted into the crimson vapor as it began to dissipate and found the source of the unexpected retaliation: a narrow air gap between two of the buildings abutting the crossroads, a passage so slim that no one had bothered to note it on any of the publicly downloadable maps of the city—and now it was vomiting Nausicaan gunmen.

Well, that's just great.

The Nausicaan reinforcements were far enough behind Harper to cut off his only avenue of retreat, and there were still enough Anticans and Nausicaans on the other side of the vehicles to make a charge just as futile. Feeling his last measure of hope falter, he resigned himself to the consequences of his final, fatal mistake.

This is gonna suck.

A symphony of pulsed plasma fire echoed down the alleyways and was answered by a guttural chorus of Nausicaan profanity and Antican roars of pain.

Harper's first surprise was realizing he wasn't dead yet. His second surprise took another half second to register: *Pulsed plasma?* Following the torrent of energy, Harper looked back toward the sliver-thin gap, past the legion of stunned Nausicaans sprawled on the ground, and beheld a modern-day Valkyrie—a tall, blonde, nigh-angelic force of nature with a pair of Talarian Stingers. Watching her defy danger, he couldn't help but grin like a fool.

My luck's gonna run out someday—but not today.

• • •

Seven strode across open ground, laying down suppressing fire every step of
the way, until she joined the Ranger behind the smugglers' vehicle. Heavy-set,
white-bearded, and late-middle-aged, he looked harried but unhurt, but she
needed to be sure. "Can you walk?"

He seemed annoyed by the question. "I'll damned well walk outta here." He
turned, pressed himself against the vehicle, then reached up and snapped off a
few more blind shots at the Anticans and Nausicaans. All his shots went high
and wide, but they still made the criminals duck. He aimed his suspicious stare
at Seven with greater precision. "Who are you?"

"The one saving your ass."

"Fair enough." He offered her his left hand. "Keon Harper, Fenris Rangers."

She used her left hand to shake his. "Seven." She listened for sounds of
movement, and then she blind-fired a few stun shots over the vehicle with one
of her Stingers. At least one of her shots struck someone, who yelped in distress
and then collapsed.

Harper nodded approvingly. "Good shooting."

"Thanks. Let's go."

"As soon as I get what I came for." He pulled a small handheld transmitter
from his coat pocket and pressed its main button. Almost immediately, the
whine of a transporter beam rang in the night air, and then the crate of medical
supplies inside the smugglers' vehicle dematerialized.

As soon as the meds were gone, the alleyway intersection resounded with
the noise of more transporter beams. Harper stole a look over the smugglers'
vehicle. "Reinforcements. We'd better move."

Seven noted what Harper was leaving behind. "What about the weapons?"

He shook his head. "Scan shielded. Transporter-proof."

"Then don't use a transporter." With one full-power shot from her Stinger,
Seven vaporized the lock on one of the crates.

Disruptor pulses tore past above her and Harper, scarring the walls of buildings with molten divots. Seven forced open the crate she had energetically
unlocked, assessed its contents in a glance, and flipped up the lid on a box of

plasma grenades. She pulled the pin from the grenade in the middle of the padded tray and pressed its trigger. Then she looked at Harper.

"Run."

They fled in alternating sprints, each of them taking turns covering the other's retreat from the nexus of alleyways. As they slipped beyond a corner at a bend in one alley, the Anticans and Nausicaans at the intersection surged forward in pursuit, bellowing as they charged.

The grenade Seven had armed inside the crate detonated. The smugglers' vehicle vanished in a flash of white-hot fire and a supersonic shock wave that flattened the pursuing Anticans and Nausicaans face-first into the rain-slicked pavement.

Harper looked both terrified and amused by the chaos erupting behind him and Seven. "Nice work," he said as they continued running, "but that ain't gonna stop 'em."

"We're outnumbered," Seven said, thinking aloud. "We need to hide."

"Wrong. If we want to live, we gotta get off this rock. *Now.*"

"This rock?"

"This *planet*. You got a ship?" He frowned as Seven shook her head to answer no. "Then we need to get to mine, before they catch up to us. C'mon!"

There was no time to argue, discuss terms, or ask questions. It was run or die. When Harper quickened his pace to a wild sprint, Seven matched his stride.

She knew what Mardani would say when he learned of this.

He would bellow that these were not her orders. That this was not the plan.

Seven found it oddly liberating that she no longer gave a damn.

Running at Harper's side, fleeing into the night of her own accord, she was flooded with a strange euphoria, an epiphany of giddy realization.

This is what it feels like to be free.

On any other day, in any other situation, Harper would have thought it was plum crazy to put his life in the hands of a stranger. But when that stranger showed up in the middle of a firefight like a guardian angel, he didn't care why—he was just thankful she was there.

They tore out of the alleyway, onto a nearly deserted street in the industrial sector of Arendel. It was an urban wasteland of empty lots, crumbling buildings, and fractured pavement. Half the streetlamps were dark, separating the intensifying banks of fog into patches of blinding haze and impenetrable wells of shadow. This was not a great place to look for a taxi, a parked aircar, or a Good Samaritan, but Harper figured it would be a great place to hide a body.

He shot a desperate look at Seven. "Now what?"

Seven cast aside a piece of debris that had been propped against the front of the building, and then she pulled away a grimy, tattered tarpaulin to reveal an idling hoverbike.

She shot Harper a cocky look. "Now we ride."

"Fine, but I'm driving."

As he had expected, she had taken offense. "Why?"

To save time, he told her the simple truth. "Because you're a better shot than me, and we're gonna have a lot of pissed-off Nausicaans behind us in a few seconds. Our best chance of reaching my ship alive is you covering our six."

"Our six what?"

"Our rear."

"Understood." She took half a second to think. "Your terms are acceptable." She pushed the hoverbike toward Harper. He swung his left leg over the saddle and took hold of the handlebar controls. As he settled his feet onto the accelerator and braking thruster pedals, Seven planted herself on the saddle behind him, her back pressed against his.

Behind them, the first wave of Nausicaans emerged from the alleyway on their own hoverbikes, followed by their aircar.

Seven drew her pulse-pistols. "Punch it."

Harper stomped on the accelerator and held on as their hoverbike shot away like a bullet. Instantly, the wind made his eyes water, and it felt as if every tiny bit of airborne grit in the city was sandblasting his face. For fear of choking, he kept his mouth shut, clenched his jaw, and tried not to scream as he raced like a daredevil above the crowded streets of Arendel.

Over the growl of the bike's engine and the roaring of the wind, he heard

Seven's plasma pistols decimating their pursuers. He wanted to look back and admire her marksmanship, but he had to keep his attention on the path and obstacles ahead, which blurred past at 270 kilometers per hour as Harper pushed the hoverbike to its limits.

Still, he saw enough to be impressed.

Harper had never seen anyone shoot like this. Seven wasn't shooting to kill—she was shooting to block, divert, or disable. Instead of firing at the pilots or riders on the hoverbikes chasing them, Seven used precision shots to bring down tangles of cabling to ensnare them, or to explode exposed canisters of compressed but nonflammable gas carried on passing vehicles, to force the other bikes into crashes or collisions. She shot at least one hoverbike out from under its pilot but somehow did it in a way that let the Nausicaan slow down enough to jump to safety before his bike hit the ground.

Within minutes she had dispatched the last of the Nausicaans' hoverbikes.

Then the Nausicaans' armored aircar appeared above Seven and Harper, dropping out of the misty night over their hoverbike like a raptor descending upon a sparrow.

Harper forced the hoverbike into overdrive, but the armored aircar matched them with ease and continued its descent, pushing him and Seven toward the street. It would be only a matter of seconds before it crushed them into the pavement and spread their remains across twenty city blocks in a flurry of sparks and blood. "I can't shake 'em!"

Seven holstered her pulse-pistols. "Then don't."

She reached inside her coat, pulled something out, and then—seemingly without a trace of fear—stood on the back of the hurtling hoverbike's saddle and lobbed something at the underbelly of the aircar. Whatever she tossed made contact—and stuck fast.

Seven turned forward as she dropped onto the saddle, and then she wrapped her arms around Harper's waist. "Brakes!"

His right foot left the accelerator, and his left foot slammed the braking thrusters into action. The hoverbike decelerated from 300 kph to just over 30 in a fraction of a second, slamming him against the handlebars and windscreen, and Seven against his back. In an eyeblink the aircar was far ahead of them, but Harper knew they would quickly—

An explosion on the underside of the armored aircar shredded its antigrav system and directional controls. Spinning, it struck the ground and rolled like a Catherine wheel through an empty construction site, leaving fiery mayhem in its wake. A skeletal, multistory building frame collapsed on top of the disabled vehicle, entombing it in a grave of warped steel.

Harper stopped the hoverbike and stared at the pillar of smoke rising from the crash site.

"Holy shit."

Seven seemed strangely sanguine. "They'll live. The armor on that aircar is four-centimeter-thick monotanium. Its passengers are likely bruised and concussed, but not seriously injured." She put her hand on his shoulder. "We should keep moving."

He looked back at Seven. "You sure you don't want to bail out now? There's a good chance these goons don't know you, but I guarantee you they know me. And there's a better-than-average chance they'll have more of their people waiting for me at the starport."

"Then it sounds to me like you still need my help."

Her candor made him smile. "I hate to admit it, but . . . yeah, I reckon I do."

"We should go, then."

He leaned down behind the windscreen and slowly eased the hoverbike back into motion. "Next stop, Arendel Starport. We'll be haulin' ass, so hang on to your hat."

Her confusion sounded authentic as she said, "I am not wearing a hat."

Harper shook his head and poured on the speed. "Miss Seven, you are one weird bird."

Seven spent the ride to Arendel Starport trying to discern what it was about Harper that made her feel so completely at ease in his company. It wasn't his looks, though he was a handsome man for his age. She thought it might be his quiet air of confidence. The man seemed to emanate calm. It was a quality Seven found most admirable; in many ways, Harper seemed to embody many of the traits she had once admired in Chakotay.

They reached the starport sooner than they had expected, mostly thanks to

Harper's aptitude for controlling the hoverbike at perilous speeds. As soon as their hoverbike stopped, Harper switched off its engine, revealing the clamor of voices and sirens that was growing closer by the moment, surrounding and pressing in upon them.

Harper got off the bike and assessed their situation. "They've got my scent. Won't be long now. Sure you wouldn't rather shake hands and say '*Sayonara*'?"

Seven dismounted the hoverbike and pushed it behind a large garbage-collection canister in front of the starport's wall. "Where is your ship berthed?"

"Bay forty-one."

"Then we should move."

"Reckon we should."

They entered the starport together, walking side by side as if they'd been doing so for years. Harper hadn't needed to tell Seven to keep her Stingers holstered, or to walk casually but with purpose, so as not to draw attention or cause alarm. She felt as if she could intuit what he needed her to do, what he wanted her to be, moment to moment. It felt good. It was comforting.

Harper was unlocking the doors to Bay 41 when Seven heard the commotion of their foes entering the starport one level below them. Alarms clanged and several distinct, masculine voices cried out in pain and distress. Seven left Harper's side to steal a look through a nearby opening in the hallway's wall, down into the towering building's lushly landscaped atrium. An entire platoon's worth of hostile faces had arrived, a mixed force of Nausicaans and Anticans, and they plowed past the starport's lightly armed and generally feck-less security personnel.

She returned to Harper's side as the door to the landing bay opened. "They're here."

He seemed unconcerned. "They made good time. Must've taken the inner loop."

Harper gestured for Seven to step inside. She moved past him, and then he closed the door and blasted its controls with his sidearm, reducing the panel to a sparking heap of junk. Fiery motes fell to the floor as a maintenance robot emerged from a low opening in the wall to squawk in mechanical noises at Harper, who dismissed it with a wave as he stepped around it. "Yeah, yeah. Bill the Fenris Rangers. Starport admin knows the account number."

Parked in the center of the bay was Harper's ship, which Seven recognized from her FSA briefing as a Starfire 500. The long, dark gray, and asymmetrical two-seat fast-attack fighter was the standard model for a Fenris Rangers prowler, which was what the Rangers called their patrol ships. This particular ship had seen more than its share of action. Its main fuselage was dented, scratched, and decorated from nose to tail with scorches and carbon scoring. Several panels on its hull had been replaced with spare parts of clashing colors. And none of its three landing struts matched. The only parts of it that looked new and fastidiously maintained were its Fenris Rangers identification markings.

Harper noticed Seven scrutinizing his ship as he unlocked its cargo panel. "She's a bit scruffy, but trust me—she packs a punch."

"I know." Seven pointed at its twin weapons arrays. "It can carry up to two dozen quantum microtorpedoes. And those are phased quantum particle cannons, yes?"

"We just call it 'the heat.'" He pulled open the cargo hatch. Inside was the crate of medical supplies he had liberated from the Anticans before Seven blew up their vehicle. Harper removed the transporter recall beacon from the crate, switched it off, and stuffed it in his coat pocket. Then he slammed the cargo hatch shut. "Got what I came for. Time to bounce."

Seven was about to ask what Harper intended to bounce, but she stopped herself as she began to infer the meanings of his peculiar idioms based solely on context.

As Harper climbed on top of his ship's arrowhead-shaped fuselage, the cockpit canopy slid open ahead of him, most likely in response to having scanned and confirmed his biometric profile or his DNA. He was one foot into the cockpit's front seat before he looked back at Seven. "Well? You comin' or goin'?"

She hesitated, for just half a second. After defying so many of her mission parameters, why not take the next logical step? If she balked now, would she ever get an opportunity like this again? Mardani had wanted her to observe the Rangers without making contact, but his long-term objectives had included Seven infiltrating the organization.

I am simply accelerating the mission's timetable.

She knew Mardani would call her actions reckless and insubordinate.

Seven called them efficient.

She climbed onto the ship's fuselage behind Harper. "I'm coming."

He pointed at the cockpit's rear seat. "Strap in tight. If you thought the hoverbike was a gut-flipper, you ain't seen nothin' yet."

Seven settled into the copilot's seat and fastened her safety harness. As soon as Harper was secured into his own seat, the canopy slid closed above them. While he powered up the engines and navigational computer, Seven familiarized herself with the onboard systems at her command from the second seat. The interface wasn't one she had seen before, but it was intuitive. Within seconds, she had sensors, comms, and the weapons array online.

The engines' whine pitched higher as Harper guided the prowler in a simple level ascent using the ship's antigrav pads. It would take just a few seconds for the ship to clear the walls of the recessed landing bay and become free to navigate.

They were halfway there when the landing bay's door—the one whose controls Harper had reduced to charred optronic pasta—exploded inward, blasted to shreds by military-grade explosives. Smoke and fire belched into the empty space beneath the prowler, and a flurry of hot shrapnel pelted the hull and canopy.

The prowler had less than two meters to go before rising above the wall into open air when a Nausicaan wearing a harness-mounted plasma cannon charged out of the smoke onto the landing pad and braced himself to unleash a firestorm.

Seven fired a single minimum-power blast from one of the prowler's quantum cannons. It hit the ground a meter in front of the Nausicaan gunner, creating a shock wave that threw him backward into the rest of his unit, tumbling them all into a sad pile of stunned defeat.

"Nicely done," Harper said. The prowler cleared the wall, and he engaged the thrusters at full power to leave Arendel behind as swiftly as possible. In less than half a minute the atmosphere faded away to reveal the vacuum of space. Harper switched to impulse power to get the prowler out of the planet's gravity well. "So, Miss Seven."

"Just 'Seven,' please."

"My apologies. Tell me, Seven: What exactly do you do for a living?"

"At the moment? Nothing."

"What is it you used to do?"

"Odd jobs."

"Secretive type, eh? That's fine. But I hope you'll forgive my presumption when I say that I think you'd make one hell of a Fenris Ranger."

Knowing he couldn't see her from the front seat, Seven permitted herself the luxury of a coy smile of satisfaction. "I imagine I would."

6

Fenris – Ranger Headquarters

The planet and its eponymous capital city weren't what Seven had expected. In truth, she hadn't really known what to expect of the home base of the Fenris Rangers. For most of the past year she had heard talking heads on various news services—some domestic to the Federation, others foreign—characterize the Rangers as rogues, renegades, and dangerous vigilantes. In her imagination she had concocted a tableau of swashbuckling interstellar freebooters, carefree pirates, and assorted benevolent outlaws. None of which had prepared her for reality.

Harper had relinquished control of his Starfire 500 on approach to Fenris Rangers headquarters, and the facility's flight operations unit had guided the prowler through local air traffic. Once the base had control, Harper's tone changed from cocky to weary. "We're in their hands now. Grab some shut-eye while you still can."

His advice had been well-intentioned, but Seven had no use for it. She gazed in wonder through the prowler's cockpit canopy at the world passing by outside. She was mesmerized by the carefully planned grids for power and comms, the well-spaced farms, the constellations of streetlights in the suburban sectors, and finally the dense clusters of increasingly large structures and denser city blocks as they approached the central district of the planet's capital. Fenris was no forgotten frontier planet. It was a well-established colony, one that likely had at least a couple of centuries of history under its belt. Not a likely home for a lawless band of regulators.

Over the comm, she heard the crisp diction of a masculine voice: *"Ranger forty-six nineteen, this is Wolf's Den flight ops. Will you need support ops on touchdown?"*

Harper keyed open a response channel. "Affirmative, flight ops. I'm haulin' medical supplies. We need to get 'em off my bird and out the door, RFN. Over."

"Copy that, forty-six nineteen. We'll have whistlers on standby."

As soon as the display in front of Seven confirmed the channel was closed, she leaned forward to ask Harper, "Whistlers?"

"Slang for medics. 'Cause of the noises their scanners make."

Seven nodded despite being mildly perplexed by the human proclivity for obscuring meanings with slang and jargon. "I see."

Her reaction seemed to amuse Harper. "Steel yourself. The patter flies fast and furious down there." The screen in front of Seven updated to indicate Harper had transmitted a data file to the Rangers' headquarters. "Before you ask," he said, "I just submitted your application."

"Most kind of you. Thank you."

Harper shook his head and let slip a good-natured chuckle. "Gotta work on your lingo. That was a lotta words when you could've just said, 'Cool, thanks.'"

"Are the two statements not semantically identical?"

"Huh? Well, I . . . Sure. I guess so."

"Then why should I risk obfuscating my meaning through excessive truncation?"

Seven saw over the cockpit divider that Harper had turned in his seat to steal a sidelong look back at her. "Girl? Are you screwin' with me?"

"First, I am not a girl. Second, if I interpret your rather vulgar inquiry on a literal basis, I have only one choice but to answer, 'No.' However, I believe your query to be colloquial and idiomatic in nature. In which case, my answer . . . remains 'No.'"

"Ain't you ever heard, *Brevity is the soul of wit?*"

After a momentary search of her memory, Seven said, "No."

"Why am I not surprised?"

"Meaning?"

"You talk too much, kid."

Minutes later, the landing struts of Harper's prowler touched down on the flight deck. Once again, Seven's expectations of raggedly dressed civilians

scrambling to maintain an illegal squadron of law-enforcement vessels was sty-
mied by a collision with reality. The moment that Harper's ship came to a halt
on the flight deck, it was swarmed by mechanics and technicians in pale gray
jumpsuits, which were marked clearly with insignia denoting each person's
rating or rank, and their role with the flight ops maintenance team. Mechanics
attached fuel lines to the prowler's fuselage, and a team of olive-jumpsuit-
wearing cargo handlers and people in white-and-blue medics' uniforms converged upon the spacecraft to unload its cargo.

By the time Harper powered down the vessel's engines and opened the
cockpit canopy, the flight deck team had already opened the crate of medical
supplies he'd captured in Arendel and was making an inventory of its contents.
"Five hundred units of isoprovoline," said an older humanoid man whose uniform insignia included a golden caduceus on his jacket's collar and shoulder.
"Two hundred doses of terakine. One hundred twenty units of trioxin. Six
liters of hyronalide." He looked over his shoulder at a younger man in a medical uniform. "Make sure all six liters reach the Freyim colony on Soroya IV.
They'll need it to purify their groundwater."

Meanwhile, a few other Rangers had gathered around Harper's ship, likely
drawn by curiosity to the sudden flurry of activity. One, a lean and weathered-
looking Bajoran man whose stubbled face was lined with fissures and worry
lines, grinned up at Harper. "Late again, Kee? What was it this time? Took a
wrong turn at the Azure Nebula?"

Harper raised his hand with his fingers arranged in what Seven assumed
was an insulting gesture as he shouted back at the Bajoran, "Kiss my ass,
Jalen."

A much younger Ranger, a handsome brown-skinned man with a brilliant
white smile, whistled when he caught sight of Seven. "Well, *damn*, Harper!
Who do we have here?"

It was easy for Seven to hear the long-suffering irritation in Harper's voice
as he replied, "None of your business, Lucan."

As Harper and Seven climbed out of the prowler and descended its lad-
ders to the flight deck, two women Rangers—one in her forties who looked
to be of mixed human and Cardassian ancestry, and the other a black-
haired, fair-skinned Trill woman in her thirties, with the hint of a stylish

and dramatic undercut above her right ear—shouldered past their male colleagues.

The half-Cardassian woman had a dry, brusque quality to her manner that Seven found oddly familiar. She caught Harper's eye and gestured at his prowler. "Did you get the latinum?"

Harper shook his head. "Sorry, Rana. Had to make a choice. Picked the meds."

Rana nodded but was obviously disappointed. "Of course you did."

The Trill woman, meanwhile, planted herself in front of Harper and Seven. "So spill the beans, Kee. Who's your rider? Witness? Prisoner?" She appraised Seven with a peculiar, curious stare made all the more intriguing by her large, wide-set eyes. "Socialator?"

Like a protective parent, Harper put himself between Seven and his fellow Rangers. "Since I know y'all won't stop asking 'til you get an answer, you might as well know, she's here as a potential recruit."

Jalen looked surprised. "Seriously?"

Rana sounded equally dubious. "What lies did you spin to swing that?"

Lucan, the hotspur of the group, waved off his elders' cynical doubts. "Ignore them, Blondie. There's no better job in the galaxy than being a Fenris Ranger. We fly free, defend the weak, and bring evil to heel—all before breakfast!"

His spiel left the Trill woman shaking her head in disapproval. "Put a sock in it, Lucan." To Seven she added, "Trust me, being a Fenris Ranger's not just an adventure—it's a *job*." She smiled and extended her open hand to Seven. "Ellory Kayd. 'Ell' for short."

When Seven touched Ellory's hand, she felt a jolt of excitement, of a kind for which she had no name. She shook Ellory's hand and stared, almost hypnotized, into the Trill woman's soulful dark brown eyes as she replied in a faltering voice, "Seven."

"Nice to meet you, Seven." Ellory raised her elegantly arched eyebrows and held Seven's hand for a few seconds longer than Seven expected, and she returned Seven's intense eye contact without blinking. It was only a brief moment of contact, but to Seven it felt significant, freighted with meaning.

Admiring Ellory's full lips, enchanting smile, and delicate nose, Seven recalled the feelings of attraction she had felt for her past romantic partners; these new sensations exceeded any she had ever experienced before.

As Ellory let go of Seven's hand, another Ranger shouldered his way into the group. The newcomer was older, a male Andorian of impressive height with cobalt-blue skin and pale gray eyes. His uniform sported more elaborate rank insignia than those of Harper and his peers, and he projected an air of authority. "Harper. The brass want to see you in ops, sharpish."

"I'll bet they do."

Lucan grinned at the Andorian. "Lookin' buff, Shren."

"I didn't ask for your opinion, Ranger Sagasta."

"No, I'm just saying, you look fit."

Shren eyed Sagasta with suspicion. "Thank you."

Sagasta folded his arms across his chest, admired Shren's form, and shook his head. "Who knew carryin' the bosses' water would be such a great workout?"

As the other Rangers muffled their laughter, Shren shot a murderous stare at Sagasta. "One more word, and you'll be carrying your own head out the door." Then the Andorian looked at Harper and added, "Get over to ops. Now."

Harper snapped a quick salute. "Yes, sir." As he broke away from the group with Shren following close behind him, he said to the others, "Take care of my friend 'til I get back."

"Count on it," Sagasta said with a broad grin.

Ellory snaked her arm around Seven's and led her away from Sagasta. "You've had a long flight, yeah? You must be hungry."

"I am, yes."

"Then let's hit the mess. The food's not exactly gourmet cuisine, but it's free."

Jalen leaned in to add, "And we *still* don't get our money's worth out of it."

The other Rangers fell in behind Seven and Ellory, all of them except Rana bantering as if they were vying for the chance to be Seven's new best friend.

Seven found the surfeit of attention awkward, unfamiliar, and more than a little bit embarrassing. However, part of her had to admit that she also found it strangely flattering. Suppressing an urge to smile, she kept quiet and let the Rangers fawn over her.

I've never been popular before . . . I don't hate it.

Keeping up with Shren when he was mad was always a challenge for Harper. Not only was the deputy chief of patrol taller and therefore gifted with a longer stride, the Andorian was also two decades younger than Harper, whose middle-aged joints grew more brittle and weary by the day.

Even at a quick step, Harper couldn't help but note the rapidly decaying state of the Fenris Rangers' headquarters. What once had been considered routine maintenance had become a luxury, and the facility was showing its age. Peeling paint, scuffed floors, random overhead lights left in place long after they had burned out—they all were symptoms of the growing malaise that was eating away at the Rangers' morale along with their reserves of operating capital. Just thinking about the group's decline suffused Harper with melancholy.

I'm surprised the brass hasn't asked us to start paying rent.

A short walk delivered Shren and Harper to the base's operations office, a heavily fortified, high-tech tactical command center located deep inside the heart of the armored complex. The three bosses who held the most direct authority over Harper's day-to-day life and objectives stood huddled around a hexagonal table, above whose center was projected a translucent hologram of a star map of the Qiris sector. Shren escorted Harper to the table, snapped to attention, and saluted his superiors.

"Commander. Presenting Ranger Harper, as ordered."

Too tired to snap, Harper tossed the brass a loose salute. "What he said."

Commander Zhang Wei, the leader of the Fenris Rangers, eyed Harper with a look between disappointment and contempt. Despite her diminutive stature and slender frame, the sixtyish human woman of mixed Asian ancestry carried herself with an air of dignity and authority. "You never change, do you, Harper?"

"Not unless it's laundry day."

From behind his shoulder, Harper heard Shren mutter, "You missed laundry day."

"Again? Dammit."

Deputy Commander Saszyk, a grizzled octogenarian Saurian whose avocado-colored hide was marked by more scars won in battle than Harper could or ever would want to count, let out a long, low hiss before beckoning Harper closer with a wave of his clawed manus. "We have reviewed your after-action report of the mission to Skånevik Prime. The death of your trainee Deputy Ranger Leniker Zehga was a great tragedy."

Hearing his dead partner's name turned Harper serious. "Yes, sir, it was."

The third member of the Rangers' command triumvirate, Chief of Patrol Yivv, was an androgynous, intersex Bolian whose gentle manner and melodious voice had a calming quality. "After a careful review of the sensor logs, our internal integrity division has concluded that Deputy Zehga's death was not one you could reasonably have foreseen or prevented. You are officially cleared of any legal culpability in this matter, and Deputy Zehga's sacrifice will be noted in accordance with our traditions by the addition of his name to our wall of honored dead."

Harper bowed his head slightly to Yivv as a sign of respect. "Thank you, Chief."

Commander Zhang's countenance remained stern. "That brings us to our next item of business, Ranger Harper. Who did you just bring unannounced into our headquarters?"

"Her name is Seven. She's a woman without a country, as they used to say."

"Why did you bring her here?"

"She wants to enlist." Harper noted the dubious expressions on the bosses' faces. "I sent in her application ahead of our arrival."

Saszyk hissed and tasted the air with his tongue. "We received it."

"Then what's with the third degree?"

Yivv struck an apologetic tone. "We have concerns about her . . . background."

Harper's temper started rising. "Which part? The one where she saved my life on Otroya II? Or the part where she served as a civilian specialist for four years on a Starfleet vessel?"

The deputy commander traded a cryptic look with the commander. Zhang wore a look of confusion as she asked Harper, "Did you notice her cybernetic enhancements?"

"Yeah. So what? Plenty of people have 'em. If memory serves, you have an artificial hand, and Chief Yivv has a synthetic liver."

"Yes," Zhang said, "but our prosthetics are corrective—and weren't created by the Borg."

The word *Borg* hit Harper like a slap in the face. "What're you talking about?"

"Your recruit is a former drone of the Borg Collective."

Harper chewed on that for a moment before recovering his composure. "So was Admiral Jean-Luc Picard. But I bet you wouldn't hold that against him if *he* applied for a job."

Saszyk shook his head. "Admiral Picard was assimilated for a matter of hours."

"In which time he killed *thousands* of his own people."

"He also helped *end* the first Borg attack on Earth. This woman you've brought into our halls was a Borg drone for most of her life. How many people do you think she killed? How many worlds did she assimilate? Their circumstances are far from equivalent."

"I don't care." Harper pointed at a display showing the unloading of his prowler on the flight deck. "See that crate of medical supplies? We wouldn't have it if not for her. And because of her, pirates and thugs operating in this sector have been deprived of a fresh cache of munitions and small arms. Don't judge her by what she *was*. Judge her by who she is *now*. By what she *does* now. We need all the skilled help we can get, and you know it."

Nodding in agreement, Yivv said, "You're right. We do need fresh blood. But we have to be cautious, Harper. Our organization, its jurisdiction, and its responsibilities all are expanding faster than we can handle, thanks to the transfer of so much Federation aid to the mass evacuation of Romulus. In our haste to grow, we must take care not to induct dangerous elements with ulterior motives."

Before Harper could reply, Saszyk added, "Even if we can draw new recruits, we are running low on ships, support facilities, provisions, and capital."

"I thought we had a new squadron of prowlers comin' in."

"Delayed," Zhang said. "Being held at the shipyard until we can pay for them."

"You've gotta be kidding me." Harper looked into the eyes of the bosses and saw they all were deadly serious. "Be that as it may, it's not a reason to reject Seven's application."

Shren, who usually held his tongue in front of the brass, spoke up. "If she still has a link to the Borg, she's a danger, Harper. What if she's a Borg advance scout? Or a Borg infiltrator?"

"She's not." Harper turned back toward the triumvirate. "Listen to me. Seven saved my life. She didn't have to. She could've walked away and let me die, and no one would've ever known. But she put her ass on the line to save the life of a stranger in trouble. And I seem to recall that's function *numero uno* in our job description."

Zhang nodded, looking almost humbled. "It is."

"Then give her a chance. Our regs say we don't discriminate based on background. So prove it. Make me her training officer. I'll take personal responsibility for teaching her how to be a Fenris Ranger."

It was clear to Harper that Saszyk still harbored doubts. The Saurian blinked his bulbous eyes a couple of times, and then he looked at Harper. "If we allow this, keep one thing in mind, Ranger: we cannot risk being held responsible for helping the Borg Collective obtain a foothold in this sector. We need your word that if your new recruit gives you *any* reason to think she might pose a risk of assimilation, to anyone, anywhere . . . you will terminate her. Immediately."

The gravity of the request left Harper mute for a second. Then he mustered his courage and nodded at the deputy commander. "You have my word, sir."

He prayed it was a promise he would never need to keep.

Lunch with a group of Fenris Rangers was not so much a meal, Seven realized, as it was an improv comedy performance. Seated at a table with Sagasta, Jalen, Rana, and Kayd—or Ellory, as Seven couldn't help but think of her—Seven listened with rapt attention as Sagasta looked into her eyes with manic intensity: "Are you ready to have your mind blown?"

"That sounds like a most unpleasant experience."

"I'll rephrase. Are you ready to learn something shocking?"

"Yes. Proceed."

"Too kind." He pointed with one dark brown hand at the shredded meat in the center of Seven's tray. "What would you say if I told you that pile of so-called meat is fundamentally indistinguishable"—he pointed with his other hand at a different-looking mound of protein that had been ladled onto Ellory's lunch tray—"from *that* pile of alleged meat?"

"That seems unlikely."

The Rangers all shook their heads. Jalen Par, the Bajoran, interjected, "It's true. We've done blind taste tests. Whatever *that* is, it goes by many names—"

"And has many faces," Rana added.

Ellory concluded, "But it has only one flavor."

"Which," Sagasta continued, "is why the only way to tell what it is you're supposed to be eating is to check the adjacent meat identifier."

Seven cocked one eyebrow in amusement. "Meat identifier?"

Sagasta pointed at the various side dishes served to the left of each heap of protein on the various trays. "If it's patridgeberry sauce, it's supposed to be poultry. If it's applesauce, it's supposed to be pork. If it's gravy, they want you think it's red meat. And if it's a cup of melted butter, it's pretending to be fish."

Seven lifted a sporkful of wilted green vegetable matter from her tray. "And this?"

The Rangers leaned in, squinted, leaned back, and declared in unison: "Mystery meat."

She put down the spork and pushed aside the tray. "I am no longer hungry."

Harper was suddenly behind her. "Told y'all she was a fast learner." To Seven he added in a more confidential register, "Walk with me."

The Rangers all said hasty good-byes as Seven got up from the table—all except Ellory, who said nothing but held Seven spellbound with her stare until Harper pulled Seven away.

"C'mon, kid, we're burning daylight."

Seven trailed Harper out of the mess hall and down a grungy hallway lined with what looked like administrative offices. As soon as they were far enough away from other people to have a measure of privacy, Harper said, "Welcome to the Fenris Rangers."

"I'm in?"

"On a probationary basis. You're a rookie trainee. And I'm the lucky duck that gets to teach you how to swim."

"I am already a proficient swimmer."

"But still struggling with metaphorical idioms, I see."

"Point taken."

"Glad to hear it."

"What's next?"

"Normally, we'd go to the armory, fit you out with some field gear. But we're on a tight budget, and you came with plenty of your own toys, so we're actually on our way back out."

"To where?"

"The RNZ. That's where the work is. And believe me, we got plenty of it. Our mission profile's been evolving the last few months. Used to be, Federation-funded NGOs—"

"NGOs?"

"Non-governmental organizations. Civilian charities. Nonprofit aid groups. That sort of thing." He noted Seven's nod of understanding. "Once the Federation redeployed Starfleet to help Romulus and its neighbors with their exploding-sun problem, all the NGOs out here pulled up stakes and went with 'em, at the Federation's request."

Seven recalled all she had seen and read about the crisis developing in the Romulan home system. "That request wasn't unique to agencies operating in the Qiris sector. The call for aid was disseminated across the quadrant."

"Yeah, but just because everybody gave something, that doesn't mean everyone gave equally, or that everyone felt it the same way. Older, better-established worlds; the core systems; the capital planets—they might've felt a little sting from what they had to give up. But they've got the wealth, the resources, the infrastructure, to weather a few years or even a decade without direct Federation support."

Seven and Harper detoured around a cluster of mechanics near the end of the long hall that led to the flight deck, and then Harper continued, "Out here, though? Take away even a little of what's been keeping dozens of colonies alive, and you've got a recipe for disaster. The fringe worlds are poor, underdeveloped. So when the Federation NGOs took back all their industrial replicators and portable fusion generators so they could send them to Romulan refugees, they left millions of people on dozens of worlds across Qiris sector high and dry.

"Think about it, kid. One day, a few million people on barely habitable colony worlds across the Qiris sector woke up and found out their chief sources of food, potable water, energy, and raw materials were all gone. Almost overnight, all those people were on the verge of going hungry, dying of thirst, and living without power, communications, or medicine."

Struck by the horror of what Harper had described, Seven struggled to reconcile the actions of the Federation with the ideals for which she had been told it stood. "But they said the transfer of resources was only temporary."

"Sure it is. 'Only temporary,' say the people who are taking everything away. And who knows? Maybe the Federation is telling the truth, or at least thinks it is. Maybe they really do mean to bring all that stuff back someday, after they get the Romulan mess sorted. But these things tend to drag on longer than anyone expects. And in my experience, even if this dry spell is as short as the Federation says it'll be, there are lots of people out here who won't be able to hold on that long. Some are being extorted by smugglers, or robbed blind by the black market. Others are being harassed by pirates. And the only thing standing between those folks and harm, the only people out here doing a damned thing to help them, is the Fenris Rangers."

They left the hallway and crossed the busy flight deck. Antigrav skiffs cruised past, loaded with cargo or ordnance, and teams of mechanics worked with speed and passionate focus to effect repairs on a line of damaged prowlers. Closest to the wide-open front of the flight deck, which looked out upon the capital city of Fenris, a line of prowlers stood ready for deployment, tethered to the ground only by their fuel umbilicals.

Harper led Seven to his ship. She noted the bright splotches of paint and sealant that concealed the scorch marks inflicted by the Nausicaans on Otroya II. As he unlocked the forward cargo hatch, Seven noticed a detail that had escaped her attention in all the excitement of fleeing for their lives in Arendel, a name painted on the nose of the prowler's fuselage. Staring at it, she asked Harper, "Who is *Lady Fly*?"

Sadness passed over Harper's face like a rain shadow. "Best dog I ever had."

She thought she had misheard him. "A dog?"

"Just a mutt, mostly border collie, but I loved her."

"A dog."

Harper threw a quizzical look at Seven, as if he were reconsidering his entire opinion of her. "You never had a dog, did you?"

"No. I have not."

"Well, trust me, kid. Someday, when you're ready, get a dog. Then we'll reach."

Harper opened the prowler's forward cargo hatch. From inside the small compartment he took out a stun pistol in a holster and handed it to Seven. "Put that on, and stow your Stingers behind your seat." Before she could protest, he added, "Regs. Trainee Rangers don't get to carry lethal weapons. But the rest of your gear—sensor scramblers, stun grenades, yada, yada—you can keep. Whatever you don't feel like toting around, you'll stow in the back of the cockpit."

"Why inside the ship?"

"Shortage of lockers, for one. And it'll spare you the hassle of deciding what to bring every time we roll out."

"So I'll be flying with you?"

"For the foreseeable future, yes."

"Will I ever get my own prowler?"

"Slow down, kid. You've been on the job five minutes. Most Rangers don't get their own bird until their third or fourth year." He reached back inside the compartment. "Last but not least—" He pulled out a Fenris Rangers uniform jacket. "Should be your size. Try it on."

Seven held the jacket and shot a suspicious look at Harper. "You just happened to have a jacket in my size in your ship's hold?"

"No, I hid it in there before I came to the mess. You gonna try it on or what?"

Satisfied with his explanation, Seven shrugged her way into the weathered, faux-leather jacket. It draped comfortably around her, as if she had been born to wear it. "Nice."

"Glad you like it. But take care of it—there ain't many left, and they ain't making any more. Now mount up, deputy. Time to earn your pay."

He helped her up to the ladder, and once she was inside the prowler's cockpit, he followed her up and settled into his seat up front. He threw switches and the engines roared to life with such vigor they made the whole ship tremble.

As he secured the cockpit canopy, Seven saw Ellory and Lucan boarding the prowler beside theirs. "Are they going with us?"

"Yup. Strength in numbers, kid. Where we're goin', we're gonna need it."

"Where, exactly, are we going?"

"Into the mud and blood, kid. Mud and blood."

7

Mercenary Frigate *Eris* – Qiris Sector

From his command chair on the bridge of the independent frigate *Eris*, General Kohgish beheld his top lieutenants with utter contempt. "You three are the reason I can't have nice things."

In less than a year's time, Kohgish had toppled a planetary government, stolen its defense forces to use as his own private army, and launched an interstellar campaign of piracy and terror. Nonetheless, true wealth and power continued to slip through his paws, and the Antican warrior was beginning to suspect he knew why.

Kohgish stared with mounting rage at his underlings' latest report of a mission gone awry. It was a litany of idiotic mistakes. A catalog of tactical blunders. A song of misjudged foes and missed opportunities. Cowardice and corruption he could overcome with intimidation. But what was he to do in the face of rank incompetence?

He flung the padd at his three senior officers. It landed at the feet of Feeno, a young Orion man who was green-skinned, black-haired, slight of build, dressed in gauzy fabrics, and effeminate in a way that had drawn mockery from Kohgish's mostly Antican crew—but only until they'd learned the hard way that Feeno was also preternaturally fast, skilled with ultrasharp blades, and an utterly ruthless, vicious killer. Feeno didn't look at the padd. He kept his eyes on Kohgish, confirming what the general already suspected: Feeno was smarter than his peers.

With slow, deliberate steps, Kohgish paced in front of his men, who stood facing him in a single rank. "I can conquer any foe except stupidity." He stopped in front of Maruuk, a male Chalnoth, and a huge one even by that

species' standards. "You were sent to Otroya II with a specific set of instructions. Sell our stolen contraband to the Nausicaans and bring the latinum
back here to me. But I'm not seeing any latinum, and all the news updates
from Otroya II are talking about a massive crime-related firefight in the industrial sector of Arendel. So why don't you try telling me what went wrong
down there?"

The hulking, auburn-maned Chalnoth cocked his head in confusion, and
then he pointed at the padd on the deck at Feeno's feet. "Already wrote it down."

"Did I ask if you wrote it down? No. I didn't. I asked you to tell me what
happened." Kohgish raised his voice as he said to his other lieutenants, "This
is what I'm talking about, gentlemen. A failure to follow even the simplest of
orders." He pivoted back toward Maruuk. "Explain to me how you lost all our
product and came back empty-handed."

"Fenris Rangers."

"Do tell. Was it an entire platoon of Fenris Rangers?"

Maruuk shook his head. "One. At first. Then two."

"Two? You want me to believe just *two* Fenris Rangers took on more than
two dozen heavily armed mercenaries, stole our medical shipment, blew up the
weapons we'd bought, and got off the planet alive?" Kohgish leaned forward,
purposefully intruding upon Maruuk's jealously guarded personal space. "Give
me one good reason I shouldn't have you garroted."

Kohgish's third lieutenant, a Betelgeusian man named Rokkash Khol, intervened. "General. There was clearly a leak in the Nausicaans' operation.
That's how the Rangers were able to set an ambush at the meeting site. And I
shouldn't need to remind you of the potential damage even a single concealed
attacker can inflict in a confined space with modern weapons."

If Feeno had served up such a defense of Maruuk, Kohgish would be staring
daggers into his eyes as a consequence, but it had been Rokkash, whose visage
unnerved him. Like most Betelgeusians, Rokkash's face had no nose, just a few
slits, and his lack of hair and prominent cranial ridges gave his countenance
the aspect of a skull wrapped in a sheath of taut gray leather. Looking toward
the deck only reminded Kohgish of the Betelgeusians' feathered, clawed feet.

Hideous species, Kohgish mused, *but sharp as swords.*

The Antican general held his ground in front of Maruuk a few seconds more, for the sake of saving face, before returning to his command chair. He settled into it, doing his best to project calm and control to his men. "The ambush on Otroya II cost us dearly, at a time when we can't afford any setbacks." He pointed at the padd on the deck and said to Feeno, "Pick it up."

The Orion man bent down and grabbed the padd. As he did so, Kohgish relayed some recent financial documents to the device. "What's happening to our cash flow, Feeno?"

"It's slowing down."

"Understatement of the century. We have a major problem. When I took control of Soroya IV, I squeezed every last drop of profit out of that rock. And I used that to grow our merry little militia into a lean, mean fighting force. One with real potential.

"But that teat's running dry. And if we don't grow soon, we'll start shrinking. Every time we fail to make payroll, more of our people go AWOL. Some have taken a few of our smaller patrol ships with them. It'll be a death by a thousand cuts unless we stop the bleeding now."

Kohgish activated a holographic star map of the Qiris sector, which appeared and rotated slowly in the open space between himself and his men. "We need to expand our sphere of control beyond Soroya and its two closest neighbors. If we move quickly, we can seize an opportunity to become the dominant political actor in this sector."

There was unfiltered doubt in Rokkash's voice as he asked, "How?"

"By acquiring a warship that can overpower anything controlled by our rivals, or by the Fenris Rangers."

Feeno crossed his arms and rolled his eyes at Kohgish. "And how are we supposed to do that, boss?"

"I've been in touch with a Talarian broker named Qulla. Classic middleman. He has a line on a battleship that his government wants to decommission and sell for scrap. He thinks he can get it for us, unscrapped, in about a week. With a ship like that under our control, this sector would be as good as ours. We could keep the Rangers at bay, quell any resistance from the remaining colonists, and compel our rivals to bend the knee."

It was hard not to hear the strain of disbelief in Rokkash's voice as he asked, "And how much will this decommissioned battleship cost us?"

"More than you'd imagine. I've been staring at the number for weeks, and even I still think it must be the Talarians' idea of a joke. But we *need* this, gentlemen. If we don't expand, we'll die—and the only way to expand is to acquire this ship. Real power is within our reach, and I intend to take it. To that end, I need you three to boost profits in all our top markets. Extort more colonists. Rob soft targets anywhere you find them. Ramp up smuggling. And do more sentient trafficking—that's where the money is.

"And last but certainly not least, gentlemen, I trust it's understood that we can't afford any more cock-ups like the one in Arendel. So, going forward, if you encounter any more Fenris Rangers? Shoot on sight—and shoot to *kill*."

Earth – San Francisco

It never ceased to amaze Janeway how much redundant and ultimately useless paperwork was generated every hour of every day by Starfleet. Everything in quintuplicate. Memoranda issued on regular schedules even when there was nothing significant to report. She had glimpsed the tip of the paperwork iceberg as a captain, but only as a flag officer had she discovered the daunting magnitude of the phenomenon.

Janeway knew it wasn't an issue unique to Starfleet. Pretty much any established bureaucracy or governmental entity would develop these maddening habits, given sufficient time and desire for operational opacity. It just seemed to her that Starfleet, like many other military organizations past and present, had elevated the practice to an art form.

She sipped her coffee, stared out the window of her office at Starfleet Command headquarters, and wondered if it might be possible to conjure into existence an all-new administrative entity within Starfleet merely by creating virtual stationery in its name and adding it to the headquarters' shared resources server.

The Starfleet Command Office of Hairstyle Management has a nice ring to it.

Her experiment in self-fulfilling bureaucratic paperwork was momentarily postponed by the chirp of her door signal. She swiveled her chair away from the vista of San Francisco's cityscape across the bay, collected herself, and straightened her posture. "Come."

Her office door slid open with a soft *whoosh*. Admiral Katya Pakaski, the deputy chief of Starfleet Intelligence, took a step inside. The blonde woman scouted Janeway's office as if to make sure they were alone. "Sorry to drop by unannounced. Is this a bad time?"

"Not at all. Please, come in. Sit."

The office door closed as Pakaski crossed the room and sat in one of the chairs in front of Janeway's desk. Janeway used a control panel on her desk to lock the door, to ensure their privacy. Pakaski took that effort a step further: she pulled a slender, stylus-shaped device from a pocket of her uniform's trousers, gave its cap a small twist, and set it on Janeway's desk. "Just to make sure no one's listening in," she explained in a quiet voice.

"Is that really necessary?"

"I'm not sure. But I prefer to err on the side of caution."

"I understand completely. So, to what do I owe the pleasure of your visit?"

The younger woman's angular features sharpened with concern. "As you requested, I made some inquiries through proper channels about the proposition Seven received. I don't think you'll like what I found."

"Tell me anyway."

Pakaski took a deep breath and calmed herself. "First, the FSA denies the existence of any field operative named Arastoo Mardani."

Janeway felt a chill of fear travel down her spine, but she fought to keep her rational side in control of her actions. She pondered a range of reasonable explanations. "Is it possible 'Arastoo Mardani' is an alias being used by one of their agents?"

"I asked that exact question. And got nothing but silence in return."

"Which means 'yes.'"

"That's how I'd read it. But now for the really bad news."

"I can hardly wait."

"The FSA has absolutely no record of any agreement with Seven, or with anyone else, about fast-tracking a Starfleet commission or expediting a petition for citizenship."

Janeway nodded. "If they deny their agent's existence, it stands to reason they'd deny the existence of a deal that agent allegedly proffered."

"True. But Starfleet Command's denying the existence of any agreement, and so is the office of the Federation Council. And not just publicly—these were deep-level sources. People I can trust, people who'd know if there was something like this in the works. There isn't."

"Maybe the FSA is playing their cards extra close on this for some reason. Is it possible they're hiding something from us?"

Pakaski smiled. "Of course they are. They're an intelligence agency."

"You know what I mean."

"My answer stands. At any given moment, half of any intelligence service is trying to hide something from its other half. It's just the nature of the beast."

Janeway made a forward-waving gesture with her hand, signaling Pakaski to move on. "I'll take your word for it. But if your intel is right, Seven's in danger. Who could've known about her rejected applications to Starfleet?"

Pakaski shrugged. "Anyone who knows how to request a search of Federation public records could find that. None of it was classified, though some bits might've been redacted."

"Which bits?"

"The ones that reveal she was rejected because the president's still terrified of the Borg, and no one wants to be the fool who let her in the door if she turns out to be a hostile asset."

"She isn't."

"Apparently, our elected representatives don't share your confidence." Pakaski frowned. "I'm sorry to have to say this, but I think your friend Seven got conned."

"I find that very hard to believe, but let's assume for the moment that it's true: Seven got conned. But by whom? And for what purpose?"

Pakaski frowned in disappointment. "I haven't a clue. Is there any way you can reach Seven? Maybe warn her about this mystery man who's recruited her?"

Janeway shook her head. "I lost contact with Seven after she left Starheim. Her comm hasn't pinged the network in over a week, and I have absolutely no idea where she was going."

Softening her countenance, Pakaski asked, "Do you want me to put some of my people on it? It'd be strictly low-key—just a BOLO, nothing hands-on."

"No. Tasking any kind of intelligence resources to find Seven might attract exactly the sort of attention that could get her killed."

Pakaski collected her signal jammer and stood. "Sorry I couldn't be more help, Admiral."

Janeway stood and briefly shook the other woman's hand. "Thank you for all you've done, Admiral. I'm in your debt."

"Anytime." Pakaski turned to leave. Janeway unlocked the office door, which opened ahead of Pakaski, who paused to ask, "What do you mean to do about Seven?"

Janeway sighed. "Be patient, and hope she knows what she's doing."

8

Soroya IV – Valen Colony

It hit Seven in the face the moment Harper opened the prowler's canopy—the kind of heat she could taste. The air on Soroya IV was hot, arid, and heavy with the dust of a world in ruins.

Harper had set them down in the middle of the Valen Colony, which he'd said was the largest and most populous of the settlements on the planet. On first look Seven thought he must have landed in the wrong place. There was nothing there. Then she looked closer.

Beyond the drifting curtains of dust and smoke, behind the omnipresent swirls of dust, she discerned the naked foundations of what had once been a cluster of buildings in the center of the town. What she had at first mistaken for dead trees were in fact the sheared-off and mangled remnants of plumbing jutting from fractured slabs of thermal concrete. The footprint of a town encompassing dozens of square blocks had been left barren and windswept. A few damaged buildings still stood along its periphery; beyond them sprawled a refugee camp of ragged tents.

Though it had set down less than fifteen meters away, Ellory's prowler was lost in the haze. Seven heard the whine of both prowlers' engines fading away as their main reactors shifted into standby. As Harper climbed out of *Lady Fly*'s cockpit, Seven caught his sleeve. She gestured at the desolation surrounding them. "What happened to it all?"

The question stirred a deeply buried anger inside Harper, one betrayed by the sudden narrowing of his gaze and the clench of his jaw. "Torn up and sold as scrap by the same prick who stole their money, their harvest, and their water."

Like ghosts rising from the ashes, colonists emerged from the tan haze. They shambled more than they walked. Dressed in tatters and rags, most of them barefoot, they all were emaciated and sunburned. In limping, halting steps they converged on the two prowlers. Ellory and Lucan had already opened their cargo hatch, and they stayed busy handing out bottles of purified water and emergency medicine packets.

More bedraggled settlers had surrounded Harper and Seven's prowler by the time they got their own cargo hatch open. Seven took her cue from Harper and focused on distributing clean water and sealed medkits as quickly and as fairly as possible, to help the greatest number of people. She had thought they might spend all afternoon on the task, and so she was shocked by how rapidly their supplies dwindled in the face of relentless demand.

She leaned toward Harper and confided, "There won't be enough to go around."

"There never is."

"But what about those who are left without?"

"We do what we can, Seven. One day at a time. With luck, we can get another pair of prowlers down here tomorrow."

Seven imagined the agony of those left thirsting for another whole day, wondering if they would still be alive when the next delivery arrived, and her pity grew into anger. "There must be a more efficient means of distribution. A freighter, or a single tanker ship—"

"Would be intercepted by Kohgish's fleet before it made orbit. He has ships watching this and other systems at all times. If we try to send in anything bigger than prowlers, we'll end up in a military engagement we aren't equipped to win."

Seven let that marinate for half a minute while she handed out more water and medicine. "How did Kohgish get so much power?"

"He stole it." Harper clocked Seven's inquisitive stare and continued. "General Kohgish used to be in charge of the militia hired to defend this colony. But when the NGOs pulled out, it didn't take him long to realize no one was watching the watchers. He ousted the government and declared martial law. Within a week he had control of the planet's weather-management system, and he brought every settlement on the planet to its knees, either by starving them into submission or murdering all their adult males."

"Why would anyone do that?"

"Where'd you grow up, a convent?"

"Hardly."

Harper looked around at the devastated vista, which stretched across dozens of kilometers of flat land, into a range of nearby hills. "He did it for the same reason countless others have done it before him: greed and ego. He wants luxuries he hasn't earned, and he enjoys hurting the weak. In short? He's a sociopath."

"Why didn't anybody stop him?"

"Societies depend on the good faith of those who govern them more than most folks realize. People count on shame to keep bad actors in line. But when someone utterly shameless comes along and just runs roughshod over the law? No one knows what to do."

From the other prowler came weak cries of dismay, followed by a rising chorus of anger and desperation. Seven didn't have to ask what was happening. Less than a minute later, the colonists amassed at her and Harper's prowler began to sing the same song of sorrow and denial.

A tall Bajoran woman whose hair had all been shorn away seized the front of Seven's jacket with a grip that was far stronger than Seven would have expected. "How long until the next shipment of water?"

"I don't know," Seven said.

The woman let go of Seven and grabbed Harper by his arms. "What about food?"

"We're trying to get a shipment together, but it takes time."

A young Bajoran boy peeked out from behind the tall woman's filthy bare leg. "When are the Ingos coming back?"

"The NGOs?" Harper clearly hated being put on the spot. "I don't know, kid. Soon."

"It's been almost a *year*," the tall woman said, rage infusing her scratchy voice with a vibrato. "How long are we supposed to wait for them to save the Romulans? How long will my children be left to *starve*?"

"I don't know, ma'am. I'm sorry. I . . . just don't know."

A Denobulan man who looked to have been robbed of his youth by a merciless sun and reduced by hunger to a hide-draped skeleton, reached out with his empty palms upturned. He begged Seven and Harper in a weak and brittle voice, "Please. My family and I are dying. Take us with you."

Harper shook his head. "I can't, I'm sorry."

"Take my children. They can fit in your hold."

"The hold doesn't have full life-support during interstellar flight. They'd die."

"At least they wouldn't die *here*."

There were tears in Harper's eyes as he closed the cargo hatch. "I can't. I'm sorry."

Once the hatch was closed, the remaining stragglers dispersed and blended back into the debris of their lives. Seven watched them stagger away and felt as if her heart had been carved out of her chest. "There must be more we can do than *this*."

Harper leaned against the prowler beside her. "Like I said: we do what we can. But large-scale relief operations? Environmental remediation? The Fenris Rangers aren't set up for that."

"Not exactly a stirring call to arms."

"I can give you truth or comfort, kid, but you only get one."

Ellory and her partner Lucan ambled over to stand with Harper and Seven. Ellory turned a sympathetic look toward Seven. "Hard first day on the job, eh?"

Seven was in no mood for small talk. She stared at Harper. "If we aren't equipped to help these people, why do we not seek aid from someone who can?"

"Because no one will take the job."

Lucan nodded. "S'truth. The Federation NGOs were the only ones keeping a lid on things out here. Once they jetted off to Romulus, Qiris sector imploded."

Ellory chimed in. "Before that, we were a patrol force, keeping the space lanes safe for commercial transport and shipping. Mainly, that meant scaring off pirates and smugglers."

Harper grinned. "And chasing down the occasional interstellar fugitive."

Despair cast a pall over Lucan's features. "We had extradition and enforcement agreements with dozens of planetary governments, but over the past year most of them have collapsed and taken their own law-enforcement agencies down with them. At this point, we're pretty much the only game left in town. But for how much longer? No one knows."

Ellory picked up the conversational baton: "That's why, from time to time, we've had to go beyond our original role in order to protect the people and keep the peace."

"And when that's failed," Harper added, "we've at least tried to be agents of mercy."

Lucan took a short puff off a vapor inhaler and exhaled a plume of bluish mist from his nose. "And if the Federation doesn't like it, or its news agencies want to call us 'renegades,' or 'vigilantes'? Fuck 'em. This ain't no popularity contest. It's life or death out here. Literally, the fate of entire worlds is hanging in the balance."

Seven shot a dubious look at Lucan. "Isn't that a bit melodramatic?"

Ellory answered for her partner. "If anything, it's an understatement. You think this planet was always like this? Who would colonize a desert? Lots of it used to be lush and green, practically a paradise. Then Kohgish took control of the weather grid and locked the people out of the control station in the mesosphere. In under a year he's baked this planet almost to death, all so he could force the colonists to pay a ransom for water."

It was all too horrifying for Seven to imagine. She looked around in dismay at the charred ground and dust-yellowed sky. "He did this much damage in under a year?"

Ellory nodded, her manner grim. "This isn't even the worst of his crimes."

"What is?"

"You really want to know?"

"Yes."

Ellory walked toward her prowler and with a tilt of her head beckoned Seven to follow. "C'mon. I'll show you."

Soroya IV – Senya Colony

Everywhere that Ellory had taken Seven as they crossed the planet's single large continent had told the same tragic story, of the cost of violent anarchy inflicted by power-hungry thugs: an ode of poverty, famine, drought, and mass suffering on a scale that left Seven feeling nauseated. Leveled settlements populated by walking shadows of the hungry and dying.

Tucked into the rear seat of Ellory's prowler, Seven was grateful for the privacy of the comm bulkhead between them as she palmed a steady flow of tears from her face.

For so many years after I left the Collective, I thought the Borg had purged me of genuine emotions. Of my humanity. Janeway always told me she believed I would find my heart. Now I wish I hadn't. . . . I wish I could be numb again. Anything but this.

As if sensing Seven's torment, Ellory said over her shoulder, "Brace yourself. I've saved the worst for last."

"What does that mean?"

"You'll see."

Ellory guided the prowler to a gentle landing on a stretch of rocky ground. Great whorls and plumes of dust swirled around the prowler as the thrum of its engines dwindled and its canopy opened. Again that slap in the face of heat poisoned with the stink of death, of dust tainted with the ash of decay. Seven hesitated to get out of the prowler, but she knew there was no hiding from this moment. She had come to bear witness to an awful truth.

She climbed down to the parched ground and followed Ellory away from the ship. They walked toward the setting sun, across lone and level sands, until they came to a broad gully, the artifact of what once had been a river. Ellory led Seven to its edge and then stepped aside.

Seven looked down into the gully.

A river of bones. Countless skeletons, stripped bare by scavengers and the elements, bleached by the pitiless sun, and left in a chaotic jumble that filled the gully and stretched away for kilometers in either direction. A few empty pockets enabled Seven to see that the gully was nearly six meters deep at its center, with steeply sloped sides.

Six meters deep, piled with unburied dead.

There were bones of more species than Seven could easily count.

Males and females. Adults. Adolescents. Children.

Infants.

Sorrow like a tourniquet on Seven's neck stole her breath. "How many?"

"At this site? At least eighty thousand."

"*This* site? How many are there?"

"Dozens, across half a dozen planets."

Vertigo washed over Seven and forced her to her knees. She gasped for air but couldn't make herself inhale. She pitched forward and put out her hands in front of her—and planted them into the jumble of bones, some of which broke like twigs or crumbled into powder.

She had spent years trying to open herself to the concept of empathy, of being receptive to the feelings of others, with little success. In her imagination, she had thought it would be the same as existing as a drone within the Collective, a single cell of the many who are one.

Only now, seeing her hands caked with the ashes of the innocent dead, did she realize how wrong she had been.

Empathy bloomed inside her. Her psychic barriers collapsed, and her emotional defense mechanisms unraveled. Her soul stood unguarded before a horror without measure. Strange, overpowering emotions crashed upon her shores and left her shaken and trembling. In her mind she imagined the pain of every life that had been snuffed out in that gorge—the fear, the grief, the confusion, the rage . . . and as she imagined the pain of one life erased, she confronted the specter of ten lives stolen . . . a hundred . . . a thousand . . . a million . . .

All of them as real as herself.

Each of them as deserving of life as she was.

Every one of them robbed of all they had known or would know.

A million lives that could have touched countless others, stolen from the galaxy. Stolen from the future that might have been.

Painful sobs racked Seven's torso even as she struggled to breathe. Tears rolled from her eyes. The harder she fought to choke back her weeping, the more terrible the pressure on her chest became. She was drowning in a sorrow greater than anything the Borg had ever imagined or could ever understand. As a drone she had been party to a number of atrocities of far greater magnitude than this, but those evils had been committed at a remove, the true scope of their consequences unseen. Here, in this blighted place, there was no ignoring the reality of this genocide. She saw it. Touched it. Felt its grit and grease on her fingers.

This is what the murder of eighty thousand people feels like.

Is this what I did to so many innocent lives?

Is this the kind of monster I am?

Her voice broke free in primal howls of sorrow. Desperate for some semblance of control, she summoned her anger, her rage, her will to vengeance, her need for justice, for the reassurance that the person responsible for this atrocity would be held accountable. Fighting for air, she drove herself almost to hyperventilating before Ellory was at her side, holding her tightly.

"Hold your breath, Seven. Hold it, and count your heartbeats until they slow."

It was hard, but Seven forced herself to do as Ellory said.

Half a minute later she could almost breathe normally, and though her heart was still racing, her thoughts were once again clear. "Thank you, Ell." She looked up at Ellory through the broken lens of tearstained eyes. "Kohgish did this?"

Ellory nodded. "He bragged about it. As a warning to everyone else."

"We need to *end* him."

"Trust me, it's one of the Rangers' top five tactical objectives. Unfortunately, he and his fleet are a bit out of our weight class, if you take my meaning."

"I do." Seven considered the disparity in the relative firepower of Kohgish's fleet and the combined forces of the Fenris Rangers she had seen at their headquarters. "But if I had a plan for taking this world, and this sector, back from Kohgish . . . would you help me?"

Ellory used her thumb to gently wick tears from Seven's face. "Depends. If there's a chance your plan might actually work? I'll have your back all the way."

"It will."

The Trill woman smiled and clasped Seven's hand. "Then let's do it."

9

Fenris – Ranger Headquarters

The briefing room inside the Rangers' headquarters was arranged like an amphitheater, with rising tiers of stadium seating in an arc around a small semicircular stage. At the front of the stage stood a lectern whose front bore the symbol of the Fenris Rangers; it was flanked by a pair of banners that also bore the Rangers' symbol, draped from the rafters upstage.

Lit by a bank of overhead lights, it made an impressive showcase for something as mundane as morning roll call. Ranger Chief of Patrol Yivv, or "CP," as their fellow Rangers referred to them, had spent the better part of ten minutes laying out the organization's priorities and duty assignments for the day while the assembled Rangers traded jokes under their breath and feigned giving CP their undivided attention. The Rangers heaved a collective sigh of relief as Yivv asked, "If there's no other business?"

Then Seven ruined the moment. "I have something."

Yivv squinted against the light shining into their eyes, and after a moment the Bolian zeroed in on the source of the voice. "Deputy Ranger Seven. If you have something to share, please do so via your training officer, Ranger Harper."

Seven stood to project her voice. "I apologize, Chief, but this is urgent."

Yivv pointed at the briefing room door and then hooked their hand leftward. "The head is down the hall, third door on the left toward the lifts."

Sniggers rolled through the Rangers' ranks, and Seven's temper began to rise when she realized she was being mocked. Not wanting to be dismissed as irrational, she drew a deep breath and then continued with renewed calm. "I wish to propose an action against General Kohgish, on the grounds that he is a major threat to life and law in this sector."

Yivv's reply was thick with condescension. "We all know who and what Kohgish is."

"Yet you have made no significant effort to halt his tyranny. Why not?"

The chief of patrol visibly bristled at being put on the spot by a first-week recruit. "Your T.O. should explain to you that we're a law-enforcement agency, not a military. We don't have the fleet power to make a stand against Kohgish."

"I'm not suggesting we engage him in direct combat."

"Then what *are* you proposing?"

"Depriving him of resources. Specifically, taking back the weather-control network on Soroya IV." As soon as she said it, she heard a low collective groan from the assembled Rangers.

Yivv shook their head. They looked tired. "Do you really think we haven't considered it? That we haven't gamed it out? Run sims? It's a nonstarter."

"I disagree."

From the front row, a male Vulcan Ranger named Tovok spoke up. "CP is correct. Kohgish keeps at least one ship from his fleet in the Soroya system at all times. Any attempt to access the weather network's main control station will draw an immediate counterstrike."

Seven addressed her reply to the Vulcan. "Thank you, Ranger Tovok, but I am aware of the disposition of Kohgish's forces. Because the control station is fully automated, I think it will be possible to overcome Kohgish's security lockout and turn the system's defenses against him."

Tovok shook his head in disagreement. "There would not be enough time. Defeating the lockout and rebooting the system would take at least ten minutes, but Kohgish's ship is never more than six minutes away."

"There's another issue," Chief Yivv added. "It's not as if it's a one-person job. It takes six people, all working in unison, with one person at each of six principal nodes, to retake command of the station. Those nodes are all on the outside of the main platform, completely exposed. Which means whoever's out there will be an easy target for Kohgish's snub fighters."

Seven absorbed the criticisms with the sort of calm that can only be earned by surviving life-or-death crises. "You all make excellent points. But what if I told you I could change the variables in your equations? Would you consider my proposal then?"

That captured the chief's attention. They moved a bit closer to Seven. "Which variables do you think you can change?"

"I possess expertise with computers far beyond anything you've ever known. I can teach you military-grade code injections that will enable us to take command of the station in as little as four minutes. As for the risk of putting a team on the platform, send the copilots of six prowlers, and let their pilots fly a combat patrol around the station until we regain control."

Yivv perked up, clearly interested in Seven's idea. "Quite the proposal, Deputy. I presume you've given some thought to an exit strategy for the team on the platform?"

"Given the extreme altitude of the weather network, the only viable insertion tactic is a free jump using orbital skydiving suits. Once we've liberated the station, we'll continue the jump to the planet's surface, and our prowlers can exfiltrate us from there."

Around the room, where Seven expected to see nods of approval, she saw more Rangers shaking their heads in refusal. Tovok seemed to be trying to keep his tone diplomatic. "Deputy, your plan would utilize at least six prowlers for a single operation, one that has a high risk of multiple Ranger ships being lost in action. Would I be correct in assuming you would also wish to have a corsair as part of your action group?"

"Of course. The corsair would give us vital sensor data and the ability to manage multiple theaters of action throughout the Soroya system, should that prove necessary."

"Have you failed to notice the dearth of combat-ready prowlers on the flight deck? Or the fact that our situation board shows only six corsairs operational in the entire sector? We simply don't have the people or the resources, Deputy."

Seven refused to give up on her idea. "It would be only a brief redeployment."

Yivv telegraphed their opposition by crossing their arms. "Putting too many Rangers in one place leaves too many other points of interest unmonitored or undefended. Semantics aside, I continue to think an assault on the weather-control station is a job for a military unit, not a law-enforcement agency. Request denied." They made a point of turning their back on Seven as they asked the other assembled Rangers, "Any other business? . . . Dismissed."

Seething quietly, Seven watched most of the Rangers file out, many of them on their way to first-shift patrol flights. When everyone else had gone, those who had stayed behind with Seven were Ellory, Jalen, Rana, Lucan, and two other Rangers whom Seven had not yet met. As the group gathered into a huddle, Ellory introduced the new faces, a clean-cut human man and a petite woman with feline features. "Seven, these are Rangers Speirs and Ballard."

Speirs shook Seven's hand. "Call me John." His grip was firm, and he had the confident smile of what Tom Paris had once called a "natural-born rocket jockey."

Next, Seven shook Ballard's hand. It was pleasantly soft thanks to a downy layer of fur. The woman had rolled up her shirtsleeves above her elbows, revealing tigerlike stripes on her forearms. She had large, catlike eyes whose irises shimmered an emerald green, and when she smiled, she seemed self-conscious about her fangs. "Hi. My friends call me Trina."

"Please call me Seven."

Ellory took back control of the conversation. "We couldn't round up an entire squadron of prowlers willing to buck the brass if they said 'no,' which they have. You're looking at everyone I could get. With you and Harper, we've got four prowlers. Enough to put six people on the control-station platform and keep one prowler flying defense. Now the only question is, when do we want to do this?"

"Right now." Seven noted the Rangers' shocked expressions. "The longer we wait, the greater the risk that one or more of our prowlers will be sent out on a call."

Anxiety put a tremor in Rana's husky voice. "But you haven't taught us your military-grade whatever-it-is to speed up the station hack."

Seven reached inside one of her coat's pockets and pulled out a fistful of isolinear chips. She handed them out to the others. "These are loaded with encryption-breaking software. When you reach one of the station's control nodes, plug in one of these. It will do the rest. Then the only thing left to do will be the synchronized initiation of the purge function, to force the station's main computer to restore itself to its default operating state."

The Rangers looked at the computer chips in their hands, nodded, and then stuffed them into various pockets for future use.

Lucan muttered, "Suits me. I always hated cramming for tests, anyways."

Jalen Par pinched the ridges above the bridge of his nose and took a deep breath. "Seven, I need to ask you a simple question, and I'd be grateful for a simple answer."

"Ask."

"Are you sure this plan is gonna work?"

"Yes."

Speirs grinned. "Good enough for me!" He gave Jalen a hearty slap on the back and headed for the door. "To hell with the brass—*let's do this.*"

"Let's just hold on a second."

Harper felt like a swimmer in the grip of a riptide. His first warning sign that something was brewing had been Seven and the other members of her heroic conspiracy arriving on the flight deck dressed in orbital skydiving suits. The second warning sign had been even more obvious: Seven asking him to warm up his prowler and plot a course back to Soroya IV.

He took Seven aside behind his prowler. "Kid, I was at the same roll call as you, and I'm pretty sure I heard the CP nix your plan to free the weather station."

"He did."

"Then what's all this?"

"We're going anyway. Better to ask forgiveness than permission."

For a moment he just stared at her in mute frustration. "Kid, the key to that strategy is not asking first, or at all. Once you've asked and been told 'no,' you don't get forgiven for bucking orders. If you blow this, it'll get you a big chicken dinner."

"A what?"

"B.C.D. Bad conduct discharge. If you're lucky, CP'll just eighty-six you. Depending on how wrong your tilt at the orbital windmill goes, you could be looking at jail time."

"And if my plan succeeds?"

"I haven't really considered the possibility."

"Consider it. You heard my plan. Do you think I've overlooked something?"

Harper stalled for time by scratching at his bearded chin and clearing his throat. "Well, no. Not exactly. On paper, it's absolutely cromulent."

"Then what is your objection?"

"No plan ever survives contact with the enemy—and, as far as I can tell, you have no Plan B. What're you gonna do out there when everything starts going wrong?"

"If executed correctly, my plan—"

"Forget about *correctly*. Forget about your *plan*. Listen to what I'm telling you: People are fallible. Combat is chaotic. We have strict rules of engagement, a duty to use nonlethal force—but our enemies don't. One mistake up there could get us and the rest of the team killed. Did you account for that?"

He wasn't sure how he expected Seven to react. He didn't think she would shrink like a violet, or wither in the face of criticism, but he certainly didn't expect what she did next. She lifted her chin and actually seemed to get a bit taller. "I am aware of the dangers posed by this mission. I've weighed the certain costs of failure against the potential gains of success. Imperiling eight lives to save eight hundred thousand is an acceptable risk-reward ratio."

Harper hated being out-argued, but he admired the hell out of the way Seven had done it. "Gotta give you credit, kid. You've really got a way with math."

"Then we are in agreement?"

"Not so fast. This ain't a sim or some kind of logic problem. This is the real world, Seven. And sometimes when you win, it only makes things worse."

At first she was confused, and then she grew angry. "I don't understand."

"I'm worried you think this is a game you can win if you just plug in the right numbers or press the right buttons. I'm even more worried you don't really understand how things work out here, or what the consequences of your actions might be. You're dealing with an enemy that has no limits, and only one answer to every setback: *revenge*."

Seven spent a moment considering what Harper had said. When she met his gaze once more, he could see that she had only hardened her resolve. "I understand why you might question my grasp of the potential fallout of this mission. But I suspect you wouldn't second-guess the other Rangers who have committed to it. If you would give them the benefit of the doubt, I ask that you show me the same respect."

He shook her hand. "Fair enough. Start the preflight while I suit up." As he trudged toward his locker, he grumbled, "Someone needs to make sure you idiots come back alive."

10

Soroya IV

Four prowlers dropped out of warp in unison, arrayed in a diamond-slot attack formation and cruising at full impulse into orbit on the night side of Soroya IV. Just beyond the curve of the planet's equator, past the terminator separating light from darkness, the first glimmer of the control station for the planet's weather network came into view.

Harper's voice emanated from the transceiver inside the helmet of Seven's orbital skydiving suit. *"All wings, look sharp. Twenty seconds out."*

Ellory was first to respond. *"Copy that, Wing Leader. Wing Two ready."*

"Wing Three ready," Rana chimed in.

"Wing Four ready," Speirs said, finishing the check-in.

Over their prowler's internal comm channel, Harper said, *"Seven, stand by to initiate CNC links to wings two through four."*

"Copy that." Seven double-checked the settings for the command-and-control system, which would enable her and Harper's prowler to remotely control the actions of the other three prowlers once their crews were deployed and their ships left in drone mode. "Ready."

"Acknowledged." Switching back to the main comm channel, Harper added, *"Five seconds out. Wing Leader dropping back. Vent and roll."*

Seven looked up through the cockpit canopy to see the other three prowlers roll 180 degrees as Harper reduced speed to give them room to maneuver. In the distance beyond them, the broad, disklike control station was now fully in view above the planet's equator.

"Rolls complete, cockpits vented, sticks released," Ellory said. *"Good to go."*

Harper replied, *"Give 'em hell, Wing Two. Seven, activate CNC."*

With a tap on a holographic interface, Seven put the other three prowlers under her control as their canopies slid open, and the six Rangers they carried all leaped away from their ships into powered dives toward the weather-control station.

On the private comm, Harper said, *"And the clock starts ticking."*

Watching the Rangers speed toward the station, Seven felt a pang of bitter envy. "I should be with them."

"Hold your horses, Calamity Jane. You're still just a rookie. Bad enough I let you run this wildcat op—I ain't lettin' you get killed doin' it."

Outside, the six other Rangers were barely visible as they neared the station, while the long-range sensors of Harper's prowler detected a mercenary frigate inbound at high warp.

Seven frowned. "My life isn't the one to worry about."

Ellory Kayd had enjoyed orbital skydiving on numerous occasions as an exciting recreational activity under controlled conditions, but until today she had never used it as a means of firing herself like a missile at a moving target in orbit of a planet.

She and the rest of the strike team were still high in the planet's mesosphere when their suits' heads-up displays told them to invert their pose and fire braking thrusters. Shifting from head-first to feet-first was harder than she had expected, and she barely triggered the thrusters in time. She hit the platform hard and rolled through the landing to avoid breaking her legs. Her momentum propelled her across the narrow section of level surface on which it was safe to land and almost carried her over its edge—until a gloved hand caught Ellory by her wrist.

Gasping for air and realizing only belatedly how close she had been to panic, Ellory looked up to see she had been saved by the keen reflexes of her partner, Lucan.

He flashed her a reassuring smile. *"You good?"*

"Five by five—thanks to you."

They hurried together away from the platform's edge in search of their respective command nodes, where they would have to use Seven's preloaded isolinear chips to override the mercenaries' lockout of the weather-management system. As they passed the others, compliments from their teammates came in over their comm channel.

Rana waved. *"Nice catch, Lucan!"* Speirs gave Lucan a jaunty salute. *"Good hands, Luc!"* Ballard just gave him a thumbs-up, while Jalen mock-criticized, *"Why can't you catch like that during intersquad softball?"*

Lucan laughed. *"Get some bigger balls."*

"I'll show you some bigger—"

"Settle down, boys," Rana said. *"We've got work to do."*

Ellory and Lucan split up as they approached their assigned nodes. As she had feared, working the controls of the nodes while wearing orbital skydiving gloves, even a pair as relatively light and electroconductive as the ones used by the Rangers, was going to be slow, clumsy work. And as the rapidly shrinking countdown timer in the corner of her HUD reminded her, slow was not going to be an option today—not if she and the rest of the team wanted to live long enough to get drummed out of the Fenris Rangers.

Everything Harper saw on his cockpit readouts looked like bad news. "Seven, did that inbound frigate pick up speed?"

"Affirmative. It used the system's outermost gas giant to perform a shallow slingshot maneuver at warp, adding three-tenths of a warp factor to its velocity."

"How does that affect the strike team's countdown?"

"Shortened by seventeen seconds. I've updated their HUDs accordingly."

He heard a *ping* from Seven's control panel, indicating an incoming comm had been received. *"We're being hailed by the mercenary frigate."*

"On speakers."

From Harper's helmet transceiver came a raspy voice. *"Ranger intruders, this is the FAS Ta-Akora. Withdraw your team from the weather platform immediately, and take your ships out of this system in the next ninety seconds. Or else."*

He needed to buy time for the team on the station. "Or else what?"

"You will be destroyed."

"That doesn't sound very friendly."

"You have been warned."

"So we have. I guess this is it, then."

"It is."

"No more second chances for us, eh?"

"None. Order your people to leave the weather station."

"Or else they'll be destroyed?"

"As we have already said."

"No, you said *I* would be destroyed."

"What? No. We were using the plural 'you.'"

"Oh. Sorry, that wasn't clear."

"It most certainly was."

"Okay. Here's my counteroffer. You turn back now, and I won't impound your ship."

"You what?"

"You heard me. I've got four combat-ready prowlers and a corsair just a few minutes away at high warp. So, you wanna dance? 'Cause I got my boogie shoes on, baby."

Seven cut in to say, *"They've closed the channel."*

"Well, now, that's just *rude*." He switched his transceiver to the strike team's channel. "Wing Leader to strike team. Pick up the pace, kids. Hostiles thirty seconds out."

If there was anything Ellory didn't need at that particular moment, it was more stress. "We're going as fast we can, Wing Leader."

"For your sake I hope you're wrong, 'cause the mercs' frigate just launched a pair of snub fighters that are comin' in hot as hell."

All she could do was mumble under her breath and hope she remembered—

"Ell," Speirs said, *"we can all hear you swearing."*

"Sorry." She muted her helmet's mic and went on cursing to herself.

Sweat dripped down Ellory's forehead, through her delicate eyebrows, and into her eyes. More sweat pooled inside her gloves, fouling her fingertips' contact with the pads inside the suit's gloves that made it possible for her to work the holographic interface on the command node, and the faster and shallower her breathing became, the more she noticed that her breath was downright hideous. She blamed herself for having scarfed all the garlic bread at lunch.

She finished keying in the last string of access codes for the node's hardwired, solid-state interface panel, which was revealed when a panel appeared on the bulkhead in front of her and then slid open. She unmuted her mic. "Node one: I'm in. Inserting isolinear chip now."

"Node two: ready," Lucan replied.

"Node four, ready," Ballard said, and Speirs followed, *"Node five, ready."*

"Node six, ready," Rana said.

It took Ellory a moment to process that the count was incomplete. "Jalen, what's your status at node three?"

"Still trying to get access. Having some—" There was a scratch of noise over the comm, followed by Jalen spewing muffled profanities in several languages. *"Having some technical difficulties with the interface."*

Ellory saw the countdown in her HUD shrinking toward zero, and when she looked up toward the stars, she saw the flash-and-streak of high-speed snub fighters on an attack vector. "Jay, get your shit fixed in the next ten seconds or we're all dead."

The frigate *Ta-Akora* and its snub fighters emerged from warp in a pulse of light and immediately opened fire, filling the space around Harper and Seven's prowler with fiery streaks of plasma.

"Break left!" Seven snapped, releasing a flurry of sensor-distracting radioactive chaff.

Harper rolled the prowler to port and then into an inverted dive, expertly evading the frigate's first barrage. *"Two snubs heading for the station!"*

"And one on our six," Seven confirmed. "Permission to engage?"

"Give 'em the heat. I'm making a run at the frigate."

Stars wheeled and the bright orb of Soroya IV blurred in and out of sight as Harper put the prowler through a series of high-speed combat maneuvers. At the end of a high-g loop, he made a perfect full-impulse strafing run that left white-hot, smoldering scars on the frigate's hull.

Seven harried the snub fighter pursuing them with regular pulses from the prowler's aft particle cannon, but between Harper's daredevil piloting and her own unfamiliarity with the system, she couldn't land a hit. "Aft gun can't get a lock!"

"I'll keep 'em off our back! Switch the other prowlers from wingmen to hunters."

"Changing modes now."

Outside the canopy, everything was moving too quickly and was too far away for Seven to see with her own eyes, but her tactical displays showed the Rangers' three drone-mode prowlers abandoning their campaign of distracting the frigate with hectoring fire followed by evasive maneuvers in favor of a coordinated attack on the lone snub fighter hunting her and Harper. "Hunters engaged."

"Copy. Stand by on countermeasures—we're taking another run at the frigate."

"Acknowledged. I suggest you target its ventral hull, just aft of its comms array. That is our best chance of crippling its warp reactor without destroying the ship."

"I'll give it a shot."

"Yes, that is what I would recommend."

"No, I mean— . . . Never mind."

There was almost no atmospheric pressure at the altitude of the control station, but when the pair of snub fighters shot past at a speed so great that all Ellory saw was a momentary wash of color across her field of vision, she imagined a sonic boom shock wave that never came.

Speirs summed up her feelings when he exclaimed, *"Damn, that was close!"*

Rana cried out, *"They're coming 'round again!"*

Ellory stared at the sync indicator, willing it to turn green. "Dammit, Jalen! C'mon!"

"The chip won't go in! I don't know why, it just won't—"

Ballard cut Jalen off. *"Is it upside down?"*

A split-second later, Jalen sounded humbled. *"Crap. Yes. Chip in, node three ready!"*

"All right," Ellory said, "on my mark! Three—"

Lucan snapped, *"Get down!"*

Disruptor pulses slashed across the control station's access platform, blasting away panels in geysers of sparks and roiling plasma flames—and scored a direct hit on Jalen Par. Ellory screamed his name almost as a reflex—"Jalen!"—as his limbs, torso, and head all were scattered by the fury of the artillery-grade disruptor pulse. Before Ellory could put words to the tragedy, she watched his savaged remains fall toward the planet, trailing dark smoke.

The pair of snub fighters streaked past, deadly silver blurs.

Lucan's voice cracked with grief. *"Ballard? I can't see Jalen's node. Is it intact?"*

"Minor damage, but it looks okay."

"Then we've still got a shot," Speirs said, *"but we're a body short."*

Ellory knew what that meant. She keyed her transceiver.

"Wing Leader, we have a problem."

Seven listened anxiously from the prowler's rear seat as Harper answered Ellory's comm. *"Go ahead, Strike Leader."*

"All nodes ready, but we lost Jalen. Hold or abort?"

It took Harper only a fraction of a second to decide: *"Abort."*

Seven cut in, "Belay that! Hold!" She keyed commands into her companels with her right hand and checked her suit's vacuum seal with her left.

Harper's temper turned sharp. *"Seven! What're you doing?"*

"Going in."

"The hell you are! Stand down and—"

"Depressurizing cockpit in three—"

"Don't do this!"

"Two—"

Harper scrambled to confirm his own suit's vacuum seal. *"God-dammit, Seven!"*

"One. Venting." She purged the cockpit's atmosphere, and then she used the emergency override to open the canopy, exposing herself and Harper to the vacuum of space. "Brake to space normal and come about, thrusters only, bearing two-zero-nine mark one-seven, sixteen degrees starboard yaw, and stabilize."

Harper executed the maneuver even as he said, *"Seven, this is crazy. Our people are sitting ducks down there. We've got to get them out."*

"I will. As soon as we free the station."

"How'm I supposed to hold off that frigate and a snub fighter without you?"

"You strike me as a resourceful person." Seven unfastened her flight safety harness and pushed herself up and out of the cockpit.

As she floated free she looked back at Harper. "You will think of something."

Seven turned toward the control station, fired her suit's main thrusters, and shot away from the prowler without a moment's hesitation or regret.

The sensible thing to do would have been to countermand Seven, halt the op, and evac the team. Instead, Harper pushed his prowler into a full-power dive so that he could get in front of Seven and chase off the two snub fighters that were angling to pick her off before she reached the station's platform. Harper almost had to laugh. *No one ever accused me of being sensible.*

The other three prowlers were close behind Harper, defending his aft quarter while he lined up a warning shot just ahead of the lead snub fighter. At thousands of meters per second, there was no room for error, no second chances—

Ellory cried out over the comm, "They've got weapons lock!"

Now or never.

Harper fired, filling the sky ahead of the snub fighters with particle-beam pulses an order of magnitude more powerful than anything the snub fighters possessed. The lead fighter charged ahead—and was torn to pieces, which fell away in smoky spirals. A fraction of a second later the second snub fighter broke off and accelerated into a recovery pattern.

That just left the fighter lining up its shot from behind Harper's bird.

He fired braking thrusters and pulled up to slow his dive, but his pursuer matched him, too sly to lose their advantaged position. So he pushed his prowler to its limit instead, thrusters and impulse drive working together to test both his and the ship's abilities to handle extreme stress. Crushing force pinned him against his seat as his ship's inertial dampers lagged a few hundredths of a second behind his maneuvers. His pulse thundered in his temples, and for a moment he was sure this was the moment he'd feared, when his skull would crack under the pressure, and blood would pour from his nose as he blacked out behind the stick—

—and then he was gulping in a breath of concentrated oxygen while banking out of a corkscrew turn into a perfect attack angle above the lead snub fighter's wingman.

He squeezed the trigger by instinct, without waiting for the targeting computer. A searing particle beam from his prowler slashed through the wingman's impulse engines, setting them ablaze, and then carved off a chunk of the snub fighter's starboard wing.

A flash of fire enveloped the wingman's ship, and then it was on its way down to the planet's surface, nothing but a burning husk in a flat spin.

Harper's sensors showed the mercenaries' third snub fighter was on its way to take the downed wingman's place in the dogfight, and the frigate was closing in on the control station.

Not good.

With one command he directed the three hunter-mode prowlers to land on the planet at the Valen Colony, where the strike team could recover them, and then he opened a channel to the strike team. "Time's up, kids! Everybody out of the pool! Proceed to evac and exfil, RFN."

Seven protested, *"Not yet! I'm just seconds away from the station!"*

"It's too late, kid! We gotta bounce. Now."

"Twenty seconds, Harper. Give me that much."

What was he supposed to say? He couldn't force her not to do something stupid. All he could do was try to make sure she and the others didn't die in the process. "Kid, if you get me killed, I am gonna be *so* pissed. Twenty seconds on the clock—*go!*" Left with no way out but through, he poured on the speed and steered his prowler back into the fray.

Seven fired the thrusters of her orbital skydiving suit at the last possible moment and slammed down onto the station's ring-shaped access platform like a hammer striking an anvil.

Agonizing jolts of pain from the impact traveled up Seven's legs and into her spine, which felt as if it had compressed on contact. *If not for the Borg nanoprobes in my bloodstream, I would likely have been paralyzed the moment I hit the station.*

A sensation like twisting eels in her gut told Seven that her body's nano-probes were knitting her organs back together, even as she sprang to her feet and ran toward the empty node station. The magnetic soles of her boots alternately hugged her to and repelled her from the station's surface with each stride. She reached the interface panel and verified that Jalen had set everything as directed. *I could have used my nanoprobes to control all six nodes at once, but I'm done using my Borg enhancements as a crutch. It's time to do things for myself.*

She set her hand above the switch that would release the lockout on the station's master-control system. "Strike team! Ready?"

Ellory answered for the team: *"Ready!"*

"On my mark! Three! Two! One! Mark!"

In synchronicity the strike team members pressed their switches, canceling the lockout. The panel in front of Seven refreshed to show a full suite of command interface tools. "Stand by. I'm setting a new access code, one the pirates won't be able to break." Again, she knew she could have done this in the blink of an eye with her nanoprobes, but as she swiftly secured the system against future intrusions, she realized that she possessed skills of her own that were already exceptional by nearly anyone's standards. It felt good to know that for a fact.

Lucan's voice warbled over her suit's comm, *"Snub fighter on attack!"*

Harper added, *"I'm on it, but y'all had better get moving!"*

Seven reset the station's operations to their default configurations and closed her command interface. "Done! Strike team evac!"

The strike team retreated from the station's core, fired their thruster packs in midstride, and launched themselves over the platform's edge and into powered dives toward the planet.

But there was no outrunning the snub fighter.

The sky around the team filled with disruptor pulses. The Rangers rolled, accelerated, decelerated, or veered away in random directions, scattering as the fighter streaked past.

A fraction of a second later, Harper's prowler blazed past in pursuit. His voice crackled over Seven's helmet comm. *"He's comin' 'round again! Get planet-side, on the double!"*

Seven saw the sky below dotted with clouds, and her team regrouping for a mad run toward the Valen Colony. She calculated multiple variables in her head and arrived at a troubling conclusion. "We will not reach the surface before his next pass. But I have an idea."

She rolled to give herself a clean line-of-sight transmission vector to the weather-control station, and then she switched her transceiver to the station's executive frequency. Using the access code she had established to secure its systems, she patched its command interface through to her suit's HUD—and initiated prioritized adjustments for the sector grid around Valen Colony.

When she looked down she saw the results of her inspiration: a swiftly gathering storm head of black clouds flashing with lightning and rumbling with thunder.

She switched back to the team's channel. "Everyone! Use the storm as cover!"

The team responded in overlapping transmissions—*"Are you crazy?" "Oh, hell no." "You've gotta be kidding!"*—until a fresh barrage of disruptor pulses from the fighter quelled dissent and spurred them all into powered dives toward the thunderhead.

"Don't cluster! Split up and regroup on—"

Another fusillade of disruptor blasts cut across the strike team's descent vector—and one tore through Ellory's thruster pack, which exploded in a burst of sparks and shrapnel.

Seven struggled to see past the inky plume of smoke pouring from Ellory's fragged suit. "Ell! Talk to me, Ell! Ell, can you hear me?"

Harper cut in: *"Her suit's offline! No power, no comms! Anyone got eyes on her?"*

"Affirmative," Speirs said. *"No movement, falling like a rock."*

"About to lose her in the clouds," Ballard said.

Seven keyed her suit's thrusters to maximum. "Everyone, get clear. I'm going in." Hands outstretched and pointed ahead of her, she chased after the unresponsive Ellory and speared her way into the thundercloud just a second behind her.

Everything went pitch-black, and then the world flared blinding white—lightning slashed in great forks all around Seven, and entire banks of black cloud pulsed with inner light, all of it followed almost instantly by crushing roars of thunder that hit her with walls of sonic force.

Her eyes pulsed with green and purple afterimages, and her head spun from the shock of thunderclaps—but she forced herself not to blink, not to pass out, not to pull inward or do anything to slow her dive. Hands first, head lowered, she arrowed through another wall of roiling black and gray vapors—to see Ellory just a hundred meters ahead of her, tumbling wildly, out of control, with no sign of consciousness.

Beneath them, the belly of the cloud flared white with electrical fury.

Seven accelerated directly into Ellory and wrapped her arms around her, and then her legs. "Computer! Shields!" Her suit's command system activated the low-power shield normally used for extra protection during the most perilous moments of atmospheric entry.

Please be enough—

She and Ellory plunged through the bottom of the cloud as it resounded with thunder and flashed—just for a few milliseconds—with sheet lightning hotter than the surface of a star.

And then the two of them were clear of the storm, back into open sky, steam and smoke trailing from both their suits as a barren expanse of the planet's surface rushed up to meet them. Seven was about to release her parachute—and then she saw the snub fighter break through the storm cloud and level out, no doubt lining up its targeting sensors on her and Ellory.

Speirs shouted over the comm, *"Seven! Release your chute!"*

"I can't! The fighter's locking—"

A bluish-white particle cannon beam lanced down, out of the storm head, and slashed across the snub fighter's wing-mounted weapons arrays, reducing them to spark-spewing junk. Then Harper's prowler burst free of the storm and dropped into a perfect kill position behind the snub fighter, which broke off and fled for orbit.

"You're clear, kid! Pull the cord!"

Seven released her chute and fired braking thrusters just in time to hit the ground at a speed that hurt like hell but which she could survive if she bent her knees and rolled through it, using her torso and limbs as buffers to shield Ellory from the worst of the hard landing.

She came to a halt, grateful to be alive—but terrified by the possibility that Ellory wasn't.

• • •

Consciousness returned in flickers. Dull waves of deep red pain. A viselike sensation of pressure inside her skull. The nauseating agony of multiple broken bones competing for attention.

Ellory wanted to speak, but her mouth was dry. She wanted to assess her surroundings, but her eyes felt as if they had been glued shut. What parts of her didn't hurt were numb.

She tried to draw a deep breath. The air was hot. It stank of fried optronic cabling, and it tasted of copper. A leaden weight had settled upon every part of her.

Am I dead? Or a locked-in quadriplegic? Where am I?

She struggled to remember how she had gotten into this state. The harder she tried to force her brain to produce short-term memories, the more confused she became. Exhaustion took hold. She was starting to slip back into the shadow. . . .

Then she felt herself being lifted and cradled by many pairs of hands. Pressure, near her neck. Something was happening. She wasn't alone.

Someone removed a helmet from her head. Muggy air that smelled of dust kissed her face. A wet cloth wiped grit from her eyes, her lips, her nose. The sweet kiss of cool water sharpened her focus. She opened her eyes.

Gathered around her, looking down with faces full of hope, were her fellow Rangers. Speirs gingerly tended Ellory's wounds with a soft washcloth, which Ballard refreshed with her canteen. Lucan, Ellory's partner, was at her side, holding her left hand. Rana cradled Ellory's head in her lap. Seven kneeled and held Ellory's right hand in both of hers.

Ellory smiled through her pain. "Can someone catch me up?"

Speirs asked, "What's the last thing you remember?"

"Liberating the weather station."

Concerned looks passed from one Ranger to another. Lucan gave Ellory's hand a gentle squeeze. "Remember the dive to the surface?"

Ellory shook her head no. She looked around; it hurt to turn her neck more than a few degrees to either side. "Guys . . . what happened?"

"You got hit," Ballard said. "Lost your power pack, and that fried your suit."

Rana added, "You were in a wild spin when you hit the storm head."

A raindrop landed on Ellory's cheek. Then came a steady patter, which swelled into a summer shower that within moments became a torrential downpour.

Her memory came back like a lightning bolt. She looked at Seven. "It was you. You caught me. Held me during the landing. . . . You saved me."

As thunder rolled and the breaking storm drenched them, Seven smiled and tightened her clasp of Ellory's hand. "You're welcome."

11

Soroya IV – Valen Colony

Hours after the deluge of Valen Colony had begun it was still going strong. The colonists' celebration of the return of their planet's weather-management system had moved indoors shortly after Harper had confirmed that the mercenaries' frigate and snub fighters had left the system in a state of full retreat. What had started as a simple round of celebratory drinks had become an impromptu dance party driven by bass-heavy club music.

Seven was content nursing a drink in a quiet corner of the colony's meeting hall when Ellory—bruised and stiff after being mostly restored to health by the prowlers' emergency medkits, but too jubilant to keep still—approached her, chasséing in time with the music thudding from speakers spread around the large open space.

Ellory extended an open hand and beckoned Seven to join her. "C'mon! No wallflowers—dance hall rules."

A look around the hall confirmed for Seven that there were, in fact, many individuals refraining from joining the bouncing, gyrating throng on the dance floor. She eyed Ellory with one eyebrow raised in mock reproach. "I see no such rules posted on these premises."

"Don't be a killjoy. Dance with me."

Seven took Ellory's hand and let the shorter, dark-haired woman lead her onto the dance floor. She felt the need to confess, "I have little experience with this kind of dance."

"What kind *do* you know?"

"Mosh-pit slam-dancing."

"Yeah, this is gonna be a little different." She pivoted to face Seven as a new song started playing. "Feel the beat, the rhythm, the syncopation. And just let your body . . . *move.*"

As if she were music come to life, Ellory twisted and turned like a slow flame. At first all Seven could do was watch her, mesmerized. Then she began to mirror Ellory's moves, and she cleared her mind to let herself experience the driving pulse of the music, the smell of dancers' sweat mingled with the scent of petrichor from rain-quenched earth, and the sight of Ellory, whose movements brought her steadily closer to Seven.

As Seven surrendered herself to the tide of sensory overload and let her body react to the music's primal tempo, she was suffused with joy and delight. This wasn't the hard, impersonal collision of strangers she had accepted as flirtation in Starheim; this was a musical courtship, seduction expressed in movement. She looked into Ellory's eyes and felt her breath catch and her heart race with the sensation of making an unspoken but intimate connection. When Ellory's hand traveled up Seven's arm to rest on the nape of her neck, bringing them nose to nose, she was sure she felt the Trill woman's pulse in her fingertips, quickened just like her own.

Ellory leaned closer and tilted her head back and to her right, and Seven felt an almost magnetic force drawing their lips together—

Until a hand landed on Seven's shoulder, breaking the spell of attraction.

She turned to see Harper, who looked worried as he said, "We need to talk."

"Right now?"

"Yes, now. In private."

He took a step away from her and waited for her to follow him. Seven looked back at Ellory, fearing that the special quality she had seen in her eyes would be vanished now—and was relieved to see that wasn't the case at all. She gestured toward Harper. "Duty calls."

Ellory lifted and gently kissed the back of Seven's hand, just above the wrist, and then said with a smile, "To be continued." Seven returned Ellory's smile as they parted, and then she did her best to resume what her *Voyager* friends called her "poker face" as she faced Harper.

"Sorry for stepping on your budding romance," he said, leading her off the dance floor, "but I want to talk while you're still relatively clearheaded."

She followed him out of the meeting hall. They took shelter from the rainstorm beneath the building's shallow roof overhang. "What is your cause for concern?"

He hooked a thumb back toward the party. "That. Everybody treating us like conquering heroes."

"Is it wrong to celebrate a victory?"

"No, but it's vital to keep it in perspective."

"I don't understand. We won." She stuck one open hand into the storm and pulled it back, a tiny puddle of water in her palm. "We gave them back their weather network."

Harper shook his head. "No, what we gave them was *hope*. And hope can be a very dangerous thing, especially in a place like the Qiris sector."

"Why? What do you think might go wrong?"

"Everything." He stole another anxious look at the colonists doting on the other Rangers inside the hall. "Out here, victories tend to be short-lived. That's because the only real law in places like this is retribution—blood for blood. Or worse. Some bad guys out here, when they've been embarrassed, don't just retaliate—they escalate."

Seven began to understand Harper's misgivings. "You think Kohgish is such a threat."

"I *know* he is. But worst of all, he's mercurial. Unpredictable. An ass-kicking like this one might drive him into retreat—but it could just as easily make him go berserk."

It troubled Seven to imagine what such a reaction might encompass, considering the magnitude of the horrors Kohgish had already inflicted on Soroya IV. But she refused to let fear drive her actions. "Harper, I understand your concerns. But I am confident we made the correct decision. By returning the weather network to the colonists, we have reduced Kohgish's leverage over them. And the damage we did to his snub fighters and frigate weaken him directly and might make him hesitate to face us again in combat."

"I wish I had your certainty, kid." He stared into the night, his mien pensive. "On Earth, there's an ancient Buddhist parable that I think is relevant here. Story goes like this:

"Once upon a time in a small village, a teen-aged boy got a horse as a present for his birthday. Everyone said, 'How wonderful!' And the Zen master said, 'We'll see.'

"Years later, the boy, now a young man, falls off the horse and breaks both his legs. And everyone says, 'How awful!' And the Zen master says, 'We'll see.'

"The next year war breaks out, and all the men and boys of the village have to go and fight—all except the young man, whose legs were permanently messed up. His neighbors all say, 'How lucky!' And the Zen master says—" He shot a prompting look at Seven.

She replied, "We'll see."

"Do you understand what I'm trying to say, here?"

"Yes. But I still think we did the right thing."

Harper sighed. "We'll see."

The party went on for hours, until the celebrants were as exhausted as the colony's supply of booze. In time the crowd on the dance floor thinned, and the songs' tempos slowed, until the last song faded away, and the rasping saw song of snoring people lying in couples and heaps was masked by the steady white noise of heavy rain pattering on the hall's scrap-metal roof.

Despite Seven's best efforts, she had been unable to replicate her earlier moment of connection with Ellory, though she was sure the spark remained alive, smoldering within her. Weary and overwhelmed by her day's overload of sentient contact, she retreated to the rear seat of the cockpit in Harper's prowler. The cushioned seat wasn't as comfortable as a bed, but in her estimation neither was anything else on this planet.

Hunkered down beneath a lightweight, temperature-regulating blanket, Seven had reclined her seat as far as it would go, and she had tried to let the staccato percussion of rain on the cockpit's canopy lull her to sleep. Instead, she had found herself staring up into the endless black, her ears registering the strike of every drop landing on the prowler's hull. The culprit responsible for her insomnia, she was certain, was Harper's damned Zen master story.

We'll see.

Why was it haunting her thoughts?

As proud as she felt about what they had accomplished on Soroya IV, Seven knew she and the other Rangers were all still going to face a reckoning when they returned to Fenris. Bad enough that they had disobeyed orders to carry out this mercy mission, but it had cost Ranger Jalen Par his life, and that was a sacrifice she knew they would be asked to justify.

If Harper turns out to be right—if this all winds up being a mistake—Jalen's death will not just be tragic; it will become inexcusable.

Seven had almost succeeded in losing herself to sleep when an indicator light started flashing on the bulkhead companel in front of her seat.

Maybe if I ignore it, it will go away.

The flashing persisted, and its bright yellow glow penetrated her closed eyelids. She restored the regular position of her seat, rubbed the sleep from her eyes, and squinted at the companel. A subspace signal had been received, marked PRIORITY, sender unknown.

Do I play it now? Or leave it for morning?

After wrestling with that choice for half a minute, she decided to kick it up the ladder, as her Starfleet friends would have said, and make it a command problem.

She leaned to port, to speak around the partial bulkhead separating the forward and aft seats. "Harper? Are you awake?" No response. "Harper?"

"Seven, what part of 'I'm pretending to be asleep' do you not understand?"

"We have a priority message on comms."

"Who from?"

"It doesn't say."

He replied with grim resignation, "Okay. Let's hear it."

She patched the recorded message to the cockpit's speakers.

"Attention, colonists of Soroya IV. This is General Kohgish, daimyo of this system and de facto governor of the Qiris sector. As you have likely noticed by now, your planet's weather network has been restored. This was not a reward any of you earned, but a privilege stolen from me by the interference of a squad of renegade Fenris Rangers.

"Understand, people of Soroya IV, that I am willing to be reasonable in the resolution of this matter. I hold the Rangers accountable for this infringement, not any of you. So I am going to offer you all an opportunity to help set matters right.

"Any colony settlement that aids in the capture or killing of one or more of the

Rangers involved in this debacle will have its water rations doubled for the next six months.

"But any settlement that I learn has willingly harbored or aided these Rangers in any way from this moment forward will be exterminated to its last soul.

"My final warning is for the Fenris Rangers who perpetrated this attack on my property and territory. Unless you turn over to me the new executive access codes you implemented on the weather-control station by high noon today in the Valen Colony, and remove yourselves permanently from Soroya IV by that same deadline, I will exact my vengeance not just upon you but upon every living soul on that planet, whether they comply with my demands or not.

"You have nine hours to make your choice. Choose wisely."

The recorded message ended, and the indicator light on the companel dimmed.

From the front of the cockpit, Harper grumbled, "Sonofabitch."

Seven felt her face flush with the heat of shame. "I'm sorry. This is exactly what you said would happen."

"Yeah, it is. And Kohgish is even more unhinged than I thought."

"I imagine the colonists will hear this message soon, as well."

"If they haven't already."

"Do you think they will turn against us?"

"I don't know, kid. Depends how desperate they are. Either way, we should wake the rest of the team and tell them to get ready to bug out."

It took Seven a moment to process the implications of Harper's statement. "Bug out? Are you suggesting we abandon these people?"

"I'm suggesting we get gone before they kill us to save their own necks."

"I will not leave these people to the capricious whims of a genocidal maniac."

Seven saw Harper's reflection on the canopy as he shook his head. "Noble, kid, but also dumb. It's time to accept that this situation has escalated beyond our ability to fix it."

"I have. Which is how I know it is time to call for help."

After four failed attempts to establish a channel, Seven was beginning to wonder whether Harper might be right. Outside the colony's comms shack, the rain had tapered to a drizzle, leaving the half-deserted town mantled in a steamy mist.

Inside the shack, it was her patience that was waning. Frustrated, she threw accusatory looks at the colony's kit-bashed assemblage of technology—antiquated signal buffers jury-rigged to work with a normally incompatible transceiver matrix, not to mention a state-of-the-art holographic projector that had no business being hooked up to a heap of junk such as this.

She checked the frequency, then told Harper, "I will try them again."

He said nothing, but at that point he no longer needed to. Seven was perfectly aware of his doubts and criticisms, but she was committed to finding a solution. To finding help.

She opened the channel. "This is Fenris Ranger—"

"*Deputy* Fenris Ranger," Harper corrected.

Seven glared at her training officer for the rebuke but kept her voice steady as she continued. "This is *Deputy* Fenris Ranger Seven hailing the *Starship T'Kala* with a priority-one planetary distress call. Please respond, *T'Kala*."

Several seconds passed. She was about to repeat her hail when an indicator light on the console confirmed the receipt of a real-time subspace signal. "The *T'Kala* is answering."

Harper shook off his cynical detachment and patched the reply into the shack's holographic transceiver. A translucent image of a Vulcan man wearing a Starfleet captain's uniform and seated in a starship's bridge command chair snapped into view inside the shack. With a few quick adjustments, Harper made the holographic image appear solid, as if the Vulcan man were actually in the room with them.

"*I am Captain Solok, commanding officer of the Starfleet vessel T'Kala. On what grounds have you invoked a priority-one planetary distress signal?*"

Seven stood to address the starship commander. "Captain Solok. I am Deputy Fenris Ranger Seven of Nine. The planet Soroya IV is in imminent danger of a global catastrophe."

Solok looked to someone on his bridge, nodded, and then returned to the conversation. "*Our sensors indicate your signal originates from the surface of Soroya IV. Is that correct?*"

"It is, Captain."

"You do not appear to be in any particular duress. What is the nature of this alleged imminent planetary threat?"

"General Kohgish, the former leader of the planet's defense forces, has become a rogue political actor in the Qiris sector, sowing terror and violence, and plundering entire worlds. He has vowed to inflict grievous, likely fatal harm on the people of Soroya IV in retaliation for our efforts to liberate them from his reign of tyranny."

The Vulcan telegraphed his aloof disdain with a single raised eyebrow. *"Are you saying you provoked this Kohgish?"*

"The provocation of Kohgish was an unintended consequence of my team's efforts to render aid to the innocent civilians of Soroya IV."

"Logic would suggest that because your dilemma is the product of actions taken by yourself and other members of the Fenris Rangers, the responsibility for addressing the consequences belongs to you and your peers."

"All true, Captain. But we are . . . outmatched. And our organization has refused to provide us with reinforcements or logistical support."

"But rather than send a general distress call, you hailed my ship directly. Why?"

"Because I know the *T'Kala* is the capital ship of the Starfleet action group closest to the Qiris sector. Your ship and its escort fleet are the only vessels with sufficient firepower to hold Kohgish's fleet at bay that can also reach Soroya IV in time to make a difference."

Solok nodded slowly. *"Logical. However, I will not bring my ship or deploy any of its escort vessels to the Qiris sector. We cannot intervene in this matter."*

Anger backed up inside Seven like bile climbing up her throat. It was a fight to keep her expression neutral and her voice steady. "Captain, I have sent a priority-one planetary distress signal. Under both Federation and interstellar law, as well as Starfleet regulations, you are obligated to respond and render aid."

"Incorrect. You proceed from a common but unfortunate misapprehension. If you were transmitting a general SOS from a vessel experiencing distress in interstellar space, then the nearest vessels receiving your signal would be required by law to render assistance. But that is not your circumstance. Though I suspect your request for planetary aid is genuine, it is, unfortunately, also invalid."

Seven's temper got the better of her. "Invalid?!"

"Interstellar law is complicated, Deputy Ranger. Any given crisis is subject to the terms and restrictions of any number of treaties, alliances, and other legally binding arrangements, some or all of which might be vying for primacy at any given moment. In this case, it is vital to note that the Soroya system is on the disputed boundary of the Romulan Neutral Zone. The Federation's current treaty with the Romulan Star Empire expressly prohibits Starfleet vessels from entering that system for any reason—even a distress signal—without the prior express consent of the Romulan Senate or the Romulan praetor."

"But these people are going to be killed! It'll be a genocide."

"An unfortunate circumstance—but the T'Kala *and its fleet are presently engaged in a top-priority operation related to the evacuation of Romulus, and I am not at liberty to abandon that mission, or divert resources from it, without direct orders from Starfleet Command."*

"Are you deranged? Whatever's going to happen with Romulus's star is still *years* away. This crisis is *hours* away. A madman who's already murdered hundreds of thousands of people is going to lay this planet waste. A planet with nearly a million inhabitants representing more than fifty sentient species, and which has no defenses of any kind. How can you turn your back on them when you know what's coming? If Starfleet ethics don't compel you to act on purely benevolent grounds, your Vulcan ethics should."

Solok steepled his fingers in front of his chest. *"That would be a most compelling argument if it came from anyone other than a Fenris Ranger."*

Seven's hands closed into fists. "Meaning what?"

"The Fenris Rangers, though they have asserted a right to enforce their own brand of justice in the Qiris sector, are not recognized by the United Federation of Planets—or by any other major power in local space—as possessing legitimate governmental authority over any system or colony world in this region. The Fenris Rangers cannot 'speak for' or act in the place of any other entity's legal government. Making matters worse, most of the inhabited worlds and systems of the Qiris sector have no functional governments due to recent coups and collapses."

"Which were caused by Kohgish!"

"Irrelevant. What matters is that most of the worlds the Fenris Rangers patrol—including Soroya IV—have no legally recognized government. Ergo, no one on those worlds has the authority to request an intervention by Starfleet or to delegate

that right to the Fenris Rangers. Put simply, I cannot render aid to Soroya IV because Starfleet has no jurisdiction there."

Seven stood mute, shocked by the cold-blooded nature of Solok's logic.

Harper stepped forward and stood next to Seven. "Thank you, Captain."

"I regret that we are unable to assist the people of Soroya IV." Solok seemed briefly on the verge of saying something more, only to decide against doing so. *"T'Kala out."*

The hologram flickered, lost its illusion of solidity, and then vanished as the channel was closed by someone on the *T'Kala.*

There was no condescension in Harper's tone, only sympathy. "I'm sorry, kid, but this is what I figured would happen. Now that Starfleet has its shiny new mission on Romulus, it and the Federation have turned their backs on this whole sector. Like it or not, we're on our own."

Seven's fists shook with an unsated appetite for violence. She fantasized about bashing the subspace comm terminal into a heap of spark-spitting junk, but she knew the colony would soon have urgent need of this tech in working condition.

Instead, she picked up a metallic thermos from the comm logs desk. It was empty but still stank of stale coffee. She closed her fist around it until the container's ceramic-polymer outer shell cracked and splintered, and its inner metal sleeve crumpled.

Still holding the demolished thermos, she muttered in desperation and rage, "There must be someone we can call. Something we can do besides give up."

Harper shook his head. "Sorry, kid. There ain't."

"But you don't *know* that."

"That's the problem, kid—I absolutely *do."*

"Any ship in range of this transmission, please respond. Repeat, this is a priority-one planetary distress signal, sent on behalf of the people of Soroya IV. Does anyone read me?"

Seven waited, hoping someone would answer her call, but there was nothing on any local frequencies except silence. She switched off her portable subspace transmitter and leaned against the forward fuselage of Harper's prowler, fuming at the indifference of the galaxy at large and also embarrassed by how abjectly she had begged for someone, anyone, to answer her.

Around her, the residents of the Valen Colony, who only hours earlier had been dancing and drinking in wild celebration, now were in a frantic scramble to abandon their homes and evacuate their settlement. Friends and families were organizing themselves into convoys, some with overland vehicles that were already speeding into the hills and mountains in search of hiding places, others with shuttles or short-hop transports that might get them as far as the next system—anywhere but Soroya IV. Watching them filled Seven with sadness and regret.

They don't even care where they're running to, as long as they get away from here.

On the other side of Harper's prowler, Ellory, Rana, and Speirs were prepping their own birds for a rapid retreat. They had all donated every last drop of water, all the meds they could scrounge, and the last of their rations to help the fleeing civilians survive whatever came next. Empty of cargo—except for Rana's ship, whose cargo hold had been loaded with what remains of Ranger Jalen Par they had been able to recover from the planet's surface—the prowlers were expected to make an especially fast exit once they were airborne.

But Seven couldn't bring herself to accept retreat.

It was irrational. When Kohgish arrived with his entire fleet, four prowlers wouldn't be a match for that kind of firepower. There was no point to making a futile last stand. There was nothing to be gained by the Rangers throwing their lives away. This fight was as good as over. Harper had said so. The colonists had said so. Even Ellory had said so. It was time to go.

But letting evil win? To Seven it felt like she was drinking poison.

Harper called down from the cockpit, "Seven! Saddle up, kid. We're leaving."

"What'll happen to the ones who *can't* leave?"

"Trust me, we don't want to know. And we damned sure don't want to be here to find out." The rumble-purr of the other prowlers' engines throttling up turned his head for a moment, and then he looked back at Seven. "C'mon, kid! There's nothing more we can do here."

Sick with guilt, Seven climbed up to the cockpit, settled into the rear seat, and fastened her safety harness while Harper closed the canopy and fired up the engines. "We could still try to make a stand in orbit. With four prowlers we—"

"Forget it." Harper initiated the liftoff sequence. "I've seen the report on Kohgish's fleet. With all three of his frigates in one place, he'll swat us away like flies."

Beneath the ship the planet's surface grew more distant and less distinct by the second. Seven stared down at the Valen Colony, remembering the dance the night before, and the way Ellory had touched her face and kissed her hand . . . and then reminded herself that the place where that all happened might be erased from existence in the next few minutes.

The colony's details melted back into the tawny expanse of Soroya IV's parched surface, and then the haze of atmosphere faded away, dissipating like a dream forgotten upon waking, until the cold light of the star-flecked cosmos welcomed Seven back into space, the environment that she had called home most of her life.

Beside and above her and Harper, the other three prowlers maneuvered once more into a diamond-slot formation. On the tactical sensor readout, Seven noted the approach of a large mass of ships. "I have Kohgish's fleet on short-range sensors. They're moving at high warp and will make orbit above Soroya IV in thirty-nine seconds."

Over the ship-to-ship channel, Ellory asked, *"Time to bug out?"*

"Not yet," Harper said. "Let's use the planet's smaller moon for cover, see what Kohgish and his goons do when they get here."

His suggestion rankled Seven. "We won't stop him, but we'll hide and watch?"

"It's called gathering evidence. We might not be able to stop whatever they're about to do, but we can document it. Bear witness to it. And someday, when we do get a chance to bring this bastard down, we'll have this to show at his trial."

It was an empty consolation, but it had just enough of the flavor of vengeance to slake Seven's thirst. "Very well." She checked the ship's sensor logs. "All passive sensors and comm intercepts functioning. Recording on all frequencies."

Harper swung the nose of the prowler toward the planet's lesser moon. "Okay, all wings, on me. Maintain silence and visual contact. Watch me for the signal to withdraw. Break."

The other three prowlers matched Harper's course, and within seconds the four ships had taken cover in the polar shadow and magnetic field of So-roya IV's moon Laertes.

"Powering down," Harper said as he switched off all the prowler's primary systems except for passive sensors and minimal life-support. "And, Seven? I need you to promise me that no matter what Kohgish and his people do, you won't do something rash and get us all killed."

It was a reasonable request, for which Seven had only one answer.

"No."

Silence. A simple directive, but so hard to obey in the face of atrocity.

Sheltered in the shadow of a misshapen moon, Seven let herself sink into her seat in the back of the prowler. On the sensor readout she watched the clustered signals of Kohgish's fleet resolve into individual signatures as they emerged from warp in orbit of Soroya IV.

A dozen ships, nine small fast-attack wings supporting three heavy frigates, assembled in formation above the planet's northern hemisphere, less than half a million kilometers from the planet's weather-control station.

Over the comm, Ballard asked on a secure channel, *"Wing Leader? How many snub fighters do they have?"*

"Enough to swamp us if we do something stupid," Harper replied. *"Everyone shut up."*

Seven watched the mercenary fleet with morbid curiosity. What was their plan? Would they expend vital hours or even days trying to break her encryptions on the control station? Or would they take the more expedient route of seizing hostages on the planet's surface and torturing the new access codes out of someone?

She wondered if Harper might know what the mercenaries were doing. "No comms yet between Kohgish's fleet and the colonies on the surface. What is he waiting for?"

Harper sounded exhausted. "Who knows?"

The mercenary fleet maneuvered into a new configuration. At first, its purpose eluded Seven. Then, all at once, she understood what Kohgish meant to do.

"Harper? I think Kohgish's fleet is targeting the control station."

"I figured they would."

"You did? When?"

"The moment you stole it back from them."

Before she could ask why he had never warned her of this potential outcome, the mercenary fleet opened fire on the control station.

Torpedoes overpowered the station's automated defenses in just a few concentrated volleys. Its shields collapsed with a momentary flickering of distortion that revealed their ovoid configuration—and then the station was a naked
target.

Disruptor beams from all twelve ships of Kohgish's fleet flensed the hull and
outer layers of systems from the control station. A barrage of precisely targeted,
maximum-power beams skewered the station's core and found its heart, the
matter-antimatter reactor and its reserves of antideuterium fuel. A cascade of
smaller explosions merged into larger detonations until, at last, a painfully
bright pulse of white light accompanied the station's fiery end.

As thousands of tons of burning, mangled wreckage fell toward the planet's
surface, all Seven could see through her tears were brilliant streaks of orange,
yellow, and crimson.

Harper's voice intruded upon her shame and grief. "Deputy? Sensor report."

Seven sleeved tears from her cheeks and forced her eyes to focus on her sensor display. "Debris from the station is falling toward the planet's surface. The
bulk of it is predicted to land near or within the limits of the Valen Colony. As
it enters the atmosphere, it will flood the upper atmosphere with smoke, ash,
and toxic and radioactive particulates with densities ranging from zero point
eight microns to three point nine microns."

Over the comm, Ellory exclaimed, *"They're firing again!"*

Adjusting the sensors on the fly, Seven noted the trajectories of the next
round of torpedoes launched by the mercenaries. "They have targeted the ancillary weather stations."

Speirs muttered in a horrified monotone, *"My God."*

For several minutes, Seven and the Rangers watched in mute dismay as
Kohgish's fleet obliterated an entire network of weather-management stations
and sent their smoking, broken husks plunging more than eighty kilometers to

the planet's defenseless surface. In less than a quarter of an hour, Soroya IV was littered with apocalyptic impact sites, each vomiting seemingly endless plumes of smoke and dust into the upper atmosphere.

Just shy of half an hour after the mercenary fleet arrived, it broke orbit and warped away, leaving Soroya IV wrapped in an increasingly dense, dark shroud.

All Seven wanted to do was shrink and disappear into herself.

This is my fault. I provoked Kohgish. Forced a conflict that didn't need to happen. I thought I could outsmart him. As if a single defeat would be enough to break his hold on an entire world. As if one little victory could change the course of history.

Perhaps sensing Seven's impending emotional implosion, Harper looked to the other Rangers to finish gathering the necessary intel. "Speirs? Can you get me an estimate of casualties on the planet's surface?"

"Copy that, Wing Leader. Prelim scans show approximately twenty-five thousand sentient fatalities since the first impact. Based on the detectable contamination of the planet's atmosphere, water table, and oceans, I project another fifty thousand will die in the next twenty-four hours, at least half a million dead in the next month, and complete eradication of sentient life on the surface within the year."

Hearing a genocide reduced to mere statistics made Seven want to vomit. All she could think about was what this catastrophe must look like from the perspective of those stranded on the surface of Soroya IV. Innocent civilians with nowhere to run, left with no recourse but to watch the sky literally fall and turn their whole world into fire and ash, smoke and death.

She raged in silence, her well of tears run dry. Kohgish would answer for this. He had to. She needed to know that. Not believe it—*know* it. As a fact. She needed to know, with the same certainty that she knew the stars were fire, that Kohgish would one day face justice.

And that she would be the one who decided what form that justice would take.

These people trusted me. And I got them killed.

No, she corrected herself. *Kohgish killed them. And in their names, I will be the one who makes him beg for mercy—and ensures that he receives none.*

After what had felt like an endless spell of watching a world in its death throes, Seven felt a small measure of relief when Harper declared, "Okay, we've got enough. Let's go home."

Without further chatter the prowlers moved back into formation, and together the four ships emerged from concealment, banked away from Soroya IV, and jumped to warp speed—leaving behind a world in ruins, along with the last shreds of anything Seven might once have dared to call innocence.

12

Earth – Starfleet Command, San Francisco

After less than two years of service as an admiral, Kathryn Janeway had learned that life inside Starfleet Command was a strictly managed affair composed of rigidly precise schedules packed with meetings (including an entire series of meetings devoted exclusively to the subject of scheduling other meetings), lunches, diplomatic functions, and more than a few carefully choreographed episodes of political glad-handing to placate some tool of the media, member of the Federation Council, or aggrieved dignitary.

Which meant that when high-ranking visitors arrived unscheduled and unannounced at her office inside Starfleet Command and breezed past her dutiful aide-de-camp Lieutenant Darusha, Janeway knew that either something serious had happened, or it was about to happen.

She remained seated as two women strode purposefully into her office. One was Admiral Pakaski from Starfleet Intelligence. The other she recognized as Keemah Geiss, the director of the Federation Security Agency. Geiss was an Argelian woman with rich ochre skin, black hair, wide-set brown eyes, and pleasant features.

Pakaski paused to lock the office's door while Geiss walked to Janeway's desk. The Argelian woman pulled from her pocket a nondescript metallic device about the size of an old-fashioned book of matches, tapped the center of a small red ring on its seamless surface, and set it on Janeway's desk. In under a second the ring changed color to bright green, and Geiss beckoned Pakaski. "We're secure, Admiral."

Janeway eyed the other women with suspicion. "What's the meaning of this?"

Pakaski and Geiss stood between the guest chairs in front of Janeway's desk.

The FSA director replied, "I apologize, Admiral. But it's vital that we preserve op-sec, and even with all these precautions, one never really knows who might be listening."

"Perhaps. But right now *I'm* listening, so I suggest you start talking."

Geiss nodded at Pakaski, who keyed commands into her padd. "Admiral, what you're about to hear is an excerpt of a conversation between your former shipmate Seven of Nine, and Captain Solok of the *Starship T'Kala.*" Pakaski started the playback.

"I am Captain Solok, commanding officer of the Starfleet vessel T'Kala. *On what grounds have you invoked a priority-one planetary distress signal?"*

"Captain Solok. I am Deputy Fenris Ranger Seven of Nine. The planet Soroya IV is in imminent danger of a global catastrophe."

Pakaski stopped the playback. "Admiral, I trust you noticed the same detail that jumped out at myself and Director Geiss?"

Janeway concentrated, processing what little she had heard and trying to imagine its larger context. "I did. Are we sure Seven was speaking truthfully?"

Geiss nodded. "It comports with witness accounts and sensor data we've compiled."

"Is that all?"

Pakaski handed her padd to Janeway. "Starfleet Intelligence also has signal intercepts of coded comms between senior leaders of the Fenris Rangers that back this up. It sounds like Seven has joined them."

While Janeway pondered the implications of that possibility, Geiss and Pakaski both sat down in the guest chairs. Crossing her legs, Geiss asked, "Admiral, can you offer any insight into why Seven of Nine would willingly align herself with the Fenris Rangers, a former law-enforcement agency that has recently devolved into a vigilante corps?"

"When I last spoke with her, she told me she had been approached by a man named Arastoo Mardani, who claimed to be acting on behalf of the FSA." Janeway scrolled quickly through the detailed Starfleet Intelligence report on Seven's recent activities. "He wanted her to act as a covert civilian asset—and for her to infiltrate the Fenris Rangers." She set down the padd. "In exchange, he claimed he could leverage the FSA's influence to reverse Starfleet Command's decision to deny her application to Starfleet Academy."

Those details piqued Geiss's curiosity. "Is that all this Mardani wanted?"

Janeway took a mocking tone. "You tell me. He said he works for the FSA."

Geiss grimaced. "It's possible, but unlikely. We have no records of anyone by that name acting on our behalf, in the Qiris sector or elsewhere in local space."

"Then an alias, perhaps."

The FSA director shrugged. "As I said, it's possible. More importantly, when was the last time you had direct contact with Seven?"

"Not since before she left Utsira III."

Pakaski leaned in to ask, "Do you have any means of contacting her?"

"Not at the moment. Her personal comm has been offline for some time now. Whether that's by intention or circumstance, I couldn't say." After a moment of consideration, she added, "If you really need to reach her, it sounds as if you could contact her via the Fenris Rangers."

That notion inspired both of Janeway's guests to roll their eyes. Geiss reproofed Janeway with a stern look. "That would be an extremely bad idea, Admiral."

"Why?"

Pakaski was quick to answer: "Because the Fenris Rangers are paranoid."

"About personal correspondence?"

Geiss said, "About infiltrators."

Pakaski, who had been nodding along, interjected, "Regardless of how Seven got herself into the Rangers' organization, at this early stage in her acclimation, even an absolutely innocuous message to her from anyone in Starfleet, never mind Starfleet Command, could get her put in prison."

"Or in front of an executioner," Geiss added.

"Bottom line is," Pakaski continued, "no matter who this Mardani person is, or who Seven is really working for, we can't risk undermining whatever trust Seven has earned with those inside this Mardani's inner circle."

Janeway shot a cynical look at her fellow flag officer. "Why not?"

"Because we don't *have* anyone else on the inside," Geiss said.

"Sadly, correct," Pakaski said.

Geiss crossed her arms. "And also because Seven is optimally positioned to tell us what the mercenaries are doing out here on the frontier."

Janeway still didn't like the other women's proposed terms, but she was equally certain she despised those forced upon her by the edicts of Starfleet and the Federation. She stood, signaling Geiss and Pakaski that their impromptu drop-in was now over. "Admiral Pakaski, Director Geiss, thank you both for stopping by."

Pakaski stood. "You'll inform us if you hear from her, yes?"

"Of course. And I'll expect you both to keep me apprised of any updates or changes in this situation."

"Naturally," Geiss said, offering Janeway her hand.

Janeway shook Geiss's hand, and then she pasted an insincere smile on her face while she watched Geiss collect her anti-surveillance device and make her exit with Pakaski.

As soon as they were gone and Janeway's office door was once again closed, she opened an intercom channel to her aide. "Lieutenant, step inside my office, please."

"On my way, Admiral."

The door slid open, and Darusha entered with a padd in hand. The lieutenant was tall, with broad shoulders, and their hair was shaved short on the right side of their head and fell in a lavender-hued bob on the left. They walked briskly to Janeway's desk and then stood, not presuming to ask why, simply ready for whatever came next. If there was one thing Janeway admired most about Darusha, it was their efficiency.

"I need you to make some discreet inquiries."

"Regarding?"

"Starships currently in the system that I can, if necessary, commandeer."

"For what purpose?"

"I'd rather not say."

"To what destination?"

"Let's keep that under our hat, as well."

"Understood. I'll have you a list within the hour."

"Excellent. But I'm not sure if or when I might need to do this."

"I'll maintain a dynamic list with hourly updates until you direct me otherwise."

"Perfect. Thank you, Lieutenant. Dismissed."

Darusha turned and left Janeway's office.

Alone once more, Janeway drifted from her desk to her office's window. She looked out across the bay at the skyline of San Francisco glittering in the honeyed light of dusk. Sailboats and hover-yachts left wakes amid the sparkling waves, and graceful aircraft painted contrails on the dome of the sky. And yet, despite being confronted with so much beauty, her mind remained fixed upon one troubled thought.

Dammit, Seven—what have you gotten yourself into?

Interstellar Space – Qiris Sector

Harper's prowler was at high warp, hurtling through a tunnel of stretched starlight that bent and curved around its warp field. The long-range sensors were clear, and the course back to Fenris was well charted and free of navigational hazards, so there was little for Harper to do as the vessel's pilot.

He had considered trying to steal a nap while letting the ship fly on autopilot, but he remained too agitated from seeing Kohgish's fleet all but destroy a planet. In the past, at times such as this, Harper had often passed the hours by striking up conversations with his partners and copilots. Tonight, however, Seven hadn't said a word since the Rangers left the Soroya system. Though Harper couldn't see her behind him, he felt her seething anger through the partial bulkhead that separated them.

I'll bet credits to quatloos she's the real *reason I can't relax.*

Her dark mood had left Harper at a loss. Would it be rude to ask after her state of mind? Would it be cold and insensitive *not* to ask? It felt wrong to just let her stew. After all, he was her training officer. He was bound by oath and duty to take an interest in his rookie's well-being. Even when it was clear she would prefer to be left alone. In fact, *especially* then.

"Seven? You all right?"

She left him hanging in silence for several seconds. "No. I'm not. I am very much *not* 'all right.'"

"That was rough back there. About as ugly as the job gets. And I can tell it hit you pretty hard." He waited to see if she would take his conversational bait. When she said nothing in the absence of a direct question, he softened his voice as best he could, and then he continued. "Wanna talk about it?"

"No."

Harper rolled his eyes. *Gotta give her credit. She's direct.* "Let me rephrase. You should talk about it."

"Why?"

"Partly 'cause it might make you feel better. But mostly so you don't pop your cork in the middle of a crisis and get people hurt or killed for no reason."

She replied with cynical self-loathing, "I've already done that. To a greater degree of magnitude than I could have expected—or could ever forget."

He reflected on some of the worst mistakes he had made as a Ranger—blunders that had cost lives and empowered villains—and was dismayed to find how fresh they remained in his memory. "I know how you feel, kid. We all take bad beats now and then. And I won't sugarcoat it: this one hurt. But if you're ever gonna be able to get on with being alive, never mind being a Ranger, you're gonna have to cope with how this bloody mess made you feel. You need to face it, not run from it."

Anger rose in her voice like a stir of flames breaking free of a pyre. "How I feel? I *feel* like I want to break necks right now. Starting with Kohgish's. And then maybe my own."

"Hrm. You started good, but you blew the dismount. Kohgish deserves to have his neck wrung—but don't go lumpin' yourself in with his kind."

"Perhaps I should. You don't know what I was. What I did."

"I got an inkling. Those implants of yours? It's pretty clear where they come from."

"So you and the other Rangers are aware that I . . . that I'm—"

"Part Borg? Yeah, we know. And I won't lie: the brass ain't thrilled. And a few of the rank and file are spooked. But they'll come around."

She sounded dubious. "What makes you so sure?"

"We need every able body we can get. Which is also why we try not to let rookies get in over their heads, like you did today."

Seven's anger turned to regret. "If you thought it was a mistake, why did you let me go?"

Shame and sorrow made Harper's voice unsteady. "Because until it went wrong, I really thought your plan might work. It was smart. Precise. I had my doubts, but I wanted to *believe* in you. So I did." He cleared his throat and fought to regain his stoic façade. "But now we have to face the fallout. *This* is why the Rangers prefer to stay out of epic battles and focus on small, low-intensity operations." He sighed. "There are major limitations on our resources, Seven. Shortages of personnel, matériel, and ships. We lack the numbers, the funding, and the ordnance to get into anything that looks like a war. We're guardians, not soldiers."

She asked in an accusatory tone, "Then what are the Rangers good for?"

"More than you'd think. We protect the innocent from piracy. Rescue those who get stuck in places no one else will go. Keep the worst of the worst contained as best we can. We're like the Dutch boy with his finger in the dam—"

"The what?"

"Old Earth legend. Not important. Point is, we're the levee holding back a flood of violence. And we're the only ones left doing this in the Qiris sector. If we fall apart, everything else falls behind us. So we need to save the lives we can and punish the crimes we're able to stop. Which means being careful to pick fights only with opponents in our own weight class. Know what I mean?"

A long, discomfiting silence unfurled. When Seven replied at last, her voice once more had regained its razor's edge of righteous indignation. "What I hear are excuses for accepting defeat. Rationalizations for failing to oppose evil."

Her unyielding air of judgment rankled Harper. "Been here a few days and already you think you know our job better than we do? Fine. Go ahead, rookie. Impress me. Tell me what *you* think our mission oughta be."

"We must bring Kohgish to justice, without delay. Every moment he walks free in spite of the enormity of his crimes, the law is weakened and justice is perverted."

Harper shook his head. "It ain't that easy, kid. I mean, maybe someday we'll get a chance to take down Kohgish. But right now? What can I say? He's just too big a fish."

"In that case," Seven said, sounding unpersuaded, "either we need to get bigger—or we need to make him a lot smaller."

13

"You have no idea how badly I want to airlock every damn one of you right now."

Harper willed himself to ignore the debilitating ache in his lower back while he and the rest of the "Soroya Seven" stood at attention inside the headquarters' command center, all of them on the receiving end of Ranger Commander Zhang's wrath. On Harper's left stood Kayd, Sagasta, and Rana. Seven stood to Harper's immediate right, and past her were Ballard and Speirs. Deputy Commander Saszyk and Chief of Patrol Yivv stood off to one side of the command center, observing the proceedings but pointedly not interfering with Zhang.

The diminutive woman paced behind the reprimanded Rangers, who all did their best to stay silent and keep their expressions blank. "You were all present when I gave a direct order not to go to Soroya. A direct order to avoid engagement with Kohgish and his fleet. I know you all heard those orders, and so does every other Ranger based in this facility. So when you openly defied me, and carried out an unauthorized commando mission to free a planet's weather-control station, that made me look weak. It gives other Rangers the idea that maybe they can ignore orders, as well."

She stopped behind Harper, who would have sworn he felt her stare boring into him like a drill bit between his shoulder blades. "Ranger Harper. What happens when the rank and file become convinced there are no consequences for disobeying orders?"

"Breakdown of the chain of command."

"Correct." Zhang circled around to pace in front of the line of chastised Rangers. "You've all humped the *targ* on this one. If the mission had been a success, perhaps we could have spun it. Said you were on a secret assignment. It might have sounded almost plausible."

She stopped in front of Harper. As she looked up at him, her stare cold and unforgiving, he did all he could to avoid making eye contact. "But you failed. The weather station was destroyed. Ranger Jalen Par was lost in the line of duty. Thousands on the surface were killed. And Kohgish and his thugs? They got away all but unscathed. Tell me, Ranger Harper: Did I miss anything?"

"No, Commander." Harper suspected it was just his imagination, but he was sure an odor of panic sweat in the room had grown stronger and more foul in the last minute alone.

Zhang turned away from the accused and walked to the command center's situation table. With a few taps on its master console, she summoned a flurry of holographic news reports that overlapped as they floated in midair, spewing condemnations in a dozen languages.

"The death of Ranger Par, coupled with the massive number of civilian deaths on Soroya IV, made this debacle the lead story on more than a few news networks. This fiasco has become a black mark on our entire organization. Starfleet and the Federation are already using it to bolster their propaganda. They're saying it's proof that, at best, we're amateurs. Dilettantes. Or, at worst, that we're a bunch of vigilantes waging campaigns of petty revenge with depraved indifference."

The commander switched off the holograms. "As I'm sure you can all understand, this wave of humiliating press has been a major blow to our *esprit de corps*, as well as a threat to unit cohesion. We can't be perceived as having endorsed your actions. Doing so would damage our credibility beyond repair. The media want someone to blame. Someone they can throw to the wolves of public opinion." She turned a poisonous sidelong look at Seven. "I'm strongly considering giving them you."

Speirs stepped forward and stood tall, his chin raised with pride. "Commander, I take full responsibility for this failed operation. I proposed it, and I persuaded the others to support it. Deputy Seven was present only as an adviser."

Before Zhang could reply, Ellory Kayd stepped forward. "I seconded Ranger Speirs's proposal, Commander. I also assume responsibility for initiating the mission."

Ballard and Sagasta stepped forward in unison.

"I volunteered for the mission, Commander," Sagasta said.

"As did I," Ballard added.

Rana took a step forward to join the *I am Spartacus* moment. "I take responsibility for the death of my partner, Ranger Jalen. I should have warned him sooner of the incoming attack."

Harper took two steps forward to put himself once more in front of the others. "I raised objections to this plan from the beginning, Commander. I joined the operation intending to serve only as an observer, and to keep an eye on my trainee, in case her expertise with the code bypass proved necessary on-site—"

"Which it did, " Kayd interrupted.

Zhang held up a hand in protest. "Enough. All of you shut up. Your show of solidarity is touching, but it doesn't bring back the dead." The commander faced away from the group for a moment, and when she turned back around she wore a resolute expression. "Rangers Speirs, Ballard, Sagasta, Kayd, and Rana: you are all reduced in rank to Ranger, third class, effective immediately. Deputy Seven, the only reason you aren't being drummed out right now is that your fellow Rangers, for some reason I cannot fathom, seem intent on shielding you from any responsibility in this matter. Personally, I think that's bullshit, but dismissing you right now would do more harm than good. However, in the interest of corps morale and good discipline, when not on active duty with your T.O., you are hereby ordered confined to your quarters for the next six weeks. Do you have anything you wish to say, Deputy Seven?"

The blonde shook her head. "No, Commander."

"Smart choice." Zhang raised her voice to say, "All of you except Harper: dismissed."

The rest of the team filed out of the command center without uttering a word. When the door closed behind the last of them, Harper found himself standing alone in front of Zhang, Yivv, and Saszyk. The Bolian chief's displeasure was evident from their expression, but the Saurian's mood was all but impossible to discern behind his leathery visage.

Yivv looked ready to chew Harper into pieces. "The truth, Harper: How much of this was your rookie's fault?"

"None of it. She's a trainee. I'm responsible for her actions."

Saszyk hissed through bared fangs. "I hear she had a reputation in Starfleet. They called her a maverick. A loose cannon."

"That hasn't been my experience," Harper said. "So far, Seven has been cool under stress. Logical. A good strategic thinker."

"Cut the crap," Zhang said. "We've reviewed the flight recorders. She's a hothead. A daredevil who acts without waiting for orders."

"So what?"

Yivv moved closer to get right up in Harper's face. "Her behavior is the very definition of reckless. Impulsiveness is not a virtue in our profession. You know this."

Harper felt long-buried resentments rising to be heard before he could stop himself. "What I know, Chief, is that Seven risked her life by leaving our prowler and jumping down to the weather platform to salvage the mission—which she did. And when Ranger Kayd was hit by hostile fire during the exfil jump, it was Seven who put her life on the line to dive through a storm head to save her. So I'll tell you what I *know*, sir: Seven is one of the bravest, smartest, and noblest people I've ever met. And if you drum her out, it'll be the biggest mistake of your life."

Zhang looked distraught. "I want to trust you, Harper. I really do. But this woman . . . was *Borg*. We can admire her virtues, but we must never lose sight of the danger she represents."

"I disagree, Commander. I think we need to stop seeing danger every time we look at her. Because the real problem here isn't that she's too hot for us to handle—it's that we're not strong enough to give her the backup she deserves."

The commander narrowed her eyes as if in suspicion, but she also seemed to be concealing the faintest hint of a smile. "We'll take that under advisement, Ranger Harper."

Seven ignored the curious glances and suspicious looks that followed her and two armed Fenris Ranger guards back to her quarters. She had learned to ignore the stares of the fearful during her first months aboard *Voyager*, and then she had learned the skill again after *Voyager*'s return to the Federation, upon her first visit to Earth. Someone was always watching her. Waiting for her to do something unusual. Waiting to see if she really was the enemy they imagined her to be.

It would almost be funny were it not so demeaning.

The guards halted outside the door to Seven's quarters as she entered. She looked back to see one of them—a tall, hirsute Denobulan—keying a code into the security access panel beside her door. The portal slid shut with a soft hiss. As soon as it was closed, she heard the low, subtle *thump* of magnetic locks engaging inside the doorway's reinforced jamb.

Locked in. I guess they don't trust me to stay put. But then, why would they?

Her assigned space consisted of a sleeping area and a tiny attached lavatory. It was windowless and spare, but also immaculately clean. Her duffel was tucked under her bunk, whose firm mattress had been covered with basic linens. She opened her duffel. Its contents had been arranged with a number of delicate hidden triggers that would help her to know if her belongings had been searched. All of them were intact. From the bottom of the bag she retrieved a passive sensor, whose log would tell her if her possessions had been scanned at any time while out of her sight. As she suspected, the Rangers had performed a rudimentary sweep of her things, most likely to check for contraband weapons, explosives, or illicit substances—none of which she had been foolish enough to bring with her.

Concealed inside the hollowed-out shell of an antiquated civilian padd was the secret FSA comm transceiver Mardani had given her before she'd left his ship for her rendezvous with Harper on Otroya II. Switched off, its sensor-scrambling shell seemed to have hidden it well from the Rangers' security inspection. Pressing its power button, Seven hoped the FSA comm's antidetection hardware and software would be equally effective.

It snapped to life, its holographic display packed with a menu of missed incoming comms from Mardani, all of them blinking red and labeled "urgent."

Tired and feeling less than fresh after two prolonged flights inside the cramped confines of a prowler's cockpit, Seven considered letting Mardani stew a few minutes longer while she treated herself to a shower and a change of clothes, but then she reconsidered.

My disheveled state should lend credibility to my report, she reasoned.

She selected Mardani's most recent transmission, and without bothering to listen to it first, she selected the REPLY option. It took the device a few moments to establish a secure subspace channel. Then came a flutter of distorted light that resolved into a hologram of the anxious face of Arastoo Mardani. *"Miss Hansen! Are you all right?"*

"I am."

"I've been trying to reach you for days."

"So I see. This is the first opportunity I have had since my arrival to make contact."

"Your arrival? Where are you?"

"Ranger headquarters, on Fenris."

"Fenris?" Mardani seemed pulled between competing emotions—surprise and admiration to one side, anger and confusion to the other. *"You were supposed to observe and report. Not engage."*

"An opportunity presented itself. I seized it."

"What kind of——?" Mardani dismissed his own question with a wave of his hand. *"Never mind. What's your status? Are you on Fenris as a guest? Or a prisoner?"*

"I am a deputy."

"A what?"

"A deputy Ranger, alternately described as a 'rookie' or a 'trainee.'"

Baffled, Mardani shook his head. *"You do work fast, don't you? All right, let's get to it. What have you seen so far?"*

"Be more specific."

"What have you observed about the Rangers' headquarters? Have you been able to get a look at its defenses? What's its offensive capability?"

Seven was about to reply when a moment of cognitive dissonance, like a twinge inside her mind, stopped her. Acquiring this information for Mardani was the reason she had come here. She had taken all these risks in service to her desire to join Starfleet—but now, at the moment of action, her conscience had intervened. She felt a sense of attachment to the Rangers. A kinship.

In the span of a breath, Seven started concocting lies.

"Their headquarters is antiquated. Most of its defenses are at half strength or less, and its offensive systems are all but nonfunctional. Without its patrol squadrons, it is a soft target."

"Really? That's unexpected, but it's also good news." Mardani looked down at

something not visualized by the holographic comm. *"How many ships do they have? And how many support personnel?"*

"Fewer than eighteen operational prowlers here at headquarters, and likely no more than thirty in service across the sector. Only two corsairs are assigned to headquarters, and only four remain viable for the Rangers at large. As for manpower, the Rangers are in the midst of a recruitment crisis. Total complement here is under six hundred personnel, and the entire organization is losing people daily."

"That's amazing news. Well done. Can you tell me anything about the specific capabilities of the prowlers?"

"No, I cannot." In the brief time that Seven had spent in the copilot's seat of Harper's prowler, she had all but memorized its technical specs, and she had observed its actual performance in combat with keen attention. But she had no intention of telling any of that to Mardani. "Because of my Borg implants, the Rangers have so far refused to grant me any close or unsupervised access to any of their ships or tactical systems. I have been forced to rely on observation and on anecdotal evidence for my evaluations."

"As I expected." He tapped his upper lip with his index finger. *"What about their leadership? Nobody outside the Rangers knows who's calling the shots in there. Have you seen anyone in charge? Heard any names?"*

"None. Just as they don't trust me with their ships, they deny me access to the command echelon or any of the organization's senior commanders. But I will continue to listen for any names that come up on a regular basis in connection with new orders."

Mardani nodded. *"Yes, good."* He squinted at something out of view and then looked back at Seven. *"We've been seeing news reports about some kind of a fracas involving the Rangers a few days ago on Soroya IV. Have you heard anything about that?"*

"Not much. Only that an op went wrong, and a Ranger died."

"Yeah—one Ranger and tens of thousands of civilians."

It took all of Seven's willpower to bury her rage, her sorrow, and her guilt to maintain her poker face. "A fiasco, then."

"To say the least." He fixed her with a hard stare that suggested he knew more about the matter than he was saying. *"Someone screwed up down there.*

Hard." When he looked away from her, Seven felt relief. She found his emotional cues difficult to read and parse, and she feared he was seeing with ease through her own hastily drawn deceptions. *"Remain alert,"* he said. *"Listen for any chatter about upcoming ops by the Rangers, anything involving more than three prowlers or any number of the corsairs. If they have something big planned, I want a heads-up, no matter how thin your details are. Understood?"*

"Understood."

"Mardani out." He closed the channel, and his holographic avatar distorted and then faded away. Seven switched off the FSA comm device and hid it back inside her old padd.

Seven sat on her bunk and started to shiver from a fear-based rush of adrenaline. Lying to both sides was a dangerous game, one she had never intended to play.

Is there some way I can still control the outcome of this mission? Some way to admit my role to the Rangers without being expelled from the organization? Or some way to sever my connection to Mardani without the Rangers finding out?

She couldn't imagine how she would cope with the shame of admitting to the Rangers that she had joined them under false pretenses. At the time it had seemed like a simple transaction. Just another move in a game, a step toward getting what she had wanted. But in the short time that Seven had been among them, she had come to like her fellow Rangers—and she had also come to like *being* a Ranger. When she wondered who she might be when this mission was done, she no longer found herself imagining a future in Starfleet. She pictured herself like a lone wolf patrolling the stars . . . in the uniform of a Fenris Ranger.

Smiling at that lingering image in her mind, she stripped off her dirty, odorous clothes while plodding into her lavatory nook for a long-overdue shower.

Lunch tray in hand, Ellory Kayd made her way from the mess hall to the sublevel one inner-core berthing area. Packed with windowless shoeboxes masquerading as living quarters, it served as home to most of the Rangers' newest recruits. Senior personnel had dibs on level six's coveted west-facing suites. Kayd's own room assignment was in level four north, whose lack of direct sunlight suited her nighthawk lifestyle. She hadn't seen the recruits' berthing area in years. Being back on the dimly lit sublevel to deliver Seven's lunch kindled memories for Kayd, not all of them bad, but the place was more depressing than she had remembered.

Confined to quarters. She shook her head at the stupidity of Seven's punishment by the brass. *As if any of us would ever refuse the extra rack time.*

She arrived outside Seven's quarters to see a pair of Rangers guarding the door. Loap, a hulking Denobulan with a beard like a garden thicket, was the muscle; his counterpart, a young Tellarite man named Boash gev Deg, was the one with rank. Kayd greeted Deg with a nod, taking care to pretend not to notice the otherwise lean Ranger's newly developed potbelly. "Deg. Been a while, hasn't it?"

He gestured with his tufted chin at the tray in Kayd's hands. "What's that?"

"Lunch for Deputy Seven."

Deg pointed at the floor across the hallway. "Leave it there."

"Why?"

"Inspection."

"For what? A plasma torch in the gravy? She's a Ranger on disciplinary confinement, not some fringe-system psycho-killer."

"Regulations," Deg said. As if that explained anything.

"Just open the door." Kayd stepped forward.

Deg put out a hand to halt her. "No visitors."

"Says who?"

Her resistance seemed to befuddle the young Tellarite. "Orders."

"I read the commander's order, Deg. Confined to quarters during nonduty hours. Didn't say a damn thing about 'no visitors.' Show me where it says that and I'll leave the tray. Otherwise, quit wasting my time and *open the door.*"

Loap and Deg traded confused looks, and then they shrugged at each other. When Deg looked at Kayd, he put on his best mask of authority. "Fine, you can deliver her lunch. But the door stays open for the duration of your visit."

"Whatever turns you on."

Deg unlocked the door, which slid open. Kayd pointedly avoided eye contact with the guards as she carried the tray inside and set it on the small desk along the left wall.

Seven sat up in her bunk and brightened at the sight of Kayd. "What's this?"

"Lunch. But don't get your hopes up: it's from our mess hall."

"Dare I ask what's on the menu?"

"The gray stuff is supposed to be sausage gravy on something that used to be a biscuit, or maybe a stale scone. I'm told the pale stuff on the right is potatoes au gratin, but I can't find anyone in the kitchen who'll swear to that. And for dessert we have . . . actually, I have no idea what that is, or what it was meant to be. Best guess would be fruit jerky."

Seven moved closer to Kayd. "Whatever it is, thank you."

Before they were close enough for contact, Kayd stepped back, out of Seven's reach. "How are you holding up?"

"As punishments go, this one is so mild as to be inconsequential." After a moment of consideration, Seven added in a less stilted manner, "I'm fine. How are the others?"

"They're good. I'll let them know you're okay."

Kayd turned to leave. Seven called after her, "Where are you going?"

Turning back, Kayd slipped into a lie like she would a comfortable pair of slippers. "Flight deck. Gotta supervise fixes to my bird."

There was sadness and longing in Seven's eyes. "Can't you stay awhile?"

"I can't. I just—" Words and emotions logjammed inside Kayd's mind. She had volunteered to bring Seven her lunch specifically so that they could have a chance to talk, but as soon as they had come face-to-face, Kayd's panic response had taken over. All the things she had wanted to say to Seven had fled from her thoughts, leaving her tongue-tied and embarrassed.

Seven's melancholy darkened as understanding took root. "You could stay. You just don't want to." She turned away, as if looking at Kayd had become suddenly painful. "Is it because of what happened on Soroya IV?"

"I'm sorry, Seven. I know I shouldn't blame you for what Kohgish did to those people. That wasn't your fault."

Shame and sorrow welled up from someplace deep inside Seven and left her shaking and teary-eyed. "Yes it was. I suggested the plan. I made it happen. And when Harper warned us what Kohgish might do in response, I didn't listen."

"You weren't alone, Seven. Speirs backed your plan, and so did I. But now I wonder if I'd have been so quick to sign on if not for the feelings I had for you."

Seven faced Kayd, her countenance one of pained betrayal. "Had? Past tense? Are you saying the connection we felt on Soroya IV is gone?"

Kayd had regretted her choice of words as soon as she had heard them aloud, but by then it felt too late to take them back. Now she was left defending her poorly chosen words when all she wanted to do was surrender. "I guess I just find it hard to muster good feelings about you—about us. When I see you, I can't help but see Soroya IV in flames. A whole world burning because we thought we could be heroes."

"That's not what I see when I look at you." Seven waited until Kayd acknowledged her with eye contact, and then she continued, "I see the hope that led us to fight back and the courage that made us take a stand against evil. My feelings for you remain . . . undiminished. But I accept that your feelings for me are entangled with those caused by the tragedy we provoked. If that means we cannot be anything more than colleagues, I understand."

Kayd turned away from Seven and strode toward the door.

"Enjoy your lunch. I'll give the others your best."

Kayd retreated down the hall, fleeing the truth in purposeful strides.

Seven sees me the way I've always wanted to be seen. And I'd see her the exact same way—if only I could forget how many people just died because I was too smitten with her to listen when Harper warned us not to play God.

I can forgive her. But how do I forgive myself?

In a flash, the answer came to her.

By finishing what we started.

During the day, the signals intelligence center, or SIC, inside Ranger headquarters was a busy place, packed with analysts, cryptographers, and engineers. The evening shift was less populated, reduced to a few comms officers monitoring the channel sweepers and an analyst or two poring through the seemingly bottomless ocean of raw information the SIC collected. But the time that Kayd liked best in the SIC was the overnight shift, when the computers were left to run themselves and there was no one else around to bother her.

In the small hours of the night the SIC was Kayd's refuge. A sanctuary. But having a place to which she could retreat was of little comfort when she brought her troubles inside with her. She had come with good intentions. Inspired by an idea how to suss out a vulnerability in Kohgish's ever-growing armada, she had let herself into the SIC. In under an hour she had written a query protocol that began searching the archives and scanning all active frequencies for any transmissions that could be positively connected to Kohgish, his fleet, or any of his people.

Then she'd set it to work . . . and realized that unless and until it yielded results suitable for review, there was little to occupy her time except to dwell on her recent mistakes.

I shouldn't have blamed Seven for what happened on Soroya IV. We all wanted to go. We'd all wanted a shot at freeing that planet ever since Kohgish put his boot on its neck. It's not Seven's fault it blew up in our faces. How could we have known Kohgish was that crazy?

Flashes of bitter memory assailed her mind from within, specters born of her own guilt. Images of the weather station disintegrating beneath the barrage by Kohgish's fleet. Its burning wreckage slamming down onto the planet. The black shroud that had swiftly encircled Soroya IV, until all trace of its surface was obscured from view by a blanket of ash and smoke.

That blood is on all our hands.

The main computer continued to process her query. Unable to coax it to work faster, Kayd slipped back into brooding. *Why did I say those things to Seven? Why did I act like I don't still have feelings for her? I can't really have blamed her for what happened. I've seen too much to do that. So why did I try to push her away?*

In her imagination she heard her mother's chiding voice: *"You did it because you like her, Ellory—and because that scares you."* When her mother had said those words to her, Kayd had been only fourteen years old but already submerged into the exquisite agony of her first crush, which, just to make matters more complicated, had been on Kaanik, a Vulcan girl a year older than her, and who would never have requited Kayd's affections, even if she had shared them.

Kayd chortled softly and shook her head. *I sure know how to pick 'em. A Vulcan girl who won't show her feelings. A half-Klingon woman whose idea of foreplay is bare-knuckles boxing. And now a gorgeous ex-Borg whose social skills would disgrace a Tellarite. It's like my libido evolved to respond to all the worst dating prospects in the galaxy.*

So why the hell can't I stop thinking about Seven?

Before she could try to answer that rhetorical question, the computer started churning out results. More than she had expected, in fact. Screen after screen of intercepted transmissions, with automated transcriptions for search indexing. Subspace communications between Kohgish's various ships, or between his ships and planets they visited, and even some that seemed to link directly to Kohgish himself. Either the Antican was staggeringly ignorant of proper operational security protocols for subspace communications, or his crews were borderline incompetent.

She smiled at her good fortune. *Either way, their lousy op-sec is my treasure trove.*

Fortified by a freshly replicated mug of *raktajino*, Kayd settled in with her mountain of newly assembled raw signals intelligence about Kohgish.

Separating useful intel from mindless chatter took hours. The vast majority of what had been caught in the wide net of the Rangers' sigint network was useless. But once Kayd began finding the figurative connective tissue that linked the most revealing bits of data, patterns quickly emerged.

In the past few weeks, a drastic shift had occurred in the routine of Kohgish and his fleet. The mercenaries had turned more aggressive, more rapacious, in their attacks on commercial shipping. Likewise, in addition to intensifying their shakedowns of the remaining civilians on Soroya IV, they had begun waging new, nearly identical campaigns of extortion on several other colony worlds throughout the Qiris sector. After each new grand-scale looting, Kohgish had made enormous deposits to his accounts at the Bank of Ferenginar—one of the few interstellar financial institutions that had tailored its services to the convenience of pirates, smugglers, arms dealers, and despots. By now he had to be sitting on a vast fortune.

So, why the rampage? Why the uptick in piracy?

The longer Kayd stared at the accumulated facts in front of her, the more certain she became that Kohgish wasn't just greedy—he was on a deadline. *He needs a ton of credits, right now. And he doesn't give a damn where they come from, as long as they pay out fast.*

She had seen this kind of desperation before. This mad scramble to assemble a lot of untraceable currency at any cost. Her years of work as a forensic accountant in the service of the Trill planetary government's treasury had led her to see this behavior a great many times.

Kayd took the list of worlds and colonies Kohgish had plundered during his current high-intensity crime spree and began plotting them out in a three-dimensional holographic star map projected from the overhead. "Let's see where you've been," she muttered as she worked, "and find out if that tells us where you might be going."

The pace of Kayd's work accelerated despite her urgent wish that everything related to her undercover operation be handled with the utmost care and discretion. She was close to something important; she felt it.

Once all the spatial coordinates were in, she added the temporal data and accounted for a wide range of cross-reference categories so that she could winnow the mercenaries' likely next targets to a manageable number. In under half an hour she had refined the search to ten worlds.

By the end of an hour, she was confident she had narrowed the list of potential next targets for the mercenaries to just three planets.

She stared at her finished tactical report. *Now what?*

The Rangers had protocols for this sort of thing, of course. Lengthy, complicated panels of review. Risk-benefit analysis teams. Not to mention a few dozen skittish intelligence analysts who would likely balk at the notion of ever doing anything that might upset anyone.

If I send my report into that bureaucratic meat grinder, I'll never see it again. If there's one thing we could use less of around here, it's red tape.

Kayd jumped to the last page of her analysis, which included lists of the specific targets she expected Kohgish and his fleet would assault, and who at each of these sites needed to be warned. Releasing her raw, unvetted intelligence file about Kohgish to anyone outside the Rangers would land Kayd in major trouble.

I'm already on disciplinary review. Do I really want to risk my badge?

She played out half a dozen scenarios in her head until she asked herself, *What would Seven do?* And she had her answer. Rolling the dice with her career as the cost of the wager, she sent her entire intelligence file on Kohgish, complete with her tactical recommendations, to the senior personnel at each of the warlord's next three most likely targets.

Then she opened a channel to Harper's and Seven's private comms and sent copies of her report to each of them, accompanied by a simple but urgent message.

"Hey, it's Ell. . . . We need to talk."

Seven stood next to Harper, who had arrived at the door to her quarters that morning beside Ellory, and stared down at the bewildering array of raw data on printed pages the Trill woman had spread out across Seven's unmade bunk. Not wanting to be rude, Seven modulated her tone carefully as she said, "If there is an opportunity to be gleaned here, I do not see it."

Harper scratched the back of his head, in what appeared to be an affected gesture meant to convey uncertainty. "Yeah, I'm sorry, kid, but I'm with Seven on this one. I don't see it."

Undaunted, Ellory replied, "That's because I haven't told you what to look for."

Her remark seemed to annoy Harper. "Well, get on with it. We're burnin' daylight."

Ellory sifted through the papers, pulled out three in particular, and set them in a row on top of the others. "Kohgish isn't being a monster just for laughs, though I wouldn't put that past him on his best day." She pointed at the first page. "Based on this sigint, I think he's in the market to buy a decommissioned warship from a Talarian broker. But that's gonna take more money than he's ever seen in his life. Plus, brokers like this one don't do credit, and odds are slim that any bank in the quadrant will loan Kohgish the latinum."

Lifting the second of the three pages, Ellory continued, "So he's got only one way forward: *other* people's wealth, and lots of it. As in, an impossible amount. He's been dumping all his loot into the Bank of Ferenginar, probably because they'll let him cash out in latinum when the time comes. If his next score is as big as I expect, he'll be ready to cash out any day now. Hell, if I were him, I'd be champing at the bit to get this done, like, *yesterday*. Which means this is the perfect chance to take him by surprise."

She lifted the third sheet. "I'm almost positive he'll raid the treasury on one of these three planets in the Qiris sector sometime in the next thirty-six hours. I've already warned all three planet's governments to expect him, and I've told them steps they can take in advance to placate him while also protecting themselves from complete financial ruin." She set down the sheet of paper. "Which leaves us as the wild card. Either we're in position, ready to take advantage of Kohgish's desperate need for a rapid infusion of capital, or we just stand around with our thumb up our collective ass while we watch him buy a warship and become the most powerful monster in the sector."

Harper looked almost pained. "The brass'll never go for it, Ell. Not after we lost Jalen. No way they'll let us risk a showdown with that maniac."

"I know. Which is why that's not what I'm suggesting."

Hearing that, Seven was intrigued. "Then what do you propose?"

"A shift in tactics. A bit of misdirection, coupled with asymmetrical warfare. Think of it as judo on a grand scale—we'll use our opponents' strength against them."

"Sounds nice," Harper said, his voice a rough growl at this hour of the morning, "but also short on details. *How* do we use their strength against them? *What* are we misdirecting? *How* do you do judo in space with starships?"

His pointed query didn't seem to trouble Ellory. "We lack the numbers to beat Kohgish's fleet in a direct engagement, but we've already shown him we're dumb enough to try. So we let him think we're *still* that dumb, just to keep him focused on the fight in orbit. Make him think that's all we've got. But while he's winning the battle, we'll be winning the war—not by overpowering his ships, but by surgically attacking his most vital resource: *his money.*"

"All of which you just said is safe inside the Bank of Ferenginar," Harper said.

"Correct. And that's where Kohgish will send all the money he steals from his next target—creating an opportunity for us to corrupt that transaction."

Harper let out a short, cynical laugh. "Dream on. The Ferengi might look like clowns, but no one does financial security like they do. Their systems have layers upon layers of defenses. It would take years to even begin planning an attack on a hardened target like that."

"For us? Sure." Ellory turned a mischievous look at Seven. "I'm guessing *you* could do it a hell of a lot faster than that . . . couldn't you?"

Seven considered the other woman's proposal. "In my experience, Harper is correct: the security systems of Ferengi financial institutions can repel any power in this quadrant." She met Ellory's gaze and smiled playfully. "Of course . . . I'm not from this quadrant."

Harper sighed. "Get serious, Seven. Assuming we've got less than thirty-six hours to pull this off, can you do it or not?"

"Yes, I believe I can."

Ellory's eyes brightened with hope. "Does that mean you will?"

Seven felt her own sense of purpose returning, like an edge being restored to a blade. Her smile widened with anticipation. "I look forward to it."

"It's bold," said Ranger Commander Zhang. "I'll give it that much."

The four bosses stood on one side of their holographic tactical table in the command center, the trio of Rangers on the other. The myriad elements of Kayd's plan hovered in midair, rendered in translucent projections through which Harper observed his superiors' deepening frowns. Saszyk blinked slowly and then barely opened his heavy eyelids, allowing his squint to convey his hesitation and suspicion. "It troubles me that this plan is based on a great many guesses and suppositions."

"With all respect, Deputy Commander," Kayd said, "I based it on analyses of hard data, from which I derived what I think is a reliable statistical model of Kohgish's next actions."

The Saurian remained dour and unconvinced. "As I said: a great many guesses."

Chief of Patrol Yivv crossed their arms and studied the intel. "Putting aside Deputy Saszyk's misgivings, this plan seems to require the commitment of a sizable fraction of our available assets. I should think that after the debacle on Soroya IV, you would be more cautious."

This time, Seven spoke up. "We need that level of engagement to convince Kohgish that it's our real counterstrike against his next robbery by extortion. But we've also taken steps to minimize our plan's risk to sentient life and to strictly limit any losses that might occur due to combat action."

Deputy Chief Shren eyed the hovering plan with disdain. His pale blue antennae quivered as he spoke. "So you've said. But we would still need to split our forces between three possible targets, leaving whichever one faces Kohgish greatly outnumbered."

Harper replied, "Not anymore, sir. Deep-space patrols located Kohgish's command ship a few hours ago. Based on his current position and what we know of his shrinking window of opportunity to purchase a decommissioned Talarian battleship, only one of the three most likely targets identified by Ranger Kayd is within striking distance for his fleet: the planet Alta, in the Kevrik system. We've already warned them what's coming."

Zhang's brow creased as her concerns mounted. "If you've prepared them in advance, why do we need to be there at all?"

Kayd answered, "Because sometimes, even when Kohgish gets exactly what he wants, he still unleashes hell on defenseless civilians. The Altan government is taking a big risk to help us. The least we can do is make sure Kohgish doesn't slaughter them after he robs them blind."

"But the most important thing," Harper added, "will be keeping Kohgish and his goons focused on us. Speed's gonna be the key. We razzle-dazzle the bastard, keep him running in circles, get him good and angry."

Saszyk flicked his forked tongue at Harper. "And that helps us how?"

"Angry people get sloppy. They make mistakes."

Yivv leaned forward, both of their blue hands on the table's edge. "If this goes wrong, our losses could be catastrophic. And Kohgish might kill every living thing on Alta."

Seven stood tall and proud, her hands clasped behind her back. "And if we succeed, we'll deal a decisive blow to Kohgish and his entire fleet—one more devastating than we could ever accomplish through force of arms."

Zhang nodded slowly. "The risk is high. But the potential reward is more than worth it."

"I disagree," Yivv said. "This isn't a wager on a game of *dom-jot*. We're gambling with people's lives here. And if we're wrong, that's a debt we can never repay."

The Ranger commander looked at her Saurian comrade. "You're the tiebreaker, Saszyk. What say you? Yea or nay?"

Put on the spot, the deputy commander lowered his head to think.

Seeing the decision fall to Saszyk, Harper prepared himself for disappointment. Over the past several years, Saszyk had proved himself to be risk averse, cautious to a fault, an acolyte of compromise and diplomacy. *If a true believer in law and order such as Yivv isn't willing to use force to stop a maniac like Kohgish, the odds of Saszyk doing the right thing are—*

Saszyk looked up. "Go get him."

"Yes, sir." Harper snapped a quick salute to the commanders, and then he led Seven and Kayd out of the command center. *Game on.*

14

Tensions were high on the command deck of the frigate *Eris* as a tunnel of light on its main viewscreen spun apart and melted away, revealing a rolling vista of stars. Watching from the center seat, Kohgish projected power and confidence. In front of him, the planet Alta rotated into view on the screen, its teal seas and ruddy continents draped in tattered sheets of white clouds.

Beautiful planet. It'd be a shame to have to kill it.

He swiveled his chair toward his tactical officer. "Raise shields. Arm all weapons." With a look at the communications officer, he added, "Order the rest of our fleet to do the same."

Muted acknowledgments of "Yes, sir" came back to him as he returned his attention to the main screen. "Sensors, assess their defenses."

A young Antican at a forward station answered while reviewing the information appearing on his console. "Planetary shield grid is limited to the capital city and two military installations. No surface-based artillery, no capital ships in the system. Three orbital defense platforms, all powering up and targeting our fleet."

Kohgish threw a look at his second-in-command. "Feeno, destroy those platforms."

"Yes, General." Feeno moved along the aft tactical stations, snapping out orders on the move. "Disruptors target platform one, torpedoes lock onto platforms two and three. Fire at will until they're gone."

Two large salvos of torpedoes raced away from the *Eris* as its forward disruptor batteries unleashed several beams that converged on the nearest of the planet's orbital defense platforms. Seconds later, as the closest platform disintegrated into a fiery cloud of twisted metal, distant flashes from beyond the curve of the planet confirmed its twins had also been obliterated.

"Platforms neutralized," the sensor officer confirmed.

"Well done. Comms, hail the planet's government. Get their leader on-screen."

"Opening hailing frequencies."

While Kohgish waited for someone on the planet's surface to respond, he noted the approach of his senior financial adviser, Rokkash Khol. Kohgish self-consciously avoided looking directly at the Betelgeusian, whose pallor and gruesome visage reminded him of myths of the reanimated dead. Khol's saving grace was that he had exquisite taste in suits and sophisticated taste in cologne. He leaned toward Kohgish to confide, "We're ready to receive an accelerated chain-code transfer."

"Good. Let me know when it's done."

"Yes, General."

Khol slipped away with the quiet grace of a professional domestic servant one who had spent a lifetime mastering the art of being inconspicuous but never far away.

The comms officer said to Kohgish, "I have Prime Minister Yaakola."

"On-screen." Kohgish straightened his back and lifted his chin just before the planet's leader appeared on his viewscreen. She was a humanoid woman in her fifties, he guessed, and she appeared to be of mixed Bajoran and Vulcan ancestry, with pointed ears, nasal ridges, tawny skin, and long black hair. Her taste in clothes suggested a preference for utilitarian simplicity.

"Prime Minister Sofia Yaakola. I presume you know what happens next?"

She kept her expression and voice neutral, but Kohgish sensed that bitter contempt simmered behind her mask of calm. *"You're going to demand the contents of our treasury."*

"Correct. And I'm going to have to insist you comply quite promptly."

"I regret to inform you that our treasury contains no hard currency of any kind."

He bared his fangs in a predatory grin of warning. "Yes, I know. You switched over to a virtual deposit archive three months ago. Which is why, for your convenience, I've set up one of my own aboard my ship. We're going to establish a secure FTL channel and initiate a chain-code transfer, from your server to ours."

"And how much are you demanding as a ransom for my world's safety?"

"All of it."

"Excuse me?"

"You heard me. I want the full value of your treasury transferred to my server in the next few minutes, or else I'll start laying waste your lovely little world."

"General, I can't let you take our entire treasury. How can we run a government without any reserves? How would we engage in foreign trade? It would be chaos."

"That, Madam Prime Minister, is not my problem. Now, unless you want to get a taste of what the ancient Terrans used to call 'nuclear winter,' I suggest you—"

"Contact!" interrupted the sensors officer. "Incoming ships!"

Kohgish growled at his comms officer and made a slashing gesture across his throat, cueing the young Antican to put the prime minister's channel on standby. Then he looked back at the tactical stations. "How many ships?"

Feeno studied the tactical screens. "A Fenris Rangers attack group."

Clenching his forepaws into fists, Kohgish fought the urge to howl. *No! Not here. Not now. Not when I'm so close to being able to bring some order to this damned sector.*

He returned his attention to the forward stations and used his chair's armrest controls to switch the secondary viewscreens to combat activity monitors. "How long until they arrive?"

"Five seconds," Feeno said. "Dropping out of warp in three. Two. One."

Dozens of signals popped into existence on the secondary screens. An entire squadron of Starfire 500 prowlers, supported by a trio of Ranger corsairs, all of them already in combat formation as they entered orbit on an intercept course for Kohgish's fleet.

The comms officer sounded almost sheepish as he reported, "They're hailing us."

"Put it on holo."

A ghostly figure of a gray-bearded male Fenris Ranger appeared a couple of meters in front of the command chair. *"General Kohgish, this is Fenris Ranger*

Keon Harper, commanding the corsair Mjolnir. *You and your fleet have sixty seconds in which to stand down and withdraw from this star system."*

"And if we don't? Then what?"

"We'll make you leave. We're done letting you run roughshod over entire planets. Done letting you just take whatever you want. It ends here, and now."

"Brave words. If you're lucky, you might live to regret them. Like you did on Soroya IV."

"Forty-five seconds, General. Stand down or be destroyed. Harper out."

The hologram flickered and faded away.

From the tactical station, Feeno said, "The corsairs are spreading out, and the prowlers are separating into squads and accelerating to attack speed."

Incensed, Kohgish bolted from his chair. "Blow them to bits! Every damn one! We haven't come this far to be scared off by a bunch of vigilante trash."

Fuming, he kept the rest of his rant to himself.

One more score and I'll be able to trade this frigate for a Talarian battleship. Once I have that, I can end this pointless fighting and rule the Qiris sector. And we'll finally have peace.

He returned to his command chair and composed himself. "Put the prime minister back on." He continued as soon as she reappeared on the viewscreen. "Prime Minister. I don't know if you summoned the Rangers or if their arrival was a coincidence. What I do know is that their intervention won't save you, or prevent me from taking what I want. You have two minutes to comply with my demands. If you refuse, I will vaporize the colony settlements on your planet's surface, one by one. No more games, Prime Minister. The choice is yours. Kohgish out."

Fenris Ranger Corsair *Mjolnir*

There was too much motion for Harper to track at once. A full squadron of prowlers, a fleet of nearly a dozen enemy warships, and three Ranger corsairs were all maneuvering for advantage. *Mjolnir* and its companion corsairs, *Gungnir* and *Ancile*, formed a blockade to defend Alta's capital from an enemy barrage. The prowlers circled the enemy ships at high speed like an angry swarm, peppering them with particle-beam fire while the enemy ships rolled, yawed, and broke away on erratic headings, clearly bereft of direction from their command ship.

Then Kohgish's fleet struck back with broad sprays of disruptor pulses meant to engulf the prowlers. Harper had to change tactics, fast. "Tactical! Increase the prowlers' speed ten percent and switch to attack pattern Echo Wide."

Kayd's longtime partner Lucan Sagasta looked up from his combat station, which was next to Harper's. "Kee? Echo uses precision maneuvers at three-quarter impulse. Push 'em that hard and Kohgish might figure out what we're doing."

"Then don't give him time to think." Harper turned away and raised his voice: "Tactical! All corsairs: Target the enemy frigate *Eris*! Full broadsides, three salvos. Fire!"

The entire ship thundered and quaked as its main guns unleashed hell. On the main screen, *Eris*'s shields flickered and dimpled beneath one brutal barrage after another.

Harper checked his chrono. Sixty seconds since Kohgish's ultimatum. Only another sixty seconds until the warlord would make good on his next genocidal threat.

I just have to keep him busy and off-balance.

Sagasta silenced a shrill alert on his console. "Enemy fleet splitting up, flanking us."

"Comms! Give the signal to abandon the blockade. Helm, come about, bearing one-one-seven mark nine, thirty degrees starboard yaw, half impulse! Tactical, shields double-front!"

A Ranger monitoring the sensors called out, "Torpedoes inbound!"

"Launch countermeasures! Helm, all ahead full!"

Sagasta winced as he declared, "Brace for impact!"

Deafening booms resounded inside *Mjolnir* and rocked its spaceframe, hurling half the command crew across the deck and into bulkheads, consoles, and one another. The overhead lights and the viewscreens all went dark for half a second, and the consoles dimmed until the rumbling in the ship's hull abated.

"Shields holding," Sagasta said. "But another hit like that could cripple us."

"Understood." Harper pulled himself up, using his console for support. "Tactical! Prowlers to full speed, active defense, attack pattern Victor!"

The Ranger executed the order as he confirmed it: "Active defense, attack pattern Victor, aye." Looking up from his console he added, "Prowlers engaging enemy fleet."

"On-screen."

It was beautiful sight, one of the loveliest Harper had ever seen: two dozen prowlers dodging and banking through flurries of pulsed disruptor fire at breakneck speeds, slashing fiery wounds in the enemy ships' hulls with elegant sweeping blasts from their particle cannons, and then spiraling away in seemingly random directions before regrouping and attacking again from a completely different vector. On the prowlers' next pass, one of Kohgish's ships broke in half and exploded, destroying another of the warlord's vessels as collateral damage.

Harper couldn't help but smile. *I love when a plan comes together.*

He stole a glance at the chrono. "All right, folks, we're down to the wire! Thirty seconds to go. Stay sharp, and make this *look good.*"

Mercenary Frigate *Eris*

Feeno shouted to be heard over the crackling of flames and keening of sirens on *Eris*'s command deck, as well as the panicked chatter issuing from the comms. "Direct hits, General! We've lost the *Tirnaq* and the *Aristan*! Prowler squadron is coming around for another pass!"

Fury and frustration collided in Kohgish's thoughts and churned into embarrassment. The damned Fenris Rangers, previously a persistent nuisance, had just become an existential threat to his fleet and his future, one he needed to deal with immediately. He turned and searched through the thickening smoke for his Orion second-in-command.

"Feeno! Tell our gunners and the other ships in our fleet to target only the lead prowler and the corsair *Mjolnir.* Ignore the others—just hit the *leaders,* with all we've got."

"Yes, General. Sending new orders now."

The image on the main viewscreen crackled with static and distorted with interference, but despite its deprecated resolution Kohgish still saw the moment his entire fleet converged all their disruptor pulses into an inescapable trap that closed around the lead prowler and blasted it into slag that sublimated into superheated vapor.

"Lead prowler destroyed," Feeno announced.

"Target the next one in formation."

The tactical officer interjected, "Torpedoes locked on the *Mjolnir*."

"Fire!"

Through his bared fangs Kohgish coughed blood, a consequence of the toxic haze filling his command deck, but he didn't care. It was still pure joy to watch dozens of torpedoes spiral toward the *Mjolnir*, tracking it even as it rolled away into a full-impulse evasive maneuver. The Ranger corsair launched another cloud of its active torpedo countermeasures, destroying or misdirecting all but the last five torpedoes—but those five were enough to collapse its shields, breach its hull, and send it tumbling through Alta's upper atmosphere while trailing plasma flames and ionized gas. *Not so smug now, eh? Serves you right, you sanctimonious fools.*

The countdown on the armrest of Kohgish's command chair ticked down to zero. "Tactical, lock plasma torpedoes onto the six largest, unshielded colony settlements on the planet's surface."

"Torpedoes locked," the officer said.

"Comms, open a channel, all frequencies." He waited until the comms officer confirmed with a nod that the hailing channel was open, and then he continued in his most imperious tone of voice. "Attention, Fenris Ranger intruders. My ship has plasma torpedoes locked onto six defenseless civilian settlements on the surface. Break off your attack immediately, or else I will vaporize all six—and then target another six. If you think I'm bluffing, remember what I did a few days ago at Soroya IV. And ask yourselves if that's an outcome you want to repeat."

The prowlers circling Kohgish's fleet ceased fire and veered away from their attack run. They fell into formation around the corsairs, which limped hastily out of orbit. Over the open channel, Kohgish heard Ranger Harper grumble, *"Your day will come, Kohgish. Count on it."* Then, in the wink of an eye, the Ranger attack group jumped to warp speed and was gone.

Feeno checked the sensors and reported, "The Rangers are in retreat, General."

"Good. Comms, get me Prime Minister Yaakola."

The Vulcan-Bajoran woman's visage appeared on the main viewscreen, almost as if she had been standing by the entire time. Kohgish spoke first, in the name of efficiency. "Madam Prime Minister—the Rangers have fled. No one is coming to save you. And my fleet stands ready to vaporize your most vulnerable communities. Unless you meet my demands *now.*"

"Very well. I've ordered our minister of finance to surrender the contents of our treasury by means of whatever frequency and protocol you direct."

With a nod, Kohgish delegated the work of transmitting the necessary details to Feeno. "A wise decision, Madam Prime Minister. We've sent you the details. Initiate the transfer."

"Transfer commencing."

Seconds later, a pleasant-sounding chime from a nearby console inside *Eris*'s command center confirmed the receipt of all funds from the Alta treasury.

Kohgish exulted silently. *One step closer to total control. To a lasting peace.*

Feeno sidled over to Kohgish's command chair to whisper, "Success, General. As soon as the Ferengi wash the money, we'll be ready to meet the Talarian broker."

"Well done," Kohgish whispered back. "Take us into the Neutral Zone so we can use the Romulans' comms network to contact Qulla." As Feeno stepped away to execute that command, Kohgish faced Yaakola once more. "This is a fortunate day for you, Madam Prime Minister. Because of your swift compliance, rather than use a few of your settlements for target practice as a warning to anyone else who might want to risk calling the Fenris Rangers, I'm going to take my fleet and go, leaving your world intact. But my judgments aren't always so charitable. So, for the sake of your world and your people, don't give me any reason to return."

Kohgish signaled his comms officer to close the channel, and then he found his first officer. Leaving a world un-plundered after a victory felt to Kohgish like leaving a buffet without eating, but he had things to do and places to be.

"Feeno, deposit all our virtual currency on hand with the Ferengi, including today's haul. Then confirm the rendezvous with the Talarians. Now, get us out of here, maximum warp."

"Yes, General."

"And, Feeno? Remind the Ferengi not to cheat us on the interest we're owed. It'd be a shame if they had to replace their Qiris sector branch manager. *Again.*"

Fenris Ranger Corsair *Mjolnir*

Ninety minutes after leaving the Kevrik system in what had been meant to look like a hasty retreat, the *Mjolnir* and its attack group dropped out of warp, back in orbit of Alta.

Harper turned an anxious look toward Sagasta. "Any sign of Kohgish's fleet?"

The younger Ranger checked his console. "No contacts within two light-years. Our outriders report his fleet dispersed after leaving the system, and his command ship is bound for the Ulrika system at high warp."

"So far, so good. Comms, hail the prime minister's office."

"Aye, sir." Within moments, the young woman at comms added, "I have them."

"On-screen."

The image of Alta's northern hemisphere switched to one of Prime Minister Yaakola in her government's situation room, hidden somewhere beneath the planet's surface. *"Ranger Harper. It's good to see you again."*

"Feels good to be seen, Madam Prime Minister. Is everyone okay down there?"

"Thanks to your warnings and intervention, yes."

"Dare I ask how much virtual currency Kohgish stole?"

The answer seemed to pain the prime minister. *"More than we would have liked, but your colleagues insisted it needed to be a convincing sum lest the general become suspicious."*

"Unfortunately, true. But I trust you were able to conceal some kind of reserve?"

"Again, yes, thanks to your fellow Rangers. It should be enough to keep our economy from total collapse for at least a week, maybe two. After that, however—"

"We'll do our best to have your money back to you before then. And if not all of it, as much as we can recover."

Yaakola looked dubious. *"I hope, so, Ranger Harper. We've taken a terrible risk."*

"I assure you, the outcome would have been far worse if we hadn't stepped in." Harper noted a look from Sagasta, who silently prompted him to move on to the next item of business. "Forgive me, Madam Prime Minister: May I have a word with Rangers Kayd and Seven?"

"Of course." Yaakola tapped a control panel on the desktop in front of her, and the vid feed switched to an angle that showed Ellory and Seven, who were in the situation room with the prime minister and her inner circle of civilian and military advisers.

"Nice work, Ell. You gamed out Kohgish's responses almost perfectly."

"Thank you, sir."

"And, Seven? Were you able to hide your malware inside the currency transfer?"

"Affirmative."

"Any reason to think Kohgish or his people noticed it?"

"None. Both sides verified the transfer as valid."

Ellory leaned forward to add, *"But we won't know for certain if our plan worked until after Kohgish deposits that block of VC into an account at a bank with links to the IFN."*

"Seven: Any chance the Interstellar Financial Network might flag our code?"

"Negative. The executable function will be completed before contact is made with the IFN. From their perspective, it will be an ordinary transaction."

Harper permitted himself a moment of satisfaction. "Well done, both of you. Get to your prowler—we leave for Fenris in five minutes. *Mjolnir* out."

Fenris – Ranger Headquarters

Back where we started, Seven mused, sitting with Harper and Ellory inside the operations center, looking across the tactical table at the senior Rangers. Ellory's eyes were fixed upon the comms screen, while the bosses' attention had wandered. Deputy Chief Shren had taken to passing the time by reviewing patrol reports that had piled up over the last few days, while Chief Yivv had put their focus on drafting two press releases: one singing the Rangers' praises in the event of success, and the other groveling with abject remorse in the event of a failure.

Ranger Commander Zhang simply glared at Ellory and Seven as she asked for the ninth time in under an hour, "How much longer will this take?"

Ellory summoned her best tone of appeasement. "There's no way to know for certain, Commander. The malware won't activate while it's still in Kohgish's virtual depository. Only after it confirms transfer to an account in an IFN-certified institution will it trigger its executable function, which Seven disguised as a verification checksum packet. Then it—"

"I don't want your life story, Ranger. I just want an ETA."

From the comms panel came a bright, loud *ping*.

Ellory grinned. "Approximately *now*, Commander."

Seven activated her console and watched her and Ellory's mission of deception bear fruit in real time. "The malware has activated from inside Kohgish's account at the Bank of Ferenginar and has linked to Kohgish's accounts at several other financial institutions throughout the quadrant. Transfers are being initiated. . . . Transfers complete. Malware package is self-deleting." The financial account data on Seven's screen vanished, and her screen reverted to its default configuration. Seven looked up. "Operation complete."

Zhang looked confused. "That's it? What just happened?"

With a smile, Ellory cued Seven to answer the commander. "We just emptied all of General Kohgish's many financial portfolios—and transferred those sums into our own primary operations account."

Harper smirked. "In other words, we bankrupted a warlord and got rich doing it."

At first, the bosses didn't seem to believe it. Yivv pivoted to a nearby console and keyed in some codes until a screen of information appeared. Their face went slack for a moment, and then a slightly manic gleam lit up their expression as they faced their peers. "Confirmed. Our operations account just received a virtual currency deposit large enough to fund our operations for the next several years—even after we return Alta's treasury funds and make donations to many of Kohgish's other victims." They flashed a broad smile. "We just pulled off a heist."

Ellory soaked up the praise. "And all it cost us was one uncrewed prowler and some repairs to *Mjolnir*. Not too shabby, if I say so myself."

Harper arched an eyebrow at her. "You did say so yourself."

"Oh, shut up."

Seven caught Ellory's eye and held her attention with a smile. "I, too, am quite impressed. How did you think of striking at Kohgish through his finances?"

"I used to work as an investigator for the planetary tax-collection service on Trill. Part of my training was in forensic accounting, so I could track money launderers. Once you know how they do it, it becomes a lot easier to recognize."

"The Rangers are lucky to have someone like you."

Ellory shrugged. "I'm not that special. Most of us had a life before we signed up."

"Were many of them also civil servants?"

"More than you might think. A few were peace officers. And we've got at least a few veterans from Starfleet and the Klingon Imperial Defense Forces. But plenty of Rangers used to be just ordinary folks: teachers, clerks, artists. The one thing we all have in common: we don't like to see good people get hurt, or bad guys win."

At the tactical table, Saszyk pored through the seemingly endless stream of metadata connected to the virtual chain currency transfer. "This is incredible. You didn't just steal a warlord's war chest—by taking it in virtual currency, you also captured a detailed transaction log. We can track the provenance of every credit in Kohgish's account. See how much of it was stolen, and how much he might have received from other criminals."

"And implicate ourselves in the process," Ellory said. "Now that we have possession of the chain currency, our name is in its metadata. So unless we want to answer some very tough questions about our sudden flush of wealth, we'd better get these funds off Fenris and into a bank that'll let us wash it clean before we move it someplace safer."

Zhang seemed suspicious. "Someplace safer? Such as . . . ?"

"An anonymous account at a mercantile bank in Stardust City on Freecloud."

"As long as we make a copy of the metadata for our own use," Saszyk said. "With this kind of information, we'll be able to break interstellar rings engaged in sentient trafficking, smuggling, illegal arms sales, bribery . . ." The deputy commander's voice fell quiet as his thought trailed off, and when the others looked to see what had muted him, they found him staring in silent horror at a highlighted patch of data on his screen.

Yivv put their hand on Saszyk's shoulder. "What's wrong, Saz?"

Saszyk pointed at the data cluster.

"Patterns of funding. Lots of Federation-based NGOs acted as intermediaries, funneling money directly to Kohgish. But look at where all these funds originated."

Seven looked over Saszyk's shoulder and felt nauseated with horror when she saw the payer Saszyk had identified as the general's chief financier:

The Federation Security Agency.

15

Fenris – Ranger Headquarters

Seven stepped back from the others but was unable to look away from the words on the screen: *Federation Security Agency.* "It must be a mistake."

Ellory shook her head. "There's no way to fake something like that in a secure financial chain code. And I've seen the FSA's metadata before. That's as legit as it gets."

The senior Rangers all wore similar expressions of concern. Zhang's was the gravest. She pointed at details in the displayed code. "The FSA put large sums of money into several different Federation-based NGOs. And within two days of each deposit, they each funneled identical amounts through a Ferenginar shell corporation into Kohgish's accounts." She frowned. "I don't know what bothers me more: the FSA funding a local warlord, or its pathetically lazy attempts at money laundering."

Not wanting to draw attention, Seven stayed quiet. Nonetheless, she felt her face flush with the warmth of anger and embarrassment. *I was a fool to trust Mardani. It cannot be a coincidence that the FSA sent me to the Rangers while also funding Kohgish's fleet.*

Yivv palmed sweat off their bald blue pate. "Why would the FSA bankroll Kohgish?"

Saszyk applied a data filter to the perplexing flood of metadata and reduced it to a more easily parsed trickle. "The first payments from the FSA to Kohgish were initiated the day after the Federation Council announced it was organizing a massive interstellar relief effort for the people of the Romulan home system."

Deputy Chief Shren added, "The same day they quietly put out a press release to say they were recalling all NGOs and available starships from the Qiris sector, effective immediately. They knew exactly what they were doing."

"On Earth," Harper said, "it used to be known as 'robbing Peter to pay Paul.'"

Ellory changed the filter set and repeated the data analysis. "Kohgish didn't waste any time, either. Within hours of getting the money, he started buying huge orders of small arms, starship ordnance, and antimatter fuel reserves for all his ships." She shot a worried look back at Harper. "No one makes that many deals that fast—not this far from the core systems. He must have had those deals lined up and waiting ahead of time."

"Which means he was expecting the funds from the FSA," Harper said. "Whoever made the deal with him knew what was coming well in advance of the announcement."

A nod from Ellory. "All the more reason to think it really *was* the FSA. But why?"

Harper called up a local star chart on the tactical table's main surface. He pointed at relevant details as he continued. "Because this sector in general, and Soroya IV in particular, are the perfect place to deploy a proxy force."

Zhang asked, with a quizzical look, "To what end?"

"Preventing a rogue faction of Romulans—like the ones that have been rumbling lately on Gasko II—from invading Federation space and disrupting the relief effort."

Seven's anger still churned and roiled inside her, but she refused to let it be seen. Mimicking a calm person, she asked, "Would the FSA have had anything to gain from Kohgish's violence against his own people? Or his increased practice of piracy?"

"I'd doubt it," Harper said.

Ellory added with mounting cynicism, "But they also didn't try to stop him when he turned a humanitarian crisis into a blood-soaked power grab."

Saszyk shrugged. "No one's perfect, Ranger Kayd."

Harper restored the flow of the original, unfiltered data to the tactical screen. "We have another problem. When we heisted Kohgish's war chest, we made a trail of our own. It won't be long before the Ferengi tell Kohgish where to come looking for his money. And once Kohgish knows, it's a good bet he'll tell the FSA. At which point we'll be in a world of pain."

Yivv's demeanor turned fearful. "He's right. The Federation has spent months smearing us. Calling us vigilantes. Imagine what they'll do if they find out we have this evidence."

"I don't have to imagine," Zhang said. "They'll burn us to the ground to keep us quiet."

Inspiration struck, so Seven spoke. "Then don't let Kohgish be the one to tell them."

Her suggestion met with a tableau of confused faces.

Shren's antennae waggled a bit as he asked, "What does that *mean*, Ranger Seven?"

"It means, sir, that we should release the information ourselves."

Ellory asked, "Which part?"

"All of it. Or a partially redacted version, at least." Seven returned to the tactical table and shouldered past Harper so she could lean on the table's edge. "Tell the people of the galaxy what the FSA did. What Kohgish did while acting as the UFP's proxy."

"Not a bad idea," Zhang said, weighing its merits behind raised eyebrows. "We can send this data, plus any corroborating evidence we can find, right to the Federation News Network."

"And the Interstellar News Service," Yivv added.

Saszyk piled on, "Not to mention every guerilla news outlet from here to Izar."

Harper nodded in approval. "I like it. Put the spotlight on them, make them play defense. If we're lucky, it might limit their freedom to act against us, at least for a news cycle or two, until we have a chance to get our act together."

Deputy Shren looked uncomfortable. "News cycles pass quickly. And once the public's attention moves off the FSA, its retaliation for this embarrassment will be all but assured."

Seven faced the Andorian. "Then I suggest we use the intervening time to make sure we're ready for them, Deputy Chief."

Her answer drew a crooked half smile of approval from Zhang. "Couldn't have said it better myself. Harper, you, Seven, and Kayd get it done. Saszyk, you and Yivv warn our people to get ready for the blowback." Bearing a look of fierce determination, Zhang headed for the operations center's exit. "And, Shren? Go grow yourself a spine."

Two hours after the intelligence trove mined from the chain codes had been sent to the media, there was nothing for Seven to do but stew in her quarters, once again relegated to disciplinary confinement.

The work itself had been simple and quick, which she had expected. What had surprised her was how swiftly the news agencies had reacted to receipt of the information. She had thought they might need several hours, perhaps even a full day, to vet the authenticity of the data, to question its provenance. Instead, all the major details had been released as parts of headline reports just over ninety minutes after Seven, Harper, and Ellory had sent them out. FNN had reacted first, but INS hadn't been far behind, and now the various independent channels were disseminating the story across the quadrant and beyond.

Someone at the FSA was, no doubt, suddenly having a very bad day.

I wonder how Mardani will react to the news.

Her hidden FSA comm device had not yet received any incoming signals. If her so-called handler had learned of the exposure of the FSA's link to Kohgish, he had not yet seen fit to make contact with Seven to discuss it. She had briefly considered using the device to contact him, to try to put him on the spot about whatever role he might have played in the fiasco. The longer she thought about it, however, the less she cared to hear his side of the story. Her gut told her she had been manipulated. Lied to. Used. In the light of such a revelation, what more was there to say?

Someone outside knocked lightly on her door.

Seven got up from her bunk. "Yes?"

The door slid open to reveal Ellory. The Trill woman beamed with joy. "Good news! Commander Zhang lifted your confinement."

"Why?"

"Does it matter?"

"I would just like to know."

"Because your plan worked. Every reporter in the quadrant is grilling the

Federation government about the Kohgish scandal. We haven't seen this many politicians trip over their own tongues since . . . well, *ever.*" She held up a metallic flask. "Come have a drink with me."

Seven peeked past Ellory and confirmed for herself that the guards who had been posted outside her quarters earlier now were gone. "Very well."

She followed Ellory through long hallways, into a lift, and then through more hallways until they reached an outdoor terrace overlooking the threshold of the flight-operations bay. Inside the bay, ground crews worked to repair, rearm, and refuel prowlers scheduled for the next shift of patrols, while deck officers supervised the landings of the last shift's returning spacecraft. But all of that paled in comparison to the distant brilliance of Fenris's capital city, a metropolis of high towers and colossal structures ranging from pyramids to hollow hemispheres.

Overhead yawned a night sky decorated with the misty sprawl of the Milky Way. Gazing up at the cosmos, it suddenly no longer mattered to Seven how much of space she had seen aboard starships. There was something magical about staring up at the stars from a planet's surface. About feeling the pull of connection to a world beneath one's feet, and the call of eternity from the endless darkness above.

Ellory removed the cap from her flask, took a swig, and offered it to Seven. "To little victories."

Seven accepted the flask and took a nip. The bourbon was sweet and smoky, and the heat of alcohol in her throat, which she had once thought so peculiar, now felt welcome. She handed the flask to Ellory. "To little victories."

Ellory tucked the flask away inside her jacket. "You say it like you're reading a eulogy."

"Forgive me. I am . . . not in a festive mood."

"Because of Soroya IV?"

Seven nodded. Ellory leaned forward and rested her arms atop the chest-high wall that ringed the terrace. "I get it. A bad beat like that? It stays with you. But you need to go forward."

"But you yourself said—"

"I know. And I shouldn't have laid all that guilt on you. It wasn't fair." She reached out and gently clasped Seven's right hand. "I'm sorry about that."

Seven pulled her hand from Ellory's, though she wasn't sure why.

Ellory looked concerned. "Did I do something wrong?"

"No. It's just that—" Seven struggled to put words to her feelings, which were all new and unfamiliar to her. "For the longest time after *Voyager*'s crew freed me from the Borg Collective, I felt cut off from my human side. I . . . didn't know how to *feel*." Unable to bear the intimacy of eye contact, she looked up at the stars. "They tried to help me, but I wasn't ready. And after we made it back to Earth, they all went on with their lives." To her own shock, she felt tears fall from her eyes, and her chin trembled. "And they left me behind."

Ellory put a consoling hand on Seven's back. "I'm so sorry."

"It wasn't their fault. They didn't know how lost I felt. Because I never told them." She closed her eyes and forced herself to pull in a deep breath to slow her pulse. "But now everything's different. Since I came here, I've felt myself changing. I'm drowning in emotions, but I don't know what they are because they're coming *too fast*, all at once, mixed together."

"Try to focus on just one thing you're feeling right now, Seven. What is it?"

Seven searched inside herself and struggled to put a name to her witches' brew of roiling emotions. "Guilt."

"About what?"

"Releasing the information about the FSA and Kohgish. I would never have suggested such a thing when I was part of *Voyager*'s crew."

"So why did you do it now?"

She dug deeper into the ugly muck of her inner self. "Because I felt angry. Betrayed. Lied to. But that doesn't make what I did right. What if we were misled? What if the evidence was fake? Or not as conclusive as we thought?"

"Then people with more time and resources than we have will uncover the truth."

"But by then the damage will be done. What if this was all just some ploy to manipulate us? A ruse to trick us into slandering the Federation, just to promote someone else's agenda?"

"If that turns out to be the case, we'll deal with it in turn. By the book."

Seven almost laughed. "'By the book.' That's a popular phrase in Starfleet."

"I know. My dad served."

"Then he was luckier than I am." Realizing that Ellory needed context,

Seven continued, "After *Voyager* returned home, I applied to join Starfleet. They wouldn't even *consider* my application."

"Because you're ex-Borg?"

"That was part of it. What really seemed to bother them was that I wouldn't use my Federation name on my application. If I had been willing to lie . . . to say my name was Annika Hansen . . . they might have let me in. But now I'll never know."

Ellory sidled closer to Seven so she could stretch one arm across Seven's shoulders and give her a gentle but steady hug. "Why did you want to join Starfleet?"

In hindsight, the answer seemed so clear: "To feel accepted."

"You have that here, with us."

"I know. And I'm starting to think I'd make a better Ranger than a Starfleet officer."

"I think you'd be amazing at anything you did."

Seven looked at Ellory. "Thank you."

Suddenly self-conscious, Ellory withdrew her arm from Seven's shoulders. "Anytime." An awkward silence bloomed between them until Ellory said, "I would've loved to have met you when we were younger."

That drew a cynical chortle from Seven. "No. You wouldn't have."

It took Ellory a second to catch up. "Oh, right. The Borg thing. How old were you when you were taken?"

"I was assimilated by the Collective when I was six years old."

There was horror and pity in Ellory's voice. "So young."

"I used to think it was a mercy that I didn't really understand what had happened to me. But I was wrong. I was a prisoner . . . a slave of the Collective for eighteen years. It wasn't until long after I was liberated that I fully comprehended all that the Borg stole from me. My childhood. My adolescence. All the years when I should've been learning who I was and what I wanted.

"Then we were back on Earth. And the more Admiral Janeway tried to help me, the more they punished her. I was sure that if I didn't leave, they would have destroyed her. I told myself I couldn't let that happen. That I needed to go away. Far away.

"But I was wrong about that, too. All I did by leaving was punish myself for no reason. . . . I was so lonely, but I didn't know how to connect with people. I couldn't figure out how to make new friends. How to feel . . . like I belonged. So I let others use me. Exploit me, as cheap labor. As a one-night stand. As a pawn in a sick game. And the whole time I told myself it was all I deserved. I couldn't see that what I was really doing was hurting myself.

"When I was on *Voyager* my friends tried to help me reclaim my humanity. Tried to teach me about love. But they couldn't give me back all those lost years. Couldn't tell me who I *was*. Now I see there were things no one could teach me—things I had to learn for myself."

"Things like . . . ?"

"Like how beautiful you are."

Ellory looked into Seven's eyes as her lips parted with a soft gasp of surprise. She seemed about to say something important—and that was when Seven kissed her.

At the moment of contact, Seven knew it felt right. They pulled together into a mutual embrace as if they had been propelled by inexorable forces of nature, souls drawn into each other's orbit by emotional gravity, spinning closer and closer until there could be no escape—

And then self-consciousness intruded upon Seven's thoughts. She pulled away, fearful that she had crossed a line. "I'm sorry."

"For what?"

"I let my desires control me."

Ellory smiled. "It's not as if I was saying 'no.'"

"But there's so much happening right now. So much at stake. Is this the right time?"

The Trill woman brushed a stray lock of flaxen hair from Seven's eyes, caressed the side of her face, and traced the edges of her ocular implant. "There's no wrong time for love. If life only ever offers it to you once, you'd damned well better take it."

Seven looked at Ellory and let herself not just see but truly *feel* how lovely she was, both in the flesh and in her soul. And then she kissed her again—deeply, slowly, tenderly at first, and then with a passion that surged to life inside her like a bonfire.

She had no idea how long their second kiss lasted, but when she and Ellory finally pulled apart long enough to gasp for breath, they both laughed with giddy excitement.

Ellory pressed her forehead to Seven's. "Take me to bed."

A name hewn in stone. It was so cold. So permanent. Looking at it, Harper felt for the first time the full weight of Leniker Zehga's untimely violent death. There was Len's full name, in both Federation Standard and his native Zakdorn, beneath a laser-cut image of his badge. And, beside and above it, more than a hundred others, in offset rows of ten, each one a tribute to a Fenris Ranger killed in the line of duty. A cenotaph for those who had given everything they'd had, and all that they were ever going to have. A roster of honored dead.

One of these days . . .

He heard laughter and bright voices from the end of the long, high-ceilinged corridor. A group of young Rangers emerged from the mess hall at the end of breakfast, their spirits bright. Among them were Seven and Ellory, who both had joined the chow line radiant with the afterglow of their first full shared night together—a love connection that half the Wolf's Den was gossiping about. With them were Sagasta, Rana, Speirs, and Ballard. They were too far away for Harper to hear what they were saying, but the group's body language suggested they were all giving the new lovebirds a gentle hazing.

Despite the distance, Seven noticed Harper's stare. She broke from the group and headed his way, while the others left in the opposite direction, toward the flight deck. Harper turned his eyes back to the wall of names, partly to hide his guilt at having unintentionally pulled Seven away from what had seemed like a very pleasant morning with new friends.

She reached him sooner than he'd expected, thanks to her long stride and fast pace. "Harper? Are you okay?"

"Not as good as you. But, yeah, I'm all right, kid."

Seven nodded toward Len's name. "Your former partner?"

"Yeah. A few more days and they'll have Jalen's name up here, too."

"I see. All the Rangers whose names are on this wall—they died in action?"

"We say 'on the job,' or 'in the line of duty.'"

"Sorry."

"S'all right, kid. Just make sure your name never ends up on here."

"I could say the same to you."

Harper felt the weight of his years bearing down upon him. "No promises."

Seven traced the outline of Len's badge with her fingertips. "What was he like?"

"Whip-smart. Crazy brave. A crusader, sort of like you. He hated seeing bullies win. But his book learning only got him so far. He was a shitty poker player. And he had a lot to learn about street smarts. He would've figured it out. If he'd had time."

Memories of the carnage on Skånevik Prime flashed through Harper's mind. Blinding pulses of detonation. The acrid bite of expended explosives; the stench of burnt flesh. Disruptor pulses flying past his head as he held Len's bloodied hand.

He was about to lose himself down a rabbit hole of bitter flashbacks when Seven said, "It wasn't your fault."

"It was. He was my rookie. I was supposed to keep him safe."

"There is no such thing. Not in this job. Not in this life."

"You don't understand. I recruited him. Promised his family I'd take care of him. And I failed. I failed them all."

"A Starfleet officer once told me that on Earth there was a saying among firefighters: the greatest act of bravery that firefighters ever perform is when they swear their oaths of service. Everything they do after that is just their duty. In many ways, the same is true of anyone who swears an oath to wear a uniform and serve others. I think Len must have known it. But he believed in the Rangers because he believed in you."

"I appreciate what you're trying to do, but you never even met Len."

"I don't have to. Because I know you."

He had a free hand but didn't bother palming away the tears brimming in his eyes before he looked at Seven. "Y'know, kid . . . before you came along, I probably wouldn't have heard those words from anyone else. I wouldn't have believed 'em. And you know what else? Just between us girls? Before I met you, I was starting to lose faith in the Rangers. In our mission. I'd been asking myself for months what we were doin' out here. I was startin' to wonder if it was all worth it. 'Cause no matter how hard we fought, or how many skells we put away, it always felt like we were fightin' a losin' battle.

"But then *you* came along. And I'll be damned if you don't just *love* shakin' shit up. You live to break rules, make messes, and drive the brass right up the wall. And I *love* it. You're a maverick, kid. And I mean that in the best possible way. With you by my side? I'm startin' to think maybe this whole shebang ain't hopeless. Maybe—just maybe—real justice might be possible out here, for the people who need it most."

His words lingered between them for a few long seconds.

Then Seven reached over and held his hand.

They traded bittersweet smiles and went back to reading the names of heroes.

16

Mercenary Frigate *Eris*

Kohgish wished he could reach through the screen and across a subspace channel to strangle the arrogant human at the other end of his current conversation. "How is this my fault?"

Arastoo Mardani shot back, *"Because* you *were the one who got hacked!"*

"By a foe *you* told me was 'under control.' Now, not only do the Fenris Rangers have my money, they're all but boasting about it! And they've given the news media proof that much of it came from the Federation Security Agency!"

Mardani's demeanor took an icy turn. *"I love how you say that, as if you were the injured party. This is turning into a major embarrassment for the Federation."*

"Who cares about the Federation? A bunch of meddling imperialists who hide behind smiles and platitudes. But without respect and fear, a warlord has *nothing.* I'm a *laughingstock*, Mardani! People who should fear me are mocking me! Saying I'm broke—"

"You are."

It stung because it was true, but Kohgish had never cared about such details before and saw no reason to start now. "Worse, they're saying I'm just a Federation puppet."

"If only you were that *useful."*

"You want to talk about usefulness? You were supposed to have an agent inside the Rangers! Someone who'd dismantle them from within, or at least keep them off my back until I had a chance to secure my position in the sector. What happened to that brilliant plan?"

"It suffered a few setbacks."

"Is 'setback' a Federation euphemism for abysmal failure?"

"If it were, 'setback' would be your new code name. Now shut up and pay attention. I don't work for you. Get it? You're the asset. I'm the handler. My job is to run you, not do your bidding. So quit whining and start thinking. Tell me how you're going to get that money back."

All Kohgish wanted at that moment was to gnaw the flesh off Mardani's skull, but he suppressed his rage long enough to begin devising a new plan of action. "The good news is that I've always kept a secret reserve of hard currency hidden on my ship for emergencies."

"I'd say this qualifies."

"I'd concur. I have enough to keep my fleet running for a week."

"A good start. But your fleet can't go into the Bank of Ferenginar and take back your money. All it can do is scare away the Rangers when they come looking to get their latinum."

"Which is the last thing we'd want to do," Kohgish said. "The longer those funds sit there, the greater the risk that the reform-minded Grand Nagus Rom might do something stupid. Like let the FSA freeze all the assets of everyone identified in the metadata."

"My greatest fear, in a nutshell."

"The Rangers share your fear. As much as they enjoyed exposing us by releasing the chain-code metadata, I don't think they're willing to part with funds they stole fair and square."

"True. They've recently had more than a few fiscal problems of their own."

"Which means they'll be looking to make a mass withdrawal any day now, and then they'll need to move all that hard currency at once."

"To where?"

"Most likely, one of the mercantile banks in Stardust City, on Freecloud. They're the only ones unregulated enough to process a cash deposit this size."

"And knowing that helps us how?"

"Eventually, the Rangers will come for their money. They might come in force, or they might try to be sneaky about it, but either way we'll know where the money is, at all times, thanks to some trusted contacts we have inside the Bank of Ferenginar on Voll."

"How do you know the Rangers will go there?"

"We know the same money-laundering tricks they do. The bank on Voll is their only option for turning that much virtual currency into latinum. But, out of respect for the bank, we won't rob them there. Once the Rangers load up, we'll let them get to neutral space, board them, and then take back our money."

"*Pathetic.*" Mardani shook his head wearily. "*That is quite possibly the dumbest plan I've ever heard in my life.*"

"Excuse me?"

"*Not the plan itself, mind you. Just the preposterous notion that you and your ragtag pack of mange-ridden curs could have any hope of pulling it off.*" Mardani rubbed his eyes, and then he pinched the bridge of his nose. "*I'm sorry, General, but your people are unsuited for this kind of work. They have no subtlety. No panache. Solving a crisis like this requires a more targeted solution, so do me a favor and keep your people out of it. I'll bring in a team of professionals. The kind who'll have your latinum back in your hands and the thieves gutted on the floor at your feet before the close of business tomorrow.*"

Kohgish felt a surge of sour bile burn his esophagus when he realized what Mardani was really saying. "Bounty hunters. You're talking about bounty hunters."

"*Look at that! You really do have two brain cells inside that furry noggin of yours, don't you? Color me impressed.*"

"I don't like bounty hunters, Mardani. I don't trust them."

"*That's a shame, General. They all think so highly of you.*"

"Do they?"

"*Of course not. They all know you're a flea-ridden sad sack who just got cash-cucked by the Fenris goddamned Rangers. Which is why* I'll *be hiring them and not you.*"

"And once they've recovered my rather prodigious war chest, how do we know they'll return it and not just take it and disappear to the other side of the galaxy?"

"*Simple. First, latinum becomes worthless if they run so far that they end up in a place where no one knows what it is—but if they stay someplace they can actually spend it, word will eventually get out about the loner who rolled into some backwater star system loaded down with more latinum than most planets' central treasuries. And, second, they know that once word gets out, nothing in the galaxy will stop me from hunting them down and gutting them like scum-fish for a chum bucket.*

"Now, go lie to that Talarian starship broker. Swear to whatever deity he believes in that you're not broke, and do it before he sells his battle-boat to someone else. Because he's actually a pretty good customer, and it'd be a real shame if I had to kill him, too."

Earth – New York City

It didn't matter how many times Janeway reminded herself that she was a vice admiral now; attending high-level diplomatic events packed with senior members of the Starfleet admiralty, elected officials and cabinet members of the Federation's civilian government, and foreign dignitaries from a dozen far-flung worlds still made her feel like a schoolgirl who had wrangled herself an invitation to the grown-ups' table for Christmas dinner.

Who am I kidding? This could be a dinner for two and I'd still feel out of place. I can't name half the things on my plate. She poked at the delicate wisps of edible lichen and the oval of colorful dots of puree arranged with asymmetrical precision around a molded cylinder composed of three disks of translucent flavored gelatin—orange on the bottom, white in the middle, and bright green on top. *And I'm still not sure if this is an appetizer or an art installation.*

If the fussiness of the haute cuisine troubled any of the other guests at her table, none of them let it show—least of all the Klingon Empire's ambassador to the Federation, Korog from the House of Kor. He was young for a diplomat with such a vital post, no more than his midthirties, a glutton, a braggart, and one of the least discreet persons Janeway had ever met. He tended to talk with his hands even when he was holding a drink, and he seemed not to notice as his gesticulations sloshed bloodwine into the lap of Janeway's dress uniform.

"So there I am, drunk and naked"—*slosh-splash*—"on the ledge outside her window, forty-eight floors above the street! With her father, the Priest-King of Antos, pacing in front of the window, while the honey dripping down my spine starts to run through the crack of my buttocks"—*slosh-splash*—"drawing a flock of the biggest birds I've ever seen!"

"You don't say, Mister Ambassador." Janeway searched in vain for a waiter. *Who do I have to kill to get a cup of coffee around here?*

"So I start trying to shoo the birds"—*slosh-splash*—"'Shoo! Shoo'!"

Janeway's patience expired. "Mister Ambassador! Please take care with your wine. It's from a vintage older than the Vulcan ambassador's father. It would be a shame to waste it."

"Bloodwine spilled is never wasted, only shared"—*slosh-splash*—"with our honored dead in Sto-Vo-Kor!"

"Spilled on the ground, perhaps. In my lap? Not so much."

"If I've offended you, Admiral, I apologize without reservation." Korog picked up his napkin and leaned toward Janeway. "Allow me to help sop—"

"Don't. You. Dare."

Before she or Korog could escalate the moment into one of interstellar consequence, a gentle hand on Janeway's shoulder diverted her attention. Her aide Darusha leaned close to whisper, "Pardon me, Admiral. Someone needs to speak with you out on the balcony." They gestured toward a nearby set of lace-curtained French doors that led out onto the restaurant's ninety-seventh-floor balcony. "They say it's urgent."

"Thank you, Darusha." Janeway discarded her wine-sodden napkin on the table as she stood. "If you'll excuse me, Your Excellency, I'm told I'm needed elsewhere. But I thank you for sharing your especially invigorating stories this evening."

"I shall look forward to our next encounter."

Janeway smiled and walked away thinking, *That makes one of us.* Once they were away from the table, she confided to Darusha, "Thanks for the rescue. Now, where's the java?"

Darusha blinked, visibly confused. "This wasn't a rescue-by-ruse, Admiral. There really is someone outside waiting to talk with you."

"I see." Janeway stopped and faced the doors to the balcony. "Can you find me a decent cup of coffee by the time I get back?"

"Of course, Admiral."

"And some of those, um . . ."

"Beignets?"

"Yes! Get me a few of those."

"Good as done."

"You're a lifesaver, Darusha. Now—" She headed for the balcony. "Let's go see if the person behind door number two has anything better to say than the one at table number four."

Janeway opened the classic doors with a half turn of their antique handles and strode out into the crisp, cool night air. Around her sparkled the gleaming towers of modern New York, a city that had barely survived the double threat of the Third World War and global sea-level rise in the twenty-second century, only to reinvent and rebuild itself into something greater, a city of architectural marvels and engineering wonders, a metropolis reimagined as a living work of art.

A woman stood at the balcony wall. Her back was to Janeway. Like many of the other guests at that evening's dinner, she was attired in elegant formalwear, a dress and a matching wrap of diaphanous Tholian silk, whose undulating weave scintillated with every flicker of light around it. The person wearing it had tawny skin and black hair styled in elegant cornrows accented with Spican fire gems. As Janeway approached, the woman turned toward her, and Janeway recognized Keemah Geiss from the FSA. Geiss extended her open hand in welcome. "Admiral. Good to see you again."

They shook hands. Janeway smiled to conceal her suspicions. "Director. My aide made it sound like a matter of life and death."

"It very well might be." Geiss motioned for Janeway to join her at the balcony wall. After Janeway settled in beside her, the director continued, "Before I say anything else, I need you to confirm you understand that the fact of this meeting, as well as this conversation in its entirety, are both classified top secret."

"I understand."

"Have you heard the latest out of the Qiris sector?"

"If you mean the report of a planetary militia becoming a rogue element after the FSA illegally bankrolled it though a number of NGOs and then tried to use it as a proxy against clandestine Romulan incursions beyond the Neutral Zone . . . yes, I might have caught that."

Geiss stewed but suffered the abuse like a pro. "We think the intel about the money laundering was leaked to the media by the Fenris Rangers."

"Good for them."

"No, Admiral. Bad for us. Because it's not true."

"You're saying the money that went to those brigands didn't come from the FSA?"

"No. It did. It's just—" Geiss struggled to find the right words. "It's complicated."

"Simplify it. And while you're at it, tell me why it's any concern of mine."

"Fine. The money came from us, but not with our blessing. It was embezzled from some of our secret operational accounts by a disgruntled ex-spymaster named Erol Tazgül. He's been using our stolen funds to bankroll arms deals, set up proxy fighters against the Romulans, and invest in a variety of criminal enterprises beyond the Federation's border."

"I'm still waiting to hear why this is my problem."

"He's been using an alias—a well-developed legend he created for himself while he still had access to agency resources. And it's a name I think you'll recognize: Arastoo Mardani."

A sickening dread twisted in Janeway's gut. "Seven's handler."

"Correct. Which means Seven might be acting as an asset for a known enemy of the Federation, for purposes unknown . . . or she might have gone rogue, in which case she's just made an enemy of one of the most dangerous, well-funded sociopaths in the quadrant. Either way, Admiral, if Tazgül has his claws into your friend, she's in grave danger."

17

Midday and the operations level was manic with activity. Media reports about Kohgish's illegal funding had begun to ask who leaked the chain-code meta-data, and the comms at the Wolf's Den were overwhelmed with requests for comment, interviews, or even fresh leaks.

Meanwhile, every two-bit thug and aspiring crime boss in the sector had reason to think Kohgish was broke and on the verge of being hounded from the sector in disgrace as a Federation stooge. Hit-and-run attacks on ships of Kohgish's fleet were being reported from multiple star systems inside the Qiris sector—an outcome that would have suited Harper just fine if only the vio-lence had been limited to Kohgish's forces. But raids on commercial shipping were also spiking. Now that Kohgish's near-monopoly on perfidy in the sector had been undermined, small-time pirates were seizing upon his moment of apparent weakness to claw their way back into the game.

But the real flood-crush of incoming signals were maydays. Distress calls from colonies tired of being harassed and extorted. Calls for help from com-mercial vessels left adrift by thieves who had sabotaged the freighters' and tankers' warp engines after robbing them of their cargoes. A chorus of victims was crying out, hoping that news of Kohgish's collapse might mean their own salvation was close at hand.

For all their sakes, Harper hoped it was. But he had another job to do.

He arrived at the door to the Ranger commander's office and pressed the call buzzer. Over the door's comm came Zhang's invitation, *"Enter."*

The door slid open. Inside waiting for Harper were the four top brass—Zhang, Yivv, Shren, and Saszyk—along with Seven and Ellory Kayd. The lot of them stood and stared at a full-wall companel that had been unevenly divided into overlapping screens of financial data, local laws, star charts, and long strings of chain code. As usual, it was Shren who took the cheap shot. "Nice of you to join us, Harper."

"Sorry I'm late, sir. Couldn't be helped."

His protest provoked a twitch of Shren's antennae. "Why couldn't it?"

Harper patted his nascent potbelly. "Plumbing problems."

"Say no more."

"To business," Saszyk said, directing everyone's attention to the data on the companel. "Time is short, and we need a plan for getting the stolen chain-code funds off our servers."

"I know I came in late," Harper said, "but what's the rush?"

Yivv summoned one of the screens of legal mumbo jumbo to the top of the stack. "Legal culpability. As clever as it was to use Deputy Seven's computer skills to rob Kohgish of his capital, that doesn't change the fact that our heist was, itself, also illegal. And that we and our entire organization could face severe consequences if anyone can prove we took it."

That seemed to spook Kayd. "What kind of consequences?"

Yivv frowned. "Fifty years in prison for Seven as the author and executor of the code. At least forty years for each of us in the leadership who approved the plan. And up to twenty-five years for Kayd and Harper as accessories either before or after the fact."

Saszyk hissed and then added, "Plus, the Fenris Rangers could be forcibly disbanded as a corrupt organization, our members arrested, and our assets impounded by an interstellar coalition consisting of the Federation, the Klingon Empire, and the Romulans."

"Right," Harper said. "So we need to get these funds anyplace else, RFN."

"Not anyplace else," Seven said. "And not simply moved."

Zhang's tone was calm and respectful as she asked Seven, "What do you suggest?"

Seven faced the companel and with gestures began manipulating the elements on-screen to support her arguments in real time with the kind of grace and surety one might expect of an orchestra conductor. "A virtual transfer of the funds from our servers to those of a bank might postpone their seizure, but transfer alone will not remove the metadata that will forever link these funds to our systems. There is no way to transmit these funds without also sending their unredacted transaction history—and that data, now updated with proof of our role in its chain of custody, would be sufficient evidence to justify our arrests and prosecutions."

Kayd stepped up beside Seven and took over, with an ease that suggested to Harper that the two women had rehearsed this routine. "To liberate this money from its history," Kayd said, "and render it immune from seizure under a warrant by the FSA or whatever entity they use for their legal dirty work, we'll need to convert it all into latinum before its next deposit. The good news is, the Bank of Ferenginar branch on Voll has enough latinum on hand to do the conversion for us. The bad news is, Kohgish and Mardani also use that bank, for exactly this reason. So they probably have someone inside who's going to tell them the moment we schedule a conversion and withdrawal."

Shren held up one hand. "Wait. Why withdraw the latinum at all?"

Seven answered, "Because the Ferengi will not expunge the metadata associated with the money until the entire sum is converted to latinum and removed from their possession. Only then can they legally delete the money's history."

That didn't seem to satisfy Shren's curiosity. "All right, then. Once the money's been turned over and its history erased, why not just put it right back into the Ferengi bank?"

Kayd shook her head. "Because we can't. The laws on Voll were written to mitigate the worst of the money laundering happening on their soil. They mandate a three-day waiting period before redeposit of any funds converted to latinum by one of their banks."

Yivv asked, "How would they know it's the same latinum?"

"Because it all gets nano-tagged when pressed. Tamper with those nano-tags and no bank in the quadrant will ever accept that latinum on deposit again.

"Plus," Kayd continued, "the law on Voll also prohibits the deposit of more than one hundred bricks of latinum per day to an account, limits depositors to one account each, and forbids the merging of accounts. Once we do the conversion, we're going to be holding over ten *thousand* bricks of latinum—and we're gonna need to get them someplace safe, fast."

Harper nodded. "And making one run to Freecloud is faster than trying to make hundreds of smaller deposits all over the quadrant. But the run to Freecloud might be a suicide mission."

Kayd muttered, "A suicide plan would have better odds."

Seven acknowledged the point with a nod. "That is the single greatest risk in our plan. Once converted to latinum and put into transit, the money becomes vulnerable to theft or destruction. And ten thousand bricks of latinum is a rather significant mass."

"If I pull out most of the secondary gear," Harper said, "I can fit that much into the hold of my prowler. I'll just have to make sure it's properly secured in case things get rough."

Zhang shot a look of mild surprise at Harper. "Are you actually *volunteering* for something, Ranger Harper?"

"Yeah. Guess I am."

Seven stepped to Harper's side. "I volunteer, as well."

He squinted at her. "You sure, kid? This could get hairy."

"You are my training officer. If you go, I go."

Harper looked at the four senior rangers. "With your permission, sirs?"

"Permission granted," Zhang said. "Get your prowler ready. We'll have Ranger Kayd make the necessary arrangements with the bank tonight, and you'll make the pickup and redeposit on Freecloud tomorrow."

"Or die trying," Harper said under his breath.

"What was that, Ranger?"

"Nothing, Commander."

"That's what I thought. Dismissed."

Seven stood back from Harper's prowler as he pulled himself inside its ventral cargo hold. His legs dangled in the air outside the ship, and his voice reverberated inside the cramped space. "Don't reckon we'll have much use for a life raft." He shoved the compact, self-inflating emergency craft back toward Seven. She pulled it out of Harper's way and tossed it on top of the jumbled pile of assorted gear they had jettisoned so far from the ship's hold.

"Is it wise to dispose of so much of our emergency equipment?"

"Not like we got a choice, kid. We gotta make room in here for a case packed with ten thousand bricks of latinum. Way we're goin', we'll be lucky if we each get to bring a toothbrush." A hard tool case clanged and then skidded across the scuffed, grit-dusted deck plating inside the prowler's hold. "Minus one dynoscanner."

She added it to the growing mound of the rejected. "There can't be much left in there." She tried to steal a look past his boots. "Is there?"

"Almost done." Something inside the hold flared and spat white-hot sparks that caromed off the bulkheads and skittered out onto the flight deck.

Trying not to sound worried, Seven asked, "What was that?"

"Nothing important. We might even pick up a couple tenths of a warp factor without it." A charred bundle of wiring and isolinear chips slid back into Seven's waiting hands.

She chucked the smoldering tangle of optronic spaghetti into a separate heap reserved for spare parts. "Please tell me that wasn't the intermix regulator."

"It wasn't the intermix regulator."

"You're lying."

"What do you want from me, kid? Truth or comfort?" Harper shimmied backward and pushed himself out of the hold. He landed awkwardly on the deck and groaned as he put a hand against his lower back. "That's all I could ditch, but I think we're good to go."

"Did we keep anything?"

Harper pulled his black-lens sunglasses from a chest pocket on his jacket, put them on, and peered into the shadowy hold. "Two heavy rifles. A photon grenade launcher with one case of ammo. Two sensor scramblers, one field medkit, and a field engineering kit."

"Sunglasses help you see in the dark?"

He pulled them off and offered them to Seven. "Give 'em a try, kid."

Curious, she put them on—and watched the dark spaces inside the prowler brighten with a monochromatic green luminance. "Most intriguing." She noticed a nearly invisible cursor that moved to follow her gaze and point of focus. With a blink she intuitively accessed some of its other settings: an infrared mode, which made the entire flight deck flare like a sun; a lidar mode, which mapped her surroundings and rendered them in three-dimensional wireframes.

"Having fun?"

"I want a pair of these glasses."

"Who doesn't? But like everything else good in this place, there ain't enough to go around." He held out an open hand. "Fork 'em over."

She gave back his high-tech spectacles and pretended to take an interest in the prowler, mostly to hide her mounting anxiety. "How much danger are we in?"

"Right now? Not much. Should be smooth sailin' till we get to the bank on Voll."

"And then?"

"Once the latinum's in the prowler, we'll have a neon bull's-eye on our back, and every hired gun in the sector usin' us for target practice."

"Making this the optimal time to abandon most of our tactical equipment."

Harper closed the cargo hatch and locked it. "This ain't the time for a stand-up fight, kid. We'll be flying heavy from Voll to Freecloud. Our best bet is to haul ass, and if anyone gets too close, you give 'em the heat."

"I see no other option, since you insist on leaving behind more than half our normal complement of microtorpedoes—a choice that will put us at a tactical disadvantage."

"Had to be done, kid. There's only so much *Lady Fly* can take."

"But unilaterally giving up a vital tactical option—"

He interrupted with a raised hand. "Stop thinking like a fighter and start thinking like an investigator." With a gentle nudge he guided her away from the prowler for a discreet chat. "We need to be fast and cautious. We've got everybody gunning for us right now: Kohgish, the FSA, Starfleet, the Klingons, the Romulans. We're like the rabbits in that old Earth story *Watership Down*. We're the Prince with a Thousand Enemies, and if any of them catch us, they'll kill us. But first—they have to *catch* us."

"I understand. And I still want a pair of those glasses."

"Slow your roll, rookie. There are Rangers who've been waiting *years* to inherit a working pair of starshades. You've barely been here a *week*."

She cracked a lopsided smile to let him know she had only been joking. "Now that you've brought it up: When do I stop being a rookie?"

He shrugged. "Usually? Six months. But I'll tell you what: If your plan works, and we survive this latinum death race? The Rangers will be *loaded*. And that'll be *after* we've given aid to those who need it most. We'd become a real force for change out here. Get this done, and I don't think anyone here will ever call you 'rookie' again. But for now?" He gave her a fraternal slap on her shoulder. "Get some sleep, kid. Tomorrow's gonna be a *long* day."

FSA Tactical Cruiser *Bolvangar*

Mardani's ready room was crowded with holograms. Avatars representing more than a dozen of the quadrant's elite bounty hunters stood in curved ranks facing his desk, listening with keen focus as he updated their assignment's details.

"As we expected, the Rangers have contacted the Bank of Ferenginar's branch on Voll to request the withdrawal of their full account balance in latinum. The pickup is going to be made sometime in the next sixteen hours. Let me remind you all: no action is to be attempted at the bank or in its vicinity. Anyone who breaks this condition will forfeit all compensation."

He called up a local star chart speckled with bright crimson dots. "This shows the current disposition of Kohgish's fleet. To assist you in your mission, his forces will undertake numerous simultaneous acts of violence and havoc throughout the Qiris sector. This will draw responses from the Fenris Rangers, limiting or preventing them from rendering any aid to the one prowler they have told the bank to expect. Alone, cut off from help, and laden with a dense cargo that will impair their maneuverability, the Rangers trying to take their group's money to Freecloud will find themselves dramatically out of their depth."

One of the bounty hunters, a hulking Chalnoth brute, shouldered forward to ask, *"What do we do with the money once we have it?"*

"Deliver it directly to General Kohgish, wherever he is."

Another hunter, the infamous Ferengi skip tracer Brunt, bared his jagged teeth. *"You've yet to specify our rate of compensation for the return of what we now know to be a veritable fortune. So, unless you're ashamed to say the price, how much is this job worth?"*

"It will be paid by commission. One quarter of one percent of all monies recovered."

"A paltry percentage!"

"But still more than enough for you to live in luxury for the rest of your days."

That reassurance satisfied Brunt, whose image fell back into line with the other illusions. Mardani gave them one last look-over, to make sure there were no lingering issues. "Distinguished guests: if there's nothing more, thank you for your time, and good hunting. *Bolvangar* out." The holographic projections faded away several at a time—until, to Mardani's mild surprise, one remained. An infamous Romulan-born bounty hunter whose reputation preceded him. Mardani acknowledged him with a nod. "Veris? What can I do for you?"

"Stop wasting my time with lowball offers. One quarter of one percent?"

"The commission was set by the client and is nonnegotiable."

"Everything is negotiable when sufficient pressure comes into play. Word in the starport dive bars is that your puppet Kohgish is in the market for a decommissioned Talarian warship. One he won't be able to afford unless his war chest is recovered. A fortune in which I've been led to understand you hold a considerable stake."

"We're burning starlight, Veris. What's your point?"

"You don't have time to wait for amateurs like Brunt and Graur to get the general's money back from the Rangers. I'm your best chance of Kohgish meeting his deadline to buy that ship, but I'm not going to work for crumbs like those other scum."

"State your price."

"One half of one percent."

"Ridiculous."

"Zero point five percent, Mister Mardani. To make sure that money doesn't wind up in the Rangers' secret numbered account on Freecloud. And to bring back every last brick, bar, and strip of latinum that was taken—before your puppet's chance to secure his position slips away forever." A dismissive shrug. *"Your choice."*

The Romulan had Mardani at a crucial disadvantage, and he was expertly making the most of it. As much as Veris's extortion annoyed Mardani, he respected its slick execution. "Very well, Centurion Veris: one half of one percent of all monies recovered."

"Thank you. If I may? One more question."

"What is it?"

"The Rangers transporting the stolen cash: Do you want them dead or alive?"

The man was nothing if not thorough. Mardani pondered the question, but only for a moment. "I'm feeling whimsical today, Centurion. Surprise me."

18

Fenris – Ranger Headquarters

A night's rest before the mission had done Seven little good. Unsettled, she had found no comfort in her bunk and no solace in dreams. Portents of doom and visions of disaster had been all that awaited her in sleep's half-remembered domain. Almost hourly, it had seemed, she had shuddered awake, each time with a cry of alarm stuck in her throat, her heart slamming in her chest, and her hair and her pillow soaked in sweat.

Now she was having trouble staying focused as Harper verified the ground crew's preflight check of his prowler. They were making a circle of the vessel. He was checking systems and calling out data. Her job was to write it all down. At some point her thoughts had drifted, and she reacted with a jolt of surprise at the touch of Harper's hand on her shoulder.

"You okay, kid?"

She shook off her confusion and lethargy. "Yes. Sorry."

"What was the last thing I told you to write down?"

She noted they were standing behind *Lady Fly*'s main engine port. "Ground crew failed to clean exhaust manifold as directed."

Harper looked at the ship and then at the blank spot on her padd where that answer should have already been. "Lucky guess."

"Sorry. I did not sleep well last night."

"Who did?" He noted her confused reaction. "Trouble sleeping before a risky mission is normal. Happens to all of us."

She smiled and nodded but didn't actually feel any better.

Looking away from Harper, Seven saw Ellory approaching from across the busy flight deck. The young Trill woman was in her duty jacket with a sidearm secured on her thigh, and her dark hair was pulled into a tight bun at the back of her head, exposing the trail of beige markings that ran from her temple and down the sides of her elegant neck. Her prowler, *Nymeria*, had been refueled and rearmed overnight, and now was on the ready line for launch next to *Lady Fly*.

Seven continued to trail Harper around his prowler, taking notes as he observed small details he wanted addressed during the ship's next round of maintenance. As Ellory approached, Seven was about to ask permission to step away, but then Ellory called out, "Hey, guys! News from ops!"

Harper cut short his inspection and turned with Seven to meet Ellory. "Don't tell me you're my new wingman?"

"Not on your life, old-timer. But that's the least of your problems. Your wingman left already. Took an emergency call out by the Azure Nebula."

Harper grumbled profanities under his breath.

Seven asked Ellory, "What about you?"

"Got my own fires to put out."

Harper raised an eyebrow. "Solo? Where's your partner?"

"He's flying Palitow's bird today. Running down some pirates harassing colony ships along the Neutral Zone. As for me, I gotta go check out an SOS from a hospital ship under attack by one of Kohgish's frigates, out by Lambda Hydrae."

Seven felt like she was a few steps behind on current events. "I thought the Romulan Neutral Zone was being abolished."

"The Romulan Senate's been *debating* abolishing the Neutral Zone, but until they issue an edict signed by the praetor, it remains very real, as well as a total pain in our ass. Strictly between us? I can't wait to be rid of it."

Harper grew impatient. "Ell—who's my wingman for the bank run?"

"You don't have one." Ellory offered Harper and Seven an apologetic shrug. "That's what I came down to tell you. The whole damned sector's blowing up. Pirate attacks, colony raids, ships in distress. It's like someone opened Pandora's box out there."

To Seven's surprise, that news drew a dark, cynical laugh from Harper. When he finished chuckling, he said, "Let me guess: dozens of level-one emergencies, all as far as possible from the Voll system but technically still inside our declared jurisdiction."

Ellory met his prediction with a grim smile of resignation. "Naturally."

As usual, Seven felt left out of the conversation. "Can someone explain—?"

"They know we're coming," Harper said.

Ellory looked worried. "Kohgish and his people have spread out across the sector, wreaking havoc to draw us all away from Voll and to make sure there aren't enough of us left free to protect whoever gets sent on the bank run."

"Which means they'll be waiting for us at Voll," Harper said. "They won't come after us on our way in. Like I expected, they'll be looking to intercept us the moment we leave Voll's sovereign territory and reach interstellar space."

Now Seven understood. "And we have to meet our foes without a wingman."

Harper tried to pretend it was no big deal. "Don't fret it, kid. A wingman would've just gotten in our way. Now we'll be free to move."

"Except that we'll be laden with ten thousand bricks of latinum. The whole reason we needed a wingman was because we won't be *able* to move."

Harper headed for *Lady Fly*'s bow. "Truth or comfort, kid."

While Harper inspected *Lady Fly*'s particle beam cannon, Ellory took hold of both of Seven's hands. "Promise me you'll be careful out there."

Seven found Ellory's request irrational. "Do *you* plan to be careful out there?"

The question was all Ellory needed to hear to understand Seven's point. "No, I guess not. *Careful* was never really part of my brand."

"Nor is it part of mine."

"Can I start over?" Ellory lifted Seven's hands and kissed her knuckles. Then she looked into Seven's eyes and smiled. "Give 'em hell, beautiful."

Seven felt so touched she almost laughed. "Kick their ass, gorgeous."

"Yes," Ellory said, leaning in, "much better."

They met in a long, soft kiss—not just one of passion but also of tender connection, soulful longing, and fear. Seven rested her forehead against Ellory's and whispered, "Be careful."

Ellory whispered back, "You, too."

Mercenary Frigate *Eris*

The command deck of *Eris* was quiet, but the silence was anything but calm. Kohgish watched seconds tick away on his ship's chrono, each one bringing him closer to a dreaded reckoning. Then came a beeping from the comms station, silenced in a flash by his Orion second-in-command. Kohgish kept his eyes on the countdown as he said, "Feeno, report."

"News from our scouts in the Voll system, General." Feeno listened for a few more seconds, and then he continued, "Confirmation of a single Fenris Rangers prowler landing at the Bank of Ferenginar. And our contact inside the bank confirms the Rangers are taking possession of a sizable, reinforced currency container."

"Large enough to hold all that they took from us?"

"And then some." Additional news on the comms screen stole Feeno's attention for a moment. "Visual confirmation from inside the bank—the Rangers who are taking possession of the currency shipment are the same two who broke up our deal with the Nausicaans on Otroya II and who hijacked our shipment of medical supplies."

That detail was one Kohgish hadn't expected. He caught Feeno's eye and pointed at the main viewscreen. "Show me."

Feeno keyed in a command, and the main viewscreen switched from an image of a static starfield to a pair of grainy vids displayed on a split screen. Both showed the same pair of humanoids: an older, gray-bearded man and a young blonde woman. On the left was a short clip of security video from Otroya II that showed the duo engaged in a street-level firefight with a mixed group of Nausicaans and Anticans. The clip on the right showed them meeting with a Ferengi bank representative and looking over a stack of currency crates on an antigrav pallet.

"How old is this vid?"

"Just a few minutes, General. The pair are still at the bank."

Kohgish bared a grin full of fangs. "Excellent, Feeno. Well done. Keep tabs on them. I want to know the moment one of Mardani's bounty hunters recovers our money. And make sure the bounty hunters know I'll pay a bonus for one or both of those Rangers' heads."

"Yes, General." Feeno started to prepare the outgoing message when another signal shrilled on his console. "General? Incoming subspace comm . . . from Qulla."

All at once Kohgish's good mood vanished. *Not the broker. Not now!*

Refusing the hail was not an option. *If he thinks I'm avoiding him, he'll assume I'm backing out of the deal. And I can't risk him selling that ship to someone else.*

"Put him on-screen."

The split-screen vids were replaced by the stern visage of Qulla Hain, a Talarian arms dealer notorious for being able to arrange the purchase and delivery of decommissioned Talarian warships. But before he had reinvented himself as a prince of the black market, he had been a formidable starship commander in the Talarian military, and his face bore the scars to prove it. His glower barely shifted as he spoke, giving Kohgish the impression that Qulla likely had never smiled even once in his entire life, and probably never would. *"General Kohgish. I have taken possession of your new flagship and am en route to your designated coordinates for transfer. My ETA is approximately twenty-two hours. Will you be ready to make payment in full, in cash?"*

"Yes, Captain."

"You don't sound completely certain."

"I am, I assure you."

"Really? Then perhaps you might explain why your fleet is suddenly dispatched across the sector on what look like nuisance missions. Or why your ship seems to be on the receiving end of an abnormally high volume of encrypted comms traffic."

"I coordinate my entire fleet from this ship, Captain. We are engaged in numerous ventures at any given moment. Increased comms traffic is an occupational necessity."

"Then I should put no stock in the news reports that say you were bankrupted by an anonymous heist? Nor should I heed the rumors that you were robbed blind by none other than the Fenris Rangers?"

"Lies and propaganda, Captain. Nothing more."

"I see. That comes as a welcome relief, General. Because I would feel quite put out if I went to all this effort to deliver you a new battleship, only to find you can't pay for it."

"That's not going to happen, Captain Qulla."

"For your sake, General . . . see that it doesn't. Qulla out."

The Talarian ended the conversation at his end, and the image on the viewscreen went back to a placid scatter of stars. Kohgish exhaled in relief and sank into his command chair. It took him a few seconds to realize his arms were trembling from adrenaline overload.

"Feeno—?"

"The moment we hear anything. Yes, General."

"Thank you, Feeno."

Twenty-two hours. That was all the time Kohgish had left to finish the most important deal of his career, and all that stood between him and glory were a rogue FSA spymaster, two crack-shot Fenris Rangers, and a dozen of the quadrant's most feared bounty hunters.

Voll – Bank of Ferenginar

Voll, like many Class-M planets, had a lovely blue sky, but from beneath the shimmering energy shield that guarded the rooftop of the planetary headquarters of the Bank of Ferenginar, it looked like a great dome of golden amber. Large flood lamps poured bluish-white light onto everything beneath the shield, compensating for its tangerine-hued cast.

Seven stood beside Harper with one hand resting on the grip of her pulsed plasma pistol sidearm. Because of the heightened risk of this op, Harper had waived the Rangers' prohibition against trainees carrying deadly weapons.

Together, Seven and Harper watched the floor number on the display screen above the rooftop's sole lift car tick upward. It was only a few floors away and swiftly getting closer.

Harper kept his eyes on the lift car's readout but feigned nonchalance for the benefit of the Ferengi-run bank's security detail, who no doubt were watching him and Seven via one or more of dozens of concealed cameras. "Remember what I said, kid."

"No heroics. Just do my job."

"Spoken like a true prodigy."

The lift doors opened. They were enormous, far too large to have been designed solely to accommodate the Ferengi for whom it had been built. When they were fully opened, it was easy to see why they had been crafted to such Brobdingnagian proportions. A lone Ferengi with a padd tucked under his left arm stepped off the lift, followed by a utilitarian-looking heavy-lifting robot.

He directed the robot, which gently propelled a long antigrav pallet out of the lift and across the rooftop to *Lady Fly*.

"Big case," Seven said.

"It'll fit," Harper assured her for the hundredth time.

The sharp-dressed Ferengi, whose suit looked to have been cut from Terran silk and embroidered with Tholian silk, stopped in front of Harper and Seven. He held out his padd and offered it to Harper, who passed it to Seven, effectively delegating to her the tedium of manifest review. This seemed to amuse the Ferengi. "You let a female manage your money, hoo-man?"

"She's better at numbers than I am." He nodded at Seven. "Give it a look, will ya?"

Seven nodded, and then she stepped forward, blocking the robot's path to *Lady Fly*. "Inspection. Open the case, please."

The robot halted and turned its tiny cylindrical head toward the Ferengi, who nodded his consent to the inspection. The robot quickly unlocked the container, opened its lid, and then took a half step away from the case. Seven stepped between the robot and the case, leaned over the open container, and perused its contents.

Harper asked, "Is it all there?"

"It appears to be." She held up a large brick of gold-pressed latinum. "By my estimate, there are approximately ten thousand seven hundred twenty-eight of these inside."

"Good. Put that one back and let the robot finish up."

"Yes, sir." Seven put the brick back into the container. After she backed away from the case, the robot moved past her, secured the lid, and then resumed guiding the pallet toward the waiting *Lady Fly*. Seven returned to Harper's side and stood with him while they and the Ferengi bank executive watched the robot heft the tremendously heavy, dense cargo into their prowler. Once the crate was secured into place inside the prowler's hold, the robot retreated toward the bank's rooftop lift while Harper tended to closing and locking the hold's hatch.

The Ferengi flashed a snaggletoothed grin at Seven. "In Ferengi banking, it's traditional for an executive such as myself, who delivers such a princely sum of latinum, to receive a tip."

Seven assessed the Ferengi with a cold look. "A tip?" She drew her combat knife and put its point against the soft tissue on the underside of his jaw. "This knife has a tip."

Hands pressed together in a gesture of supplication, the Ferengi grinned wider and retreated from the icy touch of Seven's blade in careful backward steps. "Today's services have been complimentary. Thank you for doing business with the Bank of Ferenginar."

Harper ambled back to Seven's side as the Ferengi finally turned and jogged away. "Stop playin' with your food, kid. We gotta go."

They walked back to *Lady Fly*, climbed inside its cockpit one at a time, and then Harper pressed the switch to lower the canopy. As soon as the soundproof canopy was closed, Harper set its opacity to maximum, to prevent any of the Ferengi's security cameras from being used to read his lips. "Did you get the sekenium tracer into the shipment?"

"Yes. I put it on the bottom of the brick I picked up."

"Nice work. With any luck, we won't need to use it. But I'd rather have it and not need it than need it and not have it." He started the ship's power-up sequence. "I just hope the rest of this op goes half as smoothly." The prowler purred to life, and with a nudge on its controls, Harper guided it off the bank's rooftop and then forward, through the shield dome, and out into open air above Voll's capital city, which vanished from view as he pointed the prowler's nose toward space and fired the main thrusters. "Let the games begin."

Ranger Prowler *Lady Fly* – Deep Space

It was as predictable as clockwork. Seven kept close watch on the prowler's sensor readouts as she and Harper crossed the arbitrary boundary that separated Voll's territorial space from interstellar deep space. The moment *Lady Fly* entered the legally murky emptiness between star systems, the prowler's sensor screen lit up with contacts from inbound hostile vessels.

"Multiple contacts on multiple bearings," Seven said. "All inbound."

Harper sounded almost amused. "Our welcoming committee."

Seven heard the prowler's engines thrum at increasingly higher pitches as it accelerated to faster warp speeds. Outside the canopy, starlight bent past with a noticeable curvature.

"Arm all weapons," Harper said. "Prime all countermeasures."

"Tactical systems engaged." Seven compared the number of vessels that were moving on intercept trajectories for *Lady Fly* against the prowler's limited complement of torpedoes and countermeasures. "As I feared, our ordnance appears to be exceeded by our opposition."

"We knew it would be." Up front, beyond the separating bulkhead, he keyed commands into his panels. "Which is why I loaded something extra special into your tactical suite."

A new system appeared on Seven's main console: SENSOR DISPLACEMENT.

She activated the new option and made a fast study of its various options. Almost immediately she understood its intended function. "This creates a field that fools other ships' sensors into perceiving we are somewhere that we are not."

"Correct. Don't say I never gave ya nothin', kid." He banked the prowler hard to port and increased its speed to close to its maximum-rated warp factor. "We won't be doin' any fancy flyin' with this much latinum on board, so I'll be countin' on you. Spoof their sensors. Block their shots. And use the displacer to make them confuse us with one of the other hunters."

"It can do that?"

"Check under 'advanced options: transpose targets.'"

"Copy that." She put that function on standby and began selecting likely targets for transponder-code transposition. "We are going to make them fight one another."

"Exactly. Only one of them can come back with our cargo, so they were gonna have to fight it out eventually. We're just making 'em do it *now*."

"They're targeting us."

"Good. Make 'em regret it."

Seven activated the displacer system. In a matter of seconds she created eleven custom sensor-spoofing protocols, one for each ship currently targeting them. They all went active at once, creating a protective shell of scrambled information around the prowler. Vessels one and six would target each other, as would two and seven, three and eight, four and nine, and five and ten, while vessel six's shots would be redirected toward vessel eleven—even as *Lady Fly* sent each ship fake sensor feedback indicating the prowler had been destroyed.

She locked in her settings. "Prepare to drop out of warp and drift on my mark."

"Drift? Are you crazy?"

"A necessary risk, to sell the sensor illusion of our destruction."

"You sure you know what you're doing, kid?"

"No."

"So what if you're wrong?"

"We will improvise."

"How can I argue with tactical genius like that? Fine. Standing by."

"On my mark. . . . Three. Two. One. Mark!"

Outside the canopy, bent ribbons of light retracted into cold points as *Lady Fly* dropped out of warp. "Shut down impulse engines," Seven added. "Thrusters off."

"All offline. We're adrift."

"Acknowledged." Seven released more than half of the prowler's complement of passive chaff to clutter the space around them while they drifted. Thanks to the wonders of physics, their radioactive cloud drifted with them by the grace of inherited momentum.

Seconds passed in silence. Seven looked up, scanning the heavens with her eyes, before she remembered that most of this battle was going to happen at distances up to several light-minutes away. The only reliable indicator of success would come from the prowler's faster-than-light sensors, which even then were tracking the various bounty hunters' catastrophic assaults . . . upon one another. Just as she had hoped, the displacer field had tricked their foes into crippling one another in deep space. Less than a minute after the engagement had begun, it was over.

And according to *Lady Fly*'s sensors, the prowler was the last ship left intact.

Seven reported with pride, "Threat vessels neutralized."

"Nice work, rookie. But let's give it a minute. Make sure we got 'em all."

"Understood."

Seven shut down the displacer system, and Harper powered down the rest of the ship's systems. The prowler floated for a few minutes, dark and cold, with only passive sensors running on auxiliary battery power. Outside, the cloud of chaff sparkled in the starlight.

Finally, Harper asked, "Any movement?"

Seven checked several modes available to the passive sensors. "Negative. All eleven hostile vessels have sent distress signals indicating they are dead in space."

"And how do you think we should respond, Deputy?"

She considered the circumstances, the needs of their mission, and her conscience. "We shouldn't. Authorities from Voll will assist them all within the hour. If any of our attackers turn out to be lying and continue to pose a threat, we can neutralize them using minimal force and then continue our mission."

"*Now* you're starting to sound like a Ranger." Harper brought the prowler back to full power. "Time for us to go, before any more of these goons show up. Keep an eye on the sensors while I correct our heading to Freecloud."

"Copy that. Sensors clear."

As Harper laid in a new course, Seven contemplated the eleven disabled hostile vessels they were leaving behind. Rumors she had heard—rumors she now knew were lies—had led her to think the Fenris Rangers were the kind of ruthless vigilantes who would have destroyed those defenseless ships in cold blood, rather than leave them to be rescued.

Perhaps the Fenris Rangers and Starfleet are not so different in their ideologies as I was led to believe. But if those lies about the Rangers persist, it must be because someone wants to slander them. Or needs to. Whoever it is that fears the truth about the Rangers must also fear what will happen if the Rangers and Starfleet ever become allies.

So who benefits most from feeding that fear?

And how do I stop them before they hurt anyone else?

Romulan Harrier *Nodokata*

Clever. Most clever, indeed.

The entire engagement had lasted less than a minute. Veris had anticipated several minutes of wild maneuvering by the prowler, as well as needing to finish off his competitors after the Ranger vessel had been subdued. Watching from a discreet distance, using only his ship's passive sensors, the Romulan bounty hunter at first had been perplexed by the Rangers' tactics—and then he had found himself surprised to see them using state-of-the-art experimental Romulan weapons technology.

I wonder: How did the Rangers get their hands on a displacer?

It wasn't the first time Veris had heard of the Rangers acquiring Romulan-made technology and smuggling it across the Qiris sector to the other side of the Neutral Zone, but it was the first time he had seen proof that the Rangers had found a source for military systems.

The commission on this job is going to be exceptional, but if I can recover the displacer generator from that prowler . . . that would be an amazing spoil of war.

There I go again—getting ahead of myself.

Veris reminded himself to stick to protocol. Over the years he had developed a working method that suited him. It consisted of performing diligent research and reconnaissance of his targets before attempting any kind of direct engagement. In his experience, it had often proved unwise for him to pick fights with people whose full capabilities—and vulnerabilities—were not yet known to him. If he had a mantra, it was simply *Know your enemy.*

He punched in a timecode and replayed the sensors' recorded data of the prowler's actions, starting from the moment it left the bank's rooftop. As he scrubbed forward and back to review certain moments in detail, he paid special attention to the piloting style of the Ranger identified as Harper. The human man's flying was bold, confident, but also patient and measured. This was a person with a lot of experience in the cockpit, someone who might be a formidable opponent in a dogfight were his ship not burdened with a fortune in gold-pressed latinum.

As for the other Ranger, a young woman whose name had not been included in the job's dossier, she seemed to be someone with advanced training and experience in tactical systems. Whoever she was, she had learned how to operate a displacer system and had deployed it to devastating effect. Furthermore, she had exhibited foresight in surrounding the prowler with chaff as a precaution in case any of their targets had survived the displacer attack. To a quick sensor sweep they would appear to have been hit, disabled, and left adrift in a cloud of their own debris—a ruse that might have afforded her enough of an element of surprise to destroy any foes who had come to confirm their demise at close range.

She's a thinker. One with a knack for setting traps.

Veris moved on to a detailed review of the manufacturer's schematics for the Starfire 500 prowler. It was similar in size to his Romulan harrier, a decommissioned long-range patrol ship that had been popular several decades earlier. He had upgraded *Nodokata* himself, implementing a major technical refit and a systems reconfiguration to suit his professional needs.

Normally, he would have been reluctant to risk a head-on confrontation with a ship as fast, maneuverable, heavily shielded, and well-armed as a Starfire 500, but this one was hauling a huge load of dense deadweight. That wouldn't mean much at warp speeds, but at impulse or on thrusters inside an atmosphere, this prowler would be little more than a flying brick.

Atmospheric flight—that's where they'll be most vulnerable. So that's where I'll take them—local authorities be damned. Veris laid in a course for Freecloud, the Rangers' only logical destination. *I can beat the Rangers there by nearly thirty minutes, which means I have a total of two hours to harden my sensors against their displacer module.* Confident that he would be able to nullify the prowler's only remaining tactical advantage, he brought main power back online, engaged his ship's cloaking device, and jumped his ship to maximum warp.

I'm going to enjoy being wealthy.

19

Alpha Doradus System – Freecloud

The river of warp-bent starlight outside the cockpit canopy vanished, and the colossal, brilliantly illuminated sphere of the planet Freecloud seemed to snap into being ahead of *Lady Fly*. Great constellations of light wrapped around vast regions of the planet's surface, megacities whose intense radiance was noticeable from orbit even during full daylight.

"No sign of hostile vessels," Seven said to Harper while keeping her eyes on the ship's sensor display. "Heavy flight traffic over the cities. And we're being hailed."

"On speakers."

The cockpit's speakers gave a flat, tinny quality to the man's voice that issued forth. *"Unknown vessel, this is Freecloud Orbital Control. Identify yourself and your destination."*

Harper opened a response channel. "Control, this is Fenris Ranger forty-six nineteen, bound for Stardust City."

"Hold position while we verify your transponder."

"Acknowledged." He muted the channel and said over his shoulder to Seven, "We made pretty good time, considering there's an absolutely insane price on our heads."

Seven continued to watch the sensors for trouble. "Nothing improves speed like fear. Now we need to face whoever might be standing between us and the bank in Stardust City."

"The last klick is always the hardest." Seven heard feedback tones from the ship's computer interface as Harper called up data on his screens. "Everything's quiet up here. But I'm thinking we should do a quick orbit of the planet, run some sensor sweeps, do a bit of recon."

"I would advise against that."

"Why?"

"Our scans from orbit will be detectable to ships waiting for us in Stardust City's airspace. By seeking out our enemies, we might end up announcing ourselves and lose any chance of taking them by surprise."

Harper was thinking about that when the voice of Freecloud Orbital Control returned. *"Fenris Ranger forty-six nineteen, your ID is verified, and you are clear to proceed."*

"Acknowledged, Control. Forty-six nineteen out." Harper closed the comm channel. "So you're suggesting we take the direct approach. Point ourselves at Stardust City—"

"And haul ass. Yes."

"Simple and bold. I like it." He engaged the thrusters and pointed the prowler's nose toward the planet. "Stardust City, here we come."

As soon as Harper pushed the prowler into its dive, Seven felt her guts twist in response. Maneuvers like this could overtax the small ship's inertial dampers under the best of circumstances, but when it was hauling a massive load of gold-pressed latinum, she was sure she felt the pull of several g's with every rapid change in vector or velocity. Power dives felt to Seven like falling, even though she was strapped into her seat with a six-point safety harness.

Most alarming of all to Seven was that Harper sounded like he enjoyed this madness. "Thirty seconds to Stardust City, kid! Get ready for a hero's welcome like you ain't—"

"Contact! Bearing zero-zero-four mark one-zero-five, range two hundred kilometers and closing fast! They're locking weapons!"

"In city airspace? What kind of lunatic does that?"

"One looking to collect a billion-credit bounty."

"Shields up!" Seven engaged the shields as Harper pulled up to a level attitude and then he banked *Lady Fly* hard to starboard while pushing the prowler's thrusters into overdrive. Outside the canopy, disruptor pulses shot past and vanished into the clouds. "Hang on, kid!"

The prowler shook as several energy pulses slammed into its underside, and then a salvo of disruptor fire peppered its dorsal fuselage as *Lady Fly* struggled through a high-g turn that left Seven vertiginous and nauseated. She pressed her hands against the sides of her cockpit space as Harper pushed the ship through a dizzying rolling turn.

"Jam their weapons lock!"

Startled back into action, Seven engaged the displacer system. Outside, a flurry of disruptor energy screamed past, close enough to make her wince.

The displacer system came online, but when Seven tried to target their pursuer, the system spat back nothing but error codes. "The displacer can't lock on!"

"What kind of ship is that?"

Seven checked the attacker's sensor profile. "Romulan harrier, *Mivar* class, custom refit."

"Romulan? Dammit."

"Why is that—?" At once Seven understood. "The displacer is *Romulan* technology."

"Gold star, rookie. But if we don't shake this guy—"

An explosion rocked the prowler. Cockpit consoles flickered as the ship lost speed and pitched downward. Outside the canopy, Seven saw a thick trail of black smoke spewing from their starboard thruster, and green tongues of flame from a plasma burn danced beneath a ravaged hull plate. "Fire in the main magazine!"

"Dumping ordnance!" With one tap, Harper ejected the prowler's entire complement of microtorpedoes, half of which fell away wreathed in sickly emerald flames.

"Can we still make a run for the bank?"

"Not a chance. Impulse and thruster controls are cooked. If we try to land at the bank, we'll crash into it. Or else we'll miss and wipe out half the city."

Seven ran a quick scan of the planet's surface outside the metropolis. "We can make an emergency landing to the east—"

"And get picked off by that harrier? Pass. Only one way outta here, kid." He pulled back hard on the prowler's manual controls and sent *Lady Fly* into a maximum-burn, spiraling climb toward orbit. "And that's *up.*"

The curve of the planet fell away, and then the blue haze of atmosphere thinned and vanished as the prowler broke free into the vacuum of space.

But the sensor display in front of Seven held only bad news.

"Harper! He's still on us! Range eleven hundred kilometers and closing!"

"Plotting an emergency warp jump! Buy me a few more seconds!"

Seven stared at her dwindling options. No more torpedoes. Displacer system useless. Then she saw her play. She told the defense system that the Romulan ship was itself an inbound missile, and then she launched all of the prowler's remaining chaff and active countermeasures in a single burst. They zeroed in on the harrier like a swarm of enraged bees, engulfing it in bursts of radiation and clusters of metallic debris designed to confuse and destroy torpedoes.

Then, once she was sure the harrier's pilot was momentarily blinded both visually and on sensors, she cut a fiery wound across its ventral hull with the prowler's particle cannon.

Harper whooped in celebration. "Way to give 'em the heat, kid!" He engaged the warp drive. The orb of Freecloud vanished into a muddy whorl of starlight. *Lady Fly* shuddered violently as it hurtled through subspace, its engines moaning like a wounded animal.

Seven winced at the mournful din. "That sounds troubling."

"To say the least."

"How far will the engines take us in their condition?"

"If we're lucky? God only knows where, but someplace away from that Romulan."

"And if we are unlucky?"

"In that case, I reckon they'll get us all the way to the scene of our warp core breach."

"If that was an attempt at humor, I do not find it funny. Or reassuring."

"Like I keep telling ya, kid—truth or comfort. You only get one."

Mercenary Frigate *Eris*

"What do you mean they escaped?" Kohgish was so enraged that he imagined his eyes popping out of his skull. "How did a single prowler elude twelve of the best bounty hunters in the quadrant? Especially when we told them where it would be and when it would be there?"

Looking weary and annoyed on the other end of the encrypted subspace channel, Mardani sighed and shrugged in a gesture of surrender. *"What do you want me to say?"*

"I want you to say you're going to fix this."

"Why would I? I'm not the one who botched it."

"You're the one who hired the brain trust that did."

"I've warned you since the beginning, Kohgish: there are never any guarantees."

Unable to suppress his growing fury, Kohgish let slip a long, low growl. "Wrong, Mardani. I can make you a guarantee, here and now. If I don't have the full sum of what I owe Qulla when he arrives at these coordinates in seventeen hours, not only will I *not* be buying his surplus dreadnought, I and my crew will end up floating in space with the remains of my ship."

Mardani mocked Kohgish's distress with an exaggerated *tsk, tsk, tsk.* *"Seems like a teachable moment, General. Don't offer to buy things if you don't know how you'll pay for them. Or maybe just don't make promises you can't keep."*

"I made this deal at your request, on your assurances."

"I never asked you to do anything like this."

"You told me to grow my fleet. Expand my power base."

"By absorbing other warlords' fleets into your own. Not by making foolish contracts with nefarious arms merchants known for killing people over failed negotiations."

Kohgish's paws tensed, and his black claws extended. He wished had something to sink them into—something like Mardani's smug face.

"We don't have time to argue, Mardani. We need to get this done."

"I see no reason this should be my problem."

"Let me refresh your memory. You told me months ago that you needed a new proxy force to stop rogue units of the Romulan military from sending spies and raiding parties into Federation space once the Neutral Zone falls. You wanted ships out here that could hold the line, protect the Federation from a sneak invasion via the Qiris sector, and not embroil the Federation in any kind of interstellar political crisis."

Mardani's mood darkened. *"I recall saying something like that."*

"Then you'd best recall your promise to help me build my fleet."

The frustration on Mardani's face was easy to read. *"It isn't that simple, General. Now that the media's shining a light on us, we need to be careful. Circumspect."*

"You mean cowardly."

"I mean smart. If this deal with Qulla will draw attention, avoid it. Cancel it."

"No. Acquiring this warship is the only chance I have of building a force that can hold position against a concerted Romulan attack."

"There will be other ships."

"Not like this one. And mark my words: if it falls into the hands of my rivals, whoever gets it will be able to pummel my forces. And then any chance you had of building a bulwark against the Romulans in Qiris sector will be gone."

Mardani looked disgusted with Kohgish but also resigned to needing him. *"Fine. I'll use a couple of gadgets I brought home from Alderi III. They should help me track the prowler."*

"Excellent."

"But you'd better know this changes the terms of our deal. If I need to take an active hand in fixing your problems, I want a one point five percent commission, and I'll need your word that from now on you'll stop being such a royal pain in my ass."

"I will do my best to be a loyal vassal."

"Lucky me. Stay off comms until I contact you again. Mardani out."

The screen went dark for a moment, and then one of Kohgish's command crew reverted *Eris's* main viewscreen to its customary forward angle of view. After a few seconds, he told his man Feeno, "Put the bounty hunter back on." The viewscreen switched to a close view of the Romulan bounty hunter Veris. Kohgish asked him, "Did you hear all that?"

"Every word of it, General. Thank you for being willing to share that intel."

"My pleasure, Centurion. As you heard, I did not exaggerate the facts. Our intermediary Mardani plans to cut himself in on this deal for a full point more profit than he was willing to offer you. While also being willing to cut you out entirely."

"Indeed. Most distressing. Regardless, Mardani was the one who offered the contract, and now he has rescinded it, in exchange for a generous cancellation fee. There's no point in my pursuing this wayward container. Were I to acquire it and attempt to deliver it to Mardani, he would try to kill me and take it for himself. If I capture it and try to abscond with it, I will become the most hunted target of every bounty hunter in the quadrant, if not the galaxy."

"There is a third option."

"Tell me."

"Recover the container and deliver it to me. I'll pay you the higher commission that Kohgish wants to pay to himself, and then we can join forces and destroy him."

Veris let out a snort of derision. *"No, I don't think so."*

"If we coordinate our efforts, we can avoid friendly fire incidents."

"Irrelevant."

"What do you propose, then?"

"That you and your crew stay out of my way."

Ranger Prowler *Nymeria* – Lambda Hydrae System

There were few things Ellory hated as much as being sent out on false calls. For her a false call was like foreplay without a release: just a waste of time. And that's all she had to show for her high-warp solo flight out to the Lambda Hydrae system, which was located inside the Romulan Neutral Zone. Luckily for her, there had been no sign of Romulan ships in this system for the past several months, and there was no reason to think they'd be coming back anytime soon.

I came here to save a hospital ship. Now I'm orbiting an orange giant with no planets, looking for evidence that there was ever a reason for me to come all the way out here.

Over the comms, similar reports were coming in from Ranger patrols across the sector. In the few instances when hostile ships were actually sighted, they had fled at the first sign of engagement. Some of the raiders had done a fair amount of damage before help arrived. There were now dozens of damaged colony ships packed with scared passengers, some of whom had been wounded. The only news of the day that didn't enrage Ellory was that, so far, there had been no reports of fatalities.

Be grateful for small mercies, my father always said.

She finished her third orbit of Lambda Hydrae without finding anything suspect on her sensors. Seething with resentment for the squandering of her time, she turned her prowler toward Fenris and opened a long-range, real-time subspace channel by routing her signal over the extensive network of booster relays the Federation had deployed throughout the region.

"Wolf's Den, this is Ranger thirty-five ninety-nine. Please acknowledge."

"Thirty-five ninety-nine, this is Wolf's Den. We read you five by five. Go ahead."

"All quiet out at Lambda Hydrae. No sign of recent visitation. Looks like a fake call."

"Wish we could say we were surprised. What's your status?"

"Free to move. Any new calls?"

"Negative. Quiet as a roomful of Rangers when CP's lookin' for volunteers."

"Copy that. What's the word from forty-six nineteen?"

"Nothing definite since Voll."

A chill of fearful intuition passed through Ellory. "Nothing since pickup? Did they at least make it off Voll?"

"Affirmative. Pickup was made, forty-six nineteen departed on schedule."

"But nothing since then?"

"Nothing confirmed."

"What've you got that's *un*confirmed?"

"Freecloud Orbital Control says forty-six nineteen checked in but never landed. And there were reports of an aerial firefight over Stardust City. But both ships warped out of the system before they could be positively identified."

Dread tied sickening knots in Ellory's stomach.

"Thanks for the expo, Wolf's Den. Thirty-five ninety-nine, out."

Ellory closed the comm channel and switched her attention to her cockpit's navigational display. She called up a star chart of the sector and its closest interstellar neighbors.

I have to assume it was them at Freecloud. But they didn't even try to land. That's not good. Might mean they got hit so bad, they can't set down.

She enlarged subsectors, studied which star systems were closest to Freecloud, and then asked herself what Harper would likely have done in an emergency. She had served with the man for many years, had even flown with him for a few. He was experienced, cool under fire, and could be trusted to make smart decisions under pressure.

He'll look for somewhere to regroup. Assess his ship's damage. But he can't call for help without giving away his position. Which means he'll need a safe haven. Or spare parts. Maybe both. And an alternative means of getting an encrypted SOS back to the Wolf's Den.

This wasn't going to be easy. There was a lot of space between the Qiris sector and the Iconia sector. The only safe route between them—if it could really be called "safe"—involved threading a needle's eye of legally neutral, unclaimed space between the Romulan Neutral Zone and the vaguely defined edge of the Klingon Empire. A journey of more than thirty-five light-years fraught with opportunities for detour and disaster.

Ellory stared at the map and cursed her luck until she accepted that all the anger in the universe wasn't going to make her situation any better—and that the sooner she got moving, the sooner she might find Harper and Seven. Pushing through her fear, she turned her prowler toward the eye of the needle and jumped to maximum warp.

I just hope I'm not too late.

Balduk Sector, Interstellar Space

Spacewalking wasn't something Harper did very often. In fact, he couldn't recall the last time he had gone EVA from a small spacecraft. Necessity, however, had overruled his reluctance. Without much hope of safely reaching a spaceport intact, and not wanting to give away his coordinates by sending an open distress signal while there was a bounty hunter still looking for them, he had little choice but to suit up and head outside to assess the damage to *Lady Fly.*

I'd have sent Seven, but she doesn't know this old bird the way I do. He pried open a blast-damaged hull plate to look behind it. *Like it or not, this one's all on me.*

He found it disconcerting to spacewalk in the void. Going EVA above a planet or in proximity to a starbase was no less dangerous, but at least there he could cling to the illusion of a haven somewhere nearby. Out here, in the cold expanse of the void, there was only silence and the very real possibility that a mechanical failure might become a death sentence.

Seven's voice crackled over his helmet's transceiver. *"How does it look?"*

"So far? Not good." He made sure his secondary tether was still secured before he transferred his primary tether to a rod in the prowler's spaceframe that would enable him to move aft. "We've got hits to the main impulse coil and the antimatter containment regulator. Plus, the deuterium fuel pod is cracked, and life-support is gone. Whoever hit us, they got us good."

"Can you make repairs sufficient to get us back to Fenris?"

"Beats me, kid. There could be a hundred other things wrong with this bird that I can't see, but her internal sensor matrix is fragged, and without that there's no way to run a reliable diagnostic." He shone his palm beacon inside the ship's burnt and blasted innards. "With the handful of tools and spare parts we still had room for, the best I can do is jury-rig some fixes to put us back in motion. But thruster and impulse control are both gone, so the only kind of landing I'll be able to attempt is the kind most experts simply call a crash."

"That does not sound promising."

"No, it sure don't. And I'll tell you this much: it's not something I'd want to try anywhere near a populated area. One bad bounce and our little prowler turns into an antimatter bomb."

"Then we should jettison our antimatter pod before attempting any kind of landing. Perhaps while still in orbit."

"A noble idea, kid. But that'll mean making planetfall without main power."

"An unfortunate but necessary risk."

"Yeah, I guess you're right."

He pulled himself deeper inside the guts of the ship's stardrive. Working with care, he tested several connections and inspected a few critical components. "Okay, the good news, if we can call it that, is that our ejection system for the antimatter pod is intact. So your plan might work, if we can find a planet where we won't risk innocent lives in the process."

"I am searching the local star charts now. There are not many unpopulated Class-M planets within our currently limited operational range."

"We don't need a whole planet. A barren continent would do."

"That does not improve our options to any significant degree."

"By the way, without the prowler's life-support, our survival time is limited by the air supply in our EVA gear. Which in my case is down to about four hours. But no pressure."

"Thank you. I am fully aware of our current predicament."

"Just tryin' to help."

He backed out of the prowler's stardrive and closed the exterior hull plates.

It was slow, tedious work, but he gave himself over to it in the hope that it would quiet his increasingly panicked mind. The repetition of replacing bolts and rewelding key joints had a certain Zen simplicity, a rote quality that made it possible for him to focus on the task at hand rather than be overwhelmed by the seemingly endless number of things that could yet take turns for the worse.

When he finished putting as much of his ship back together as he could with the few resources he had available, he checked the chrono and realized neither he nor Seven had said a word in over ten minutes. He made sure his helmet's transceiver was still on. "Seven?"

"Yes?"

"Just making sure you're still with me. *Lady Fly*'s patched up best I can manage. Any luck finding a place to set her down?"

"Perhaps. I had to check some older charts, but I found an unpopulated Class-M planet just a few light-years away, with a thin atmosphere but zero point eight-five standard gravity, which should take some of the pain out of our . . . less than fully controlled landing."

"Nice work. Does this lucky ball of rock have a name?"

"It is listed as Zirat."

The moment Harper heard the name, his mind went blank with fear. He had grown up hearing ghost stories about Zirat. Tales of hauntings and exiled madmen. All just fantasies, of course. When he got older, he'd learned that adults told those stories to children to discourage them from visiting Zirat, which frequently was scoured for spare parts by ruthless salvagers, desperate pirates, and all manner of lowlifes, who all knew it by its nickname.

The starship graveyard.

Where hope and spacecraft both go to die.

Thankful that Seven couldn't see him wince, he took a moment to steady his voice before he replied, "Perfect. Nice work, kid."

Seven was not an impatient individual, at least not by nature, but the time she had spent alone in the cockpit of the prowler, listening to her own breathing inside her helmet, felt interminable. It wasn't the absence of the ship's chrono that fueled her anxiety; one of the many lingering aftereffects of her long assimilation by the Borg was that she had a fairly keen sense of time's passage. No, the great unease that stirred within her came from another place: fear.

She told herself it wasn't a rational response. That she had every reason to be calm. Harper had made the best repairs he could, under the circumstances; there was no cause to think the bounty hunter who had so deftly routed them at Freecloud knew where they were now. And she recalled having faced many perils of a more dire nature during her time on *Voyager*.

So why am I so nervous this time?

There were many possible explanations, but the one she thought most likely was that she was reacting to her sense of isolation. Left behind in the cockpit, with only Harper's voice over her helmet's transceiver for company, she had dared to gaze at the stars—to face the black and unblinking stare of eternity.

And it had made her feel so small . . . so powerless . . . so helpless.

She refused to be afraid any longer.

She shut her eyes and cast out her fear. *I am not alone. My friend is still here. I am still here. We will survive. I am not weak. I am not powerless. I am Seven of Nine.*

She opened her eyes and saw her dilemma clearly—as well as a means of confronting it. The prowler's comm control circuits were badly damaged; it would not be able to get a real-time signal back to Fenris, not even with the aid of the subspace relay network. But the encrypted comm device that Mardani had given her—it worked on different frequencies, employed different technologies, and would connect to a completely different network than did the prowler's comm system.

First, I will sync its transceiver with the prowler's. Seven pulled optronic cables from beneath her console in the cockpit's aft seat and grabbed up assorted pieces of hardware to construct an adapter that would enable the FSA comm device to make use of the prowler's superior transmission power. *Next, I reconfigure the FSA device's encryption matrix to bypass the prowler's filters. Then I just need to find Starfleet's emergency network frequency and open a channel to . . .*

The comms display in her half of the cockpit fritzed and awoke with a flurry of static and distorted lines. Visible behind the interference was Starfleet's emblem. Short, repeating tones at four-second intervals indicated Seven's hail was being sent to its intended recipient. Whether she would answer, and whether she would be willing or able to help, were different questions entirely.

Then the call connected, and a familiar face appeared on Seven's screen.

"Hello, Admiral. Forgive me for calling at an inopportune hour."

Bleary-eyed beneath a wild, asymmetrical crown of sleep-shaped hair, Kathryn Janeway blinked and leaned closer to her comms unit. *"Seven? Where are you?"*

"Stranded in deep space."

"So, not a social call, then."

"Regrettably, no. I was hesitant to contact you, after the way I left, but—"

"Nonsense. I'm just glad you're all right. It's been so long since we last spoke."

"Yes, I know. I made myself difficult to reach. Now, however, I find myself in need of . . . an ally. One who has the resources to help me, and who won't judge me."

Janeway's face was a portrait in heartfelt concern. *"Are you all right?"*

"Not entirely, no. My friend, Harper, and I are in great danger."

"Dare I ask what sort?"

"Bounty hunters—employed by a would-be dictator. Our vessel has been badly damaged, and we do not expect it to survive our imminent crash landing."

"Which will be where?"

"An unpopulated Class-M planet called Zirat, in the Balduk sector."

"Ah, yes—the 'starship graveyard.'"

"You know it?"

"I know of it, but only by reputation."

"We are running low on air, so Zirat is our only viable option. Is there a Starfleet vessel anywhere nearby that can pick us up from Zirat?"

"Not at the moment. There aren't any ships to spare at Starbases 173, 105, or 234." Janeway's eyes gleamed with mischief. *"But I have access to one that can be there in about ten hours. How will we know where to find you on the planet's surface?"*

"I am sending you the Rangers' SOS frequency."

"Understood. Now, as long as I have your attention, there's something you need to know. The man who introduced himself to you as an FSA handler named Arastoo Mardani? Is actually an FSA spymaster gone rogue. His real name is Erol Tazgül, and in addition to being the Beta Quadrant's most ambitious new black-market arms dealer, he is currently number four on the Federation's most-wanted list of interstellar criminals."

Seven processed that news only to find herself too numb with shock from recent events to react strongly to it. "I see. He lied to me. Played on my recent failings to manipulate me."

"Don't let it upset you. That's what people like him do. Professionally."

"Regardless, I feel annoyed at myself for not heeding my initial suspicions about him, which in hindsight I see were justified." She composed herself into a semblance of calm. "Thank you for the warning. I will terminate all dealings with him, effective immediately."

FSA Tactical Cruiser *Bolvangar*

"See that you do," Janeway said, over the channel that apparently neither she nor Seven knew had long since been tapped by the FSA. *"And if you encounter him again, run. He's more dangerous than you realize. Leave him to Starfleet, or the Federation Marshals Service."*

"Understood," Seven replied. *"Harper and I look forward to your help on Zirat."*

"Keep your heads down and stay warm. I'll be there as soon as I can. Janeway out."

The channel closed, but Tazgül had what he needed: a lock on the transceiver in Seven's comm device and her declaration of where she was going next. He had intruded late upon the conversation between Admiral Janeway and his renegade asset because of the supplemental encryption the ex-Borg had used. *Clever, Miss Hansen. But not clever enough.*

He left comms and crossed the command deck to the tactical station. "Calligaris, bring up a local star chart. Show me where Zirat is."

Daphne Calligaris, a former FSA operative who had followed Tazgül into his new life of private enrichment, called up a three-dimensional holographic chart of the adjacent eight sectors. The Swiss-born woman pointed at a tiny spark of light in the narrow patch of unclaimed territory between the Federation's outer reach and the Klingon Empire's coreward annexation. "Here."

"Has anyone put a flag on that rock?"

"Not yet." Calligaris called up a sidebar of data about the Zirat system. "Several recent treaties have made a point of keeping it neutral for salvage purposes."

"Good. That helps." He relayed the coordinates from Hansen's comm unit into the holographic display. "Looks like our gal and her Ranger friend are just a quick hop away from Zirat. Count on them being there by the time we arrive."

"Already factored in, sir. What's our plan for engagement?"

Tazgül weighed his options. "An ex-Borg should never be underestimated. She has abilities that Starfleet doesn't talk about, for fear of causing a panic in the civilian populace."

"Such as?"

"Most notably, enhanced strength and endurance. And her nanoprobes can be used to take control of a wide variety of computers and devices, among other functions. She can also use them to assimilate other people and put them under her control—which is why we are not sending any flesh-and-blood operatives down to Zirat."

Calligaris shrugged. "Why not just lock onto her and Harper with a transporter beam, dematerialize them, and then scatter their matter and energy matrix in a wide-dispersal beam?"

Tazgül highlighted a detail in the sidebar data about Zirat. "The planet has a natural transphasic distortion field. The only way our decades-old transporter could get a lock on anything down there would be to plant a transport enhancer on it—and if we're going to the effort of laying hands on our asset and the Ranger, we might as well just neutralize them on-site. But that does give me a good idea about recovering their stolen shipment of gold-pressed latinum. Which *is* our chief objective."

"Understood. Recovery first, termination second."

"Correct, but both are vital." Tazgül used an ancillary companel to pull up files from the ship's memory banks. "Daphne, do you remember the name of the urban-defense project the FSA cooked up after the Borg attacked Earth in '73?"

"Operation: Erinys?"

"Yes! That's it." He keyed in that name and pulled up a collection of tactical dossiers, accompanied by several sets of engineering schematics. Leafing quickly through the technical drawings, he smiled. "Yes, this'll do nicely." He looked at Calligaris. "Power up the vehicle replicator. We have work to do before we get to Zirat."

"I thought we weren't sending anyone to the surface."

"We aren't. The vehicle replicator is perfect for generating huntsman drones." He saw by her reaction that she didn't recognize the name. He called up a top-level schematic of the arachnoid-looking machine and added it to the holographic projection between them. "Modeled on the Terran huntsman spider, but much bigger—about the size of a rhinoceros. Made to be dropped onto a planet from orbit. Once on the ground, it's a hunter-killer unlike anything you've ever seen. It has modes for physical combat as well as beam weapons and explosive projectiles." He relayed the schematics to the industrial-grade replicator. "Four ought to do it, I think."

Calligaris regarded the engineering diagrams with a dubious expression. "Seems like overkill. Are you sure this is absolutely necessary?"

"It is. Our renegade asset Miss Hansen is an ex-Borg drone. These things were made specifically to hunt and destroy Borg drones in *any* environment: wilderness, urban, starship, Borg cube, you name it. And the huntsmen's beam weapons pack a little something extra, put in special just for the Borg and their pesky nanoprobes. Trust me, this is the right tool for the job. As for it being overkill?" He keyed in the command for the replicator to begin fabricating the four killer drones. "Sometimes, overkill is *exactly* what's called for."

20

Zirat

Seven couldn't see what was going on in the front half of the prowler's cockpit, but she heard it with perfect clarity. Wind and turbulence hammered the small ship as it plunged through the storm-wracked atmosphere of Zirat. Within seconds of Harper starting their descent, nearly every warning alarm on his master console had begun to beep and whoop, and he had finally given up trying to mute them because he clearly was too busy trying to prevent *Lady Fly* from disintegrating in midair.

Strapped into the second seat, Seven knew there was nothing she could do to help except stay quiet. Outside the canopy, colossal sheets of lightning bent through endless valleys of black clouds while the prowler pitched and spiraled through the maelstrom.

Her sensor display flashed a warning as it lost track of the prowler's anti-matter fuel pod, which Harper had ejected while they were in orbit prior to their descent. The pod had continued on its original heading, in a regular orbit around Zirat, thanks to momentum inherited from the prowler. Now it passed out of sensor range, behind the mass of the planet that seemed to be racing up to meet them with alarming speed.

The ship's damaged thrusters roared for a second, and then they sputtered. Up front, Harper grumbled a string of profanities while fighting to level the prowler's attitude, but his swearing only grew louder and more vulgar as the wind tore blast-scored hull plates off the ship's fuselage and cast them away into the darkness.

He shouted over the chaos, "How're the shields?"

Seven hollered back, "Twenty-five percent and falling!"

"Transfer all power to forward deflectors! We're taking this one on the chin."

Rain and sleet lashed at the prowler's canopy as the ship penetrated the lower levels of the storm. Great forks of violet lightning bent and danced around the ship, whose nose dipped as their speed increased. More cursing from Harper told Seven something else had gone wrong.

He banked the ship hard to port—and a moment later the prowler shot through a narrow gap separating a terrifyingly close pair of ice-capped mountain peaks.

Seven leaned right to look past the cockpit's center bulkhead and sneak a peek at the terrain ahead. On the other side of the fast-receding mountain range sprawled a vast, snow-covered, forested basin littered to the horizon in all directions with tens of thousands of wrecked starships of all kinds, origins, and sizes, most of them at least half-buried in the frozen landscape.

The prowler's spaceframe trembled and groaned as Harper pushed it to remain level for just a few moments more. "And for my next trick, I'm gonna try to set us down without turning us both into chunky salsa. Wish me luck."

"Good luck," Seven said as if by reflex, but for once in her life really meaning it.

A bolt of lightning ripped through the starboard thruster and set it on fire. The engine spewed flames and smoke for a few seconds before it exploded and pelted the rest of the ship with its debris. The prowler slowed and stalled into a precarious starboard dive. Its port thruster fired in overdrive to compensate, and for a moment *Lady Fly* righted itself—until its ailerons and secondary thrusters all broke apart and the prowler's nose pitched toward the blur of the ground speeding past below.

Harper called out, "Brace for impact!"

Seven crossed her arms over her chest and bowed her head.

The moment of contact was as loud as an explosion.

Seven heard Harper fighting to control the ship's crash landing, but she knew his efforts were futile. Parts of the prowler were torn off as it skidded over snow and ice and caromed off rock formations and the hulls of long-derelict starships. Waves of snow and dirt surged over the canopy. A collision sent the prowler into a wild tumbling roll across the icy ground. Then came another impact, against something solid. Something unmovable.

Stillness. Silence. Shock.

She heard the hiss of something leaking somewhere inside the ship's compromised systems, and the sickly creaking of a twisted spaceframe settling into its chaotic new form. A lone beeping alert, weak and slow, emanated from Harper's console. From outside the canopy, Seven heard the patter of rain and the banshee howls of wind assailing their downed ship.

Seven took a few moments to assess her own condition before releasing herself from her seat's safety harness. "Harper? Are you all right?"

The older man groaned. "Nothin' an induced coma on Risa couldn't fix."

"Is that a yes or a no?"

She heard him unfastening his own safety restraints. "Let's just grab our survival kits and get out of here." Something on his console answered a request with a dysfunctional chirp. "Great. Canopy controls are offline. Can you trigger the emergency release?"

"Yes. Cover your face."

"Go for it."

Seven lowered her helmet's protective visor and pulled the manual control lever beneath her seat. The explosive charges under the canopy's contact points detonated.

BOOM. Tooth-rattling, spine-shaking, turn-your-guts-into-a-milkshake loud.

A gust of bitterly cold air washed over her, followed by a spray of freezing rain. Seven opened her eyes and saw the shattered remains of the canopy arc away through the downpour and then tumble over the wreckage-strewn ground.

The remains of the prowler were wedged into the side of what once had been a much larger ship but now was just a small hill composed of monotanium and empty spaces. She sat up to get a better view and was rewarded by the sight of a lush, boreal forest with a high canopy and thick, tall fronds and other primitive green flora on the snowy ground. Branches and ship hulls were dusted with freshly fallen snow, which was developing an icy shell thanks to the misting rain. An omnipresent cold fog reduced anything more than ten meters away to a sketch of itself and erased from sight entirely anything beyond fifteen meters.

Harper climbed out of the cockpit and descended the ship's downward-angled fuselage with caution. "Watch your step out here. Hull's slicker than a Ferengi used-starship salesman."

"I will take appropriate care." Seven retrieved the emergency survival kit from under her seat and then got out of the ship. Standing beside the wreck with Harper, she wondered if the moisture on his face was rain or tears. "Are you all right?"

"I'll be okay." He pointed at a nearby large derelict whose outer hull appeared to be mostly intact. "We should shelter in there. Get out of the rain. Phaser some rocks for heat."

"A reasonable plan."

He started walking, and she followed him. As they passed other wrecks, she noted how the forest seemed to have grown through and around so many of them, in effect transforming the cast-offs into part of their ecosystem. She was about to comment upon it when she saw Harper activating a small, chip-sized comms device. "What is that?"

"Personal emergency beacon. It doesn't have the greatest range, but if our people come looking for us, this should help 'em find us."

"I did tell you I've already shared the Rangers' SOS frequency with my friend Admiral Janeway."

"Yeah, you did. No offense, but the day I put my trust in Starfleet ahead of my fellow Rangers is the day I turn in my badge." He flashed a playful smile at Seven. "If you like, we can place a few bets, make a wager out of it. Who do you think'll find us first? Rangers, Starfleet, or the bounty hunter?"

"I would prefer not to speculate."

"Fair enough." They reached a tear in the hull of the ship they intended to use as a shelter. Harper stuck his head through the gap and shone his palm beacon around inside. "Let me go in first, make sure it's clear. Last thing we need is to find out something big and ugly already lives here." Edging through the narrow space, he added, "Be right back."

Seven waited until he was gone, and then she took the FSA-issued comm from inside her jacket and wondered whether it might betray her location to Mardani—and the bounty hunter.

She crushed the device in her fist and scattered its splintered debris across the rocks.

Better safe than sorry, as Janeway would say.

Sleep proved elusive for Seven and Harper in spite of the comforts of shelter and heated rocks. Frigid wind snaked in through cracks in the derelict's hull and bulkheads, a constant reminder of the bleak, frozen wilderness that surrounded them for hundreds of kilometers in every direction. Harper had suggested playing various card games to pass the time, but Seven had been unable to resist applying her enhanced cognitive and computational abilities to seize the advantage by mastering the odds at speeds Harper couldn't hope to match.

After losing several dozen successive hands of poker, blackjack, and rummy, Harper put away the cards. "I think that's enough practice for now."

"Are you certain? It seems you could benefit from a bit more."

"Yeah, kid. I'm sure." He dug in his emergency kit and pulled out a self-warming meal ready to eat, or MRE. He squinted at the picture on its peel-away lid. "I can't tell what this is."

Seven peeked at the box. "The red stuff looks like cranberry relish. So I'd say it's turkey."

A smile conveyed Harper's pride. "Deducing the entrée from the meat-identifying side dish. Your peers have taught you well."

"Well enough that I'll trade you any meal in your pack for the one I pulled out." She showed him the MRE, whose cover's text was illegible, and its image was scuffed and faded.

Harper squinted at her MRE. "What's the meat-identifier?"

"Creamed corn."

"Oh, man. Salisbury steak. Tough break, kid."

"So you won't trade with me?"

"What am I, a rookie? Get real."

She opened her self-warmed Salisbury steak meal. Poking at the rubbery oval of synthetic meat, Seven grumbled, "You are a cruel teacher."

"Life's the cruel teacher, kid. I just grade the homework." He dipped a forkful of his meal's replicated turkey in its sludgy gravy. "On the bright side, yours has a brownie for dessert. Mine has a pile of snot masquerading as flan."

Seven refused to look at him. "If you are attempting to elicit pity from me, you should at least wait until I've finished eating this . . . *whatever* this is."

"Fair enough."

They were both about halfway through their dinner when a faint sound emanated from the emergency comm unit in Harper's gear—a hailing frequency request. They both cast aside their unfinished meals and hurried over to kneel beside the comm unit. Harper switched it from its power-saving standby mode to full function and checked its readouts. "It recorded a repeated greeting." He initiated a playback, and they both leaned close to listen.

The voice that issued from the speaker sounded like Janeway's. *"Fenris Rangers, this is Admiral Kathryn Janeway, responding to your distress signal. Please respond."*

Harper reached for the device to open a reply channel.

Seven caught him by the wrist and stopped him. "Don't. Something's not right."

He pulled back his hand. "What's wrong? Talk to me, kid."

"Her greeting was . . . odd. She didn't identify her current vessel."

"So?"

"This comm isn't strong enough to pick up signals from anywhere but orbit." She looked upward, as if she could see through the hull of their derelict shelter. "And there is no vessel to which Admiral Janeway would have access that could have traveled here from Earth so quickly. Not even the new quantum slipstream drives are that fast."

Her certainty fueled Harper's mounting dread. "You're sure?"

"Completely." She pulled the comm unit toward her. "Let me try something." She set it for a reply frequency and opened the channel. Raising the pitch of her voice and infusing it with a vibrato of fear, she said, "Kathryn? Is it really you? This is Annika. Please respond!"

The delay in the response was brief but, for Seven, telling.

Then came the reply.

"Yes, Annika, it's Kathryn. Are you all right?"

Seven turned off the comm, even though she knew whoever had sent the reply already had her and Harper's coordinates. She stood and helped Harper to his feet. "We have to go."

He put on his Ranger-issued tactical lenses and grabbed his rifle. "Go where?"

"Anywhere but here." Seven strapped on her double-holster rig. "They're coming, so we need to move. *Now.*" She slung her bandolier of Gorn shock grenades across her torso, activated her sensor mask, and handed Harper his. "We need to hide our life signs and heat signatures."

They hurried out of their adopted shelter, into the screeching, ice-knife wind of a night darker than any she had ever seen before. As soon as they stepped out into the darkness, her ocular implant augmented her perception with monochromatic night vision enhanced by an infrared overlay. "Keep moving. Use the wrecks for cover."

Jogging alongside Seven, Harper adjusted the settings on his starshades with a few taps on the left rim. "Why are we running from Janeway? I thought she was your friend."

"She is. *That* was *not* Admiral Janeway."

"Who was it?"

"Mardani, the rogue spy who funded Kohgish."

"What the hell is *he* doing here?"

"He's here for the latinum—and to kill us."

21

Zirat

Seven and Harper sprinted through numbingly cold, ankle-deep snow. She had
no idea where they were going. There had been no time to reconnoiter the area
during their crash or since their arrival, and accurate maps of the surface were
all but nonexistent. All she saw were thickets of dense coniferous trees entwined
with the gnarled remains of long-lost starships and shuttlecraft. In theory, the
trees would offer some measure of concealment, but once the shooting started
the only real cover was going to be the twisted metal husks around them.

They emerged from the forest into an open space at the bottom of a hill
strewn with the corpses of lost ships. Harper tapped Seven's upper arm to get
her attention and pointed at the top of a nearby slope. "This way! High ground
and cover! Might be the best chance we'll get."

"Too open. We'd take fire from multiple directions and never see the enemy."

Harper started up the slope in spite of her warning. "Never give up high
ground."

She followed him up the snow-dusted, debris-covered knoll, if only to give
herself another chance to tell him he was making a mistake.

Thunder rolled from one side of the world to the other as the sky glowed red.

Above the low-lying clouds, something blazed in flickering hues of crimson. It
grew brighter by the second, until the clouds overhead turned the color of blood.

Four shuttle-sized objects cocooned in flames fell through the clouds. Nearly
in unison, they smashed down into the surrounding forest with ground-shaking
booms, bracketing Harper's and Seven's position. Smoky plumes climbed sky-
ward from each point of impact.

Harper's face contorted in horror. "What was that?"

"Nothing good." Seven grabbed the sleeve of Harper's jacket and pulled. "Forget the high ground, keep moving."

"Are you sure? We—"

Massive pulses of green energy shot through the forest toward Harper and Seven, disintegrating countless trees before being deflected at the last moment by the hulls of nearby derelict ships to blast smoldering chunks out of the hillside around the duo.

Harper sprinted with Seven, back into the forest. "No high ground! Got it!"

"Stay near the hulls! They're our only cover!"

"Copy that!"

Seven set her rifle to full power. Whatever was coming for them wasn't shooting to stun, so neither was she. She pulled a Gorn grenade from her bandolier and poised her thumb over its black trigger, which would arm it for use against hardened targets.

More pulses ripped through the forest, clearly tracking Seven and Harper as they fled deeper into the starship graveyard. Green blasts shredded the bases of massive tree trunks and set them ablaze. Within seconds, enormous ancient trees were falling like burning avalanches in every direction around Seven and Harper. Everywhere Seven turned, all she heard were the piercing shrieks of the pulses and the leaden thuds of falling trees.

Then she saw a massive hemispherical section of starship hull jutting from the ground, like the remnant of a collapsed bandshell. Inside its curve were heaps of metallic debris and the bent remains of other, smaller craft long since abandoned there. She pointed at it, and Harper nodded his understanding. Even though it was open on one side, it still would give them something to put their backs against, at least for a moment.

They darted and slalomed through the maze of debris inside the half shell until they found a slab of metal that seemed dense, solid, and firmly entrenched. More energy pulses flew past over their heads as they dove to cover behind their newfound rampart.

Harper stole a look over the top of the slab, then ducked as another flurry of pulses screamed past. "I can't see them. Can you?"

"Not yet," Seven said. "But I hear them." She closed her eyes and listened for the sounds beneath the chaos of weapons fire and the collapsing forest.

"Mechanical. Articulated. Too fast to be people or even manually controlled vehicles."

A grim nod of understanding from Harper. "Attack drones."

"Correct."

Harper winced as a wild fusillade of green pulses from the trees scoured the metal maze beyond their cover. "How the hell are they tracking us through our sensor masks?"

"Best guess? Sonic ranging. Target anything of sufficient mass that moves."

"That's old-school."

Seven had no idea what that idiom meant, so she ignored it. "This position is defensible, but not for long with our limited armament. Do we have any stronger weapons on the prowler?"

"Just the grenade launcher."

"We should get it."

"You want to break cover now? Are you nuts?"

A fresh salvo of energy pulses slammed against the other side of their rampart. Seven ducked low to the ground as the slab shook and warmed with each hit. "You lay down suppressing fire. I'll run for the prowler."

"The hell I will. And last time I checked, I was the one giving—"

Seven sprang from a crouch into a sprint. As she'd hoped, Harper unleashed a barrage of plasma rifle fire into the forest while she zigzagged through the labyrinth of metallic debris.

Then came the next barrage of energy pulses. She pivoted to cover in the nick of time, only to see one pulse ricochet off a nearby hunk of tritanium straight toward her. She spun and dove toward the ground, but not before the caroming bolt grazed her left arm.

By the time she hit the dirt, her arm felt as if it were on fire from within, and she reflexively cried out in pain and fear. The fingers of her left hand curled into a rictus like a dying spider, and the searing agony inside her arm paralyzed it for several seconds.

Harper called to her, "Kid! You okay?"

"Yes!" she lied. "Stay down!"

Seven tried to focus the healing properties of the Borg nanoprobes in her bloodstream—and when they refused to respond to the injury, she realized what had hit her was no ordinary energy weapon. Whatever else it might be, its pulses were infused with omicron particles, which Starfleet had learned could be used to neutralize Borg nanoprobes.

She took a few deep breaths and concentrated on relaxing her arm, on letting the pain pass through her and out of her. A few seconds later, the worst of the pain abated and she uncurled the fingers of her hand, but her arm remained numb. The nanoprobes in her blood still were not responding to the damage in her arm.

Those aren't just any killer drones, she realized. *They were designed to kill Borg. Which means Mardani sent them specifically to kill* me.

She forced her left hand to make a fist, and then she picked up the Gorn shock grenade she had dropped when the ricocheted pulse hit her.

Very well. War it is.

FSA Tactical Cruiser *Bolvangar*

The lack of timely information had Tazgül anxious and annoyed. "Dammit, Calligaris. What's going on down there?"

Keying commands into her panel and getting back nothing but empty screens had the tactical officer looking as frustrated as Tazgül felt. "There's no way to be sure. Contact with the drones is sporadic at best." She frowned. "It's a good thing they're fully autonomous once deployed, because I can barely make contact with any of them for more than a few seconds."

Tazgül moved to loom over the shoulder of his comms and sigint specialist, a male Zakdorn named Kael Dornik. "Can you boost the drones' signals? I need real-time intel."

The mercenary recruit shook his head. "Not much we can do, sir. We're getting major interference from Zirat's natural transphasic distortion field. And the millions of metric tons of sensor-scattering alloys covering the surface definitely aren't helping."

"Just our luck our prey goes to ground in a starship graveyard," Calligaris muttered.

Not yet ready to give up working the problem, Tazgül crossed the command deck to Hadon Saro, his science and engineering specialist. "Hadon, tell me you have a fix for this."

The blonde Bajoran woman didn't even look up from her console. "Wish I did. But any sensor readings we make from orbit are less than reliable. And that's being generous."

"Dammit." Tazgül returned to his command chair and considered the image of Zirat on the main viewscreen. "What if we reduce our range to the surface? Zeiss, can you take us into a lower orbit? Maybe skirt the planet's thermosphere?"

Flight control officer Yulen Zeiss looked back at Tazgül in vexed disbelief. "And risk losing helm control due to transphasic interference? I'd advise *against* that, sir."

"Does anyone have a damned telescope? Maybe I can find a viewport and—"

"Too much cloud cover," Calligaris interrupted. "No surface visibility from orbit."

"I was being facetious, Daphne, but thanks for stepping on my—"

"Contact! Drone Delta found the Rangers' prowler."

"Is the latinum on board?"

Calligaris checked her console. "Affirmative. Shipping crate confirmed intact. Transport enhancers are affixed and active."

Hadon chimed in, "We have a transporter lock on the latinum container."

"Energize!" Victory was close; Tazgül could almost taste it.

"Transport complete," Hadon said. "Engineer Krenz confirms the case is aboard, and the full payload is inside."

"Well done, people. Calligaris, instruct the drone to leave antipersonnel mines with proximity fuses near the prowler, then put it back in the hunt for the Rangers."

"Yes, sir."

"Any more updates from the drones?"

"None. But all four remain active."

"Good. Then it's just a matter of time."

Zeiss looked back at Tazgül. "Speaking of time, sir: General Kohgish's meeting with the starship broker is just hours away. Do you want to break orbit now to make our rendezvous with the general and come back later to check on the drones?"

Tazgül considered the suggestion. It wasn't entirely unreasonable. They and

Kohgish were on a tight schedule, and there was little they could do to affect the outcome of the battle currently underway on the planet's surface. But Tazgül had learned the hard way that bad things happened when people became overconfident, took their attention off critical matters before they were finished, and allowed their focus to become divided.

Tazgül reclined his command chair. "No. We don't leave before the job is done. Not until I confirm the Rangers are *dead*."

Zirat

A storm of green bolts hammered the clamshell above and behind Harper, showering him with hot sparks and metallic dust. For every shot he fired back at the pair of fleet-footed arachnoid drones skittering through the debris maze, they sent dozens screaming back at him.

I'm startin' to think this ain't a fair fight.

More pulses pounded the slablike rampart Harper was depending upon for cover. Lying low, he stole a look toward Seven's last position. He caught only a glimpse of her. She was pinned down, as he was, by the swiftly advancing drones.

"Kid! We can't stay here!"

"I know!" She popped up from cover to hector the drones with a flurry of blasts from her rifle, drawing both of the drones toward her. As they bombarded her position with an insane volley, she caught Harper's eye with frantic hand signals: COME TO ME. I HAVE A WAY OUT.

He gestured back: I WON'T MAKE IT THAT FAR.

She denied his refusal: I'LL COVER YOU. MOVE.

Before he could argue, she blindly lobbed a pair of her Gorn shock grenades over her cover into the maze. Each landed close enough to one of the drones that their blasts knocked the mechanoid horrors off their eight feet. The moment the monsters stumbled, Harper ran. Seven laid down a withering spray of rifle fire while he zigzagged as she had, darting from one piece of cover to the next until he reached her.

He collapsed beside her, gasping for breath. "What's your plan?"

She pointed at a low break in the rear wall of the clamshell, a hole in the ancient starship's hull that was exposed just enough for them to crawl into. Harper bent down and looked through the passage. It looked wide enough for them both to get through, but it was nearly four meters to the other side. "No way we clear that before they're on top of us."

"You go first. I'll hold them back."

"They'll shred you."

"They will try." She slapped his back and pointed into the passage. "Go."

She resumed shooting, so he slung his rifle across his back and scurried. Scrambling on elbows and knees, he scuttled through the ragged space, not looking back, all his focus on reaching the end. In a matter of seconds he emerged onto the other side, unslung his rifle, and from a prone position made a fast check of the area for signs of the other drones.

He looked back through the passage. Seven was already halfway through, her own rifle on her back. When she was close enough, he reached in, took her hand, and pulled her free.

Then one of the drones slammed into the other side of the clamshell and wedged its spiderlike, multi-eyed head into the passage's far opening—where a Gorn shock grenade, magnetically attached to the metal above the drone's head, blinked in readiness.

The grenade exploded.

A burst of fire laced with shards of metal and stone erupted from the passage's opening, while Seven and Harper stood on either side of it and looked for any debris that resembled the drone. Not seeing any familiar components in the smoldering aftermath, he shook his head. "I think we missed. But it's a good bet we made it angry."

Seven pointed toward a dense cluster of trees on a short hill. "The prowler's just over that rise." She started running, and Harper forced himself to keep up.

Blurs in the darkness followed them through the forest as they ran up and over the hilltop. From every direction came echoes of the chittering clanks of metallic legs scurrying over broken duranium. Harper wondered why the drones weren't firing, and then he realized his worst fear was likely coming true: he and Seven were being herded, like lambs to a slaughter.

The forest thinned on the other side of the hill, which Harper now saw was an ancient starship fuselage mostly smothered in dirt and overgrown with lichens, shrubberies, and trees. Resting at the base of the hill, at the end of a long, fresh scar cut into several kilometers of the landscape, was his prowler—or, at least, what remained of it. He and Seven jogged toward it, and this time he took the lead. "Can you see the cargo hatch?"

After a moment, Seven said, "Yes. It's been opened."

"No! The latinum—!"

"Is gone."

"This is *not* turning out to be our day." He paused at the bottom of the slope to tell Seven, "Use that boulder for cover while I grab the launcher."

Without waiting for her to acknowledge, he ran toward the prowler.

He heard Seven's voice: "HARP—"

An explosion turned his world into white light and crimson pain. He felt weightless for a moment, in spite of every nerve in his body being lit up in agony—and then gravity returned, and his momentarily airborne body crashed to the ground.

Burnt, bent, and broken, Harper lay in a heap, staring into an endless darkness, unable to speak through the frothy blood pooling in his mouth.

He felt an arm wrap around his shoulders. Someone sat him up, leaned him forward to drain the blood from his mouth. It took him a moment to remember where he was and who was with him. "Seven?"

"I'm here," she said, her voice quaking. "I'm so sorry. I thought you saw the mines. I tried to warn you, but—"

"S'okay, kid. Not your fault." He recalled poor Leniker Zehga and his own fateful encounter with an antipersonnel mine just a couple of weeks earlier, when the young Zakdorn had counted on Harper to look out for him, and he let out a bitter chuckle. "Call it Karma."

"I'm not calling it anything." She picked him up and scrambled while carrying his full weight away from the burning prowler to a nearby heap of debris. She set him down behind the mound of junk and propped him up in a sitting pose against a heavy chunk.

Harper gurgled through fresh blood and spit, "What're ya doing, kid?"

"I will come back for you."

"Leave me. Save yourself."

She cupped her hand behind his aching head and looked him in the eye. "We don't leave our people behind."

He smiled. "Spoken like a Ranger."

Seven stood and picked up a large, warped circle of something metallic that sparkled. "This contains chimerium. It will block the drones' sensors." She rolled it into place like a stone blocking the mouth of a sepulcher, and then Harper was alone in the dark.

He knew she couldn't hear him, but he still had to say it, for luck.

"Give 'em hell, kid."

Seven was an engine fueled by rage. Legs pumping, heart pounding, blood surging through her veins, she ran, her speed only increasing as she neared the top of the low hill. She willed her Borg nanoprobes into overdrive to repair tissue, enhance strength and agility, and suppress pain. *No more half measures. No more pulled punches.*

She heard her prey moving in the woods below, on the other side of the hilltop.

A running start downhill, then a daring leap through the shadows, and she landed on top of the arachnoid machine like a cannonball.

Momentum carried her over the top of it, and she let gravity help her. She took hold of one of its legs as she tumbled. With a fierce pull she flipped the drone over her, ripping out its leg and sending it past her to slam into the base of a tree.

The drone twitched and jerked against the tree trunk, then it started to right itself. Seven charged, using the severed leg and its fearsome talon as a spear.

The drone parried her first thrust with one leg and slashed a deep wound across her torso with another, exposing her body's layer of silver-and-black Borg-created biomechanical tissue and synthetic muscles. A third attack made Seven duck and roll to avoid being decapitated.

She had only just hit the ground but already the killing machine was above her, stabbing divots into the snowy ground with its talon-tipped limbs as Seven rolled, tucked, and used her improvised spear to swat away blows meant to impale her.

The drone's latest thrust left it with a limb stuck fast in the permafrost. It bent lower to get leverage to free itself—so Seven tucked her knees to her chest, put her feet against the drone's underside, and with an excruciating effort launched it backward, off of her.

It scrambled as it hit a patch of ice, lost its footing, and skidded backward.

A pivot, a stride, a jump, and a parkour bounce off a tree put Seven on the drone's back. With one thrust of its severed leg, she drove its own talon through its head. Sparks flew from the wound, and a black ichor that reeked of industrial chemicals burbled out moments later.

The forest echoed with the metallic clangor of approaching drones. Seven turned and seized the disruptor cannon mounted on the first drone's back. She kneeled, gave the gun a hard twist, and tore it free of its mount. Through the freshly wrought hole in the machine's shell, Seven extended the nanoprobe tubules of her left hand and released hundreds of nanoprobes into the drone. In seconds she usurped control of its tactical system and its gun's trigger.

In a flash, she understood that the drones were using a system called identify friend-or-foe, or IFF, to avoid targeting one another on the battlefield.

Dozens of meters away through the trees, she spied a second drone, charging straight toward her. She pointed the first drone's cannon at her new attacker and commanded it to fire. The weapon flared hot in her grip as it unleashed a furious barrage on the second drone, whose IFF—conflating Seven with drone one—caused it to hesitate in returning fire for a crucial tenth of a second. Which was all she needed to blast drone two into a heap of molten slag.

Beneath her, drone one shifted, its auxiliary systems kicking in to continue the fight.

She turned drone one's weapon on itself and kept firing until its disruptor cannon sputtered and went cold. Only then did she feel reasonably sure the machine was neutralized.

Two down, two to—

A talon burst out of her right flank, spraying blood and shredding the resilient fibers of her Borg-tissue layer. Using her body's durability against her, the third drone flung her into the air—and then, with a blindingly fast spinning maneuver, two of its legs swatted Seven as she fell. She heard some of her ribs crack as she was hit, and a few more snapped when she caromed off the corner of a derelict starship's metal husk and landed facedown in the snow.

Rage abandoned her, leaving only panic in its wake.

Where is my weapon?

Seven looked around but saw no sign of the drone leg she had used as a spear. It could have flown in any direction, she realized in dismay. But there was no time to search for it or draw the rifle still slung on her back: the drone that had just batted her a few dozen meters into the forest was already bearing down upon her. Her primal instincts took over.

Run!

Standing sent waves of pain through Seven's gut and up her spine. Nausea came in flashes of violet and sickly green as she ran, arms flailing. Bile pushed its way up her throat and made her fight against the urge to vomit.

Green pulses pulverized the trunks of trees on either side of her and made smoking craters of her footsteps. She heard the drone close behind her, bashing through trees it had felled, peppering her path ahead with disruptor shots—

A steely talon arced toward Seven's face. The fourth drone had been lying in ambush, waiting for its partner to chase her into its trap.

She let herself fall backward, twisting her body as gravity took her, and watched the fourth drone's deadly strike miss her face by millimeters. She landed on her back with one of her Stinger pistols drawn and fired a quick burst of five shots at drone four's thorax, only to see her counterattack bounce off without effect.

Drone four snap-kicked her with another limb and launched her through the air, toward a cluster of starship wrecks that jutted at peculiar angles from a vast span of treeless ground. When she landed and slid across a slick surface, she understood why the ships here stood strangely—they were all partially submerged in a frozen lake dusted with snow.

The two remaining drones charged out of the forest in pursuit.

Triggering an overload in her pulse pistol, Seven ducked low and fled in a crouch onto the frozen lake, skulking quickly between the noses and wingtips of a dozen drowned starships. She heard the ice crack and groan as the drones followed her, one on each of her flanks.

Ahead of her, a large section of starship fuselage with ragged gaps on either side revealed that she was almost out of cover and therefore running out of time. Beyond the large derelict there was nothing but open ice for hundreds of meters, until more wrecks thrust upward from the shallows along the lake's distant shore. She had to make a decision now.

The drones made it for her.

Drone three bounded over a bent wedge of hull behind Seven and leaped high into the air, its arc of descent aimed squarely at her. Drone four charged from Seven's left in a bid to cut off her sole path of retreat.

She sprinted toward the great open wound in the hull ahead of her. Drone four raced to cut her off. At the last second Seven threw herself into a slide on her hip, ducking under drone four's swinging talons as she glided into the gap—and lobbed her Stinger pistol, with its nearly-overloaded prefire chamber, backward into drone four's path.

The pistol exploded, and the blast wave threw Seven the rest of the way through the derelict ship and out into the empty middle of the lake, while the ice beneath drone four turned to slush and swallowed the machine in one frigid gulp.

Three down. One to go.

She stood and assessed her wounds. Numerous scorches as well as multiple lacerations, some of them serious, one of them possibly critical. Blood spilled in heavy pulses from the wound in her side, and a quick moment of internal reflection confirmed her nanoprobes were struggling to keep up with the damage the drones had inflicted.

Seven clenched her jaw to stifle a cry of agony as she unslung the rifle from her back. Every nuance of the movement aggravated the searing pain in her ravaged tissues, torqued joints, and fractured bones. With a calming breath, she set her hands into place on the weapon.

Creeping back toward the large derelict ship, she remained alert for any sign of the last drone. Was it tracking her? Setting another trap? Falling back to pick her off from a distance?

Whatever its intention, I must find it soon. While I can still fight back.

Stealing through the darkness, powdery snow muffling her steps, Seven made her way past the cluster of ships along the shoreline, back to solid ground, without a glimpse of the last drone. It had left her nothing to follow: no heat path, no unnecessary data signals. Like the predator on which it had been modeled, it was hunting with stealth and patience.

Where are you?

A crash like a hundred windows breaking spun Seven back toward the lake. Drone four punched through the ice along the shoreline and scrambled awkwardly onto dry land. Tendrils of charged plasma danced around the wide fracture in its thorax that had been caused by Seven's exploding pistol. She raised her rifle to target the open wound in its armor.

The drone fired first.

A green pulse hit Seven's upper chest and threw her backward.

Lying on her back in the snow, Seven's vision dimmed, and all she could think about was the burning pain in her torso and the paralysis that seemed to grip the rest of her body. Over and over she told her limbs to move, but none of them obeyed. Reaching out for her nanoprobes, she sensed there were still a few inside her that had not yet succumbed to the omicron particles that had just bombarded her, but they likely wouldn't remain functional much longer.

Her own body had become her enemy.

Fight! Get up and fight, damn you!

She forced her left hand to move one finger. It felt like knives of fire were being driven through her armpit and out her shoulder. If she'd had any air in her lungs, or been able to move her mouth, she would have shrieked like a child.

But her finger *had* moved. And if she could move her finger, maybe she could move her hand. And if her hand obeyed, why not her arm? After all, the only price to pay was horrific pain.

She marshaled all her strength for one last strike, knowing she might never get to use it. But she had watched these machines at work, and seeing how they hunted had told her something about the people who had made and programmed them. The creators of these horrors hadn't just wanted a machine that would neutralize Borg. They clearly had built a machine that would avenge them upon the Borg. They didn't just want the drones' victims to die— they had designed these things to make sure their victims *suffered.*

These were machines programmed by sadists.

And if sadists were nothing else . . . they were *predictable.*

The drone with the cracked thorax crept into position above Seven, as if inspecting its prey and claiming its right to deliver the death stroke. It scanned her. Nudged her.

It raised one taloned limb to finish her off.

Seven thrust her left hand into the drone's open wound crackling with plasma creepers, a knife-hand strike designed to extend her reach as deep inside the drone as possible.

And then she let loose every last nanoprobe she could spare.

Tell your masters your targets are all confirmed dead.

The damaged drone stumbled backward. Staggered. A few of its limbs buckled under it. Its dorsal cannon swiveled but seemed unable to find a target.

Battling through her body's countless agonies, Seven pushed herself up from the cold, hard ground. First to her knees. And then to her feet. Gingerly, she touched the blackened wound on her chest and marveled at how it had just barely missed her bandolier of Gorn grenades. She probed her exposed Borg biomechanoid tissue and thanked it for saving her life. Again.

Then she froze.

She didn't need enhanced Borg senses to hear the heavy, clanging steps behind her. Slowly, deliberately, one hand still on her chest, she turned to face the last drone.

It was a few dozen meters away. Many dozens of trees at irregular intervals and angles prevented it from taking a clean shot at Seven, as it had done lakeside.

She shifted her weight left. It moved with her. She shifted right. It did the same. When she took a step back, it took a step forward.

It's waiting for me to run.

Seven turned to show it her side, the narrowest profile possible. With her left hand covering the scorch on her chest, she extended her right arm, fist closed, and adopted the combat stance she had learned from the Hirogen hunter who years earlier had taught her the Norcadian martial art of *Tsunkatse*. She beckoned it with a repeated, slow curling of her fingers.

"Come and get me."

Suitably provoked, it charged. Gained speed with each stride, even as it slalomed between the trees, barreling directly toward Seven. Who didn't move at all.

She stood her ground. Calm. Centered. Ready.

It crashed through the last several trees in its way, snapping them like toothpicks.

And in the fraction of a second that its view of Seven was obstructed by the trees it was trampling, she detached her bandolier and flung it into the air, knowing that the grenade she had concealed beneath her hand had been armed.

The drone dashed directly into it as if it posed no danger.

The grenade exploded and triggered its half-dozen siblings in sympathetic detonation. The blast wave hurled Seven away from the fireball that shattered the drone into shrapnel and scrap, flattened every tree in a twenty-meter radius, and set ablaze every bit of flora on the blast zone's perimeter. Seven slammed against a thick-trunked tree that survived the shock wave and felt her left ulna and radius break on impact. Stunned, she dropped to the ground.

Smoking chunks of the drone fell from the sky and pattered down into the snow around her for several seconds while the post-explosion haze cleared.

Admiring her handiwork, Seven only belatedly discovered the hunk of burnt metal lodged in her gut. It perplexed her. *How odd. I don't remember feeling it happen.*

Bleeding, her consciousness hanging on by a metaphorical thread, she staggered over to the last drone, the one infected with her nanoprobes. It was so hard to hear them now. So hard to make herself heard. But she focused her mind. Pierced the silence.

Is it done?

The nanoprobe-possessed drone answered, *It is done.*

Your mission is over. Engage self-destruct.

Seven's nanoprobes inside the drone had told her the machine's self-destruct system was designed to prevent needless collateral damage in populated areas. It wasn't going to explode.

It was going to *implode.*

It took only a few seconds for the drone to destroy itself. Its internal systems turned against one another and reduced the once-formidable hunter to a smoldering pile of spare parts.

Alone in the forest, Seven stood and listened. All was quiet.

Her foes were vanquished. Her greater enemy was, she hoped, deceived.

Burnt, bone weary, and bleeding, Seven limped into the forest to go save Harper.

• • •

FSA Tactical Cruiser *Bolvangar*

Tazgül watched the sensor readouts at Calligaris's tactical station, because he had no other source of information on which he could rely. Comms remained useless, and ordinary sensors were still no use against Zirat's transphasic field and nearly omnipresent cloud cover.

Even thermal sensors are worthless from up here, he brooded. *All this tech and still we're as good as blind half the time. What's the point of it all?*

Urgent feedback tones and blinking indicators on the tactical console snapped him back into the moment. "What have we got?"

Calligaris quickly assessed the new intel as it came in. "Sensor feed from one of the drones. It shows two drones left, and only one life sign." More flashes on the display. "Correction, one drone left. And it's reporting the second of two confirmed kills."

Tazgül perked up at the rare delivery of good news. "So, both Rangers are dead?"

"Yes, sir. Drone Delta sent sensor logs documenting both kills."

Another blinking alert lit up on the tactical panel, but then it went dark, and a flood of machine-language gibberish flooded across an ancillary screen for a few seconds before going dark. Tazgül furrowed his brow at that sequence of events. "What now?"

It took the tactical officer a few seconds to sort through the chaotic influx of data. "Drone Delta suffered catastrophic damage in the battle, so it self-destructed. Looks like a standard security protocol, to prevent the enemy from capturing and analyzing the tech."

"Huh. Isn't that something?" Tazgül processed the mission's outcome with a rare sense of pride and accomplishment. "So, to recap: we recovered all the lost latinum, both Rangers have been eliminated, and all it cost us were four expendable machines?" He nodded and smiled. "Sounds like a damned good day's work to me. Well done, everybody."

Tazgül returned to his command chair and settled in for what he imagined was going to feel like a victory lap. He pressed a button on his chair's armrest to record a log entry. "Commander's log, supplemental. Operations on Zirat have been successful. Vital resources for our ongoing operation have been recovered from the Fenris Rangers, and the renegade asset Annika Hansen has been de-activated, with prejudice." He thumbed the switch to end his log entry and felt strangely optimistic. "Helm, set course for the rendezvous with General Kohgish—and make it maximum warp. We've got a big day ahead of us."

Zirat

Every step was an act of will overcoming inertia. Lashed by wind so cold it burned, Seven limped through the forest, seeking her previous footsteps to guide her back the way she had come. Her good foot made crisp new prints limned in fresh blood, while the leg she dragged cut a ragged, wavering line in the snow.

Flashes of the ravaged forest came and went between long stretches of pure darkness as her ocular implant fluctuated between working and failing. Tattered curtains of acrid smoke drifted between the trees.

The throbbing pain in her broken left arm made it feel large and clumsy. Unable to move it, she clutched it tenderly against her body to keep it as immobile as possible. Each lurching step she took sent new jolts of pain through her arm and coaxed fresh blood from the wound in her side, and more from around the hunk of metal in her abdomen. She couldn't tell if her other wounds were still bleeding; she was so cold now that her whole body felt numb, as if she were a disembodied soul floating through a nightmare.

More than once she shut her eyes and tried to listen for the nanoprobes within her bloodstream, for the comforting subconscious buzz of their presence . . . but all she found was crushing silence, and she started to fear the worst. *What if my nanoprobes don't recover?*

What if that part of me is gone?

Who would I be then?

Familiar patterns in the snow caught her eye. The circular patterns of someone working, moving pieces into place. She stopped. Pivoted to either side. And saw the makeshift camouflage she had laid around Harper. From what little she could see in the dark without her night vision, it seemed to be intact. Defying the pain it caused her, she hobbled quickly toward it.

Please be alive.

Without her Borg-enhanced strength, the sheets of duranium proved much heavier than she remembered from just a few hours earlier. With her one good hand she struggled to move the chimerium disk. As she had hoped, its shape proved helpful, and when she used her weight as leverage, the disk rolled slowly aside, revealing Harper huddled in the tiny shelter behind it. Seven crouched, and then she crawled awkwardly to his side.

Harper's eyes were closed, and his head was drooped toward his chest.

She touched his shoulder. "Harper?"

He cracked open one eye, to barely a squint. With what seemed like terrible effort he raised his head and turned it slightly toward Seven.

His voice was a dry rasp. "How'd you do?"

"I won."

"That's my girl."

A gentle patter of precipitation against the stacked pieces of metal above them developed into a soothing background of white noise.

Seven reached out and took Harper's hand. "I'm sorry."

"For what, kid?"

"For causing all this. All my plans. This is what they led to." The sting of her failures welled up inside her, and tears fell from her eyes. "We've lost the latinum. And your ship. And failed all those people who counted on us. On me."

He shushed her. "Stop. Not your fault."

"But I—"

He stopped her by raising his free hand. "Quiet. I ain't got much breath left." He reached inside his jacket and fished through the inside pockets. "Got somethin' that belongs to you." His hand emerged, holding something. He pressed it into Seven's open palm. Something compact, flat, stiff, and bound in synthetic animal hide.

She looked down. Opened the leathery fold.

Inside it was a Fenris Rangers badge. With her name on it.

Beside it, a Rangers calling-card transceiver chip.

Harper cracked a bloodied grin. "I was gonna give it to ya on Freecloud, after the mission. But like I say—"

"No plan survives contact with the enemy."

"You got it."

She tried to push the badge back into Harper's hand. "I don't deserve this."

"The hell you don't."

"But all this? I failed so many—"

"We all fail. You'll fail again. But I know you'll get back up. You got more fire in you than a supernova. You're what a Ranger should be. Smart. Tough. Fair. And best of all? You actually give a damn."

There was a smile on Harper's face but tears in his eyes.

"Give 'em hell, kid."

Then his eyes turned empty, and the strength left his hand.

Something inside Seven stirred, and when she spoke, her voice was like that of a frightened child. "Harper? . . . Harper?"

In her voice she heard an echo of her past. Dark memories flashed through her mind.

Borg drones boarding her parents' ship, the Raven *. . . her father screaming her name as the Borg dragged him away . . . and all young Annika could do was cower and hide. . . .*

Her voice, that same terrified whimper: "Papa?"

Sleet and rain drizzled through the gaps in the cover above Seven's head, slowly drenching her while she huddled beside Harper and wrapped her arms around him, even though he had no more warmth to offer her.

There was nothing more to be done. Her strength was gone, and even if her nanoprobes hadn't been blasted into dormancy, she didn't have access to any of the medical technology she would have needed to use the nanoprobes to revive him. It was over.

Grief welled up from somewhere deep inside her, an ocean of sorrow she couldn't hold back. She let herself sob, then wail, then scream in fury . . . but none of it could fill the aching emptiness Harper's death left within her. No matter how long she let herself cry and rage, she couldn't forget that her friend was gone, forever.

22

Zirat

Ellory had been five light-years out from Freecloud when her prowler's comm picked up Harper's distress signal. A quick course correction had been sufficient to help her get a lock on the beacon, which her sensors had said was on the surface of Zirat, the starship graveyard.

As soon as she had confirmed the distress signal she had called it in. Fenris was sending reinforcements, but they were hours away at best, and there was no way of knowing how long Seven and Harper had been in trouble. Every second mattered now.

She kept her prowler in a hard dive through the dense storm cells that covered the planet's surface. Her lock on the mayday beacon remained strong and clear, even as wild twists of violet lightning bent around her ship while dancing from cloud to cloud.

Hang on, guys. I'm almost there.

Her prowler shot free of the storm head into the wild downpour beneath it. Even free of the clouds, visibility was near zero. Dawn was many hours away on this slow-turning rock, and the persistent storm cover made its night side as dark as a grave. But the real hazard was the cyclone-level wind and the inescapable freezing rain, which even now had started to glaze the prowler's fuselage and canopy with ice.

Unassisted landing is definitely out. Instruments, it is.

Ellory engaged the holographic terrain wireframe overlays in her HUD and set her bird's sensors for a wide range of proximity alerts. There were hills, tree clusters, lakes with dangerously thin ice coverings, and more starship wrecks than she could count. She knew that finding a place to land without damaging her prowler in the process might prove challenging.

Then she confirmed the distress beacon was stationary and less than ten kilometers ahead of her, and she no longer cared about what might be in her way. She pushed her ship's thrusters to full burn and reached the site in a matter of seconds rather than minutes.

As she had expected, the irregular spacing of trees in the area near the beacon, as well as the presence of several derelict ship hulls and great swaths of swirling mist roaming the surface like ghosts, had left her without a safe place to land.

Let's make a landing pad.

Ellory raised the tail of her prowler until its nose was pointed almost straight at the surface. She raised her shields, set them for double-front, and then she rotated her ship slowly around a fixed central point while using its particle cannon to vaporize all the trees and melt the defenseless metal debris into discrete pools like a scattering of silver mirrors.

That'll do.

She leveled the prowler and guided it down to a feather-soft landing. As soon as the struts touched the surface, she released the cockpit's canopy, grabbed her field medkit, a palm light, and her scanner, and scrambled out of the ship and down the ladder.

Once down, she switched on the palm light and moved quickly away from the ship. The ground was searing hot there, having been swept bare by her particle cannon and left steaming from the boiled permafrost beneath the topsoil.

Where are you, guys?

Ellory kept one eye on her hand scanner and the other on the path ahead, which was lit by the broad but still intense white beam cast by her palm light. Ahead she saw signs of recent battle. Damaged trees. Scorched patches of ground. Banshee winds howled as she pushed ahead.

And then she saw blood in the snow.

She sprinted to it. A footprint about the same size as Seven's. Traced in crimson. Ellory cast her palm light upon it and followed the trail to a ramshackle lean-to of ship debris that had been arranged to look random. *Industrial camouflage—a skill one might expect in an ex-Borg.*

Circling around it, she found its entryway wide-open. "Seven? Kee?"

Her palm light's beam found Seven and Harper, and Ellory gasped.

Seven and Harper sat huddled together beneath their meager cover. She was shivering violently. Her face was pale almost to a deathly gray, and her blonde hair was stringy, wet, filthy, and matted to her head, some of it crusted with ice and flecks of sleet. Her fingertips, clutched so tightly around Harper, were blackened from frostbite, and so were her lips. An ugly wound in her side was wet with fresh blood, as was her tunic around a chunk of metal wedged in her gut.

It was clear to Ellory that Harper had been dead for hours. His face was coated in ice from the rain and bitter wind, but beneath his frozen mask he wore a serene expression.

Ellory clambered inside the lean-to and checked Seven's vital signs with her scanner. "Seven? It's Ell. Can you hear me?" Seven didn't respond, not even to look at Ellory, so the young Trill woman continued her scan. "Seven? You're hypothermic. You've got frostbite on your extremities, and you've lost a *lot* of blood. We gotta get you outta here."

Quaking from her plunging body temperature, Seven finally looked at Ellory. Her voice vibrated with her tremors, but her resolve was unmistakable. "We. Bring. Harper."

"Damn right we bring Harper."

Ellory fumbled through the medkit for the right ampoule to load into the hypospray. Once she had it, she put the device to Seven's throat and delivered the injection. "That'll bring your core temperature back up at a safe rate and stop your bleeding until I can get you to a hospital. Can you walk?" Seven shook her head no. "No worries. Get your arm across my shoulders. I'll put you in the prowler, and then I'll go back for Harper. Okay?" Seven nodded.

She was about to stand when Seven rasped, "Thank you . . . for . . . finding me."

Ellory couldn't hold back her tears of relief and sorrow as she gently kissed Seven's brow, then touched her own forehead to Seven's. "Anytime. *Every* time. I promise."

A mad gust of wind slammed into them, and Ellory knew it was time to go. She helped Seven out of the lean-to, and once they were clear of it they both stood. Watching Seven limp while cradling a broken arm above the metal debris in her abdomen filled Ellory with anger, but also a need to protect. "Easy steps, love. It's about thirty meters straight ahead to my prowler. Just put one foot—"

Ahead of the duo, at the edge of the palm light's effective range of illumination, something small, cylindrical, and metallic arced down out of the night, clinked as it bounced off the hard ground, and rolled beneath Ellory's prowler.

Then it exploded.

23

Zirat

The blast consumed Ellory's prowler in one huge fireball and flung white-hot shrapnel in all directions. Ellory pulled Seven to the ground and draped herself around her as a living shield. Chunks of hot metal rained down upon them. Several pieces bounced off Ellory's jacket. Thanks to its durable blend of ablative and antiballistic fibers, it was like light armor.

After a few seconds, Ellory tried to pull Seven back toward the lean-to. It wouldn't offer any real hard cover, but sometimes concealment was the best one could get.

They had barely turned around when a disruptor shot—from a Romulan-made rifle, if Ellory's hearing could be trusted despite her post-explosion tinnitus—cut a fiery streak into the ground in front of their feet. The meaning of the warning shot was clear: *Freeze.*

Ellory had no patience left for this. "Whoever you are? You've made your point. Show yourself and tell us what you want."

She heard movement and turned, aiming her palm light reflexively. On a low slope just a dozen meters away—much closer than she had expected—a Romulan man dressed in gray-and-white winter camouflage and dark goggles stood from his concealed position, his rifle squarely trained upon her and Seven. He shouted back, "I want your friend there. And her partner."

"You mean Harper?"

"That's the one."

Seven found her voice. "You're too late. He's dead, and the latinum's gone."

The Romulan seemed confused by her response. "Excuse me?"

"Harper is dead."

"I caught that."

"And the latinum is gone."

"So what?"

Ellory was sure she must have misheard the man. "You aren't here for the latinum?"

"You mean the general's war chest? No, that was a fool's errand. But the bounty on your friends? It pays out whether they're dead or alive."

Nothing but open ground around us, Ellory realized. *And this guy has clean sight lines and the high-ground advantage. If we try to run, we're as good as dead. Have to stall.*

"You got a name?"

"Veris of Haakona." He seemed quite proud of himself, as Romulans often did. "I assume you've heard of me."

Seven and Ellory shared a look, and then they both shook their heads in denial. "Nope," Ellory said. "Can't say I have."

Seven added, "Your name is not familiar to me. But I am new to this region of space, so that is to be expected."

"Regardless, I still intend to kill you. You're far too dangerous to try to take alive."

"You flatter me."

Ellory tried to bargain. "Whatever the bounty is on these two, the Fenris Rangers will pay you *double* for their safe return."

The Romulan laughed. A lot. Long, loud, derisive howls. "Are you serious? The Rangers? Pay a double ransom for *them*? With what? They just lost all their latinum to Tazgül and his Antican puppet. The Rangers are *bankrupt!*"

Ellory grumbled to Seven, "Just our luck: we get the galaxy's only smart bounty hunter."

Veris collected himself, and then he braced his rifle against his shoulder and took aim. "Well, ladies, this has been most entertaining. I almost regret having to kill you both."

Ellory reflexively hugged Seven to her, and Seven reciprocated.

Then came the shot—not of Veris's disruptor, but of a compression phaser rifle, which landed a pulse of orange energy in the ground between Veris's feet.

From the other side of the hilltop a man called out, "Veris of Haakona!

Drop your weapon!" Moments later a tall human in a Starfleet lieutenant commander's uniform appeared from out of the darkness, his compression phaser rifle braced for battle and aimed at Veris, who stubbornly seemed unwilling to relinquish his own weapon.

Then a dark-haired human woman of average height, attired in a Starfleet lieutenant's uniform, manifested from the shadows, on the other side of the bounty hunter. She held a Starfleet pistol phaser, aimed with a rock-steady hand at Veris's head.

"You have lovely hair," the human woman said to Veris. "It'd be a shame if I had to blast it clean off your skull. Drop. Your. Weapon. *Now.*"

This time Veris slowly removed his finger from his rifle's firing stud, took his steadying hand off the weapon, and with a slow, careful motion tossed the disruptor rifle into the snow.

The lieutenant commander with the rifle shouted, "Hands above your head!"

Veris complied but continued to act nonchalant. "Out of your jurisdiction, aren't you?"

The female lieutenant slapped a magnetic manacle onto one of Veris's wrists and pulled it down behind his back. "We hadn't noticed. Give me your other hand, or I'll break this one."

Again the Romulan did as he was told. As soon as the lieutenant had him fully manacled, the lieutenant commander asked, "You got him, Benson?"

"Yeah, I've got him. And *Dauntless* has his ship. We're all clear."

The lieutenant commander whistled and waved to someone else in the forest below. Moments later, more Starfleet personnel emerged from the misty darkness, all of them jogging toward Seven and Ellory. Unlike their compatriots up on the hill, none of these people were armed. They all wore uniforms with blue accent colors, which Ellory remembered was Starfleet's current color for medical and scientific personnel, and came bearing field medkits much better equipped than the one she had brought from her prowler.

They all swarmed around Ellory and Seven, wrapping them in self-warming thermal blankets, giving them both hyposprays to protect them from the cold, and scanning them both with those amazing state-of-the-art Starfleet medical tricorders.

A tall Andorian man in a red-accented command division uniform approached her and Seven. He offered Ellory his open hand. "I'm Lieutenant Commander Tysess, first officer, *Starship Dauntless.*"

She shook his hand. "Fenris Ranger Ellory Kayd."

"Good to meet you, Ranger Kayd." He directed his next remarks to Seven. "Seven? You've been critically wounded. You need immediate medical attention. Our sickbay and medical team stand ready to help in any way we can. May we have your permission to beam you up and provide emergency medical care?"

Seven nodded weakly. "Please."

"Very good." He tapped his combadge. "Tysess to *Dauntless.*"

"This is Dauntless,*"* answered a woman with a patrician voice. *"Go ahead, Commander."*

"Admiral, we found her. Three to beam directly to sickbay."

Ellory gently took hold of Tysess's forearm. "Four." She nodded toward the lean-to. "Ranger Harper comes with us."

Tysess nodded. "I understand. . . . Correction, *Dauntless.* Three living subjects and one body to beam directly to sickbay, on my signal."

"Acknowledged. Standing by for transport."

A pair of medical technicians retrieved Harper's body, sealed it inside a Starfleet standard-issue body bag, and rested him gently at Seven and Ellory's feet. Then the medtechs withdrew to a safe distance, to avoid getting accidentally caught up in the transporter field.

Tysess said in a clear voice, *"Dauntless*: Energize."

Ellory tensed as the restrictive embrace of the transporter's annular confinement beam took hold of her in the instant before dematerialization.

I have to admit, this isn't how I thought this day would go. At all.

U.S.S. Dauntless NCC-80816 – Thirty Seconds Earlier

Awaiting the arrival of Seven and the return of the away team, Janeway paced between the rows of biobeds in sickbay. She tried not to fear the worst about Seven's condition, but how could she not? Ever since Seven's liberation from the Collective, she had never been away from Janeway for so long without supervision.

Self-awareness kicked in. *Listen to yourself. You're acting like a nervous parent with empty-nest syndrome. You can't treat Seven like a willful child. She's an adult with her own life.*

An adult. Chronologically, that was true. Biologically, Seven was thirty-two years old, though she appeared younger thanks to the regenerative properties of her Borg nanoprobes. But did her age accurately represent her degree of socialization? She had been robbed of so many years of her life as a Borg drone. So many aspects of social development that her new peers took for granted likely remained alien to Seven.

In so many ways, she's still adapting to her human identity, still navigating the uncharted waters that separate a person's adolescent identity from that of their fully adult self. How could I have let her leave at such a crucial juncture?

Janeway paused her self-recriminations when she heard the start of an incoming transporter signal, like a faint hum of music in the air. She stepped to one side of the room, clearing the middle for the arriving group. Three standing figures sparkled into existence and turned opaque as they materialized, with a fourth form wrapped in a cadaver pouch at their feet.

On the right was Lieutenant Commander Tysess. The slender Andorian towered over the two women beside him.

On the left was an attractive, dark-haired Trill woman in her early thirties, wearing the uniform jacket of the Fenris Rangers. She was holding Seven upright, bearing most of Seven's weight on her left side, with Seven's right arm draped across her shoulders.

And Seven—the sight of her filled Janeway's eyes with tears of empathy and sorrow. She was slashed, burnt, and bloody. The shape of her left arm betrayed its savage breaks. Frostbite had cracked and blackened her lips, and her once lustrous golden hair had become a matted mess of filthy ice. An ugly hunk of scorched metal was lodged deep inside her abdomen, and she reeked of wet dirt, industrial chemicals, sweat, and blood.

Pity swelled inside Janeway until she couldn't contain her dismay. "My God, Seven."

Seven reacted to Janeway's voice, detaching herself from the other Ranger and all but falling into Janeway's comforting, quasi-maternal embrace. As Seven pressed her face against Janeway's shoulder, Janeway realized Seven was quietly crying.

Janeway looked at Tysess. "Let's get her on a biobed."

Tysess helped Janeway guide Seven to a nearby biobed, which he shifted to a nearly vertical position behind her. With his help, Janeway eased Seven back against the cushioned mattress, and then Tysess slowly returned the biobed to its normal, near-level orientation. As the readouts on the panel above the biobed switched on, Tysess tapped his combadge. "Tysess to Doctor Noum. You're needed in sickbay, stat."

The ship's chief medical officer responded over the comm, *"Already on my way."*

Janeway stood to the left of Seven's bed, and the Trill woman stood on the right. The vital signs on the readout above Seven fluctuated wildly and then started to sink, something Janeway knew from bitter experience was not a good sign. She clasped Seven's left hand in both of hers. "Seven? Are you in much pain?"

Seven deadpanned, "I am experiencing moderate discomfort."

Translation: "I'm in agony. Don't ask stupid questions."

Tysess summoned a pair of medical technicians and pointed at the body bag on the floor. "Take Ranger Harper's remains to the ship's morgue." Noting a sharp look from the Trill woman, he added, "Make sure he is accorded all the honors appropriate to an officer killed in action."

The technicians acknowledged the order quietly, transferred the bagged body onto an antigrav stretcher, and carried it out of sickbay without another word.

On the biobed, Seven slipped in and out of consciousness. Janeway noted the Trill woman's obvious dismay and alarm, and realized they had not been introduced. She offered the younger woman her hand in greeting. "Admiral Kathryn Janeway."

She shook Janeway's hand. "Ranger Ellory Kayd."

"Welcome aboard the *Dauntless,* Ranger Kayd."

"Thank you, Admiral. We're lucky you came when you did." Kayd turned a worried look at Seven. "She's told me a bit about you. You mean the world to her."

"Seven is quite dear to me, as well. Are you and Seven close?"

The question left Kayd searching for words that proved elusive. "Um . . . well, yes . . . I'm . . . that is to say, we . . . um . . . we haven't exactly said what—"

Seven, abruptly half-awake, clasped Kayd's hand. "We are . . . *together.*"

Kayd's sadness was dispelled by a broad smile. Seeing how they looked at each other, Janeway felt the profound bond between them, like an electric potential in the air. The blush of new love.

Overjoyed for Seven, and feeling a bit less guilty now that she knew Seven wasn't completely alone in a strange and hostile galaxy, Janeway smiled. "I understand."

The main doors of sickbay parted open, and Doctor Noum rushed in. The stout Tellarite surgeon hurried to Seven's bedside. "Apologies, Admiral. I came as soon as I could."

Kayd asked, "How bad is she hurt, Doc?"

"Pretty bad. Major wounds and internal injuries." He tapped his combadge. "Nurse Chong! Prep OR one for surgery, stat! We're on our way now."

"Acknowledged," a woman answered, even as Noum activated the antigrav function beneath the biobed platform and detached it from its base.

Noum set his hand on Seven's shoulder. "Don't worry about a thing. You're in good hands, here. Give us a couple hours, you'll be good as new. I promise."

Seven nodded her understanding.

Kayd leaned down and shared a tearful kiss for luck with Seven, just before Noum whisked her away, guiding the antigrav biobed platform toward the nearby surgical suites.

Then Janeway and Kayd were left standing beside each other, staring at the doors to the surgery suites as they drifted closed. The Ranger wore her self-consciousness with quiet good humor. "Should I stay here? Or maybe there's a waiting room with six-month-old holomags?"

Janeway put on her most ingratiating manner. "I think we can do better than that." She turned to face Tysess. "Commander, would you please arrange accommodations for the Rangers? One of our diplomatic staterooms, perhaps?"

"Right away, Admiral." The Andorian looked at Kayd and gestured toward the door. "If you'd please follow me, Ranger Kayd."

Kayd palmed a tear from the corner of one eye, and then she gave Janeway a bittersweet smile. "Thank you, Admiral."

"You're more than welcome."

Tysess led Kayd out of sickbay, and Janeway stood alone once more.

Not the homecoming I wanted for my prodigal daughter.

But at least she's finally home.

24

Seven was only half-awake, but she was aware enough to detect the antiseptic, filtered air of a Starfleet sickbay recovery ward. After four years of living aboard the *Starship Voyager*, much of it spent socializing with the Doctor, it was a scent she knew all too well: cool and aggressively devoid of anything remotely organic in odor.

She remained still as she took stock of her body's cues. No restraints on her limbs or torso. The worst of her pain was gone, replaced by a dull, bearable full-body soreness. The cool touch of bedsheets on her skin told her she was wearing only undergarments. Her pulse was normal, and when she reached out with her mind to contact her body's nanoprobes, she caught just the faintest whisper of a reply. There were at least a few left intact in her blood.

Then she heard the soft cadence of another person's breathing, less than a meter from her. By the second round of inhalation and exhalation, she recognized whose it was.

Slowly, Seven opened one eye.

Seated beside her recovery bed was Janeway, tapping and scrolling through something on her padd. When the admiral noted Seven's one-eyed stare, she beamed with joy and stood to be next to Seven. "Welcome back to the land of the living."

When Seven spoke, she was surprised by the dryness of her own voice. "Thank you." She coughed to clear her throat. It helped, but not much. "Am I still on *Dauntless*?"

"Yes." Janeway set her padd in an open space on the side of Seven's bed. "How do you feel?"

"My physical injuries have been expertly remedied, thanks to Doctor Noum." She sat up and looked around. "Where is Ellory?"

"Ranger Kayd is waiting for you down the corridor, in the diplomatic suite. But I was hoping you and I could speak privately for a moment."

"Of course."

"I want to give you some information about the man you met as Arastoo Mardani."

"You mean the FSA traitor, Erol Tazgül."

"Precisely." Janeway picked up the padd, loaded a new document, and handed it to Seven, apparently so she could follow along as Janeway walked her through its contents. "Starfleet Intelligence acquired an unredacted copy of Tazgül's service dossier. As you can see, he was involved in numerous covert foreign operations over the course of nearly two decades."

Paging swiftly through the dossier, Seven was aghast. It read like a demon's résumé. "According to this, he destabilized at least three alien governments and sabotaged our enemies' civilian infrastructure, inflicting hundreds of thousands of fatalities as collateral damage."

Janeway gestured at the padd. "Skip ahead to the part of his service after he was promoted out of field ops."

Seven jumped to that section of the dossier. "He served in counterintelligence."

"But not just any part of it. He was an interrogator. One who specialized in breaking foreign spies. In turning them into double agents against their own people."

"I see. He is an extremely dangerous person."

"And a criminal." She reached over the top of the padd and clicked a link that took Seven to a classified set of files from the Federation Department of Justice. "Before he went rogue, he embezzled vast sums of Federation credits and laundered Ferengi latinum, and used it to set himself up in business as an arms dealer and political fixer."

It was a staggering and brazen list of achievements. Seven was both appalled and impressed. "How did the Federation fail to detect his crimes when they occurred?"

"He concealed many of his transactions by processing them through third parties—"

"Middlemen," Seven interrupted, starting to understand.

"Yes. His middlemen did his dirty work. But his best trick was faking his own death."

Seven raised her eyebrows in genuine surprise. "How long did that ruse last?"

"Long enough for him to escape with all the money he stole."

Picking up the narrative, Seven felt confident she had heard this before. "Let me guess: He went solo. Started making big sales on the black market. Bided his time."

"Bingo. Now, because the Federation and its neighbors are moving everything they have to help organize the evacuation of Romulus and Remus—"

"It has left a power vacuum. One that Tazgül is exploiting by propping up a warlord and aspiring dictator, General Kohgish."

Janeway nodded. "No doubt, once this general's position in the Qiris sector is mostly secured, he'll become Tazgül's chief buyer of starships, weaponry, and munitions."

Seven sat forward and felt strength returning to all her limbs. "Kohgish is even more ambitious than you realize. He is hoarding food, medicine, water, construction supplies—everything he can get to create a complete stranglehold on the Qiris sector's economy."

"Delightful." Janeway took back the padd and tapped at its screen as she continued. "The FSA was watching Tazgül for quite some time, but they lost track of him. Now they're scrambling to figure out what his next move will be."

"I might be able to help with that." Pangs of hunger gnawed through Seven's gut. "Tazgül attacked us on Zirat to recover a shipment of . . . *confiscated* latinum. It is my understanding that he plans to deliver most or possibly all of it to General Kohgish—if he hasn't already." She looked around for the ship's chrono. "How long was I unconscious?"

"Just over two hours."

"Then there is still time to stop them. Ellory uncovered proof that Kohgish plans to use the latinum to acquire a new, more powerful warship. One that will make him all but impossible to remove from power once he has it. We must find their rendezvous and stop that transaction."

"Easier said than done, Seven."

Seven got up from the biobed. Her first step was off-kilter, but she quickly found her balance. She detached a few small sensors from her fingertips and temples. Deprived of input, the biobed's readout flatlined with a shrill whine.

Janeway observed Seven with mounting annoyance. "What are you doing?"

"Going after Kohgish."

"You're in no condition to go anywhere."

"I will be the judge of that."

"And how do you expect to find this secret rendezvous? You have no ship."

"I don't suppose—"

"We're not loaning you a runabout. Not even a shuttle."

"I was going to ask for the Romulan bounty hunter's ship."

Janeway looked shocked. "Are you serious? You want us to just let you fly away in a custom-refit, military-grade Romulan harrier?"

"Yes."

"Perhaps Doctor Noum should run another set of scans on your brain."

As if on cue, the doors to the recovery ward slid open, and Doctor Noum ran in. "What's happening? Why did her—" He halted when he saw Seven conscious and standing. With an aggrieved wrinkling of his snout, he said to her, "You should be in bed."

"I have places to be."

"Is that so?" Noum picked up a medical tricorder from a nearby table. He switched it on as he moved to stand in front Seven. "Let's see how you're doing first, shall we?"

As the surgeon performed his exam, Seven said to Janeway, "Give me one good reason you will not let us borrow the harrier."

"For starters, Starfleet wants a long look at it."

"I promise I will give it back when I am done."

"Well, maybe you shouldn't be doing what you plan to do."

Seven bristled. "What are you saying?"

"I think you should stop working with the Fenris Rangers."

Anger bloomed inside Seven, and she feared that if she didn't find it an outlet, she might do something regrettable. She started to search the room. "Where are my clothes?"

Doctor Noum pointed at a closet door on the bulkhead next to her recovery bed. "In there. Everything except your weapons. Security took those."

"Of course they did." She opened the closet door with a gentle push that released it from its magnetic clamp. As promised, her clothes were inside. They were bloodstained, singed, and torn. She dressed as quickly as she was able without falling over her own feet.

Her urgency perplexed Janeway. "Wouldn't you prefer some new clothes?"

"I would not."

Janeway sounded desperate. "Seven, please. This is ridiculous."

"Not to me."

"Why are you suddenly so attached to a bunch of outlaws?"

Seven glared at Janeway while pulling on a filthy, bloodied shirt. "Do not believe the Federation's propaganda. The Rangers are a legitimate law-enforcement agency."

"I disagree. Their legitimacy came from the agreements they signed with the governments of several worlds in the Qiris sector. But those governments no longer exist. Some collapsed into anarchy. Others were replaced by entities that have no ties with the Rangers. That means the Fenris Rangers are acting as an armed law-enforcement agency without any civilian oversight, and no accountability to anyone but themselves. There's a word for that: *vigilantes*."

Mostly dressed in her battle-ruined outfit, Seven pulled on her boots one at a time. "Call us whatever you like. At least we're still there."

Janeway turned defensive. "Meaning what?"

"The moment the Romulans cried for help, the Federation abandoned the people of the Qiris sector. Took your Starfleet patrols, your NGOs, and all the industrial and medical supplies you'd given the colonists on worlds like Soroya IV, and you moved it all to Romulus without so much as a farewell. And in the process, you left *millions* of innocent people to die at the hands of monsters like Kohgish."

She fastened her boots and then she reached into the closet for the last item: her Fenris Rangers jacket. She put it on as she continued, "For millions of vulnerable civilians in the Qiris sector, we're the only protection they have left. So if you, Starfleet, or the Federation don't *approve* of the Rangers? I really don't give a shit."

"I see they've taught you some colorful new vocabulary."

For better or worse, Noum chose that moment to intrude on their argument. "Well, the good news, Ranger Seven, is that your injuries have healed perfectly. You're welcome, by the way. Expect to be sore for a few days to a week. That's normal after the body endures something as traumatic as surgery, to say nothing of what you endured *before* surgery. And, because I know you're probably wondering, your Borg nanoprobes took a beating. They will regenerate, but it's going to take a few months, so if I were you, I'd rest for a while. Because for the next few days, like it or not, you're pretty much 'only human,' if you take my meaning."

Seven kept her angry stare on Janeway as she said, "Thank you, Doctor. I shall take your counsel under advisement."

"What more could I ask? Take care, and remember to hydrate." Sensing it was past time for him to extricate himself, he headed for the exit in quick strides and abandoned the medical tricorder by lobbing it onto a biobed on his way out the door.

Fuming, Seven stepped forward specifically so she could loom tall over Janeway and glower down at her. "If there's nothing else, Admiral?"

Equally resolute and just as angry, Janeway held her ground. "Dismissed."

Seven stepped around her and walked out of sickbay. She wanted to steal a look back at Janeway as she left . . . but she didn't permit herself that solace.

I made my choice; she made hers.

Now we live with the consequences.

Mercenary Frigate *Eris*

The small warship's shuttlebay was abuzz with activity. It looked to Tazgül as if half of Kohgish's crew had come to see him reclaim his war chest. Most of them were Anticans, but at least a handful of Kohgish's crew hailed from other species. Tazgül had never bothered to learn any of their names, because none of them were important enough to merit his attention. The only reason he knew Kohgish's name was that he might need to use the fool as a scapegoat someday.

The general was down on one knee beside the open shipping crate, obsessively counting each brick of latinum. At random intervals he would pull a brick out and subject it to a verification scan. He had immersed himself in this tedium nearly ten minutes earlier, and he showed no sign of tiring—at least, not yet.

"I assure you, General. It's all there."

"So you say. I've learned to trust my own counsel. And my own arithmetic."

"You have less than four hours until Qulla arrives to finish the sale of that battleship. Do you plan to be sitting here counting when he arrives?"

"No, I'll be finished well before then. But I intend to have exactly the agreed-upon sum on hand when Qulla arrives—that much and not one strip of latinum more."

Tazgül considered the fortune sitting in front of them and imagined all the ways that day's business could go wrong. One scenario in particular nagged at him. "I'm not happy about you conducting this transaction in cash, General."

"Nor am I, Mister Mardani. But fate has left us no other recourse. We don't have time to deposit our funds in a Ferengi commercial bank and get back to the rendezvous before the Talarians arrive." Kohgish paused his counting and looked up at Tazgül. "Pray tell—where are *you* going to be?"

"Just a few seconds away at high warp."

"Thank you. I appreciate your support."

Tazgül gritted his teeth while purging the sarcasm from his reply. "It's less support than insurance, General. After the string of mishaps that led us to this moment, I have no intention of seeing you bungle the most important step of our plan so far."

The Antican bared his fangs, and the fur on the back of his neck stood up. "Are you implying I lack the business acumen to simply hand Qulla a crate full of latinum?"

"Implying? No. I'm stating it outright. Sending you to that meeting with the purchase price in latinum is tantamount to sending Qulla a printed invitation to rob you. Which is why you're going to put a force field around the crate—so that sneaky bastard doesn't beam it out from under you before handing over the command codes to your new battleship."

Still sulking, Kohgish cooled his temper a few degrees. "A sensible precaution."

"Yes, I know. We're just a few hours away from becoming the masters of this sector, and richer than either of us ever dared to imagine . . . as long as you don't screw this up."

U.S.S. *Dauntless* NCC-80816

Ellory watched Seven pace in front of the suite's long row of arched viewports, outside which starlight slipped around the *Dauntless*, bent into gentle arcs by its warp field. Seven had been agitated from the moment she walked in, minutes earlier, and had only gotten angrier since then.

"Janeway's stubbornness can be maddening! She won't even *consider* that my opinion might be just as valid as her own."

"I get it," Ellory said, trying to be the voice of reason. "My mom drives me crazy, too."

Seven stopped and trained a harsh stare at Ellory. "Janeway is *not* my mother."

"Could've fooled me. But look—forget that. She said we're guests, not prisoners. There's no guard on our door, and it isn't locked. So why won't she let us use the subspace comm to contact the Rangers?"

The ex-Borg's mood shifted from furious to quietly seething. "If you ask her, she will conjure some arcane regulation. Operational security, for instance. But I think the truth is . . . she doesn't trust me anymore."

"If that were true, she'd have deactivated all the companels in the suite. But they're all up and running. The only function we can't access—"

"Is subspace comms."

"Right. Which is a bitch, because we're running out of time to stop Kohgish's deal. If we could just get word to the inbound Ranger squadron, they might still have time to reach Kohgish and shut him down *before* he gets his hands on a battleship."

Seven looked away from Ellory, out one of the viewports. "Unfortunately, that is no longer an option."

"Are you sure?"

"The admiral made her wishes explicitly clear."

Ellory shrugged. "So what?"

"Excuse me?"

"You heard me. Who cares what Janeway wants? We have our own mission." She pressed her left hand against the cool, smooth, glassy surface of a bulkhead-mounted companel. "You spent four years serving on a Starfleet ship. You must know some way to bypass the lockout."

"Theoretically, yes."

"Then do it, already! Let's call in the cavalry while it can still make a difference."

Seven looked torn between her will to action and her Borg-induced desire to obey. "I cannot repay Admiral Janeway's hospitality with betrayal."

Passivity was a quality Ellory hadn't seen in Seven before now, and it troubled her. *We've only just met. There's still so much I don't know about her.*

Ellory collected herself. "No offense, Seven, but why are you breaking your back to show Janeway this much courtesy when she clearly won't do the same for you?"

"You don't understand how much she and the crew of *Voyager* did for me." Seven returned from the viewport to stand beside Ellory at the deactivated companel, which in its dormant state resembled a dark mirror. "They were the ones who liberated me from the Borg Collective. Janeway set me free."

"Well, now she's the one holding you in a gilded cage."

Seven looked at Ellory. When Ellory looked back, she saw the bottomless abyss of pain and sorrow that hid behind Seven's blue eyes. "When they freed me, I didn't appreciate the magnitude of the gift they had given me, or of those that would follow. The crew of *Voyager* welcomed me back into human society. Back into life. . . . They are all I have."

Ellory put her palm softly against Seven's cheek. "And yet, their Federation Council disavowed you; they won't even call you a citizen. And after all you did to prove yourself on *Voyager*, the Starfleet brass turned you away. You deserve better than that."

"Yes, I do." Seven rested her hand atop Ellory's. "I won't lie. Those rejections . . . hurt. It stung to be treated that way by those Janeway said would welcome me." She gently removed Ellory's palm from her face, though she kept holding Ellory's hand. "But those slights do not reflect on Admiral Janeway, or my other *Voyager* shipmates. Every one of them knows the real me. Each of them cares about me. And it's *because* they see me as I really am that

I still believe there will come a day when the Federation Council and Starfleet will learn to see me, as well."

Something about Seven's hidden spark of childlike faith in the goodness of others made Ellory's eyes brim with tears of compassion. "I think you're right. Someday they'll see what a huge mistake they made in letting you go. But today is not that day. And you shouldn't have to wait a lifetime to be treated with the respect you deserve. Because in case you've forgotten, the *Voyager* crew aren't your only kin anymore. You have hundreds of brand-new brothers and sisters on Fenris, and they're all waiting to welcome you home."

A tear fell from Ellory's eye. Seven brushed it away with a whisper-soft touch of her finger, and then she took Ellory in her arms and kissed her. They lingered in each other's embrace and let the kiss last. When their lips finally parted, Seven rested her forehead against Ellory's. Seven's voice was rich with renewed confidence. "We need to warn the Rangers about Kohgish, right now. But we can't do that while we're still on *Dauntless*."

Ellory looked up into Seven's bewitching blue eyes. "Is this the part where you tell me you have a plan?"

Seven's face brightened with a mischievous smile. "Yes. It is."

Janeway settled in behind the desk of her office. Her ready room on *Voyager* had been a rather cozy space. *Dauntless*'s captain's office was larger and comfortably appointed, a space befitting an admiral on her flagship. *Rank does have its privileges,* she mused with satisfaction.

"Janeway to Lieutenant L'Kel."

Dauntless's young Vulcan female communications officer answered, *"L'Kel here. Go ahead, Admiral."*

"Get me a secure real-time channel to FSA Director Keemah Geiss, on Earth."

"Yes, Admiral. I'll patch her directly through to your office."

"Thank you, L'Kel."

Waiting for the real-time channel to be established, Janeway picked up her padd and sorted through all the raw intelligence her crew had obtained from debriefing Seven and from interrogating Veris of Haakona. Between the two of them, it was as if a dam had broken, releasing a reservoir of raw information that had been held back for far too long.

The holographic image projected above Janeway's mirror-perfect black desk switched from the delta-shaped emblem of Starfleet to the face of Keemah Geiss. *"Admiral. I didn't expect to hear from you again so soon."*

"There have been developments." With a tap on her padd she sent all of her crew's recently acquired intelligence across the encrypted channel to Geiss. "With permission from Starfleet Command, I'm sharing with you everything we learned from debriefing Seven of Nine, and also from our interrogation of Romulan bounty hunter Veris of Haakona. Everything I'm sending you has been vetted and confirmed."

Geiss's eyebrows arched high in surprise. *"This is impressive, Admiral."*

"Thank you. Now I need to ask a favor in return. I need any tactical intel you can provide about your rogue spymaster Erol Tazgül. We have reason to believe he's in the process of facilitating the purchase of a decommissioned Talarian battleship by a Qiris-sector warlord."

"You mean the Antican? General Kohgish?"

"That's the one."

"We've been wondering who the Talarians' first bidder would be. My office has been tracking their Fystrel-*class battleship* Yamanok *since it was decommissioned last year."*

"Unfortunately, Director, now we know. My crew and I are doing all we can to stop the sale from taking place, but we suspect the Fenris Rangers are withholding intel that could lead us to the transaction's coordinates."

"I see. That raises a sensitive subject, I'm afraid."

"Sensitive in what regard?"

"Your latest report suggests the individual known as Seven of Nine is currently aboard your ship. Is that the case?"

"It is."

"Admiral, Seven is suspected of withholding key information about the sale of a foreign warship to a group known to be hostile to Federation interests. Furthermore, because of her extensive knowledge of Starfleet technology and protocols from the years she spent aboard Voyager *as a senior member of its crew, she is considered a risk to Federation security. On behalf of the Federation Security Agency, I insist*

that you take Seven into custody and secure her in your brig, pending her transfer to civilian authorities on Starbase 234."

Janeway straightened her back and hardened her countenance. "No."

Now it was Geiss who turned prickly. *"Tread carefully, Admiral."*

"Spare me your 'concern.' Seven has been nothing but forthcoming and helpful since she and her fellow Ranger came aboard. As far as I can tell, she's done nothing wrong—and I won't condemn her merely on your say-so."

The Argelian woman was aghast. *"Nothing wrong? Admiral, working with Tazgül to further his objectives, even unwillingly, has made Seven an accomplice after the fact to several of his crimes. She needs to be arrested in the name of civil order."*

Janeway rejected that assertion with a huff. "Utter garbage. Even I can see you're clutching at straws. I won't have any part of it. I won't help you violate Seven's civil rights."

"What rights?"

"Pardon me?"

"Your gal Seven isn't a Federation citizen. Her 'rights' within Federation space are extremely limited."

Anger and suspicion mingled in Janeway's frantic thoughts. "I refuse to believe Seven's not a citizen. Both her parents were Federation citizens, and she was born in Federation space."

Geiss shook her head. *"She might have been born a citizen, but she lost that status after being assimilated and serving the Borg as a drone most of her life."*

Janeway found the director's argument sickening for both its cynicism and its hateful xenophobia. "Preposterous. She can't be held accountable for being enslaved when she was a child! And the length of her assimilation is irrelevant. She has no remaining loyalty to the Borg."

The FSA director regarded Janeway with dubious condescension. *"How can we be sure, Admiral? Would even you have made that same argument six years ago? In the first two years after the crew of* Voyager *liberated Seven from the Collective, how many times did she resort to violence in her effort to rejoin the Collective? Your own logs say it happened at least three times, maybe more. Even when Seven wasn't trying to resume her former life as a drone, she repeatedly put* Voyager's *crew at risk through her attempts to resume prior associations with other members of the Collective, such as those who were part of Unimatrix Zero."*

"That's not fair. Seven was experiencing culture shock and post-traumatic stress disorder. And some of her attempts to reestablish contact with other Borg drones were motivated by a desire to help liberate them so that they could become ex-Borg, like her."

Geiss didn't seem persuaded. *"Even if that's true, it doesn't address one of the most damning choices your friend made. When offered the chance to reclaim her identity as Annika Hansen, she refused. She chose instead to retain the designation imposed upon her by the Borg: Seven of Nine, Tertiary Adjunct of Unimatrix 01. She chose to retain the identity given to her by avowed enemies of the Federation. The moment she did that, she de facto renounced her Federation citizenship."*

"That's outrageous."

"That's the verdict of the Federation Council. What? You thought they rejected Seven just because she had a few lingering enhancements? No, Admiral. Your girl got herself branded a noncitizen by rejecting the one thing that would have shown she was with us *instead of* them. *And if that hadn't done it, her latest dalliance sealed the deal. She might've been able to argue she was tricked into an association with Tazgül, but she willingly enlisted in the Fenris Rangers, which is currently listed as a clear-and-present danger to our border security. So, as far as the FSA is concerned, Seven of Nine is now an agent of a hostile foreign power. We've issued a warrant for her arrest—and we expect you to enforce it."*

Janeway glared across the subspace channel at Geiss. "I will do no such thing."

"The law demands otherwise."

"I'm not so sure. Even if I didn't think your entire argument was built on fear and lies, I still wouldn't do what you're asking."

"Why not?"

"Because if Seven's not a Federation citizen, and hasn't been since before returning from the Delta Quadrant, then she owed the Federation no allegiance and was free to join whatever foreign entity she pleased. Furthermore, in case you can't read a star chart, Director, *Dauntless* is presently outside of Federation space and therefore is beyond its legal jurisdiction to apply Federation law or serve its warrants. I couldn't legally arrest Seven here even if I wanted to—which I most emphatically *do not*."

"You don't want to pick this fight with me, Admiral."

"I could give you the same advice, Director."

"I can make life very difficult for you."

"You don't know the meaning of 'difficult.' You might know how to use the law, but I know how to use the *bureaucracy*. Come after me or mine and I'll make you jump through a thousand procedural hoops inside the civilian government, and then I'll make you jump through a thousand more at Starfleet Command, all just to wind up back where you started."

"You think you're clever, don't you?"

"I'm better than clever, Director—I'm *famous*. I know for a fact the shine hasn't yet worn off my celebrity as *Voyager's* captain. And if you think I won't stoop to manipulating public opinion to tie your hands and make you look like a petty villain . . . think again."

Geiss frowned and then nodded in resignation. *"Have it your way, Admiral. But I promise you, I'll remember this."*

"I'm counting on it."

"Just tell me this before I go: Why? Why risk blowing up your public image, your career, your entire life over one renegade ex-Borg?"

Janeway knew Geiss would never understand the truth, but she told it to her anyway: "Because this is what I do for *family*."

25

". . . and I hope that when all this is over, you will know that I did this for noble reasons. Seven, out." Sitting alone in the work nook of the diplomatic suite's main room, Seven ended the recording of a personal message and programmed it to be delivered later, after an interval just long enough for her and Ellory to make their exit before it would be heard.

I can only hope it is received in the spirit in which it was made.

She left the nook and joined Ellory in front of one of the suite's bulkhead-mounted companels. "Have you found an optimal route?"

"I think so. I have to say, the computer's pretty helpful. I asked it to plot the shortest walking route between these different points, and then it asked if I wanted to know about routes that were technically longer in total linear distance but faster to traverse." She threw a befuddled look at Seven. "It's almost like the ship *wants* us to win."

"Indeed. Show me what you think is the best route."

Ellory called up the floor plan for their current deck of the *Dauntless*. "We go left from our suite. Split up here, at the fork. I take the port-side corridor to objective one. You take the starboard corridor to emergency ladderway B and slide down to H deck aft and objective two."

Seven studied the route and nodded. "Excellent. Using the ladderway is a very good suggestion. It will help me avoid triggering any alerts for unauthorized turbolift access to the shuttlebay." Seven pointed out a subtle detail in the deck plan. "Use compartment C-LC8 to reach compartment C-LC7 via this internal connecting door."

"Why? Wouldn't it be faster to stay in the corridor?"

"Yes, but if you use the main corridor you will be visible from the entrance to the ship's armory when you enter C-LC7. Armories are often guarded, and we cannot risk you being challenged for moving around the ship without an escort."

Ellory absorbed all that with a slow nod. "Got it. But are we sure C-LC8 will be empty?"

"No. But the risk of your being stopped is much lower if you use the detour."

"Copy that. Now, what about final extraction?"

"Once you are in position, activate your Ranger SOS beacon. I will use it to find you." Seven reverted the companel to its regular standby mode. "Remember, when we leave the suite, walk. Do not run. We are guests, not prisoners. Most of this deck is considered nonclassified. So there should be no reason for our presence to draw suspicion as long as we remain calm."

"I'd be a lot calmer if they hadn't taken our weapons."

"If our plan works as intended, we won't need them. And I would prefer that we not harm any Starfleet personnel if we can avoid doing so without compromising our escape."

Ellory grinned. "I promise, I won't even use sharp words."

"Good enough." Seven checked her chrono. "Time to go." She led the way to the suite's door, which slid open ahead of her. Outside, C deck's forward corridor was quiet. Seven and Ellory left the suite, turned left, and walked together, side by side, their strides slow and casual.

A young female Bolian ensign in a blue-trimmed uniform with a sciences division emblem on her combadge passed them heading in the opposite direction. She offered the Rangers a pleasant smile, and Seven and Ellory returned it with equal warmth.

Less than ten strides after leaving their suite, they arrived at the fork in the corridor and paused. Seven leaned in close and whispered, "Remember, the door marked C-LC8. Don't pass C-LC7 or enter the transverse corridor that leads to turbolift two."

"I'll remember," Ellory said, her voice also hushed. "Three minutes, right?"

"That's the plan."

"Don't leave me hanging, Seven."

Seven kissed her. "Never."

They clasped each other's hands once for luck, and then they split up.

Seven strolled down the starboard corridor as if she had not a care in the galaxy, despite knowing that her and Ellory's freedom was going to depend upon the swift execution of a desperate plan with almost no margin for error. Drawing a calming breath, she rounded the turn into the transverse corridor, and then she opened the disguised panel that led to emergency ladderway B. She stepped inside. Pulled the panel closed behind her.

And then she slid downward, gaining speed by the second, using the ladder's outer edges like a pair of firehouse poles.

Time to see just how well Voyager*'s crew taught me about Starfleet.*

No matter how many times Ellory reminded herself to be calm and not show any anxiety, her body refused to listen. Sweat trickled from beneath her hair down the nape of her neck. Her pulse raced, and with each step she felt her breaths getting faster and shallower.

It didn't matter that Ellory had a reasonable cover story and plausible answers for any questions her movements might provoke. Nor did her body seem to understand that Starfleet was about as benign an opponent as she had ever faced. All her adrenal system seemed to understand was that she was alone and moving through a figurative lion's den with deceptive intentions.

If I ever wondered, now I know—I'd make a terrible spy.

She paused at the door Seven had pointed out to her on the deck plan. Next to it on the bulkhead was posted a simple piece of signage indicating its compartment number and its designation: C-LC8 SICKBAY / OFFICES.

Seven had promised her the door wouldn't be locked, but there was only one way to find out. Ellory stepped forward. The door slid open. *So far, so good.*

She proceeded inside and let the door close behind her. As she and Seven had hoped, the physicians' administrative offices were dark and empty during the ship's overnight watch. If anyone had been there and asked what Ellory was doing, she had been prepared to say she had come looking for medical attention in sickbay and in her confusion had used the wrong entrance.

No need for that now. One perfectly good lie, wasted.

Alone in the shadows, she moved like a ghost, her steps soft and quick.

She passed one glass-walled office cube after another, checking the names on the plaques beside their doors. At the end of the row, after the offices for the orthopedic surgeon, the ob-gyn, and the chief medical officer, she found the one for which she had come: that of Doctor Valarius, M.D., *Dauntless*'s chief of forensic pathology.

Like most Starfleet officers' workspaces, Valarius's office was uncluttered and all but immaculate. Its one peculiar characteristic was that it also harbored a faint but still pungent odor of formaldehyde, which somehow persisted despite the prevalence of strong disinfectants. Ellory held her breath and settled into the chair behind the pathologist's desk. A tap on his desktop activated his holographic interface with the ship's computer.

Then the interface abruptly deactivated as a monotonal, feminine voice told Ellory, *"Attention: biometric identity scan failed. This station is locked pending reauthorization."*

Ellory sighed but felt a grudging respect for her hosts. *Contrary to reports, Starfleet's op-sec isn't a total joke. Now I just need to find another way to get the intel I need.*

She poked around Valarius's office, hoping to find a clue. Or a written manifest of the ship's morgue. Or perhaps an unsecured padd that would conveniently be open to the page of information she happened to need. None of those things materialized.

This is starting to get annoying.

Frustrated, she muttered to herself, "I don't get it. The ship's computer seemed so helpful just a few minutes ago. I mean it's not as if I can just say, 'Computer, please tell me the location of the body of Fenris Ranger Keon Harper.'"

The feminine computer voice replied, *"The body of Fenris Ranger Keon Harper is in the morgue: C deck, compartment C-LC7, stasis chamber nineteen."*

Ellory looked up toward the source of the voice and smiled. "Thank you."

So much for their op-sec not being a joke.

She skulked out of Valarius's office and back the way she had come, to an intersection whose yet-untaken path led to the morgue. Once more, Ellory prepared herself for the door to be locked, only to have it slide solicitously out of her way as she drew near.

At its threshold, she peeked around the jamb in one direction and then another, checking the corners and listening for any sounds of activity from the compartment beyond. All was quiet. She stole into the morgue, as quiet as fog, but not trusting her apparent good fortune.

I guess it makes sense the door wouldn't be locked. Why would it be? It's a morgue. There aren't any open criminal investigations aimed at us. And nothing brought in with Harper would be tagged as evidence, because Starfleet's not investigating anything about his death.

She stayed low and darted from one forensic examination station to another, using their conglomerated investigative equipment and drainage systems as cover.

At the back of the large compartment she found a wall lined with rows and columns of stasis chambers. Most were dark, but a few were filled with intense blue light. Those were the ones whose stasis fields had been engaged to inhibit decomposition of a body for long periods of time—in some cases, years, if that was what was required.

Halfway along the wall, in the fourth row of chambers, was 19.

Ellory checked its readouts, and then she double-checked its holographic record of contents. She didn't want to risk opening the chamber only to find she had disturbed the repose of some soul other than Harper. Two looks confirmed it was him.

She opened the chamber and stood aside as its sledlike platform glided out of the bulkhead, until all of Harper was laid out in front of her, lying atop the Starfleet body bag in which he had been shrouded before being beamed up from Zirat.

Ellory wiped a tear from her cheek, and then she placed her palm against Harper's chest. "Hey, Kee. Sorry I was late to the party on Zirat, but Seven and I are gonna make it up to ya." With a press of her thumb, she activated her Fenris Rangers SOS beacon. "Just hang in there, old man. You wouldn't want to miss the good part, would you?"

Seven landed on her toes at the bottom of the ladder. With a graceful pivot she turned and opened the emergency-access panel. The ladderway ended at G deck, but this far down in the center of *Dauntless*'s arrowhead-shaped primary hull, there was no actual deck to speak of—just a junction for intersecting Jefferies tube crawlways, and the cramped, dark confines of the ship's mechanical infrastructure: EPS conduits, massive bundles of optronic cables, and thousands of other systems, all hidden away in the parts of the ship few souls ever saw.

To borrow an old Earth saying: time to take the low road.

She ignored the access hatchway to the Jefferies tube network. Newer ships such as *Dauntless* frequently monitored their Jefferies tubes for signs of intrusion or sabotage. If she were detected down here, in the bowels of the ship, moving through the Jefferies tubes beneath such restricted sections of the ship as main engineering or the aft magazine, where torpedoes for the ship's aft launcher were stored, it would almost certainly trigger a red alert. That would put the ship on a combat footing—exactly what Seven did not want right now.

Using both her hands and her feet for traction and balance, Seven navigated through the superstructure and auxiliary systems like a spider traversing her web. She recognized various systems as she clambered past them. Using them as landmarks against her eidetic memory of the ship's nonclassified schematics, she orientated herself and adjusted course as necessary.

Her preparations brought her to a ventilation node. She bypassed its security sensors with a few deft rearrangements of its wiring, and then she entered the broad airway. It led her to a grate that looked down into the ship's spare parts depot on H deck, just aft of the point where the ship's primary and secondary hulls met. She slipped her fingers through the grate, took hold of it, and with a push ripped it free of the bulkhead. Rather than let it fall, she pulled it back into the airway with her and tucked it behind her, out of her way. Then she climbed out of the airway and landed in a low crouch inside the depot.

By Seven's mental count, close to two minutes had elapsed since she and Ellory had parted. She needed to make up for time she had lost slithering through the ship's tangled innards.

She moved to the compartment's door. Using the override functions on its control pad, she unlocked it, and then she manually slid it open just enough to peek out at H deck. Directly across the corridor was the door to the shuttlebay's preflight area—a fancy name for an airlocked compartment with lockers for storing EVA suits and other gear.

The door was clearly marked with a red warning label, on which bold white letters declared RESTRICTED AREA / AUTHORIZED PERSONNEL ONLY.

That door, she knew, would almost definitely be locked.

Until it wasn't.

A male human ensign who looked barely old enough to need to shave approached the door to the preflight area and pressed his hand to a biometric sensor on the bulkhead beside it. "Dehler, Ensign Brody. Authorization two nine chase fox run blue."

A masculine computer voice replied, *"Authorized."*

The light on the panel beneath the ensign's hand changed from red to green, and the door to the preflight area unlocked with a gentle *thunk* of magnetic seals being released.

As the door in front of the ensign slid open, Seven opened the depot's door.

Ensign Dehler stepped over the threshold into the preflight area as Seven strode across the corridor with pantherlike stealth. She snaked her right arm around his throat and used her left hand to cover his mouth. He thrashed and struggled until Seven applied gentle pressure to his carotid, rendering him unconscious within seconds. She lowered him gently to the deck and then she stepped over him to survey the shuttlebay through the preflight area's windowed hatch.

As Seven had expected, *Dauntless*'s shuttlebay had been cleared of Starfleet auxiliary craft to make room for Veris's captured Romulan harrier, which was parked with its port hatch open. A trio of Starfleet engineers stood beside the expertly refitted ship, arguing over something displayed on a padd and occasionally pointing at the harrier. Of the three engineers, the insectoid Kaferian seemed to be the one in charge. Its subordinates, a bronze-skinned Vulcan woman and a Benzite wearing an old-fashioned external vaporator, did not seem to like the Kaferian very much.

A more careful check confirmed for Seven that there were no other personnel inside the shuttlebay—just the three engineers.

She opened the airlock hatch. Slipped into the shuttlebay. Closed and secured the hatch behind her. *No going back now.*

The engineers, consumed by their debate about some trivial bit of techno-babble, paid no attention to Seven's arrival. She ducked behind a long row of triple-stacked cargo containers and used it as cover as she scampered to a huge, bulkhead-mounted companel. With a few taps she accessed the refueling system and commanded it to flood the shuttlebay with highly volatile, explosive hydrogen. Predictably, a fail-safe caused the system to refuse the order.

Seven entered an override code she had learned from B'Elanna Torres on *Voyager.* She had no idea if the code would work on a different, more advanced ship, several years after—

The system accepted the override and began pumping odorless, flavorless, invisible hydrogen into the shuttlebay, in quantities that would swiftly become hazardous.

Time to go.

Using the companel, Seven set a timer on a ten-second countdown, at the end of which part of her override code would be canceled—specifically, the part that kept the ship's internal sensors blind to the threat. The part of the override that blocked them from stopping the leak, she left in place. Then, counting off the seconds in her head, she prepared herself to sprint.

A stentorian alarm resounded inside the shuttlebay, followed by a masculine voice declaring on a loop, *"All personnel, evacuate the shuttlebay immediately. Imminent explosion risk. Repeat: Evacuate shuttlebay immediately. Imminent explosion risk. . . ."*

The three engineers bolted toward the preflight area.

Seven dashed across the shuttlebay and into the harrier. She slapped the panel switch to close its hatch on her way in and kept running toward the cockpit.

Dauntless's automated emergency response would activate within seconds, as soon as the ship's sensors confirmed there were no personnel left inside the shuttlebay. Seven had only that long to do what needed to be done.

She threw herself into the pilot's seat. With the flip of a toggle she manually deactivated the harrier's magnetic docking clamps, but deliberately left the ship cold and dark.

Outside, red warning lights flashed, and the shuttlebay's outer doors snapped open. Seven knew that time was up when she felt the pull of artificial gravity disappear, and the harrier, like every other loose object in the shuttlebay, floated like a feather dancing on a warm breeze.

The force field holding in the shuttlebay's atmosphere crackled—then it deactivated, explosively decompressing the shuttlebay and ejecting into space the shuttlebay's dangerous buildup of hydrogen, along with a few dozen cargo pods, two sets of engineering tools . . . and one unsecured Romulan harrier.

26

Romulan Harrier *Nodokata*

Seven felt her stomach revolt at the sudden loss of gravity, coupled with the disorienting tumble of the harrier as it was ejected from *Dauntless*'s shuttlebay. The ship rolled and yawed, turning everything outside the cockpit viewport into a muddy whorl of colors.

Eyes on the controls, Seven reminded herself. Flying by instruments alone had come easily to her during her years on *Voyager*, a fact for which she was now thankful. She averted her eyes from the dizzying external view and activated the master console. In a flash she had a sensor report of her position relative to *Dauntless*'s nacelles and secondary hull, as well as confirmations that all of the harrier's systems were online and fully operational.

She powered up the harrier's small transporter platform, which was located in the aft compartment, through a currently open hatchway. A quick sweep of the frequency band used by Fenris Ranger beacons instantly locked onto Ellory's transponder chip inside *Dauntless*—which had not yet raised its shields but no doubt would do so in the next several seconds.

We'll just have to be gone by then.

"Computer: Lock transporter onto the SOS beacon and energize."

The computer responded in a man's Romulan-accented voice, *"Energizing."*

A coruscating pillar of light filled the space between the harrier's transporter pad and the overhead, and the resonant, almost melodious sound of the transporter beam washed through the ship. Ellory materialized on the platform in a seated pose, cradling Harper's body in a dark-blue Starfleet cadaver pouch. As the materialization effect dissipated, Ellory gave Seven a thumbs-up.

Seven raised the shields, programmed a course into the helm, and pre-charged the harrier's warp coils. She was about to engage the cloaking device when the harrier lurched, disturbed by a tractor beam from *Dauntless* being deflected by *Nodokata*'s shields.

Janeway's voice issued from the console's main speaker. "Dauntless *to Seven of Nine. Seven, I know you're on the Romulan harrier. I don't know what you think you're—*"

Ellory switched off the speaker with a tap on the master console as she settled into the copilot's seat beside Seven. "Ready?"

"Ready."

"Hit it."

Seven engaged the harrier's cloaking device. The cockpit's interior lighting shifted to a dim ruby glow. Outside the viewport, the cosmos seemed to ripple almost imperceptibly for a fraction of a second. With the cloak at full power, Seven made a series of drastic course changes at impulse speeds to thwart *Dauntless*'s attempts to guess their trajectory, and then she jumped *Nodokata* to warp speed. "And we're away."

"What's next?"

Seven recalibrated the harrier's sensors. "We find Kohgish."

U.S.S. *Dauntless* NCC-80816 — Thirty Seconds Earlier

A padd's blank screen held Janeway captive. Seated in the command chair on *Dauntless*'s bridge, she struggled to find the right words for the report she would, inevitably, need to submit to Starfleet Command, explaining her perspective on the day's events. Rationalizing her decision to refuse to cooperate with the Federation Security Agency was going to require extreme tact. And maybe a few spins on the truth. But first she had to choose where to begin.

An insistent beeping from the operations console interrupted her deliberations. The ship's senior operations officer, Lieutenant Brooks, a human woman with a tawny complexion and close-cut, tightly curled black hair, silenced the alarm and checked her readouts. "Hazard alert in shuttlebay. Critically dangerous levels of hydrogen detected."

At the adjacent console, female Trill navigator Lieutenant Asencia looked up in alarm. "Hydrogen? Mixed with the oxygen? One spark in there—"

"And we could lose the entire shuttlebay," Brooks said, finishing the thought.

Janeway sprang to her feet. "Sound the alarm. Evacuate the shuttlebay!"

Tysess arrived at Janeway's side. "Shuttlebay clear. Emergency venting engaged."

"On whose order?"

Brooks looked back at Janeway. "It's an automated response, Admiral."

Janeway sensed something was amiss. "Yellow Alert."

Tysess triggered the alert, which set yellow panels flashing on the bulkheads. From the ops console, Brooks reported, "Shuttlebay decompressed. Hydrogen dispersed, along with some cargo pods and small items left behind in—" Her expression turned to one of shock and embarrassment. "Admiral, the Romulan harrier was also ejected. It's in a chaotic tumble heading aft."

"On-screen!" Janeway watched as Brooks changed the main viewscreen to an aft angle showing the gap between *Dauntless*'s warp nacelles. The small Romulan ship was tumble-rolling away into the void. "How the hell did that happen? Weren't its docking clamps engaged?"

"The engineers' report said they were." Brooks reacted as more alerts shrilled from her station. "Admiral, the harrier's engines just came online. There's someone on board."

Janeway felt her temper rising. "And I bet I know who it is. Get a tractor beam on that ship! Put it back in the bay."

Her tactical officer worked quickly, but as Janeway feared, *Dauntless*'s shimmering golden tractor beam bounced away from the harrier rather than taking hold. Brooks looked back again. "The harrier's shields are up, Admiral."

"Hail them!"

The communications officer responded almost instantly, "Channel open."

"*Dauntless* to Seven of Nine. Seven, I know you're on the Romulan harrier. I don't know what you think you're doing, but let's talk about this before you do something that can't—"

On the main viewscreen, the harrier faded from view.

Her tactical officer reported with dry efficiency, "The harrier engaged its cloaking device, Admiral. We've lost them."

She aimed a reproachful glare at the Vulcan man. "Thank you for captioning the obvious, Lieutenant Dokar. Who knows to what wild assumptions we might have leapt to without you?" Walking back to her command chair, she said for the entire bridge to hear, "Someone tell me something about this debacle that I *don't* already know."

Tysess returned to stand beside Janeway's chair. "Sensor logs show Seven beamed someone and some*thing* out of *Dauntless's* sickbay just before the harrier cloaked."

Janeway started to understand not only what had happened, but why. "Computer, is Fenris Ranger Ellory Kayd still on board this ship?"

"Negative."

"Is the body of Fenris Ranger Keon Harper still in our morgue?"

"Negative."

Her first officer reacted to the computer's reports with a look of confusion. "The Rangers' tactics puzzle me, Admiral."

"How so?"

"Why did they substantially increase their risk of detection and capture by splitting up, just so one of them could retrieve a dead body?"

His question made Janeway crack a wan smile. "Honor, Commander." Seeing that he still wasn't putting the pieces together, she added, "Because either Seven, the Fenris Rangers, or both share a core philosophy with Starfleet: we don't leave our people behind."

Tysess nodded slowly. "Now I understand. Thank you, Admiral." He looked away, toward the forward duty stations. "Should we ask Starfleet for reinforcements to help us find the stolen harrier?"

"No. We're already outside our jurisdiction and testing the limits of interstellar law as it is. I see nothing to be gained from escalating the situation."

"Understood. Orders, Admiral?"

"Set course for the Qiris sector, slipstream ten. Stay alert for any sign of the harrier, General Kohgish, or Mister Tazgül." She stood and smoothed the front of her uniform's tunic. "I'll be in my office. If you find anything, let me know. Commander Tysess, you have the conn."

"Yes, Admiral."

With the crisis of the moment utterly bungled but also effectively over, Janeway walked to the turbolift and got in. "B deck, aft."

As the lift made its brief descent, Janeway's thoughts turned inward. *I ought to be angry. I should feel betrayed, or at least disrespected. But I can't. If my back had been put to the wall under equivalent circumstances, I'd have done the same thing, and I know it.* The turbolift halted and the doors opened. She exited, crossed the corridor, and entered her office. Planting herself behind her desk, she chortled softly at the irony of her circumstances. *You learned my teachings well, Seven. Never let what's lawful stop you from doing what's right.*

The holographic interface for the ship's computer system appeared above her desk, having activated itself after automatically verifying her biometric data when she sat down. At the top of her incoming messages queue was an internally recorded missive flagged as URGENT.

It was from Seven.

Janeway checked its metadata. It had been recorded a short while earlier and had been set for delayed delivery. *Clearly, Seven wanted to tell me something, but only after she and Ellory had made their escape.*

Curious and oddly hopeful, Janeway played the message.

Seven's face appeared inside the holographic frame. *"Admiral. By now, Ellory and I will have left* Dauntless, *without your permission, in the Romulan harrier. I apologize for departing in this manner. I know it can only add to the professional and political difficulties you have endured because of your friendship with me, and for that, I am truly sorry.*

"But I hope that when you hear what I need to say next, you might yet find some way to forgive me. . . ."

Romulan Harrier *Nodokata*

Cloaked and lingering in the polar magnetic field of Achlys, a rogue star transiting the endless darkness, *Nodokata* was like a shadow in space. Hunkered in its cockpit, Seven watched the sensor display and listened for intercepted comms traffic. The mercenary frigate *Eris* and the tactical cruiser *Bolvangar* were both just a few light-minutes away, orbiting the rogue star's equator—far enough away that neither was likely to detect a cloaked vessel at this range, through this much interference, but close enough that the upgraded sensor package and comms suite Veris had installed during his refit of the harrier could keep close track of their every word and action.

Ellory sat apart from Seven, conserving her energy but still sweating like a Risan socialator in a Bajoran temple. The cockpit was warm and getting warmer by the minute because Seven had insisted on "running silent," minimizing the harrier's sensor profile by limiting its energy usage and emissions. Though Seven had agreed to maintain atmospheric support inside the ship, she had reduced thermal maintenance to its minimum level, which left the temperature inside *Nodokata* at the mercy of the rogue star's erratic radiation output.

Unable to contain her curiosity, Ellory asked, "What're they doing now?"

"They are maintaining an equatorial orbit of the star."

"'Hurry-up-and-wait.' When I was a kid, that was how my dad described his life in Starfleet. I never understood what he meant—until now."

Seven looked up from the sensors. She wore the expression of someone trying not to let on that they were annoyed. "I presume that's a commentary on our current mission?"

Ellory sighed. "It's just been a bit choppy."

"Choppy."

"I'm just saying, we hauled ass away from *Dauntless* and zeroed in on *Bolvangar* in minutes, thanks to you having salted the latinum with sekenium before leaving the bank. Speaking of which, whose idea was that? Yours or Harper's?"

"Harper's. He called it 'screw-up insurance.' I think he anticipated our being robbed."

"Sounds like Harper." She climbed back aboard her train of thought. "Anyway, after that mad flurry of action, we've been sitting here doing nothing for almost an hour."

"We're waiting for the right moment to strike. The moment when our prey will be divided. Distracted. At their most vulnerable."

"Which will be . . . when?"

"Hang on." One of her screens indicated active comms traffic. Seven used the harrier's military-grade decryption technology to break through the signal's security coding and patched it through to the cockpit's speakers so she and Ellory could listen to it together.

The first voice from the speaker was smooth, smarmy, and condescending. *"We have Qulla and his ships on short-range sensors, coming in on bearing four eight mark seven. ETA, eight minutes. Are you and your men ready?"*

Seven whispered to Ellory, "That was Tazgül."

A voice like a growl replied, *"Ready. But are you sure he won't just rob us?"*

Ellory whispered back, "Kohgish. I'd know his voice anywhere."

"Just do as I said." Tazgül sounded vexed. *"Keep your men and his on opposite sides of the bay, and the latinum between you. Don't let them flank or surround you. And no matter what, do not lower the force field around the latinum until after you get the codes for the ship."*

"I know the drill. But what if Qulla pulls some kind of surprise?"

"Then sound the alarm on this channel and I'll intervene. But for both our sakes, try to get this done without me. Show your men—and me—that you're ready to lead."

"I will. But make sure you stay close."

"I assure you, General, I wouldn't have it any other way. Good luck. Mardani out."

The channel went quiet. On the sensor display, *Bolvangar* accelerated away from *Eris*, maneuvering to put the mass of the rogue star between them and conceal *Bolvangar* from the incoming pair of Talarian vessels.

"Now we strike," Seven said, restoring power to the engines. "I will move us into position. Go aft and select an appropriate loadout from Veris's small-arms locker."

Ellory started to head aft, then stopped and turned back. "Define 'appropriate.'"

"Nonlethal, but with powerful wide-field effects."

"Rifles or pistols?"

"Pistols, two each. Small, lightweight. Good for tight spaces. Our strategy will be to hit fast and keep moving."

"Got it." Her objective clarified, Ellory hurried aft to the weapons locker.

Seven engaged the harrier's warp drive to make a microjump to within a few thousand kilometers of the frigate *Eris*. *Nodokata*'s arrival caused no discernible change in *Eris*'s orbit, nor did it provoke any frantic messages to *Bolvangar*, so Seven took the lack of reaction as confirmation that the harrier's cloaking device continued to perform as intended.

She eased the harrier forward at quarter impulse, cautious not to stir up any eddies in the solar wind currents. In under half a minute she had *Nodokata* parked and holding station precisely fifty meters beneath *Eris*'s main hull. A quick check of passive sensors confirmed where its crew were located. Four had been left on its command deck. Another cluster of eight remained in main engineering. Two were in the sickbay. But the majority of the ship's complement, twenty-six persons, was heading to the aft lower decks—the ship's main shuttlebay.

Seven recalled Tazgül's instructions to Kohgish and deduced that the big meeting between Kohgish and the Talarian broker was going to take place in the shuttlebay. After a quick, final review of the frigate's deck schematics, Seven settled on her plan of attack.

She headed aft and met Ellory at the transporter pad. "We're in position. We have just over five minutes until the Talarian broker arrives." Seven handed Ellory two small disks. "Transporter recall triggers. One for you, one for the latinum in case we get separated."

"Copy that." Ellory pocketed the disks and handed Seven a pair of Romulan-made disruptor pistols. "Small and light, with a wide-field heavy stun that can drop a charging *hengrauggi*."

"A what?"

"Really big predator."

"Perfect." Seven stepped onto the transporter pad. "Computer, stand by to beam us directly onto the command deck of the frigate above us."

"Coordinates locked. Standing by."

Ellory took her place on the pad beside Seven. "What's the plan?"

"Start at the top, work our way down."

"Sounds good." She drew her disruptors from their holsters. "Let's rock."

Seven mirrored Ellory's pose, disruptors at the ready. "Computer—*energize.*"

27

First came light, then justice. The transporter beam had only begun to fade away around Seven when she pressed the firing studs on her disruptor pistols. Ellory did the same, and together they filled *Eris*'s command deck with a heavy-stun field that hit the four Antican officers like the hand of an angry goddess. It enveloped them in flashes of white light as it knocked them out of their chairs. Three were out cold before they struck the deck. Only the largest of them, the one who had occupied the command chair, clung to consciousness as he lay on the deck, twitching and gasping like a landed fish.

Seven knocked him out with a short disruptor pulse in his torso on her way to the forward consoles, whose smooth interface surfaces were cracked and sparking—collateral damage of Seven's and Ellory's overlapping barrages of disruptor energy. She was relieved to find that the panel continued to accept input despite having been fractured by small-arms fire.

Ellory visited each of the command deck's three aft stations, inflicting minor bits of sabotage at each one before moving on to the next. "Warp drive, weapons, and shields offline," she declared proudly. "Internal comms disabled. Should I knock out the subspace transceiver?"

"No. We need it." Seven finished her work at the ship's operations console and then joined Ellory at the comms station. "Call up a copy of Kohgish's voiceprint while I prepare a message for time-delayed transmission."

"On it." As she navigated the frigate's computer system to get the voiceprint file, Ellory stole glances at what Seven was doing. "Let me guess: you write it, but the computer says it with Kohgish's voice."

"That is the general idea, yes." She finished writing the message and set it to broadcast on a loop once transmission was initiated. "Do you have the voiceprint?"

"Applying it to your text now. . . . Done. How long until it sends?"

Seven checked her awareness of time's passage. "The Talarians arrive in three minutes and fifty seconds. Begin transmission in four minutes."

"Done."

"Let's keep moving. Sickbay. One deck down, one section aft."

Side by side they left the command deck and strode down a short corridor to a ladderway. Seven descended first and held her disruptor ready, covering the passageway ahead while Ellory followed her down to deck two. Using hand signals, Seven directed Ellory to head aft and to look for their target on the left side of the corridor.

They neared the door to *Eris*'s sickbay. Ellory raised a hand and made a fist, signaling Seven to stop. As they paused, Ellory pulled a compact Romulan stun grenade from her jacket's front pocket. With an irritated look Seven asked, *What are you doing with that?*

Ellory smirked, shrugged, and then armed the grenade.

The tiny device beeped softly as it counted down to detonation.

With a tilt of her head, Ellory cued Seven to leapfrog past her to the far side of the sickbay door. Seven darted down the corridor and put her back to the bulkhead next to the portal. With barely any time left on the grenade's fuse, Ellory pivoted in front of the sickbay entrance. The door slid open, she lobbed the grenade inside the medical bay, and then she ducked back against the bulkhead on the other side of the doorway.

A *snap-bang* and a searing flash of veridian light was followed by the crackling of lightning run amok as the grenade lit up the sickbay with stunning tendrils of electricity, frying both equipment and personnel into submission.

When the commotion ceased, sickbay was choked with thick white smoke that stank of scorched polymers and burnt fur. Seven surveyed the scene and offered Ellory a grudging nod of approval. "Most efficient."

"Thank you."

The pair resumed heading aft.

"Do you have any more of those?"

"Sorry, that was the only one Veris had."

"Unfortunate. Had I known, I might have recommended we save it for main engineering."

Ellory rejected that idea with a small shake of her head. "Not ideal. Multi-level and too much open space. That kind of electro-stunner works better in confined spaces."

"Noted." Seven stopped at the next ladderway and let Ellory pass her.

The Trill woman descended the ladderway without hesitation, as if she understood what Seven wanted and needed from her without having to be told. At the bottom of the ladder she took up a covering position while Seven followed her down.

They arrived in the middle of a longer corridor than the ones on the upper decks. Ellory pointed aft, toward the entrance to the main engineering compartment, and Seven nodded. Together they advanced, shoulder to shoulder, disruptors level and steady. Every few steps Seven looked back to make sure they weren't being targeted from behind.

Several strides shy of the double doors to engineering, Ellory's expression betrayed a hint of anxiety. "How do we play this?"

"Eight targets, four on the upper level, four below. I will breach the door. You cover the four up top, and I will take the four below."

"How exactly do I—"

Seven jogged toward the double doors, which parted ahead of her, and then she sprinted, vaulted over the low safety railing that encircled the engineering compartment's ring-shaped upper catwalk, and landed hard in a low squat on the lower level's deck—much to the surprise of the four Antican engineers who were there monitoring the ship's impulse and warp reactors.

She fired her disruptors, bathing the lower level with heavy-stun pulses.

Two of the engineers were slammed back against bulkheads and crumpled to the deck like cheap sacks stuffed with raw meat. But two slipped behind cover—one behind a bank of control stations, the other behind the warp core reaction chamber.

Plasma bolts screeched down at Seven from above, scorching the deck in front of her and caroming off hard surfaces behind her. She dove for cover behind a boxed junction of EPS conduits. Lying on the deck, she blind-fired a few stun pulses at her attackers on the upper level.

Then, from above, a sound sweeter than music: the *vwap* of heavy-stun disruptor pulses followed by the *thumps* of bodies hitting a grated catwalk. *Two down up top, two to go.*

Fiery streaks of plasma raced past close enough to singe Seven's hair. Noting the angle of the shot's ricochet, she realized it had come from the Antican behind the control stations.

And two more down here.

She made a mental time check: she had just over two minutes until the Talarian broker was expected to arrive. Two minutes to deal with these troublesome engineers, and then an entire platoon-strength gang of mercenaries in the shuttlebay.

Another burst of plasma tore past her.

Seven laid down a blind salvo of suppressing fire as she stood, and she kept firing as she charged across the lower engineering deck, hammering the bank of consoles and the warp core with stun-force blasts from her disruptor pistols, forcing both her opponents to stay behind cover.

Then, as she passed the warp core and neared the consoles, she remembered her fight on Zirat and threw herself into a slide across the smooth metallic deck, firing all the way.

She slid into the view of the engineer behind the consoles—and flattened him with a heavy pulse before he realized what had happened.

Then she rolled over, reset one weapon to full power, narrow beam, and targeted the coolant conduit above the other Antican engineer's hiding place. One shot ruptured the conduit and doused the area behind the intermix chamber with freezing-cold chemicals, flushing the hidden Antican into the open—where Seven dropped him with a stun blast from her other pistol.

She looked up and saw one Antican emerging from a nook behind Ellory. No time to shout a warning—Seven fired and put him down with a stun pulse. Then she heard Ellory's weapon discharge. The last of the Antican engineers tumbled over the catwalk's safety railing and landed on top of the deuterium injector assembly beside the intermix chamber.

Moments later, Ellory slid down the ladder from the catwalk and joined Seven on the lower level. "How far to the shuttlebay?"

Seven pointed out two doors along the compartment's aft bulkhead, one each to port and starboard. "Through either door, straight aft into who-knows-what. We've got ninety seconds and a target-rich environment."

"Let's split up. Hit 'em from both sides at once."

Seven consented with a nod and a smile. "Good luck."

"You, too. And don't waste time being careful."

"Wouldn't dream of it."

They kissed quickly, and then they sprinted in opposite directions—Ellory to the starboard hatch, Seven to port.

The corridor from engineering to the shuttlebay was mercifully empty.

The hatch at the far end was unlocked. It opened as Seven approached.

She charged through it, knowing she had seventy-five seconds left.

Eris's shuttlebay was mostly open space, but its forward end, near the two hatchways, was a cluttered, disorderly mess. Tall stacks of cargo pods and crates of spare parts were clustered in uneven heaps, creating an asymmetrical labyrinth of blind intersections. Loose bits of junk littered the deck, and dozens of untended cables and hoses curled over and around one another like a serpentine orgy. Passing through it, Seven glimpsed Ellory advancing along its opposite side, but she quickly lost sight of her in the maze of industrial refuse.

As Seven neared the end of the mess, she chose a pod to use as cover, crouched behind it, and surveyed the group of heavily armed mercs surrounding Kohgish and the shipping crate full of latinum. Wide-field stun blasts would be useless at this range in such a cavernous space, and she was fairly certain the mercenaries would not be using stun settings when they returned fire.

But I promised Harper I'd play by the rules. Or that at least I'd try.

Seven reset her pistols to narrow beam, maximum stun.

Sixty seconds left.

She popped up from cover and opened fire. Even from a distance, she peppered the clustered platoon of mercs with ease. Each shot she landed slammed another goon to the deck. From the other side of the junk maze, Ellory joined the assault. Watching the Trill's disruptor blasts level one merc after another, Seven knew Ellory had made the same adjustments to her weapons as she had.

By the time the first eight mercs fell, the rest had scattered, and Kohgish had taken cover behind the shipping container. Seven had expected the goons to retreat to cover—but instead they charged toward her and Ellory, zigzagging to evade incoming fire, their weapons blazing, lighting up the stacked pods and crates with plasma, phaser pulses, and particle beams.

Ricochets caromed around Seven's position, and the mercs' barrage rained white-hot motes down upon her as their weapons slagged the crates into molten junk.

She fell back, flooding the zone with disruptor blasts to cover her movements.

Ducking and darting through the chaotic maze, she heard the mercs barking information at one another as they tracked her and Ellory. Their footfalls and the echoes of their voices revealed that they were splitting up to cut off all avenues of escape.

In other words, Seven mused, *you just divided yourselves.*

Now we conquer.

There was no time to think about tactics, no master plan. For Seven the battle became a dance, an improvisation, a work of inspiration as she took her cues from every shifting shadow, every reverberating sound. She turned a corner, fired—and down went a merc. She climbed on top of the stacks, alighted soundlessly from one heap to another, and then leaped down into the midst of her enemies and mowed them down with speed and precision, pinning some, using others as shields before stunning them with point-blank pulses to their chests.

The whine of weapons fire and the *thud-grunts* of large thugs meeting the deck told Seven that Ellory was cutting her own swath through Kohgish's troops.

Moving through the labyrinth, Seven felt alive. Powerful. Here in the dark, skulking in close quarters, she knew in her bones that she was this jungle's apex predator.

She holstered her pistols. Stalked the last few mercs in silence and put them down by hand. A palm-strike put an Orion's head against a metallic pod. A knife-hand attack into a Betelgeusian's temple knocked him out before he knew Seven was beside him.

An eerie silence filled the shuttlebay.

Ten seconds to spare.

Seven walked out of the maze to find Ellory was several meters ahead of her, scuffed, bloodied, but mostly unhurt, standing perfectly still in the open space of the shuttlebay.

Then a lone figure stepped out of the far end of the maze. It was Kohgish, no more than four meters behind Ellory, with a particle-beam pistol aimed at the back of her head.

The Antican general beckoned Seven with a curl of his free paw. "Miss Hansen, I presume? Mardani told me quite a bit about you. Do come say hello."

Seven walked slowly toward the showdown, taking care to keep her hands away from her holstered disruptors. "General Kohgish. Let's not do anything foolish."

"I think we're past that. Don't you?"

"I suppose we are."

"Let me tell you what's going to happen now, Miss Hansen. You—"

"My name is *Seven*."

The general snarled. "Impudent little *stroyk*! Mardani gave me your dossier. I *know* your real name is Annika Hansen."

"That name belonged to someone who no longer exists. *My* real name is *Seven of Nine*."

"Tell yourself whatever you want, Miss Hansen. But if you defy me again, your friend dies. Now, as I was saying, here's what will happen next. You will both remove your weapons. Set them on the deck. And kick them back to me."

Seven stared Kohgish in the eye. "We will do no such thing."

The general grinned to show his fangs. "I warned you, Miss Hansen."

Kohgish fired.

A brilliant white beam leaped from his weapon's muzzle—

—and slammed into an invisible barrier three meters in front of him.

Golden ripples of distortion shimmered across the hemispherical surface of the force field . . . which sat over Kohgish like a dome.

Enraged, he fired again.

Once more the force field shimmered—but now it was half a meter smaller in diameter. Kohgish stared in wide-eyed shock. "What is this?"

Seven nodded at Ellory, who walked quickly to the latinum crate. Then Seven paced in a slow orbit around Kohgish's gradually shrinking invisible prison.

"This, General, is the force field you set up to protect the latinum from the Talarians. I reprogrammed it while I was on your ship's command deck."

Ellory affixed a transporter recall beacon to the shipping crate, triggered it, and stepped back. Half a second later, the crate full of latinum dematerialized on its way to *Nodokata*.

"Right about now, your starship broker, Qulla, is probably wondering why you and your crew won't answer his hails. I expect he'll wait a few minutes before he beams over here to investigate the matter for himself."

Kohgish slammed his paws against the contracting force field, only to be punished by harsh shocks. Then it began to touch the top of his head, shocking him into a low crouch. "What are you doing? Let me out!"

"You're a wanted man, General. The only place you're going is to prison."

He growled like a wild animal as the force field started to crackle against his whole body. When he spoke, he sounded as if he were choking. "Hansen, you *guvok*! You'll pay for this! You hear me, Hansen, you filthy Borg *soka*?"

Kohgish writhed in agony on the deck as the force field crushed the air from his lungs, pushing him toward unconsciousness. Seven kneeled beside him. "You're right about one thing. I *am* part Borg. I will *always* be part Borg. But I will *never* let anyone shame me again for being who I am." She leaned in close and savored the fear in his eyes. "And I will never, *ever* let anyone tell me again that I don't know *my own fucking name*."

Seven stood tall above the Antican and composed herself as he gasped for air inside his invisible cocoon. Ellory stepped up beside her. Seven pulled out her badge and declared, "Kohgish of Antica, I am Fenris Ranger Seven of Nine— and *you* are *under arrest*."

28

Romulan Harrier *Nodokata*

Seven and Ellory materialized inside the still-cloaked harrier, each holding one arm of the unconscious, manacled Kohgish. Together they dragged him aft to a stasis pod and shoved him inside. Ellory slammed its door closed, and Seven activated its suspended-animation protocol.

Clapping her hands clean, Ellory said, "Let's finish this."

Seven walked to the cockpit and took the pilot's seat. Outside the forward viewport, a small Talarian transport vessel and an enormous Talarian battleship loomed large beside the frigate *Eris*. Ellory dropped into the copilot's seat, took silent note of the newly arrived vessels, and flipped on the comms-interception system.

An angry man's voice issued from the overhead speakers: "*. . . please respond! Repeat, General Kohgish, this is Qulla. Are you receiving this? Why aren't you answering?*"

Ellory muted the channel. "He sounds pissed."

"Not as much as he's about to be." Seven checked the status of the signals she had programmed *Eris*'s ops console to send on timed delays. All three had gone off as scheduled, one after the other, in the last sixty seconds. "If Mister Tazgül remains as punctual as I remember him being, he should be arriving right about . . . now."

On cue, the tactical cruiser *Bolvangar* dropped out of warp and cruised smoothly into orbit, directly behind the Talarian ships.

Seven nodded at Ellory, who fiddled with the controls on the comms intercept. The next voice they heard was Tazgül's. "*Qulla! What kind of double cross are you trying to pull?*"

Qulla sounded perplexed. *"Mardani? What are you talking about? Where's Kohgish?"*

"I was about to ask you the same question, Qulla! What did you do to him?"

"Are you insane? We've been trying to raise him on comms. We haven't reached him."

"Then why did he send me a distress signal saying you ambushed him?"

"That's absurd! What kind of scam are you two trying to—"

The argument between the Talarian broker and the rogue spymaster came to an abrupt halt as the *U.S.S. Dauntless* dropped out of quantum slipstream in a burst of light, directly above Mardani's ship, *Bolvangar*. Almost instantly, *Dauntless* disabled *Bolvangar's* engines with two precision phaser blasts, and then snared the cruiser in a tractor beam.

"Attention, Erol Tazgül. This is Lieutenant Commander Tysess of the Federation Starship Dauntless. *Surrender your vessel and prepare to be boarded."*

Ellory smirked at Tazgül's predicament. "Wow. That was fast."

Seven permitted herself a satisfied smile. "It's almost as if someone told *Dauntless exactly* where to find Tazgül and his ship."

An alert chirped on the harrier's main console. Ellory muted it and checked the readouts. "Looks like the Talarians are making a run for it."

"Naturally." Seven stole another look at the chrono. "Three. Two. One."

Bam. More than two dozen flashes of light appeared in front of the Talarian ships—and from those brilliant flares emerged a squadron of prowlers, backed up by three heavy corsairs, in a battle formation poised to encircle the Talarian battleship.

Courtesy of the comms intercept, the deep and melodious voice of Ranger Lucan Sagasta spilled from the harrier's speakers: *"Attention, Talarian vessels and mercenary frigate* Eris. *Surrender and prepare to be boarded, by order of the Fenris Rangers."*

A different man answered. *"Fenris Rangers, this is* Dauntless. *No offense intended, but you're a bit outside your jurisdiction."*

"No offense, Starfleet, but so are you. But, hey—we won't tell if you won't."

A momentary silence. Then Tysess replied, *"Your terms are acceptable."*

The next voice over the comm was Admiral Janeway's, on a general hailing frequency. *"Seven, we know you're out there somewhere. Please show yourself."*

The two Rangers shared a knowing look: *The party's over.*

"Ell? Please detach the general's stasis pod and stand by for transport."

"You got it." Ellory headed aft.

Seven opened a response channel. "*Dauntless*, this is Fenris Ranger Seven of Nine aboard the harrier *Nodokata*. Decloaking in three. Two. One." She disengaged the ship's cloaking device. The view outside flickered momentarily, and the harrier's internal lighting switched back to its normal hue. She switched her comm to a Ranger frequency. "*Nodokata* to corsair *Laniakea*. Please stand by for transport, three persons, one in stasis, plus one body and one very large crate of latinum."

A woman's voice replied, *"Acknowledged,* Nodokata. *Standing by."*

Seven switched back to the main hailing frequency. "Admiral, I trust you had no difficulty tracking the sekenium traces?"

"That information was most helpful, Seven. Thank you for that."

"My pleasure."

An encoded message from the lead Ranger corsair appeared on the harrier's console: TALARIAN BROKER, TALARIAN PIRATES, AND CREW OF ERIS IN CUSTODY. READY TO TRANSPORT.

Seven shifted her focus back to her conversation with Janeway. "Ranger Kayd and I are ready to abandon this vessel. We remand it to your custody, with our apologies, and our thanks."

Janeway's reply had a contemplative tone. *"I can't exactly say 'You're welcome.' . . . but I will say thank you. Not just for returning the harrier, but for showing us that maybe Starfleet and the Fenris Rangers can do more good in the Qiris sector as partners than as adversaries."*

"My thoughts exactly, Admiral."

There was so much more that Seven needed to say to Janeway, but there was no time for that now. She switched back to the Ranger frequency. "*Laniakea*, this is Ranger Seven on the harrier *Nodokata*. Ready for transport in five seconds."

"Acknowledged, Nodokata. *T-minus five seconds."*

She strode aft to the transporter pad, where Ellory waited with Kohgish, asleep in his stasis pod, and Harper, enshrouded at their feet. Seven took her place beside Ellory. In the moment before the transporter beam took hold, Ellory's and Seven's fingers entwined.

Time to go home.

U.S.S. *Dauntless* NCC-80816

A palpable sense of relief settled over the *Dauntless* bridge crew as the crises around them came to swift and orderly conclusions. In the center of the action, and most thankful of all, Admiral Janeway relaxed in her command chair as one report after another reached her.

The communications officer looked up from his post. "Security Chief Gresh confirms Erol Tazgül is in solitary confinement in our brig, and the rest of his crew are in custody."

"Excellent. Tell Mister Gresh 'Well done.'"

As her compliment was relayed belowdecks, second officer Lieutenant Shawna Benson arrived at her side. "Admiral? Sensors confirm the Ranger corsair *Laniakea* has beamed all personnel off the Romulan harrier. The vessel is officially abandoned."

"Splendid. Lieutenant Dokar, get a tractor beam on the harrier and tow it into our shuttlebay, on the double."

"Tractor beam to shuttlebay," the tactical officer replied. "Aye, sir."

Lieutenant Commander Tysess approached Janeway's chair. "The Rangers have arrested starship broker Qulla Hain, as well as his skeleton crew from the Talarian battleship. They're all in custody aboard the corsairs *Amarok* and *Okami*."

"And what about the Talarians' ships?"

"About that—the captain of the *Amarok* would like a word with you."

"On-screen."

Tysess relayed her command with a nod at the comms officer. A moment later, a Catullan man's smiling face appeared on the bridge's main viewscreen. His receding hairline drew her attention to his high forehead as well as his dark-violet hair and matching, enormously shaggy eyebrows and handlebar mustache. He wore a synthetic leather jacket emblazoned with a Fenris Rangers patch over a casual ensemble of civilian clothing. *"Admiral! Well met. I'm Ranger Captain Sorno Kel, commanding the corsair* Amarok.*"*

"A pleasure to make your acquaintance, Captain. What can we do for you?"

"We'd like you to take something off our hands."

"And what, precisely, would that be?"

"This gigantic Talarian battleship. We don't want it floating around out here and falling into the wrong hands. But at the same time, to be honest, we wouldn't know what to do with it. So if it wouldn't be too much trouble . . . would you mind?"

"Sure. We're already towing one ship. Why not two?"

"Thanks, Admiral. I'm glad we reach. Safe travels. Amarok *out."*

The transmission ended, and the main viewscreen switched to an image of the Talarian battleship, adrift in orbit of the rogue star.

Tysess regarded the colossal vessel with a skeptical eye. "Are we really going to tow that all the way to Starbase 234?"

Janeway shrugged. "You have a better idea?"

"Scuttle it into the rogue star and call it an accident?"

"Tempting. But no. Even decommissioned, it might still be of interest to Starfleet Intelligence. Take it in tow alongside the *Bolvangar* and keep us under warp seven."

"Yes, Admiral."

As her bridge crew wrangled the battleship into position behind *Dauntless*, Janeway watched with a secret melancholy as the squadron of Fenris Ranger ships turned in unison like a flock of birds and then leaped away to warp speed in a prismatic flash.

Be safe out there, Seven.

Fenris – Ranger Headquarters

After nineteen hours in *Laniakea*'s hold at high warp, General Kohgish's stasis pod was none the worse for wear. Seven and Ellory walked on either side of the pod and guided it on its antigrav sled through the broad double doors of the Rangers' oldest building, the Justice Hall.

Inside, their fellow Rangers had formed two long lines, leaving open between them a broad path that led straight to the booking sergeant's desk. Everyone remained silent as Seven and Ellory escorted their prisoner toward his long-overdue reckoning. Their crisp footsteps on the marble floor echoed off the stone walls and ceiling in the cavernous old building, a relic of the Rangers' earliest days.

They halted two meters in front of the sergeant's elevated desk. Ellory deactivated the antigrav sled, which sank slowly to the floor. Once the sled had settled, Seven triggered the stasis pod's rejuvenation sequence. Its transparent lid retracted into its shell, and a cloud of wispy vapor rose from its interior. The machine hummed for a second, and then the display of vital signs on its outer panel confirmed that General Kohgish was alive and conscious, with his manacled wrists at his waist.

Seven grabbed one of the Antican's burly arms. "He's awake. Help me stand him up."

Ellory took hold of the general's other arm. Together, she and Seven hoisted the hulking brute up and out of the pod and then they marched him forward to present him to the sergeant. Disoriented from his ordeal on the *Eris* and the aftereffects of suspended animation, Kohgish swayed; his balance clearly had been compromised. Ellory steadied him with a hand on his chest. "Stay still. Try not to puke."

Looking down from the desk was Ranger Sergeant Caro, a stern-faced Kelpien. He squinted his small, close-set eyes at Kohgish. "And what do we have here?"

Seven didn't need to look at the charge sheet. She had memorized it.

"This is General Kohgish of Antica. He is hereby charged with sedition and treason against the government and people of Soroya IV; acts of genocide that resulted in the deaths of at least three hundred thousand persons on Soroya IV; extortion of the government of Alta; the sabotage and subsequent destruction of Soroya IV's weather-control network; ordering an attack that resulted in the death of Fenris Ranger Jalen Par; and contracting with bounty hunters to commission the murder of Fenris Ranger Keon Harper, and the attempted murder of myself, Fenris Ranger Seven of Nine. Plus such other charges as the prosecutors' office deems proper."

"The charges are so registered. Guards, take the prisoner to processing."

A trio of Rangers approached to accept custody of the general.

Kohgish struggled against his manacles and tried to retreat from the jailers as he succumbed to panic. "Stop! You can't do this!"

Sergeant Caro asked, "Why can't we?"

"Because I'm an Antican! I'm a Federation citizen! I have rights!"

Seven seized Kohgish by his tunic's collar and pulled him down to her level. "So did the people you *murdered*."

He thrashed but could not free himself from her grip. "I won't be condemned by a Borg and a bunch of vigilantes! I *demand* to be extradited to the Federation! I—"

Seven twisted the general's shirt collar into a tourniquet to shut him up. "You *committed* your crimes here and you'll *answer* for them here." Disgusted, she released him with a push that landed him in the jailers' arms. "Book him."

Kohgish flailed and ranted like a madman as the jailers hauled him away.

Seven and Ellory ignored every word he said as they left the Justice Hall together, with their heads held high and their strides in perfect sync, basking in the cheers and applause of their fellow Rangers.

29

Fenris – Ranger Headquarters, One Week Later

Ellory stood with Seven and held her hand as they watched an artisan burn the names of Jalen Par and Keon Harper onto the Fenris Rangers' wall of honored dead.

Dust and white smoke curled away from the point where the radiant yellow beam struck the wall. Watching the plasma cutter carve letters into the stone, Seven reflected on the past few weeks of her life. On how she had come to this place, and this life, with these people.

I will make you proud, Harper.

Perhaps sensing the maudlin turn of Seven's thoughts, Ellory gave Seven's hand a gentle squeeze and shot her a sympathetic look. "You okay?"

Seven nodded. "I will be. I just . . . miss him."

"Me, too."

"Harper was one of the few people I have ever known who truly believed in me. Who saw me as the person I am, and not the monster I once was."

"You weren't a monster."

"I was. For thousands of innocent beings across the galaxy, I was the last thing they saw as they were assimilated. I've seen holograms of myself as a drone. I looked like a walking corpse. Like something from a nightmare." She closed her eyes to hold back tears of regret, and bowed her head. "I was just a tool of the Collective . . . but I remember it all. Every life I took. Every life I stole. And I can never make it right. No matter how much I atone, I can never be redeemed." She opened her eyes and focused on Harper's name. "But I still have to try."

"Well, I know what he'd say to you right now." Ellory waited until Seven looked at her to add, "'One day at a time, kid. One day at a time.'"

Seven had to smile through her tears. "That's exactly what he'd say."

Ellory gave Seven a gentle tug. "C'mon. Let's go meet our new bird." They turned away from the wall and strolled slowly down the long passage to the flight deck. "One question: Didn't I hear you swear you'd never be shamed again for being part Borg?"

"That was about accepting all the parts of me that make me who I am. About not hating parts of myself that I can't change. The things I did when I was a drone . . . I feel shame for them because those were things I *did*, whether I wanted to or not. I will always regret the atrocities I was forced to commit. . . . But I will not be shamed because I still have some of my old Borg implants, or because I still have nanoprobes in my blood. Those are just part of who I am. What matters isn't where they came from, but what I do with them."

Saszyk, the old Saurian deputy commander, was leading new recruits on an orientation tour of the headquarters. The sight of it seemed to make Ellory happy. "New blood. It's amazing how much a high-profile arrest and seizure can improve recruitment."

"Indeed."

Seven and Ellory ambled past the half-empty mess hall. Inside, Ballard and Speirs were lingering over breakfast, trading tall tales with Rana and her new half-Klingon, half-human copilot, Korag Toranzo. For a change it was Rana holding court, and when she hit her punchline, the whole table roared in laughter.

The administrative offices were busy, as always. A holoframe mounted high in one corner of the office played a steady stream from the Federation News Network, which had finally broken the story of "a joint operation by Starfleet and the Fenris Rangers to strike a blow against piracy, arms trafficking, and crimes against sentient rights in the Qiris sector," as well as a new emergency mission by the Federation to evacuate the surviving colonists of Soroya IV.

Seven stifled an urge to huff derisively at the news.

Nice of them to notice. Finally.

As always, the flight deck was a chaotic mess. Refueling teams seemed to hurry in all directions at once, while munitions crews raced to reload prowlers with full complements of microtorpedoes. Mechanics had scavenged a wrecked prowler for parts and left its naked spaceframe in a corner of the deck like a carcass abandoned by a sated predator. Now they were using those salvaged components to make last-second repairs on the prowler parked next to Ellory and Seven's new bird—a brand-new Starfire 500, fresh off the assembly line.

Ellory ran her hand along its fuselage as she circled the spacecraft. "Is she a beauty or what? Look at those lines! And look at the hull! Not a scratch. Not one dent. I could cry."

Following a few paces behind her partner, Seven arched an eyebrow at the new prowler. "It is a well-made vessel."

At the rear of the prowler, Ellory asked her ground crew, "How's she look?"

"Like a dream," the crew chief said with a thumbs-up.

Returning along the other side of the craft, Ellory and Seven were on the receiving end of envious stares from Lucan Sagasta and his new copilot, Tovok. Sagasta's broad, gleaming white grin of perfect teeth contrasted so dramatically with his deep-brown skin that it reminded Seven of an old Earth story about something called a Cheshire cat. "Look at that shiny new ride! Why'd you two get the squadron's first new bird in five years?"

Ellory shrugged, as if the truth weren't obvious. "I don't know, Lucan. But the next time *you* recover a crate packed with enough latinum to balance our budget for the next decade, maybe you'll get a new bird, too."

He teased her with a rude flip of his arm. "Showoff."

She replied with a vulgar two-finger gesture.

They both laughed like teenagers.

Lucan's ground crew detached the refueling lines from his prowler, and Tovok climbed up into the cockpit to begin a preflight check. Ellory noted the activity with curiosity. "Hey! You're not on the patrol schedule. You guys goin' somewhere?"

"Special assignment." Lucan leaned back against his prowler and crossed his arms. "Heading out to a secret meeting with some Starfleeters."

"Something wrong?"

Lucan shook his head. "Nah. They want to set up an orbital defense system on Vashti, but they can't get the parts they need. Guess why."

Seven knew the answer. "Because they're only made in the Romulan Star Empire."

"Correctamundo, Blondie! Starfleeters can't go into Romulan space to get what they need, so that's where *we* come in." He turned and started up the ladder to his ship's cockpit. "It's a brave new day, children! Starfleet and Rangers, workin' together. What *will* they think of next?" He settled into the pilot's seat. As he shut the canopy, he added, "We're gonna be gone awhile. Don't wait up." Lucan and Tovok's prowler warmed up with a rising whine from its impulse drive and thruster package.

Seven and Ellory turned away to face the port side of their new prowler. Painted on the fuselage beneath the canopy's frame was their ship's nickname, which they had chosen together:

Harper's Hope

Looking at it, they held hands and smiled.

They enjoyed a bittersweet moment of silence.

Seven turned a hopeful look at Ellory. "I'm thinking of getting a dog."

Ellory scrunched her brow at Seven. "A dog?"

"A dog."

The Trill woman pondered that. "What kind of dog?"

"I don't know. A mutt?"

"Good choice. But what would you call it?"

Seven looked at their ship. "How about Hope?"

Ellory nodded. "Not bad."

A few seconds of strange silence followed.

Seven turned another look at her lover. "So . . . ?"

Ellory chuckled and shook her head. "I guess we're getting a dog."

U.S.S. Dauntless NCC-80816

Janeway gazed out of a curved viewport in the main compartment of her stateroom, sipping from a mug of coffee while watching warp-bent starlight slip past. In contrast to the emergency slipstream mode she had used to reach Zirat from Earth in a matter of hours, she had ordered a more conservative approach to its return, restraining it to warp velocities of factor seven and below. Her official rationale for doing so was to limit stress on the ship's propulsion system. The truth was that she had missed the experience being on a starship, out amid the stars, and simply wanted to prolong her time away from Earth.

It's not as if anyone's waiting for me at home. Everyone's moved on now. To new assignments, new commands, new lives. As they should.

Professing to loneliness while surrounded by people at all hours of the day and night felt to Janeway like a fate as ironic as it was tragic.

A soft double-chirp from the overhead speakers was followed by the voice of Lieutenant Benson, who was acting as the ship's overnight officer of the watch. *"Bridge to Admiral Janeway."*

"Janeway here. Go ahead, Shawna."

"Admiral, incoming live comm for you. Marked personal."

"From whom?"

"Seven of Nine."

"Patch her through, please."

"Yes, Admiral."

Janeway turned away from the viewport in time to see a life-sized hologram of Seven manifest in the middle of her quarters. The younger woman wore her recently cleaned and heavily patched Fenris Rangers jacket over civilian garb, and her long blonde hair spilled in carefree waves over her shoulders. She greeted Janeway with an uncertain expression and a cautious tone. *"Admiral."*

"Seven." Janeway smiled, hoping to expel some of the awkwardness between them. "You're looking well."

"I am fully recovered from my physical injuries on Zirat."

"Glad to hear it. And your partner? Ellory?"

"She . . . We are doing fine."

"Good. So, to what do I owe the pleasure?"

For a moment, Seven seemed on the verge of saying something major, but then she backed away from it. *"I just thought I should check in."*

"Check in?"

"The end of our last conversation felt . . . incomplete."

"I suppose it did." Janeway wondered how much she could risk trying to influence Seven. "You know, a lot has changed in the year since you left Earth."

"Such as?"

"A young male ex-Borg you helped liberate has been accepted into Starfleet."

Seven's face lit up with joy. *"You mean Icheb? Icheb is in the Academy?"*

"He was granted advanced placement."

"*That makes me very happy, Admiral. Thank you for telling me.*"

"It also changes things, Seven. Icheb is winning hearts and minds. Thanks to him, I can finally get you a spot at the Academy, or maybe even a special officer's commission from the Federation Council."

Seven shook her head. "*I would prefer you didn't.*"

"But isn't that what you wanted?"

"*It was. But I've started to question whether my interest in joining Starfleet was genuine or just something I taught myself to want because I thought it would make you happy to see me take that path. Even now, looking back, I'm not sure which is closer to the truth.*"

"I wouldn't have recommended you to Starfleet if I didn't think you'd make a superb officer. Nor would I have encouraged you to join Starfleet if I didn't think you'd be happy there. I thought so before you left, and I still do."

Seven turned away, as if on her end of the conversation she was looking out a window. "*I understand. And I respect your devotion to Starfleet.*"

"But?"

"*Its ability to act, to do what is right and necessary in the moment, is often constrained in ways that I find maddening. And its jurisdiction frequently is defined by the petty concerns of politics, rather than by the needs of sentient beings.*"

"No organization is perfect, Seven. But despite its flaws, I still think Starfleet is, overall, a force for good in the galaxy."

"*I agree. But its way is not the only way. As much as I respect Starfleet and what it stands for, the Fenris Rangers are where I need to be right now. They let me act more freely. Help people more directly. With them, I can make a difference, right here, right now.*"

It was difficult for Janeway to mask her disappointment. "Seven, I want you to know that I genuinely admire your commitment to helping others and your desire to serve something greater than yourself. But I have to question whether the Fenris Rangers are really the best avenue to fulfilling that mission."

"*Why can't you accept the Rangers as they are?*"

"Because however they might have started, they operate now without oversight. Without any laws other than the ones they themselves choose to enforce and live by. That's not law enforcement, Seven. That's vigilantism."

Seven's expression hardened with anger and denial. "*You don't know them.*

The laws the Rangers enforce were codified before they became independent, and the Rangers haven't changed them. They aren't a lynch mob. They're investigators. Regulators. Fugitive hunters. And, when necessary, judges and jailers."

"And you don't think that's too much power to invest in one organization?"

"The enforcement and legal divisions operate independently of each other. The legal division holds trials, imposes sentences, and polices the Rangers themselves."

"For now, perhaps. But how long do you think it can last without a source of funding? Or be taken seriously without some kind of official sanction? History has seen this kind of thing before, Seven. It degrades over time. Loses its way. Becomes something else."

"Then so be it. But even if it turns into just a bunch of outlaws using a famous name to do some good . . . so what? Isn't it better to have someone, anyone, keeping the wolves from the door rather than letting them run wild?"

"Is that how you see your role with the Rangers?"

"As long as governments abandon their people to predators, I plan to be there, a firewall defending the innocent from evil."

There was no denying the passion of Seven's sense of mission, and Janeway realized there was nothing more to be gained from debate. "That's a commendable sentiment, Seven. And I can understand why you find the immediacy of the Rangers' methods more gratifying. But I'm afraid I simply can't condone it."

"I'm not asking you to. I'm just asking you to trust me."

There was a pleading note in Seven's voice, and a purity to her expression, that moved Janeway deeply. She wished she could touch Seven's cheek. "Always, Seven. Always."

Seven mustered a sad smile. *"Thank you, Admiral."*

"Seven . . . call me Kathryn."

A bittersweet silence lingered between them until Seven said, *"Tell the others I said hello and that I'll be in touch again soon."*

"I will." Janeway's eyes misted with emotion. "Be careful out there, Seven."

Seven mirrored Janeway's teary expression. *"You, too . . . Kathryn."*

30

2386

Fenris

Closing time at The Kettle. Last call had come and gone, and only the hardest of the hard-core drunks and derelicts still lingered, along with the smoke and the mingled reeks of a floor soaked in puke and spilled booze. Outside the front door, the gray light of predawn in Fenris's capital was yielding to a morning sky streaked with pink clouds.

Seven and her new, dark-haired acquaintance were still seated at the bar. Their latest round of drinks—she had lost count of how many refills the woman had ordered on her behalf—were almost empty. The brunette sipped her rainbow-hued Belgarian Sunset through a spiral straw that was barely tall enough to clear the top of the drink's tulip-shaped container, while Seven emptied the bourbon from her lowball glass with one quick tilt.

"That was quite a tale." The stranger's beguiling dark eyes captivated Seven's attention as she continued. "So much loss. My condolences on your friend Harper."

Seven waved off the offer of sympathy. "That was long ago. Another life." She got up from her barstool and stretched her arms high above her head. "And I never look back."

"A wise philosophy." The woman finished her beverage. "So, it sounds as if Starfleet came to its senses about your past just in time to be too late."

Any mention of her status as an ex-Borg put Seven on a defensive footing. She had learned to hide the truth for her own good. "Starfleet was only willing to forgive my past because my implants and nanoprobes were permanently neutralized by the fight on Zirat," she lied.

"Really? But you said they let a former Borg drone join Starfleet."

Seven nodded. "Yes, Icheb. He was one of several drones I helped liberate from the Collective during my time aboard *Voyager.* He's special, though. Remarkable in every way."

"Are there others like him?"

"A few, but more are being freed all the time, both in and beyond the Federation."

The dark-haired mystery woman looked awestruck. "It's incredible to think there are former drones of the Borg Collective who have been set free and now live among us, still packed with Borg technology but trying to live like regular people."

"Not really. What's incredible is that even after I told you how underfunded and overworked the Rangers are, you still want to enlist."

"Like I said. I want to help."

"Well, I should warn you. Some of the predictions Janeway made have started coming true. Every year the Rangers get a little less organized. Used to be, there was a sense of who was in charge. These days? Not so much. A few more years and the only thing the present-day Rangers will have in common with the original Rangers will be the name."

"I can live with that."

"Well, then, maybe this *is* the job for you." Seven felt suddenly embarrassed. "I'm sorry. I just realized I've been talking to you for *hours* and I never even asked your name."

The brunette shook Seven's hand and flashed a bright white smile tainted by a glimmer of wickedness. "Call me Bjayzl."

ACKNOWLEDGMENTS

My deepest gratitude goes first to my wife, Kara, for her unflagging love and support, not just during the writing of this novel, but always.

I offer my sincere thanks to my good friend Kirsten Beyer, whose suggestions during story development helped elevate so many of the ideas that were foundational to this tale. Her sage counsel helped make it more than just another action story and more than just another tale of interstellar politics. It was Kirsten who made me dig deeper into learning what made Seven who she is, so that this story could be about Seven finding her way in the galaxy as both a newly independent adult and also a newly out queer woman.

I'm grateful to my editors, Margaret Clark and Ed Schlesinger, for their patience and for helping me obtain the research materials I needed for this book. My thanks are also owed to the team at CBS Studios for making those materials available.

I'm thankful for the assistance of *Star Trek* historian Larry Nemecek, who helped me acquire some behind-the-scenes star charts created for the production team at *Star Trek: Picard*, in order to help me pin down a location for the Alpha Doradus system and, with it, Freecloud.

Lastly, a special word of thanks to the readers of these tales—and this time around, especially to all of the LGBTQIA+ readers who have found hope and inspiration in *Star Trek* over the years. This one's for all of you, with love and respect.

Live long and prosper, my friends.

ABOUT THE AUTHOR

A medium says David Mack remains at large on a small planet.

Learn more on his official website:

davidmack.pro